BOOK ONE

# Call Me Captain

LILLIEANNE BROWN

Published by: Silver-Compass Press
lillieannebrown.books@gmail.com

Cover Design: LillieAnne Brown & Marissa Empey

ISBN-13: 979-8-9992720-1-0

Printed in the United States of America

*To my sister,*

*my fiercest cheerleader,*

*who read every version*

*and always asked for more.*

# Foreword

A NOTE TO THE READER—

This story takes place in 1727, at the tail end of the Golden Age of Piracy. Although this tale is fictional, I've always been fascinated with history. Many names that appear in this book were real people, and my extensive research allowed me to craft them, the setting, and even the legendary treasure as true to life as possible.

Let me entertain you with the real life legends that inspired this book.

It begins with an Irish woman named Anne Bonny, who ran away with Captain "Calico" Jack Rackham to escape her abusive husband, not knowing she would eventually become one of the most notorious pirates in history. Among his crew was Mary Read—disguised as a boy. The two women immediately became friends. (Theirs is a story you'll learn as you turn these pages.) One fateful evening, they were captured by a brutal pirate hunter named Jonathan Barnet. The story of their arrest is also true, but I do add embellishments. Although Bonny and Read claimed pregnancy to avoid the hangman's noose, Read died of gaol fever in prison. But the fate of Anne Bonny and her possible child is unknown, as she escaped her cell and disappeared...

*Call Me Captain* is the story of that child.

Now go curl up with a cup of hot cocoa and dive into this world of pirates, danger, and romance!

— LILLIEANNE BROWN

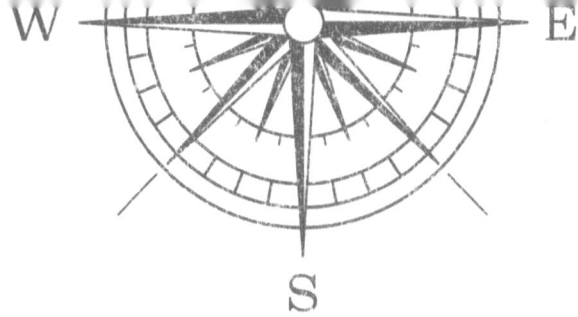

# Prologue

TEARS STREAMED DOWN MY FACE and my heart beat wildly as I tried to pick the lock on her cuffs. I struggled with the hair pin in the stuffy darkness, the hot stench of bilge water, sweat, and urine filling my lungs.

"It's no use," she whispered, her voice tight.

A loud *thud* sounded as the hatch was thrown open, and light streamed in. I dropped the pin, shielding my eyes as I stared up in fear. Two men pounded down the stairs and roughly hoisted me up by the armpits. I struggled against them and screamed, my thin arms flailing. They hauled me onto the deck, my legs kicking uselessly in the air, then forced my arms behind my back as my parents and the rest of the crew were dragged up after me.

My eyes, deprived for so long, feasted upon my surroundings. We were in some sort of harbor, about one hundred yards from the dock, and the sounds of the town drifted across the water. Goats braying, people yelling, auctioneers calling, horses clopping down the streets.

It was all foreign to me. I was used to the quiet life at sea.

"How many will the governor buy?" the man with frightful black eyes and a fancy tricorn hat asked.

Another man replied, "Thirty-one in total."

"And how many do we have?"

"Thirty-five."

"Take care of it then."

My heart seized with fear. My mind flashed with the nooses I'd seen drawn in newspapers. With cages and gibbets and crows picking at skeletons. I clasped my shaking hands. *Is that our fate?*

They'd lined the crew up on deck by now. I looked at Aunt Mary, at her hard-set face. I could see no fear at all in her brown eyes. She had lost her hat, and her auburn hair flowed around her shoulders. She nodded to me, and I put my shoulders back.

*If she can be brave, so can I.*

My eyes traveled around the rest of the crew, all clapped in irons. Seeing them cowering like that made it hard to keep my chin up, so I looked at my mother and father instead. The pirate hunters had forced them to their knees, and they, along with Mary, were chained more heavily than the rest of the crew: cuffs around their necks, ankles, and wrists. My father wore a sour expression.

*Mum still hasn't forgiven him.*

I watched as she leaned toward him and hissed, "Had you fought like a man, you need not be hang'd like a dog."

My lower lip trembled. *Hanged?*

The man talking to the captain walked across the deck and pulled out a pistol. My muscles tensed.

BANG.

Zach keeled over, and moved no more. My breath caught in my throat, and I curled in on myself. Fear and grief choked me. *I'm sorry Mary. I can't be brave no more.*

My parents stood up, yelling, as the man reloaded his weapon, and it took four men to push them down. The captain walked over. "Why are you angry? He is a pirate, and so are you. I thought pirates were ruthless and merciless."

"He was a good man!" my father yelled, beside himself.

The captain punched him in the face. "He deserved his death."

"*You* deserve death!" My father received another blow to the face for that.

My mum spat in the captain's direction. "If I weren't bound by these infernal chains, I'd run ye through."

"I am well aware; that is why I put you in chains." Chuckling, he turned away and flicked his wrist. "Continue."

*BANG.* Isaiah collapsed to the deck. I screamed and fought against my captor, a river of hot tears running down my cheeks. Blood began to pool on the polished wood. I had grown up with these men. The crew was my family. The killer pointed his weapon at William, and Mary screamed, trying to run at him, but the chains at her ankles tripped her, and she landed on the deck with a thud.

"And what exactly were you planning to do?" The captain held his hands behind his back and stared down at Mary.

"Stop this. Don't shoot him. Please."

"You're all going to die anyway. Why do you care?"

She sucked in a trembling breath. "Please. It's a terrible way to die. No honor."

"Honor? You can't speak of honor; you're pirates."

*BANG.* Will fell, and Mary screamed. I'd never seen her cry before, but her face was contorted in anguish. "Will! Will!" She rounded on the captain and sobbed angrily, "Your life I will take, yours and everyone you love. You will pay for what you've done. I will make you know the meaning of pain!"

A sob tore through my throat, my sight blinded by tears.

"Shut up!" The man gripping my arm shook me vigorously until I started choking on my own spit. He threw me to the ground.

"*Child,*" a voice cut through my tears.

I pushed myself up with shaking arms and found my father's dark gaze on me. "*Stand tall,*" Calico Jack ordered quietly, his gruff voice comforting.

With great difficulty, I did as he said. *I wrap all my sorrow in a canvas sail. I tie a cannonball to it. I watch it sink below the waves. My chin is raised. My shoulders are back. My gaze is steady.*

One more of our men fell before they were satisfied. They tossed the bodies of my shipmates overboard like fish carcasses, denied an honorable death and a funeral.

Our captors washed the deck of all evidence of their crimes before anchoring and lining us up on the dock. I was allowed to stand next to Mum, which was my only comfort as I watched a fat man in a big white wig shake hands with the captain.

"Jonathan Barnet," the captain said. "I'm here to hand over these gallows birds. You have the money?"

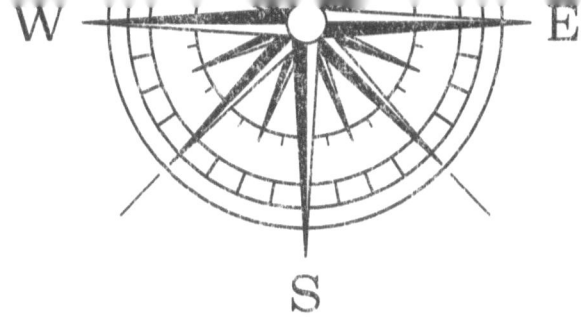

# *Chapter 1*

THE THOUGHT OF SPIDERS crawling up my arm brought me no dread. I had no fear of rats, nor any monster that lurked in the seas. I didn't cower before the swordpoint, nor did I tremble when the sea brought violent, stomach-tossing storms. But living on this ship, with that crew... I spent my days and nights with a dread gnawing at the back of my skull.

The lid of the tiny chest clicked shut, locking the fragile parchment inside. How many hours had I spent staring at it? Countless days, comparing it to every sea chart I had. Wasted time—while my crew's respect for me slipped like sand between my fingers. I hung the key around my neck and tucked it beneath my shirt.

I readjusted the brim of my hat and roughly pushed through the squeaky cabin door.

The sun beat down and the smell of dead fish wafted through the air. My eyes squinted as my pupils adjusted to the sudden change. I headed immediately to the side of the

ship, listening to the water lapping at the hull. I traced my cal-
loused fingers along the grain of the wooden rail—and sighed.

*The Mirage* was my one true companion on these waters.
She knew me before any of these men did—since the day
I bought her with stolen jewelry. She knew the sweat that
dripped from my back as I pounded nail after nail to make her
seaworthy. She counted each drop of blood I spilled removing
those blasted barnacles from her hull.

That's why the failure last week cut so deep.

I glanced up to see the toothless cook smiling down at
me, one eye scarred shut by a fight. A bandana kept his thin,
wiry hair out of his burnt face. He smelled filthy, just like the
other members of my crew.

"How's the patchwork coming, Tommy?" When two ships
were in our sights, we had chosen the more heavily-armed
one, believing it would carry plunder. Not so.

My beloved ship had suffered, for little reason.

"Well, Cap'n Blade. We slowed the leak. It's barely nut'in'
now." His yellowish mustache twitched as he snorted like a pig,
then shuffled away to hock a loogie over the side of the boat.
I strode past him as he yelled across the ship, "Hey Bones! I
spit farther'n you!"

I rolled my eyes as Bones huffed. He was a large man,
who'd earned his nickname by fighting with clubs made
from femurs. *Cow? Human?* I never asked. He was my Master
Gunner, the most experienced at shooting cannons and other
weapons. Much too valuable to toss overboard. "How d'ya
know you spit farther than me, ya scurvy dog!"

A sizable figure approached me from behind. I stiffened.

"Don' fret over last week, Cap'n. Every great leader makes
a few boyish mistakes now and then."

I turned slowly on the spot, and lifted my chin to meet
Axe's pale green gaze. He was twice as wide and a foot taller

than me, but I refused to be intimidated. "Boyish?" I demanded, my eyebrow arched.

He grinned faintly. "Aye. We all had high hopes. Easy to get a little reckless when the scent o' loot's in the air."

*Reckless?* I folded my arms. "You voiced your agreement. We took a chance—now you say it was a mistake?"

Axe dipped his head. "I'm just sayin'—we've all got yer back. You're young, sure, but the crew stands with you. A few think an older cap'n would be better fit, but I think we've just had a bit o' bad luck."

My spine stiffened. I could hear the undercurrent of his words. "I have more years at sea than most men here, including you, Axe. Trained under Calico Jack since I could barely reach the deck rails. If you disagree with me, say so. But don't twist your words to match the wind."

"Wouldn't dream of it," he chuckled, but his eyes were sharp. "Jus' lookin' out for the ship, same as you. That's all."

I gave a short nod and a tight smile. "'Course."

As he walked off—footsteps heavy on the deck—my gut roiled like storm-tossed water. I slipped back into my cabin. I couldn't lose my cool in front of them. Not with half the crew having heard every word Axe said.

I took a slow breath. We hadn't seen a proper prize in weeks—just a few sorry coastal ships and barely a handful of coin. Even that fat merchant with guns stacked sky high only carried sailor rations. No gold, no spice. Just crumbs. The crew was restless. And Axe?

Axe was circling like a shark.

I stepped in front of the small, cracked looking glass that sat on my desk. My own reflection stared back at me, but two years ago I would not have recognized it. My hazel eyes, flecked with green amidst deep caramel, had lost the shine they once held. My face was smeared with grime—but unlike my filthy crew, most of it was purposeful.

*They* had nothing to hide.

My fingers flexed, itching to unlock that box and hold the map again. But staring at the old relic any longer would be fruitless. *It's not like I'd magically gain the ability to read.* I turned around and stared at the tiny chest on the table, my hand closing absent-mindedly around the key at my neck.

*If only I could read.* The words on the map would surely tell me which direction I should sail—at which island I should drop anchor. My heart longed for the vast treasure that awaited me. It would mean power—and true freedom.

I wouldn't have to worry about crafty quartermasters who thirsted after my position. No one knew about the map—if Axe ever laid eyes on it, he'd be wearing my hat before the sun rose the next day.

*I'd have to sleep with the crew.* My stomach twisted at the thought, and my gaze dropped to the woven rug on the floor. Beneath it, a trapdoor led to a tiny, hidden room—my last resort if things went south. I'd built it myself, stashing away supplies and an escape plan no one knew about.

*But it won't come to that.*

I *had* to find out where the treasure was buried.

---

"Who's in for a tale?"

My crew shouted their approval. I sipped my water, silent.

Night had fallen, and we'd gathered below decks to enjoy the grub Tommy had *so carefully* prepared for us: a small piece of cod, complete with scales. I had to pick at it carefully to avoid the bones. A morsel of cheese and a stale biscuit accompanied it. We'd run out of pickled vegetables weeks ago. How *sorely* I missed them.

"Alrigh' then," Bart said, rubbing his dirty hands together. "Not too long ago, a fishin' boat floated off the coast o' Grand Cayman. Five fishermen were pullin' in their nets, when all o' the sudden—a giant wave outta nowhere washes one o' the men outta the boat an' drowns 'im. The wind picked up and started howlin', but the sea was as calm as can be. No ripples, no nothin'. Then a second wave hit—and killed another. The last three fishermen huddled together, scared to their bones. Finally, the wind blew off a fisherman's hat, an' the rest realized why the sea was so angry."

"Why? Why was the sea angry?"

Bart leaned forward. "The one who's hat blew off? She was a *woman*."

Some of my men gasped. "No!"

I felt like the cod in my stomach wanted to swim back up.

Bart nodded. "Aye. She'd tricked those poor fishermen and made the sea angry with her dumbness. So do ya know what they did?"

"What?"

"They slit her throat and tossed 'er in the ocean, as a sacrifice. The sea sure calmed down, then. No more waves came to kill 'em."

My biscuit turned to crumbs in my fist. I took a tight breath to suppress my fury, then forced my body to loosen. As the other pirates nodded, satisfied, I asked, "You gonna finish the story, Bart? Or should I?"

Bart grunted. "What d'ya mean? That's it."

"You didn't hear?" I feigned surprise. "They thought all their troubles were gone. But as soon as they reached land, they were plagued. When they went to the market, their fish disappeared. When they returned to their boat, the sails were torn and their equipment gone. All that was left in the boat was one hat. The same hat that the woman wore, before the wind blew it off. Every time something went wrong for them, they would see that hat. It would follow them everywhere, just like their misfortune, a reminder of their horrible deed so long ago."

My men glanced at each other, unsure. Axe was watching me closely.

"That ain't true, is it?" one asked.

I shrugged, then dumped my empty dishes into Tommy's arms. As soon as I was out of sight, I raced into my cabin, breathing hard as I locked the door. My hands were slick. I wiped them on my jacket like it'd help.

*I think we've just had a bit o' bad luck.*

*She tricked those poor fishermen and made the sea angry...*

*They slit her throat and tossed 'er in the ocean.*

I stepped in front of the mirror. My hat came off first. I yanked the pins holding up my hair, my breath coming faster. My long, dark locks cascaded down, and I ripped off my mustache and goatee, my hands shaking. The paint thickening my brows and the soot masking my feminine cheekbones were the only things left. I stared at myself in the mirror, my heart beating wildly.

*They can't ever know.*

My hands clenched into fists. I wanted to scream. *Captain in name. A ghost below decks.* One wrong word, one slipped mask, and I'd be tossed into the sea like yesterday's scraps. *Or worse.* Who knew what my men were capable of?

When I was a lass, I feared nothing but death. I wore no disguise, but still I'd laugh alongside my parents' crew.

But they were all gone now, and that life along with them. Bitterness held me fast, like a dead man's grip. I shed my coat in one fluid motion and plucked my sword from the wall. I held it out with my left hand.

Breathing deeply in through my nose, I closed my eyes to center myself. When I opened them, it was easy to imagine the enemy in front of me, ready to strike. A gray wig under a fancy tricorn hat, a clean-shaven face and cruel black eyes. His face, frozen in time, filled me with a fiery loathing.

I slashed the air, mindful of my form. I spun around, practicing my back-hand, then rolled away. I leapt up again, deflecting multiple strikes. I pushed harder and harder, until my muscles began to burn. The pain helped me think. Helped me feel alive.

Finally, I knocked the sword from his hand. Imagined my silver blade sinking into his black, black heart.

I knelt, sword point resting on the ground, sweaty hands wrapped around the handle. *Dear Mother*, I breathed, my lips moving silently with the thought. *How shall I ever avenge you? How, when I lack a destination? I have no money, no way to learn where the pirate hunter hides.* Sweat dripped down my brow, anguish simmering inside me. *I thought captaining a ship meant freedom, but nay, it is bondage.*

I raised my eyes and pushed myself up with great effort. Would I die in a man's boots—with no one alive to mourn my real name?

---

A loud bang on the door yanked me out of my dreams. I sat up, disoriented. After a moment's hesitation, I cleared my throat and yelled, "What?!"

"Uhhh, Cap'n, Sir. There's a ship on the horizon."

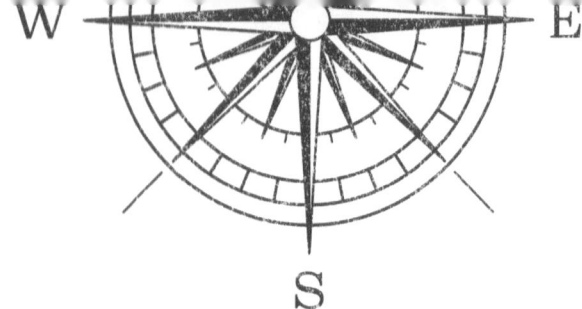

## *Chapter 2*

MY HEART BEAT a fast rhythm in my chest. I ran to the mirror and tied my hair up, piling it atop my head. *Please let this be a shift in my luck*, I prayed. I shoved my hat on, combing the feather straight as visions of canned vegetables briefly drifted through my mind. Once properly weighted down with weapons, I smeared some grime on my cheeks, fixed my mustache, and put on my mean face.

I opened the door and squinted in the early morning sunlight. My crew was running around, preparing the weapons. Cutlasses, pistols, muskets, cannons.

I turned and took the stairs two at a time to the poop deck, where my boatswain stood at the wheel. We called him Wyatt, because none of us could pronounce his native name. He was an escapee from one of the slave trading vessels that often traversed these waters. He looked worlds healthier than when I had first plucked him out of the water—half dead from starvation and exhaustion. He'd jumped overboard seeking death, but instead he found a new life.

Shielding my eyes, I gazed out to sea. Sure enough, there was a large dot on the horizon. I liked my men's eagerness, but it would be a couple of hours before we caught up.

I looked back at Wyatt. "I'll take it from here." I grasped the wood and watched a line of men ferry pails of water to the side of the boat, where they dumped them into the sea. *That stubborn leak.*

"Hands to the ratlines! Loose the topsails and heave out the staysails!" I shouted. Soon enough, *The Mirage* was gliding along at a good clip, the bilge empty and sails full.

I shielded my eyes against the sun and glanced up at the Jolly Roger fluttering and snapping in the breeze. The skull and crossbones was an ancient tradition we kept alive. They were the bones of Jacques de Molay, a symbol of rebellion from the oppressive Church. To me and many other pirates, it represented defiance against any oppression, be it unfair levies or trade control.

The colors struck fear into the hearts of our prey.

I held the wheel with one hand and gazed through my spyglass. It was a large ship, with three masts and billowing white sails. A Red Ensign rippled in the breeze. *Perfect.* A British ship sailing away from North America was sure to have plenty of goods and supplies.

We waited in anticipation as the gap narrowed. "You ready, girl?" I whispered to her, giving the wheel handles a little squeeze. "You shouldn't take too much of a beating this time. They don't have much cannon."

*Closer. Closer.* The minutes ticked by. My heart beat faster, as if it knew it might be pumping its last. There was always the danger of that.

An alarm bell tolled across the water. Soon we were near enough to hear our opponents' urgent cries as they prepared for battle.

"Axe!" I shouted. "Fire a warning shot!"

A single cannonball soared through the air and splashed a few yards from their starboard side. I lifted my spyglass to look for any changes—would they raise a white flag?

All I saw were men loading the few cannons they had. Passing muskets around.

*So be it.*

"Alright men!" I screamed, drawing my cutlass and brandishing it. "This is the moment we've all been waiting for!"

A chorus of cheers responded.

I gazed down at them all, soaking in their excitement. But if we were going to win this battle, I needed more. "What is our power?"

To this, they knew the answer. "FEAR!" they screamed, raising their weapons in the air.

"Fear!" I repeated. "We will make their knees tremble and their stomachs drop. We will strike such fear into their hearts, no blood will be spilled before we take what is ours!"

A fearsome racket ensued, full of "rah!"s and "aye!"s and chest-beating.

I stomped my foot. "I can't hear you!"

*Louder.* We were nearly on top of them, and I knew this was our time to make an impression.

"I want beasts, not ladies! I want lions, not housecats!"

The ruckus grew to a fervor. They were snarling, beating their chests, running to the guns and slashing their swords through the air. Bones was brandishing his gruesome clubs and Axe was loaded down with pistols.

My crew was armed to the teeth.

"All hands ready!" I screamed at my men. "Prepare the chase gun!" My master gunner and two other men stood at the bow, impatient to cripple the large ship and board. I filled my lungs with air and screamed, "FIRE!"

My men cheered as the cannon went off, a loud bang that left my ears ringing. The first cannonball whistled as it sailed through the air, punching a hole in the back of the ship. Splintered wood flew, and the opposing ship began to turn, so their few cannons could be aimed at us.

"Once more! Fire when ready!" My command echoed down the men, and I waited for the cannon to boom. My hands started to feel slippery around the handles of the wheel. *Any moment now.* Our bow was almost in their line of fire—we had gained considerable ground.

The cannonball missed the ship entirely, instead sailing just over the heads of the sailors and splashing into the water on the other side. No damage done, but nonetheless had the intended effect: some had thrown themselves to the deck in fear. I spun the wheel hard, our ships only a dozen meters from each other, now parallel. Their captain screamed orders; white faces stood ready at the artillery. Poor sods.

"FIRE!" The opposing captain yelled.

"FIRE!" I screamed in response.

Our ship rocked with the force of a dozen cannons going off at once. Clouds of white billowed into the air. A chain shot crashed into their fore mast, and it creaked and groaned as it fell, narrowly missing *The Mirage*. My crew cheered.

Their cannons punched holes in my ship as we returned fire. As splinters flew and smoke filled the air, I knew they were no match for us. Although their ship was bigger, it was not made for war.

"Grapples at the ready!" I screamed. On my command, they were tossed as far as they could go. Some hit their mark. Some were drawn back to try again. The strongest of my men strained against the rope, their muscles rippling as they pulled the merchant ship closer.

I cupped my hands to my mouth and called, "Surrender! Surrender, and no harm will come to you!"

The few muskets they had were aimed, and my crew dove for cover. Shots echoed in the breeze. *I guess that's a no.* I watched a young man with sandy hair rush forward and take a sword to each grapple. Headless ropes slithered into the water. *Too late.*

"Lower the gangplank! Prepare to board!" I yelled. I abandoned the helm, locking the wheel in place before bounding down the stairs. Drawing my swords, I yelled like a maniac as I charged across the gangplank and into the chaos.

The sound of the battle surrounded me. Swords clashed and clanked, yells from both sides filled the air. The cannon and musket fire ceased as the battle concentrated on the deck of the enemy ship. I slashed with my swords, aiming to injure but not kill. Intimidation was the key to a victim's surrender; besides, I always offered a place in my crew if they'd rather join me.

I scoured the deck and spied an older man with a short graying beard, navy blue coat, and a decorated tricorn hat. *The captain.*

I knocked two men out and swept another off his feet as I charged across the deck. As soon as my crewman saw me, he ducked out of the way of the captain's strike—eager to find a new fight. I'd lost one sword, but my remaining blade was enough. I met the captain blow for blow, steel flashing, my parries clean and fast.

I took notice of his form: the way he favored his right side and how he would always take a bigger step forward when he went for my legs. He wasn't bad—but I was better. I sidestepped, then slashed at his arm. He yelped as a line of red seeped through his coat.

I scowled, trying to look meaner. "Just surrender, Old Salt. You're no match for us, and you'll save your men's lives if you do." My next swipe grazed his cheek.

"Surrender?! Never!" He fought with renewed vigor. I felt a sharp pain in my side as he managed to get under my defenses, and instinctively stepped back.

Mistake number one.

I saw close movement out of the corner of my eye and ducked, feeling the rush of air as a thin blade slashed the space where my head had been a moment before. Finding myself fighting two people at once, with naught but a single cutlass, I leapt out of the captain's reach and drove my sword into the less experienced man's calf.

His scream was cut short as the hilt of my sword thudded into his noggin. I kicked him forward, hoping to slow my opponent down.

I stepped backward without looking, and my heel caught something.

That was mistake number two.

I fell backward, softening my fall as much as I could. My hat slipped, and I hurriedly shoved it harder on.

*Mother's love*, I was having a bad day.

Rolling out of the way of a fatal strike, I snatched up my fallen blade and leapt to my feet.

"You'll have to try harder than that to get rid of me, Old Salt." I spared a glance around me at the savage pirates and courageous sailors. *Damn* their bravery. I didn't want lives lost, on either side.

I didn't wait for my enemy to advance. I lunged, and he barely deflected. I panted, trying to catch my breath. "Call off your men, man. No need for useless bloodshed."

I stopped his sword inches from my face and leaned into it, wondering why a skilled fighter such as he wasn't a general. With a little extra effort I forced my blade down his and twisted it fast and hard. His wrist rotated as much as it could go before he was forced to let go, and his sword clattered to the ground.

I held my sword to his throat, having a good look at his face. Sweat glinted on his forehead. He had a weathered look to his visage, and his narrowed blue eyes told me he was not one to back down. "What's your name, *Captain*?" I felt the mood shifting around me as the sailors realized they were outmatched.

"It's Captain Callaway, you shabbaroon. And if you take anything on the *Britannia* or cause any more damage to her I'll cut your heart out." He spat at my feet.

Anger bubbled in my stomach, and I nursed it. "I accept your challenge, *Captain Callaway*," I sneered. "But I don't see your sword. Did you lose it?" I pressed my blade harder against his throat, making him flinch. He was half a foot taller than me, but I was unafraid. I had beaten bigger men before.

"Turn around and put your hands behind your back." I whipped out my gun, sliding my sword back in its sheath with a *shink*. I pointed the pistol at his head.

"This ship is one of King George's personal trading vessels. He is sure to notice it didn't return, and once he does, you will feel the wrath of the royal navy!" he growled, turning.

I cocked the trigger. "Call off your men."

He begrudgingly complied, and swords clanked as they dropped to the ground. Wyatt handed me a rope. Relieved, I shoved the captain against the mast and secured him.

Red was smeared across the main deck, and one sailor was kneeling over another, as blood pooled around them. I felt a twang of guilt as I watched Bones yank him up and tie him to the others, leaving the dying sailor on the ground. Blood soaked the front of his clothes, and he groaned as he lay there.

My eyes found the man I'd tripped over. He looked young, and very dead. *Did he have family? Someone he loved that was waiting for him back home?* My eyes moistened against my will. We didn't usually receive so much resistance. Was there an unseen force testing me? Seeing how far I was willing to go? When I set out on this course, I hadn't intended to be responsible for innocent deaths. It made me feel sick.

Johnny limped toward me, his jet-black hair hanging in his face and one hand clutching his side. I was pleased to see him largely in one piece. He was the quiet type, and didn't engage in any of the brawls Tommy or Bones started. "Johnny, stop that man's bleeding. He still may be useful to us."

He raised an eyebrow, and looked down at me. "Useful?"

"Are you questioning my orders?"

He shrugged. "Naw. Just know as well as you do, a man don't need to be useful to be worth savin'." He limped toward the sailor, who was too weak to refuse his help.

I stared after him, relieved, in more ways than one. The skirmish was over.

Or so I thought.

An angry wail as loud as a cannon blast rang out, and I looked up in surprise. Tommy the cook had collapsed a few feet away, his chest bloody and his yellow mustache stained with red. He groaned, but my attention was drawn away by Axe barreling toward his comrade's killer, who was already engaged with Wyatt and Bart. The young man, with dirty-blonde hair and a nasty cut on his cheek, kept his own against all three of them. He was dressed as any ordinary sailor—tall boots, white shirt, worn brown vest—but his expression bore no fear, instead, rage. His mouth was twisted into a snarl, but something struck me about it. I'd seen it before, and my heart shuddered with suppressed emotion. It was the kind of rage borne from grief.

The boy slashed and blocked, using a sword in both hands. I watched with interest as I stepped closer. He had shorter hair than most men I'd seen; it wasn't even shoulder-length and fell in his face as his arms moved lightning fast. I felt in my bones that when he set his mind to something, he would be ruthless in his efforts to accomplish it. His fighting technique was the result of hundreds of hours of practice.

I realized my mouth was hanging open, and I closed it quickly.

Axe, crazed with anger, took out his gun, but before he had a chance to pull the trigger, the boy sliced his hand, and Axe dropped the pistol with a yelp. He kicked it, sending it skidding out of reach, leaving Axe with just a sword. It was impressive, but I could see the boy was tiring. His blocks slowing, he was being forced back towards the cabin walls at the rear of the boat. His comrades, held at gunpoint or tied by ropes, watched helplessly as he was overpowered. Wyatt and Bart teamed up, knocking both his swords to the ground, and Axe threw a punch.

I winced, knowing the pain.

The boy shook his head, stumbling backwards. Wyatt and Bart grabbed his arms and forced them behind his back. He struggled and kicked, and although they had difficulty holding him, he could not break free.

"Get off me, get off me, disgusting arsworms! Filthy pirates!" he yelled, his voice deep and his British accent pronounced. His other insults were cut short with another blow in the face from Axe.

"You will pay for what you've done!" Axe screamed in his face. "You will— you will get the Keelhaul! By the time I'm done with you, you will be begging for *his* fate!" Axe pointed to the ground, where Tommy lay with his eyes rolled up into his head. A slight pang of sadness hit me. I hadn't liked him very much, but that didn't mean I would ever want him to die. He wasn't sadistic like *certain* crew members of mine, he was just...brainless. And a terrible cook.

The boy's deep blue eyes shone with a familiar fiery light. Despite his split and bloody lips and his bruised eye, he showed no fear. "He deserved his fate. He murdered my friend."

*Tommy was the one who killed that sailor?! Maybe he* did *deserve his death*, I thought. I had gone over this multiple times with my crew. Most of what we do is for show; we don't kill unless *absolutely* necessary.

Axe raised his cutlass to deliver a fatal blow, his face almost purple with rage. I stepped over our fallen sailing master, and barked, "Axe!"

Axe froze, then turned to me. "Did you see what he's did!? Don't tell me he don't deserve to die. He killed Tommy and hurt Johnny an' me." He held up his bloody hand.

"Tommy's death grieves me," I told him. "We will give him a proper sea burial when we are done. But killing this man isn't going to bring him back."

"Are you saying this lad is worth more than Tommy!? He's the enemy!" Axe's face turned a darker purple and he flexed his bulging muscles.

My eyes narrowed. "I said no such thing. But he *is* a fine fighter, so I will give him the *ultimatum*. If you kill him before he can decide, I'll throw you overboard." I turned my attention to the boy. "What's your name, sailor?"

The sailor glared at me, and kept his mouth shut. Axe punched him in the stomach, which didn't help because now the boy had no breath in him. I rolled my eyes, waiting. "Alexander," he finally gasped.

"Alexander what?" I snapped.

He looked at me. "Alexander Callaway."

I raised my eyebrows. *That's* where I recognized his eyes. "Well, well, well. You're the captain's son, then."

The crew members closest leaned in with interest. "Does that mean I can kill him?" huffed Axe.

"You can kill him if he decides he doesn't want to work with us." I gently fingered my mustache. Alexander Callaway was the finest-looking boy I had ever laid eyes on, but Axe was dangerous for more than just his strength. He was admired by all the other crew members. If he thought I was going soft, he could convince them of that, dispose of me, and Alexander would just die anyway. "What do you choose, sailor? Would you like to meet an untimely, painful death, or serve under my leadership?" I stared him down, hoping he would choose the latter option.

He set his jaw. His voice was low, shaking with rage. "I'd rather die."

Axe's swordpoint rose a little higher, but I demanded, "Are you certain? Your father would be awfully heartbroken. And Axe won't make it pretty. Are you sure you want to do that to your dear old pa?"

Alexander glanced behind me at his father, his eyes softening. "Won't you kill us all anyway?"

"If we wanted to do that you'd be dead already. We'll just take what we need and the rest of your friends can go on their merry way. I'll give you ten more seconds to decide. Nine. Eight. Seven."

"Fine!" He shouted, yanking his arms angrily, as if trying his last hope. "Fine. I'll go. Just leave everyone else alone."

I nodded, satisfied. "Axe, take the rest of the crew and go below decks. Plunder it all!" That got his mind off of revenge for the moment, which was a relief. After they pounded down the stairs and out of sight, shouting with excitement, Wyatt and I were left alone with our prisoners. When Wyatt forced Alexander down next to his father, I realized how similar their features were, besides the age difference. I scowled at them, adjusting my hat. "My name is Captain Blade, son of Anne Bonny and Calico Jack. You and your ship are under my command, now."

"You have no right to come aboard our ship!" shouted a sailor. My eyes drew to a skinny boy, with brown eyes and short curly auburn hair, who glared fiercely at me. He had a small nose and freckles, and looked to be Alexander's age. "Have any of you even *heard* of the word hygiene?!"

I arched an eyebrow, my lips tweaking upward. *Funny, this one*. "No right to board your ship? We're pirates! No law commands us, which means we have more rights than *you* will ever have. Savvy?" The curly-haired boy scowled darkly at me. "Now, who wants to join me and who wants to be a prisoner for the next few years?"

Alexander looked betrayed. "You gave your word—"

"The only *word* I gave was that your life would be spared," I told him.

"I'd rather die," Curly Hair spat.

"All right, then." I pulled out my pistol and pointed at his head. "Are you sure?" I put my finger on the trigger.

"No!" Alexander shouted, struggling against his bonds. "Please!"

I looked at him, cocking my head. "But he wants it. I wouldn't deprive a sailor of such a desire." Behind me, my fellow buccaneers came up the stairs, loaded with crates and baskets, sacks and barrels. They stomped past me and across the gangplank, back to *The Mirage*.

"*Please*. If you understand the meaning of mercy, don't shoot him."

I looked at Alexander. His dirty-blonde hair glinted in the sunlight, and his eyes remained narrowed. There was an unwelcome warmth in my chest, but I didn't know where it came from. He was British. He was the enemy. *Focus*.

Of course, I wasn't going to shoot Curly Hair—unbeknownst to my victims, my threats were often idle. "Alright, since *you* killed our navigator and cook," I said to Alexander, "we need a new one. Who volunteers?" No one did. I sighed and raised my pistol at Alexander's friend again. "Do I really have to threaten?"

Captain Callaway snarled. "None shall be joining you. Don't bother with threats— my crew is loyal to King George and no one else."

I didn't waste a glance at him, instead studying Alexander's friend. "You're right handed?" I took his silence as my answer, and lowered my gun slightly. "I think I'll start with your left forearm. You can do without, can you not?"

Curly Hair paled.

"*Fine*," Alexander snapped. "I'll do it."

I brightened. "Can you read the stars? A compass and map?"

"Yes."

"Brilliant! Who's your cook?" I aimed my pistol at another sailor.

"The one you just threatened!" He yelped, squirming.

"Peter!" Alexander said sharply.

"I'm sorry, man, I just don't like finding myself at that side of a gun!"

I quelled my laughter before it started, knowing it would give me away.

Tucking my gun away in its holster, I looked back at my ship. To my great delight, it was loaded with baskets and barrels. My mouth watered watching two of my men walk across the gangplank carrying more crates. Soon, we would have a great feast, with food loaded into heaping piles on each man's plate, celebrating our victory after a hard-fought fight. My crew would no longer doubt me. A huge weight was lifted off my shoulders, my anxiety from the past few weeks whisked away in the breeze.

"That's the last of the goods, Capt'n. What should we do now?"

I turned around to see Johnny standing there, his weight shifted to one leg, the other with blood seeping down it.

"I'm keeping some of the men, but the rest we can send on their way."

"Dead men tell no tales, Capt'n," boomed Axe from my ship. He was standing on the side, holding onto the Pilot ladder. "I say we either kill 'em all, or keep 'em all as prisoners."

"Prisoners means more mouths to feed." I gestured to Alexander, his best friend, his father, and two other strong-looking sailors. "Lock them in the brig. We'll leave one barrel of water for the rest, so they can survive the journey back to land." Johnny and two others forced the men I chose across the gangplank, while Axe reluctantly rolled a barrel back to the trading vessel. "Johnny!" I called after him. He stopped in his tracks and turned. "Go get cleaned up. I don't want that wound to fester."

"Aye, Aye, Cap." Then he grinned. "You ready for a feast?"

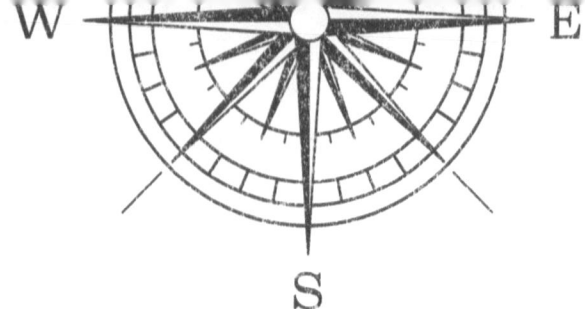

# Chapter 3

A S MY BOOT LEFT the last step of the ladder, sunlight that streamed through the hatch above me glinted off something in Weasel's hand. *A bottle.* His back to me, he was sneaking off.

I intercepted him and snatched it out of his hand. He squeaked.

"Where did you get this?" I demanded, my jaw tight. He cowered under the force of my gaze, glancing between me and the bottle of amber liquid I brandished.

"C-Cap'n, sir," Weasel stammered. "Been savin' it for months."

I raised a brow. "For some reason I find that hard to believe."

"It's the truth! I wanted to celebrate, is all."

My grip tightened around the neck of the bottle. "Remind me of my rules."

"Uhh...killin's bad?"

"And?"

Weasel's face fell, sullen. "No rum."

"Aye." I nodded curtly. "Get your arse back to your duties."

He scrambled up the ladder. I turned to the nearest gun port and hurled the bottle into the sea.

The last time my father drank, half the crew was too deep in their cups to fight. That's when the pirate hunter came. I wouldn't let the same thing happen to this ship.

I took a slow breath. I needed a clear head for what came next.

———⊙·⊙———

I hooked the oil lamp on the wall. Rustling echoed in the dim as the prisoners stirred. The captain and his son each had their own cell. Even from across the hold, I saw Alexander watching me—eyes narrowed, sharp. Too sharp for comfort.

I stopped in front of Captain Callaway and cleared my throat. "Will you be willing members of the crew and obey orders without argument?"

"Willing?" the captain growled. "Nay."

I nodded. "Thought so. Very well. Then I want news. What do you know?"

Silence.

I pressed them with questions, but not one of them spoke.

"Has someone come down here and removed your tongues?" I demanded.

Alexander's voice cut through the dark. "How old are you?"

"That does not concern you," I snapped. Then I smiled. "All I want is a little information. I won't use it for evil, I swear. Your conscience will remain spotless."

"I pity you," Alexander said. His arms folded, his gaze burning. "For your despicable way of life. And for thinking we'd believe your lies."

I stepped closer. "I pity *you*," I murmured. "Locked in chains while the rest of us walk in the sun." I straightened. "I'll return tomorrow. In case your pride thaws by then."

I made my way up to the deck and found my quartermaster. "Axe!"

"Aye?" he said, stepping up.

I cut straight to the point. "Is there rum aboard this ship?"

He raised a brow. "Rum? You don't allow it."

"Did any come from the merchant?"

"No. We know your rules. Where's your faith, Captain?"

My smile was tight. "Just checking."

———

I stared in disbelief at the mess before me. The card table was overturned and so was a food crate, spilling out precious rice. Cards and dice were strewn everywhere. *Broken glass.* I ducked under some empty hammocks, and spied Johnny, Bones, and Gabriel lying on the floor, out cold.

*Oh no.*

The empty bottle a few inches away from Johnny's hand confirmed my fears. "*Sink me*," I murmured in dismay.

I heard another shout—the same that had woken me from my slumber—and I felt my temperature rise. Not only did they bring alcohol onto *my* ship, and they went and trashed it! *And Axe had lied to my face.*

I pressed the facial hair on my upper lip harder to my face. My last mustache was starting to lose its stick. *Jolly. Another worry to add to the list.* When I climbed down to the last level, I stopped in my tracks, speechless.

The prisoners were still locked in the cells lining the sides of the ship. Well, all but one. The pirates were lounging on crates and boxes, whiskey bottles in their hands. They watched the scene and laughed—except Wyatt, who stood off to the side, anxiously curling and uncurling his fingers.

Axe and Bart were taking turns landing blows on Alexander's skinny, curly-haired friend. My stomach twisted as I saw his puffy face and bloody lips. Held up by his armpits, he looked at Bart and mumbled, "I lub what you'b done wit your hair. How'd you make it come out o' your nostrils like dat?"

I shook my head, impressed that he kept his humor in a situation like this.

My eyes drifted to Alexander. Tear streaks glinted in the light as he watched with horror, knuckles white as he gripped and shook the bars. "I'll kill you!" he screamed at them. "If you kill him I'll kill you! All of you!"

When I first saw him, he radiated fearlessness and power, but now—I couldn't help thinking about the way I felt all those years ago, so powerless when my friends were picked off one by one. Their bodies tossed into the water like excess cargo. Rage boiled in my stomach. *These boys are my age.* They didn't deserve this.

"YOU LILY-LIVERED, BILGE-SUCKING PIGS!" I screamed as loud as I could.

Axe stopped mid-swing. Everyone went dead silent and frozen, but I didn't stop there. Anger was power. Power meant control. Control meant safety. *For Curly Hair. For Alexander. For me.* I stomped up to the nearest carouser, grabbed his bottle, and smashed it over his head, drenching him and sending him keeling over onto the floor.

"YOU FOUL-BREATHED—" I drew my sword and slashed the nearest bottle. "PEG-PUFFED, TEWLY-STOMACHED—"

I grabbed another one and flung it at the opposite wall, narrowly missing one man's head. It shattered, spraying everyone around with amber liquid. I paused, searching for my next insult.

"Squiffy heapth ub gull droppingth?" Curly suggested.

The next blow sent him unconscious. I was glad he was out of his misery for the moment, but I sent a death glare at Axe, putting my hand on my sword hilt menacingly. I saw movement out of the corner of my eye, and turned to see Weasel slinking toward the stairs. I hurled my sword through the air, and it stuck into the wall right in front of his face. Weasel froze midstep, watching the blade vibrate back and forth, inches from his nose. "No one goes anywhere!" I shouted. "Until I'm done with YOU." I stomped over and jabbed my finger at Axe, who had dropped his victim to the ground.

Axe growled, but I cut him off before he could speak.

"We do NOT beat our prisoners to death, you cracked wench! And you *lied* about the rum." He towered over me, and I didn't think I could make his face hurt badly enough from this angle, so I punched him in the soft spot instead. He doubled up, and then I brought my knee up to his nose. "If this EVER happens again, you're going straight to Davy Jones's Locker with a bullet in your skull. Savvy?"

Axe just scowled, holding his nose.

"Savvy?" I repeated, turning around to the rest of the crew.

They nodded eagerly, eyes wide. Except for one, who slumped drunkenly off his chair and thudded to the floor, out cold.

"Now all you bilge rats, go upstairs to your hammocks and stay out of my sight. And leave all of your drinks down here." I waited impatiently while they staggered past me, all of them three sheets to the wind.

I walked over and knelt by the poor boy, my stomach twisting again as I looked at him. His nose was swollen and gushing blood, and greenish-purple bruises were swelling up on his face. There was a small cut on his forehead. His loose, white sailor's shirt was partially ripped open, and smeared with more blood. "What's his name?" I asked, my voice a little hoarse from yelling.

"Why do this?" Alexander whispered. "Why help him?"

I looked up at his handsome face, marred by tear tracks. "Sailor, not *all* pirates are what newspapers and books describe us to be. Believe it or not, most of my crew are decent people. But they're scared of Axe and will do anything to please him. What's his name?" I repeated, a little more forcefully, trying to put some gruffness into it.

"Preston Beckworth," the captain murmured.

I slid my arms underneath his back and knees, and lifted him up. *Ohhhh*, I groaned internally. He was heavier than I expected. My arms were already burning as I shuffled toward the ladder, away from Alexander, his father, and the other two sailors.

"Let me out. I'll carry him," Alexander's smooth voice washed over me.

*Blast.* His keen eyes had seen my struggle. Even though I didn't want to admit it, I was going to grow a real beard by the time I got him up the two ladders and into my cabin, where I kept medical supplies. I paused, and finally my fatigued muscles won the debate. I carefully set him down and dug in my pocket for the keys. "Fine." I gritted out as I fit the key into the lock. "But you have to promise me that you won't kill any more of my men."

He nodded.

"If you break a promise you gave me, you're a dead man."

"Noted."

"And while you are helping your friend, I want your Old Salt to clean up down here and throw all the full bottles overboard."

"I am a captain," Callaway cried indignantly. "I will not—"

"He will be happy to help." Alexander gave his father a meaningful look. They seemed to have a silent argument for a few seconds, and then the captain nodded solemnly at me.

I opened the door. Alexander burst out and knelt by his friend's side, his eyebrows knit with concern. "You're going to be alright, Pres. I won't let this happen again. I'm so, so sorry." He gently picked him up, and followed me through the boat into my cabin.

I lit a second oil lamp. Alexander placed Preston on the ground as I quietly went to my desk and pulled out some of the drawers. I found bandages and medicinal alcohol, both a little dusty. I fetched a knife, a cup, and the large jar of clean water I kept for myself, setting everything down beside Alexander. I know it was selfish not to share with my crew, but they were filthy men.

In a couple of minutes we had him cleaned up and his cuts bandaged. Alexander had offered to help, but soon realized I didn't need it. He sat cross-legged and watched me, which made me minorly uncomfortable. Finally I sat back and admired my handiwork. I wasn't the best doctor, but my skills sufficed.

"You have my thanks, Captain," he said begrudgingly.

I shrugged.

Alexander's eyes searched my face. "There's something different about you," he decided. "Different from all the men I've met at sea. Especially from the pirates."

Alarm bells rang in my head. "It's my personal hygiene," I replied stiffly.

He chuckled softly. I seized the moment to change the subject—before he learned too much. "How did you end up on a trading ship with your father?"

He hesitated. "It's a long story."

"I have all night."

He sighed. "I suppose you'll threaten me with death if I refuse to tell you?"

"That is more or less correct." I bared my teeth.

Alexander fingered the edge of his jacket. "I liked astronomy, and my father...he works for King George the Second, as part of—"

"King George?" I made a face.

"What, you don't like him?"

I shook my head. "Keep going."

"When King George ascended the throne a few years ago, he wanted to increase the wealth of the throne, so he hired good-standing merchants to be his 'Royal Traders.' Since my father is friendly with a noble, he had a foot in. After my studies, I joined my father as a sailor."

"Where'd you meet Preston?"

"Cambridge."

"Cambridge?"

"It's a university in England."

I nodded, filing those facts away for future use. I never knew when little details would come in handy when trying to get what I wanted. Alexander may have been book smart, but he didn't know how to deal with pirates. "So you studied all that time just to become a sailor?"

"Navigator," he corrected. "And yes. Astronomy alone doesn't pay well. And I was intrigued by the thought of travel. I didn't realize how boring it truly is." His face turned dark. "Or was."

I suppressed a grin. "Life at sea is often boring. But it's much better than on land."

"Why?"

I cursed myself for giving him that opening. My mother's words rang in my head. *Do not trust Englishmen. They are insolent, deceitful pigs. I trust your father, but he is different.* Alexander was the enemy. The more he knew, the better he could predict my actions. I couldn't take those words back, so I needed to give him just enough to be satisfied. Besides, if Alexander trusted me, maybe I'd get more out of him.

"There's more freedom on the sea. Land has too many rules."

He nodded, and interlaced his fingers. "Is that all? Did you grow up on land? Or did you always live at sea?"

"As my prisoner, all you need to know is that I do not tolerate rulebreakers or rum-drinkers on my ship."

He scowled. "First of all, I thought I was going to be your navigator, not your *prisoner*."

"You will be my prisoner *and* my navigator until I can trust you."

"When will that be? When will I not have to sleep in your disgusting prison cells?"

"When I decide."

He scowled and mumbled something I couldn't understand.

"What was that, boy?" I asked sharply.

He looked at me incredulously. "You call me *boy*, yet you're clearly younger than I am. And your gait—there's something unnatural about it."

I was taken aback. "What do you mean?" I demanded.

"It changes. Sometimes, you step daintily."

I nearly gasped but growled instead. "I do not."

"I've watched you."

I gave him an ice cold glare. "Get. Out."

"Fine," he spat, returning my glare two-fold. "It is your fault I am here in the first place." He gathered up his friend and headed out the door.

I forcefully threw the supplies into a corner of the room, and they bounced and scattered. I stomped to my desk, pulling off the bandana around my head and pushing my fingers through my hair. It was a terrible idea to bring him aboard my ship.

Very terrible indeed.

I sank down into my cot and thought about my next move. We were headed down south now. Tortuga would be a good place to stop and pick up more supplies. I'd ask the locals about that treasure, perhaps find someone who can read.

I froze, and the corners of my lips crept up.

Alexander.

He can read.

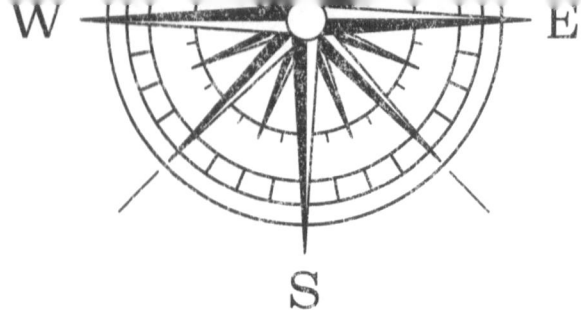

*Chapter 4*

I YANKED OPEN A DRAWER. Nothing. I tried a few more, then found what I was looking for. I pulled out an old quill, a bottle of ink, and a sheet of parchment before heading back to the table. I could barely contain my anticipation, but I couldn't let myself get carried away. After all, Alexander was intelligent, so I had to act carefully, and give him one random word at a time. He couldn't find out what I was really doing. I studied the map, but *blast it*, the cursive was tiny and slanted—I could hardly tell when each word ended. I took my best guess and copied the first three lines. Then I ripped the parchment between each word, so I had thirty-three paper scraps. I gathered them up, and with the exception of the first word, placed them in my safe-box. I practically ran out of my chambers, a single morsel of paper in hand.

I searched for Alexander on the deck, but found Axe instead.

"Where's Callaway, the captain's son?"

He folded his thick, tree-trunk arms. "Why d'ya wanna know?"

"I have a special job for him." I smiled evilly, pretending I had a punishment in mind.

Axe nodded, satisfied. "He's below decks, checkin' the traps."

I found Alexander bent over a little cage in the corner. "Sailor," I barked, and he turned around.

"Hello, Captain... What was it again?"

"Captain Blade."

He snorted disrespectfully.

I narrowed my eyes. "What's so funny?"

"You're not serious, are you? Blade? What kind of name is that? Is that supposed to strike fear into your enemies? Because it's not doing anything of the sort to your *captive*."

I folded my arms, my jaw ticking. "I don't need a name to strike fear into the hearts of my enemies. They cower at my actions alone."

"Well, you'll have to excuse me," he said pointedly, "I'm too busy *cowering*, so you'll have to come back another time." He picked up the cage by its handle, holding it away from him in disgust. The huge rat inside squealed and scratched at the bars, its red eyes alight in panic.

I intercepted him, glaring, before he could take more than a step. "You don't just walk out on your captain when he is trying to speak to you."

"You're *not* my captain," he retorted.

"Your captor, then."

He raised an eyebrow. "What do you want?"

I gave him the scrap of paper.

"What's this?"

"A word."

He scoffed. "I know that. Why are you giving it to me?"

"I want you to read it."

This time, both his eyebrows went up. "You can't read? I suppose that makes sense, since you're a *pirate*." He almost spat the last word.

I pulled out a knife from inside my sleeve and started cleaning out my fingernails. "If you're only going to mock me, then I really have no use for you."

"Certain, are you? I was under the impression you needed a navigator."

I clenched the handle of my knife, *really* wanting to use it. My threats didn't seem to work on him, and it was really starting to annoy me. "If you were smart, you'd want to gain my trust."

"Oh really? And why would I want that? I don't see you treat your crew much differently than you treat me."

I scowled, not wanting to admit he had a point. "You'd get better jobs. You could officially become a member of my crew, which means better food, break time, and even a share in the spoils. And lastly...you'd have more say in what we do, where we go. I might eventually let you go."

He looked at me for a moment, thinking. "Fine. Just so you know, I want *nothing* to do with you or pirates. I want my freedom." He looked me in the eyes, making sure I understood before adding, "It says, 'nights.' Why do you need to read it? What's it for?"

"That's none of your business." I turned, but hesitated as I realized I needed him to clarify. "What kind of nights? The ones in shining armor, or like the opposite of day?"

"The latter." He studied me closely. "'The latter' means—"

"I know what it means." I turned around and ran up the steps, smiling to myself. *This might actually work.*

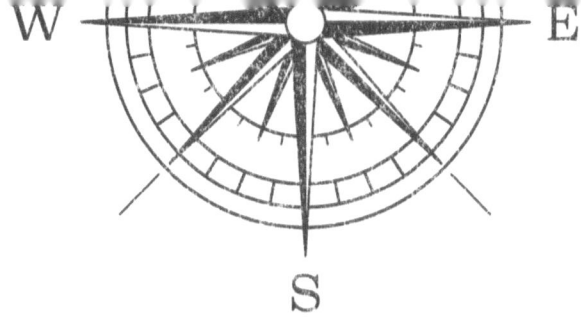

## Chapter 5

I STARED UP AT THE CEILING, paying close attention to the subtle rocking of the ship. *Back and forth, back and forth.* It was well past dark, almost midnight. The room around me was pitch-black, except for a thin strip of moonlight through the window, which reflected off the water and brushed the ceiling. I took a deep breath, in through my nose and out through my mouth, closing my eyes. My muscles relaxed as the familiar, comforting veil of sleepiness gradually descended on me.

*Creeeeak.* It came from the far side of the room, jolting my senses into alertness. I turned my head towards the door but stayed where I was, my muscles tense, by brain whirring. *There wouldn't be anyone awake at this hour, would there?* The sound came again, only slightly higher pitched.

*That could only mean one thing.*

I crawled out of bed as quickly and quietly as possible, picking my sword off the ground. Cursing myself for forgetting to lock the door, I widened my eyes to better see in the dark. I scurried toward the door as a stream of soft yellow light hit the floor, angled away from me. A normal girl might have run to the farthest possible corner.

I was not a normal girl.

I pressed myself against the wall as the door opened towards me, blocking my view and casting a dark shadow upon me. My heart was loud in my ears as the candlelight fell upon a heap of my clothes at the foot of my bed. I moaned inwardly. It was too late to grab my coat and hat. I'd have to stay hidden the entire time—nigh impossible!

My mind raced through the possibilities. *Do I give away my position by threatening to shoot him?* I stared at the pistol across the room, cursing. My wool pants itched, distracting me as I tried to formulate a plan. I couldn't see a way out of this without giving away my identity.

I stood frozen as the intruder stepped forward, revealing himself, his back still turned to me. His silhouette stood a head taller than me, and I recognized his short hair.

*Alexander.*

He held a stolen sword in his right hand. I narrowed my eyes. It was either brave or very stupid for him to try to kill me. Of course, it could be called cowardly to make the attempt in the dead of night, when I would likely be asleep.

I moved closer to the door, grateful for the shadowed protection it gave me, and wondered what was going through his mind as he gazed at my empty bed. I hid my sword behind my back in case it would catch some of the light. He turned on the spot. I could only imagine the fear he must've been feeling he searched—unless he was unaware how deadly I could be. His eyes passed harmlessly over the spot where I stood. I debated the best way to go about subduing him. I had seen him fight. He was good.

But not, unfortunately for him, good enough to beat me.

I came to my decision. "What were you planning to do, kill me?" I mused, hiding any unease behind a mask of composure. I'd wiped off the makeup on my eyebrows and removed my facial hair.

My only disguise was the shadow I stood in.

He whipped around. The light hit the left side of my body, but nothing more. He still couldn't see my face.

I dropped the lightheartedness. "Take a step closer and I will blast the brains right out of your skull."

He swallowed. "I'm no killer."

"Then why come in here in the middle of the night, when you assumed I'd be sleeping?"

"I... I didn't think you would let us go, and bring us to land, unless I forced you to."

I forced a laugh—one I hoped sounded manly. "First of all, you are an idiot to think that would actually work. Second, I'm not without reason."

"What do you mean?"

"There is a possibility that I will set you free, but..."

"But what?" I could hear hope in his voice. Naive hope. It almost made me pity him.

"I see nothing in it for me. I would waste days bringing you back to the coast, and any port over there is dangerous for pirates."

"Don't you like danger?"

"Only a fool takes unnecessary risks."

He looked crestfallen.

"Now that I answered your question, you are free to go."

He hesitated, then shook his head. "Apologies, but I can't just leave."

"If you're planning to fight me, I really would, from the bottom of my heart, suggest otherwise."

"The bottom of your black heart," he retorted, taking a step closer and holding the lantern higher. "You don't care about anyone but yourself."

I shielded my face with my arm as the glow descended over me. "Don't!" I yelped, scooting as close as I could to the door, and then grabbing the handle and pulling it closer to me. *Blast.* I'd let some emotion slip out through my voice, and now I was going to pay. I prayed to any god that was out there that he hadn't seen me—hadn't heard the panic in my voice.

*No one can know.*

"Are you trying to hide?"

"No," I snapped. I desperately needed a way out of this situation.

"Are you afraid?" he asked, with a hint of surprise.

"No! I just...your lantern is too bright. It's the middle of the night, for crying out loud!"

"So..." he said slowly. "You can walk into battle without batting an eye, but you flinch from my lantern like it's searing your skin. Did I get that straight?"

*Blast it.* He had me trapped—and worse, he *knew* it. If I stayed hidden, I'd look weak. Like I was afraid of *him*. And that would be far more dangerous than him knowing the truth. The last thing I could afford was to seem like prey.

"I'm not afraid of you," I said, my voice sharp as flint. "I just... didn't want anyone finding out."

"Finding out what?" His curiosity had peaked—I could hear it in his voice.

My pulse roared in my ears. This was madness. I'd guarded this secret for years, through battle and bloodshed. And now, I was considering handing it over to a boy I'd barely met?

But if I backed down now, if I stammered or ran or lashed out like a cornered animal—he'd own me. He'd *never* fear me. And that could end in my death.

I gripped my sword tighter and stepped out of the shadows.

The light fell on my face, and Alexander's eyebrows slowly raised, higher and higher, until they almost disappeared behind his sandy-brown hair.

"You're a... a..." The tip of his sword dipped toward the ground, his mouth slightly open. His gaze traveled up and down in disbelief, over my wavy brown locks, loose linen shirt and black woolen pants.

It seemed he had forgotten all about what he had come to do.

I stepped forward boldly, chin raised, my expression hardening. "If *anyone* finds out, I will cleave you to the brisket. Savvy?"

"Sorry, I'm not quite familiar with—"

"It means I will cut you open, all the way from your shoulders," I used my sword to draw an imaginary line down his chest, "to your stomach."

"Alright, I get it." He took a step back, looking a little disgusted.

"And then, I will throw your guts—"

"I told you, I understand!" He yelped, stepping back again, remembering I was the same ruthless pirate captain he had first met. "You don't need to go into all the details."

I shrugged. "You asked for it, sailor."

He backed up and set the lamp on the table, his eyes not leaving me. "So *this* is why you didn't want to tell me your story."

I nodded.

"What is your real name? Pray tell me it's not Blade."

"Of course not."

"So..."

"It's Cassandra," I snapped. "Now, it's nearly midnight, and I need my beauty rest, so if you will get out, both of us will benefit. If not, you will have a *very* bad night. Possibly your last."

"There are other ways to get what you want, you know, besides threatening."

"Like what, seduction?" I stepped closer to him, so we were only separated by a foot, and gave him the most seductive smile I could manage. It felt strange, after years of not using it. Funny, I used to flirt to get what I wanted.

Alexander swallowed, the knob on his throat bouncing up and down. "You could just—just ask," he stammered.

I gave a small laugh, as Alexander shook his head.

"You're an... interesting woman, Cassandra. But I still need my freedom."

"Fine. I'll let you go in a couple years."

"That's not going to work."

"Well, what are you going to do about it?" I asked sweetly, enjoying this.

His eyebrows knit together as he debated. "Well, I was planning on fighting you, but..."

"But what?"

"Now I can't. I would never hurt—"

"A woman?" I asked dangerously.

He chewed his bottom lip nervously. *Ah. I was right.* I stepped back, narrowing my eyes. I needed to teach this man a lesson. I lashed out, lightning fast.

He caught my blade with his, narrowly avoiding a serious injury. His eyes went wide. "Woah! What—"

"I am your captor." With every sentence I striked; each time I found my blow deflected. "I am your captain." *Clang.* "I am *not* helpless, and do *not* need your pity." *Clang.*

"My sincerest apologies, Cassandra." He wasn't even breathing hard. "Just because you are a woman does not mean you are weaker."

I paused my attacks, but kept my sword pointing at him. "You're exactly right. Which means, if you find my leadership unjust, feel free to fight me. But are you certain you want to do that? I can beat every single member of my crew."

"Impressive. However, you've never fought *me* before."

I smiled. "That's what they all say."

The idiot raised his sword.

He held one hand behind his back as he took the offensive position. I didn't settle for defense, though. I was fighting to win. My mind became laser-focused, as it usually does when engaged in a fight. I took in every detail: his expression, the way he moved, his footwork; all things became a tool for me to use, telling me where he was weaker, which moves were his strengths, his level of energy and fear.

Meanwhile, I kept my expression under control. I needed him to see only what I wanted him to see. My smile told him I was completely calm, and even having fun. His expression and the way he aimed each strike told me he didn't want to injure me, but desperately needed to win.

"You'd do better if you weren't so afraid to hurt me," I told him.

I swung my sword at his leg, and he was just able to catch it and force it away.

"I'll keep that in mind."

He tried to step in closer and obtain more leverage, but I knew what he was doing. I was not going to let him disarm me. My mind wandered down below, as I wondered if any of the crew had woken with all the clanging. A searing pain erupted on my upper arm, and I realized he had managed to slice me. I narrowed my eyes, chiding myself for losing focus. Just because he wasn't planning to kill me did not mean I shouldn't care as much.

We were in the center of the room now, our shadows dancing around the walls. I managed to get under his defenses and graze his side. He flinched. I advanced, and he stepped backwards toward the open door.

I could feel droplets of sweat forming on the back of my neck and along the top of my forehead. Alexander took a swipe at my legs, and I blocked it automatically. He was becoming more aggressive as he realized that he couldn't beat me by fighting half heartedly.

His strikes came with more power, and I had to leap backward to avoid a gash near my knee. I grinned, liking the challenge. "Where'd you learn to sword fight?"

I caught his blade with mine and shoved it aside, my grin widening as I pressed the advantage. I noticed it was harder for him to parry attacks at the lower right side of his body. If I ever had to actually kill him, I could use that, but for now I was just having fun.

"My father taught me, until I arrived at Cambridge and took lessons."

"Interesting," I told him, sending a volley of strikes his way. "You're not bad, I suppose. But you're at a disadvantage."

"Is that true?" He defended himself from each strike, but I kept them coming.

"You weren't taught by a pirate."

I gave his arm a shallow cut, expecting him to flinch away, but instead he leaned in, forcefully sliding his sword down mine until it stopped at the guard. Then before I could process what was happening, he twisted his blade and my weapon clattered to the floor.

I stared at him, stunned. My fingers twitched, aching for the hilt I'd just lost. Heat flushed my cheeks—part frustration, part awe. He'd disarmed me.

"And why," he said between breaths as he leveled his sword at me, "is that a disadvantage?"

I swallowed. Had he been holding back before?

Managing to regain my composure, I sent him a mischievous smile. I tried to step closer, but the sharp swordpoint against my sternum prevented me from doing so. I let the small cold blade slip down my sleeve until the handle hit my palm. Then I lashed out, reaching under his outstretched arm, ignoring the small cut I got in doing so, and slashed his wrist. It wasn't deep, but it was enough to make him drop his sword with a surprised yelp. I wrapped my arm around his neck and pressed my knife to his throat.

"Pirates don't play by the rules." I stared into his eyes. The deep blue was flecked with gold, a detail I'd missed until I was mere inches from his face.

"That's not fair," he replied, trying to push me away, but I pressed the blade harder against his neck.

"It would be best not to struggle," I told him. "You're going down to the brig for the night, as punishment for delaying my rest. Or maybe I'll keep you there for the next few days. As for your freedom... since you're a worthy opponent and have provided me with quality entertainment, I will say... one year."

"An entire *year*? But—"

"If you complain I'll make it longer."

He let out a breath. "Very well. I will accept your offer... for tonight."

I rolled my eyes and stepped back from him, still keeping my knife to his throat. "Well, you have ample time to think about it." I grabbed his wrist, ignoring his flinch. I yanked him to where I'd left my gun, and, upon picking it up and pulling on my effects, I forced him out of my room.

The bars clanged as I shut them. Alexander held my gaze in the faint candle light, his eyes dark and intelligent. He had leverage, and he knew it.

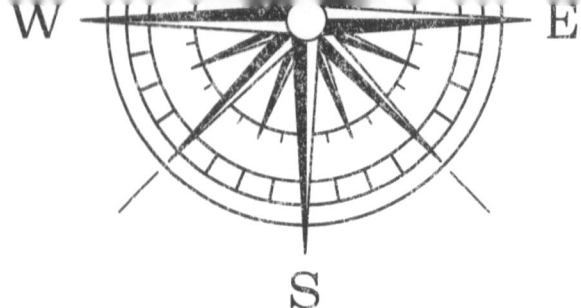

## Chapter 6

**T**HE WIND CARESSED MY FACE, and I inhaled deeply, the fresh sea air going in and out of my nostrils. I stood before the prow, gazing toward the horizon. It was two days since Alexander discovered my secret, and the air was getting warmer as we traveled farther south. I pulled out my compass, the last thing my mother gave me before she told me to run away and hide. Before the guards pulled her away. Before I never saw her again.

I turned around, stuffing the little navigation tool into my pocket. My crew worked hard, scrubbing the decks, pulling on the ropes, and tightening the sails. I watched with unease as Axe shook his whip, threatening two of the new sailors. I knew with little doubt he was sewing seeds of discontent among the crew members after I'd thrown the rum overboard. *Was it not enough that we filled our bellies with a feast?*

I pushed away from the rail, remembering my prisoners and their need for sustenance. Weaving in between my crew members, I made my way down to the galley.

"Hello," Preston said after he pulled open the door.

I nodded in greeting. "Get me two plates of—"

"Your maker didn't waste any time giving you a decent personality, huh? It's not difficult to begin a conversation with, 'Good afternoon'."

I rolled my eyes. "Oh, shut up. I forgot to order someone to feed your friend and his father, so I came to pick something up before heading down there."

"I already fed them."

I nodded. "Good." I paused, looking him over. "You've recovered nicely. I can hardly see a sign you were beaten."

His expression soured. "Don't remind me."

"Have they bothered you since?"

"Not much. And when they do I just lock myself in here like a coward." He gave me a lopsided grin.

I chuckled, shaking my head. "I'd call that intelligence." My thoughts drifted to the secret compartment under my room. I wasn't above hiding if it meant survival.

Preston leaned on the doorway, gaze drifting away. "Alexander's always been the brave one. I like adventure, to be sure... but I'm not a lover of the life-risking variety."

I turned to go. "At least by the end of this, you'll come away with a very intriguing tale."

"Will there be an end to this?" His tone was hopeful.

"One year, and I'll let you go. You can thank Alexander for that."

On my way toward the hatch, I heard hushed voices. Creeping towards the sound, I caught some of the conversation.

"Axe is right, ye know. He's too small and slight. Hardly a grown man."

"But would Axe be a better captain? I want real riches, and I don't care who helps us get it or what they look like."

"Look at us. We're in rags—"

"Just like any other man who sails the seas!"

"Hear me out, man. Axe has a plan. He says Cap'n is hiding something. An' Axe is stronger, and can intimidate our prey. And once we hit the jackpot, we'll split everything evenly."

Silence.

I crept away, feeling slightly sick. *Axe would* not *be a better captain...* But I had a moment of self doubt. Was I not the leader I thought I was? *How long had this disloyalty been festering?* I fought down the lump in my throat as I looked up at the taught white sails through the hatch. I longed for my mother. Someone I could talk to.

Someone loyal.

Johnny's frame appeared in the hatch and he picked his way down the ladder. "Which way's the wind blowin', Cap'n?"

I sighed. "Against me."

He eyed me as he perched himself on the seventh step down. "Somethin' wrong?"

I chewed my lip. "What's your take on the crew's state? How many are for Axe taking over?"

He sighed. "Almost half, I reckon. Some of us were wonderin' if you got a plan to get wealthier. This job ain't givin' us the freedom we wanted. We're barely scraping by, know what I'm sayin'?"

My face hardened. *It wasn't* my *fault none of the ships we captured carried gold.* "So you're against me, too?"

"Never said that. I ain't rootin' for no blunderin' idiot. He's not gonna live up to what he boasts, fer sure."

I breathed a sigh of relief. "I'll try to figure something out. And Axe is lying. He wouldn't give you equal share. But *I* would."

He nodded, and I climbed the ladder, wishing I was a man. Beefy arms and a deep voice would really come in handy right now. If my crew feared me more, I wouldn't be having this problem.

———○○●○———

The galley door rattled as I pounded my fist against it. It was a new day, and I was determined to make the most of it.

"Who is it?" Preston called from inside.

"Your captain."

The latch was drawn and the door opened. I pushed past him, my eyes roving over barrels of water and food. "How are we doing?" I asked curtly, counting the water casks.

"Enough for a good eight weeks, plus some to sell."

"Good. You're an intelligent cook, I'll give you that." My thoughts drifted to the conversation I heard yesterday, and I wiped sweaty palms on my overcoat.

"Is that the first compliment you've ever given someone?"

"What?" I said, pulling myself from my thoughts. He raised his eyebrows, and his comment registered. I narrowed my eyes. "I take it back. Maybe you're not so intelligent."

He laughed, and I shook my head. I didn't even mind his jab. I had too many things on my mind. I fought the urge to run a hand through my hair. I couldn't— it was pinned up and stuffed in a hat. I stepped toward the door, wishing I had all the keys to finding the treasure. I could use it to buy back the loyalty of my crew.

"I'm impressed, you know. You're the captain of a ship, yet you look younger than me—er, besides the facial hair. I don't know what's going on with that." He paused. "How did you manage it?"

"The facial hair?"

Preston threw back his head and laughed. "Being a *captain*. I can grow my own bushy facial hair if I wanted, thanks."

I raised a brow. "Are you sure?"

He folded his arms, grinning. "Don't insult my manliness. I'm taller than you. Now tell me how you managed to become a captain at such a young age."

I rolled my eyes. "By means you nor your friends would approve of."

"Such as?"

I looked at him curiously. "Violence, deception, thievery, and the likes."

"Respectable." Preston nodded thoughtfully. I couldn't tell if he was serious or not. "You're on edge," he noticed.

"Nothing's the matter," I replied gruffly.

"If nothing's the matter, you wouldn't be acting strangely."

I eyed him, feeling defensive. "Meaning?"

"You're fidgeting. Something's obviously on your mind. Care to tell?"

"No." I turned to go, anger bubbling up at his observations. I hadn't noticed I was fidgeting.

"I know about Axe's plans," he blurted.

I looked at him sharply, wondering why he asked me to tell him when he already knew.

"I know he's trying to convince the crew that you're a muttonhead and that *he* should be the one in charge."

I turned away. "Aye. It's a bit of a problem."

"For us both," Preston agreed. He glanced around and leaned in like he was sharing a secret. "I was the one who put that glass shard in his fish."

I laughed, even though I'd already guessed as much. "So that fish didn't *actually* swallow a bottle of rum?"

He grinned. "Just know I'm rooting for you, mate."

I left the galley, not even bothered he didn't call me captain. Preston had a knack for lifting spirits.

My feet hit the lowest level of the ship. With the single lantern to light the room, I had to strain my eyes against the dim. Alexander and his father stopped talking when they heard me approach.

"How's your day going?" I asked with a little mirth.

"Quite wonderful," Alexander responded, his tone flat. "I love spending all my hours down here in this dank, smelly place, with not a drop of sunlight to be seen. You should try it sometime."

I chuckled, then my smile dropped. "I've brought some news, if you'd care to hear it."

"If you want to share it, I shan't stop you."

"What news?" Unlike his son, Callaway didn't bother masking his interest.

"Axe wants more power, so he's looking to demote me. He has many others convinced he'd be a better captain." I already knew that Alexander held a grudge against Axe, because of what he did to Preston, but for some reason I needed some validation. "If I am demoted, you might have to declare your full loyalty to the pirates or be killed. And I wouldn't trust moral-less, bored pirates to give you a quick and painless death."

Alexander leaned back on his hands. "What will *you* do once you're demoted? How will you keep your secret safe?"

"What secret?" Captain Callaway demanded.

Alexander dropped his voice to a whisper, his eyes locked on mine with a dangerous gleam. "The captain..."

I gave Alexander my most menacing look. "Don't. You."

"Is..."

"Dare." I seethed, banishing any trace of fear from my face. *He wouldn't dare.*

"A *girl*."

"Come again?" his father said, shocked.

I clenched my fists so hard my nails cut into my skin. "I *hate* you," I growled. *That blasted man.* I should've thrown him overboard the first chance I got.

Alexander gave me a pointed look. "You don't have the gift of my trust, nor my respect. It was your mistake to assume I would keep such a secret from my own father."

I narrowed my eyes. "Yet you didn't tell him until I was standing in front of you. And you didn't tell anyone else. Which means—"

"Who would I have told, whilst being left to rot down here?"

"Preston."

"In truth, I completely forgot about you until you walked into my line of sight."

Somehow, I doubted that. I fished the keys out of my pocket and held them up. "I came to release you."

"Oh good. So you can force me to do your bidding."

"Absolutely not!" Callaway growled. "Do not come anywhere near my son, whore!"

I was really fighting for composure, now. "I am no whore," I hissed, keeping my hand away from my gun. "I am a girl with a dream of freedom. There's a very big difference." I looked at Alexander. "As for you, *boy*, you can do whatever you wish... as long as it's within the roles of a deckhand and navigator."

He raised an eyebrow. "If you really need me, unlock this infernal cage."

"Not so fast." I held up a slip of paper. "This is your ticket."

He took it from me, understanding. His father leaned closer to see what it was.

Alexander's eyes found mine, and he flipped the paper between his fingers, a slight smile playing across his lips. "You know... I have a feeling these aren't just random words. You've obviously been copying them from somewhere."

"Well, I don't care about your *feelings*. Read it and give it back." I shifted my weight uncomfortably.

"You don't want me to find out what they really mean, do you?"

"I said, give it." Anxiety coursed through me. I'd under-estimated him—one of the worst mistakes a person can make with their enemy. I was going to have to alter my plan if I wanted to keep the map's contents a secret from him.

The old captain was watching us with curiosity, undoubt-edly trying to figure out what was going on.

"If you want what's on this little piece of paper so badly, then I assume you are willing to make a trade."

I scowled. "Name your terms."

"Let my father out as well. Don't chain us up again, and treat us like part of the crew."

"Only if you—"

"Actually," he cut me off, "I take it back. Don't treat us like part of your crew. Treat us like...your guests. Respect us. There is a reason your crew's turning on you. You treat them like garbage."

"That's because they *are*—"

Alexander's father held up his hand. "Let me give you some advice, captain to... captain. You need a loyal crew. You need to give them a reason to trust you and do what you say even in times of great tribulation. Respect their beliefs and share their joys. If you're harsh, at least don't be distant."

"Thanks, Old Salt," I grumbled. "I accept your terms—I'll treat you the best I can."

"Good. Your word is 'warm.'"

I nodded, taking the parchment and repeating the word in my head. So I had '*nights*' and '*warm*'. There was a short, three-letter word in between, but I would have to figure it out later.

*Creeeak.*

I looked toward the ladder, where the sound had come from. Large boots disappeared from the top step. My stomach sank. Who was it, and *how much had he heard?* I shoved the key in the lock and turned. I didn't wait for them to step out before flying up the stairs. Quietly I followed him through the darkness, listening. His pattern of steps told me it was my quartermaster. *Damn it.*

I squared my shoulders. "Axe!" I snapped.

He turned. "Yes, Captain?"

I caught up to him, and we kept walking, side by side. His use of my title told me he hadn't heard the revelation of my secret. *Whew.* "Is there something wrong? Why did you follow me to the brig?"

"Nothing's wrong, Cap'n." He sounded far too upbeat. "Just wonderin' if there was a plan of action for the next couple of weeks."

"In fact, there is. We're heading to some warmer weather in the Caribbeans. I was thinking we'd try our luck with the sugar trade."

"Aye, aye. Good idea."

I bit my tongue to keep from responding something less than kind as we climbed up to the main deck.

Striding to the edge of the boat, I looked out at the horizon. Would I be the captain, the next time we raided a ship?

A large gust of wind blew in my face. It ripped my fake mustache loose and carried it into the air. I grabbed desperately at it, but all in vain. Horror filled my stomach as it landed on the surface of the waves, gliding farther and farther away. I stood there, clenching and unclenching my fists. That little piece of facial hair was a key feature in my disguise. I supposed I could say I shaved it, and I still had my goatee... But I was getting dangerously close to revealing my secret.

I snuck into my room and stared at myself in the mirror. I still looked like a boy, albeit slightly younger. Sighing, I touched my top lip. *Dinner tonight will be a nightmare.*

True to my prediction, I was the center of attention when we sat down to eat our grub.

"What rot got into your head to make you shave your mustache?"

I raised my chin, steeling myself. "Go hang by your toes from the yardarm."

They roared with laughter. I smiled, feigning confidence.

"How do we expect our prey to cower, with you leading the charge? You're a wee little lad!"

I narrowed my eyes, heat flashing up my face. "I can beat you all in a sword fight. People who underestimate me *always* pay." Before they could say anything else, I added, "Bart, I saved your life, don't you forget. That monster of a sailor would've turned you to fish food, if it weren't for me."

Axe leaned back against a support column and took a bite of biscuit. "Who got him into that sticky situation in the first place, I wonder?"

I threw up my arms and exclaimed, "We're pirates! Do you honestly expect to accomplish anything without facing a little danger?"

"Cap'n's got a point," Johnny said.

I was aware of Preston's silence from the corner or the room. *Is that what* 'rooting for me' *meant?* Although, he'd admitted that his friend was the braver one. But did I expect Alexander's support?

Not at all.

"What *have* we accomplished?" Axe argued. "We've been out at sea for two years, and rarely do we go ashore. All we've gained is a price on our head, and nothing to show for it!"

"And no rum," Bart growled.

"And no women!"

Alexander met my eyes when a chorus of agreement followed. He knew as well as I what would happen if my secret was discovered.

"We have our freedom," I argued, anger laced in my tone. "And you've each gained coin! Do you not remember where the money you gamble between yourselves came from?"

"That's not enough!" Axe spat on the ground.

Furious, I whipped out my pistol. On a normal day, it would've hardly bothered me. But at the moment, I was high strung and ready to snap. "Wipe that up."

Axe narrowed his eyes, refusing.

*Too humiliating, was it?* "Who's ship is this?" I demanded.

No answer. The crew was watching, buzzing with energy.

"I said, who's ship is this!"

"Yours," Axe snapped, eyes glittering with hatred.

"Good. Now if you'd prefer to leave this ship without a bullet in your skull, you'll want to wipe that up."

Axe gazed around at the rest of the crew, shaking his head. I couldn't tell his expression, but some of the other faces reflected disgust, and a few glared at me.

I put my pistol away as Axe bent to the floor, using his sleeve to clean up his saliva. My anger simmered down, revealing unease.

I much preferred anger.

A tickling at my neck pulled me from a light sleep. I held still for a moment, gazing through my lashes. Someone was looming over me, hands near my throat.

I grabbed his wrists and twisted, throwing myself out of bed and knocking him to the floor.

It was Weasel.

I reached over to grab my gun, and he wiggled out of my grasp, scampering back. "Freeze!" I ordered, holding him at gunpoint and blinking the sleep from my eyes. "How did you get into my room?"

"Yer a girl!" Weasel exclaimed.

Dread pooled in my stomach. In my daze, I hadn't realized the weight of what his intrusion meant. *That merchant ship wasn't a boon. It was a curse.* Ever since, things started to fall apart. I swallowed. "I think I should kill you."

He cowered.

"You picked the lock, didn't you?" I demanded.

His silence was answer enough.

Feeling violated, I kept my voice steely calm. "You snuck into my room and tried to rob me. But tell me what you were planning to do with my key, and I'll let you live." I waited.

He said nothing.

I cocked the gun, desperately pushing down the fear that was threatening to consume me.

"Axe sent me!"

I narrowed my eyes, my heart pounding. "Why?"

Biting his nails, he explained, "He told me to find somethin' with words on it. He said it migh' be hidden. He said he'd give me half of his coin."

Cold washed over me. *Weasel knows. He's loyal to Axe.* The threat of death or slavery was very real now. "He doesn't have any money, you blithering idiot. He gambled it all away two nights ago. And I don't know what he means by *something with words on it*. You know I can't read. Why in the seven seas would I keep a book on board?" If Axe got ahold of the map, my dreams would be lost forever. I was no longer safe aboard my own vessel. As soon as we touched land, I'd take the few items I owned and escape. It hurt to abandon such an expensive vessel, but the treasure was worth more.

"Leave. If you tell anyone I'm a woman, I'll gut you." I watched him go, knowing he would blabber.

Knowing it might cost me everything.

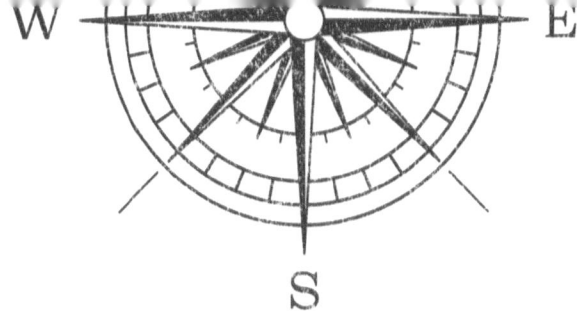

## Chapter 7

I HUMMED TO MYSELF as I brushed my hair, wondering how long Weasel would keep my secret. I'd made it through the day without incident, but I'd taken a biscuit to my room instead of heading to dinner with the crew.

How much longer would I have to speak in an unnaturally low tone? I tested a higher pitch and muttered something. It'd been so long I'd forgotten what I used to sound like. I settled on a tone in between—*yes*.

I massaged my scalp with my fingertips, trying to forget the problems with my crew and letting my mind drift to the map instead. Only about thirty more words to go. Maybe I'd ask multiple at once, just out of order. Alexander had figured out I was up to something, but as long as he didn't put them in the correct order, and as long as I didn't accidentally make him read the word, "treasure," he wouldn't connect the dots.

*Tap, tap.* I whipped my head towards the door. *Tap, tap, tap.*

I set down the brush and hurriedly pinned my hair up, shoved my hat on, and slipped my coat over my shoulders. "Who's there?"

"It's Alexander." His voice was muffled through the door.

I sighed. "Listen, sailor, I already gave you one chance. Are you really going to ask for a rematch? I thought you were intelligent."

"I am unarmed. I simply came to talk. You'll really want to hear this."

I pursed my lips, then walked to the door and let him in. "What?"

"There's no need to pin your hair up. Everyone already knows."

I froze.

He nodded, closing the door behind him. "They know you're a girl. And well... if the crew found out I warned you, they would surely take my life."

I looked at him intently. "Warned me about what?"

He opened his mouth to reply, but a loud *BANG* on the door made him whip around.

My eyes widened. "Did you lock the—"

"Yes. This is what I was going to tell you," he said, his words rushed. "Your crew's un—" *BANG.* "—happy," he finished. "They were planning a mutiny."

"A mutiny?!" I exclaimed.

"Shhh!"

"Why didn't you tell me this before?" I whispered.

"I didn't know until supper today! And I didn't know they were going to do it so soon!"

I took my compass out of my pocket and ran to the table. *Just in case.* I fumbled with the key around my neck, then grabbed the little box and fitted the key into the lock. I quickly opened the lid, put the compass inside, and locked it again.

The door shook again as I ran back to Alexander, adrenaline pumping through my veins.

There was one last BANG, and the lock snapped, the door crashing open. I pushed Alexander down, and he fell into the shadows. Axe appeared before me, his form filling the entire door frame. I grabbed my sword, hoping to distract him before he noticed there was anybody else in my room. Alexander stayed where he was, not daring to move.

Axe stepped forward and smiled grotesquely down at me. "Hella, ya little wench. Would ya like to die or warm up that bed for me?"

Rage shot through me, and the next second I was slashing at his face with my sword. He moved his knife to block it, but too slowly. A splatter of blood, and a chunk of flesh went flying.

Axe let loose a blood-curdling scream, and I dove under his legs, my stomach churning. I stood up to a wall of large bodies.

Who were all *very* angry.

"Hey there, maties! Fine night for sailing, don'tcha think?" I said breathlessly. Maybe if I spoke like them they would forget I had just cut one of their maties' noses off, but I didn't stop to find out. I ducked my head and plowed through them, only succeeding because I caught them by surprise. I lost my hat, but I didn't look back as I ran down the deck, listening to them pound after me. My heart raced, and so did my mind. Where could I go?

And then it hit me: I had planned for something like this. I had built that little secret room years ago. *Why did I not remember sooner?* Now it was too late. I looked wildly around. The sun had already disappeared behind the horizon, but the sky still gave off a faint light.

They took their time, knowing I had nowhere to go. I backed up, my heart thudding. Bart licked his lips, his bald head shining with the last of the light. I kept my sword high and pulled my gun out, making them hesitate. But who would I kill?

I only had one shot. One kill, and what would that accomplish? There were too many, and it would just make them angrier. Alexander and the other captured sailors were nowhere in sight, most likely fearful of this violent version of pirate politics.

No, not politics. This was personal.

Finally the person I most dreaded to see pushed his way through the crowd, more furious than I had ever seen him.

The front of his shirt was steeped with blood, his eyes were murderous, and his muscles bulged as he passed his long knife back and forth between his hands. His nose wasn't there, there was just blood, so much blood, running down the front of his face and dripping from his chin.

"You made a grave mistake, lassie," he growled. He spit blood out of his mouth before he continued. "For cuttin' off me nose. For gettin' rid o' all the rum. An' for comin' aboard at all. You ain't no cap'n. Yer a WENCH. A GIRL!"

"A whore," one sniggered.

I struggled to find the right response.

"Girlies ain't allowed aboard a ship. So we voted, and you ain't the cap'n no more. You could've stepped down peaceful-like. But now..." He gingerly touched his face. "Now, after you provide each of us a little fun, yer goin' to Davy Jones's Locker, you are."

"Then I will haunt your dreams, scabby sea bass. You will wake up every morning screaming for your nose," I growled, pointing my gun at his heart. "But I won't go down that quickly."

"Oh I wouldn't do that if I were ya." Bart grinned savagely. "If you shoot me matey, I'll make sure your death is as painful as it can be."

I hesitated, then lowered my gun. I was mentally grasping at solutions now, any situation that didn't end in my death—or worse—becoming their nightly entertainment. If I could just get past them, I could run up the stairs and hide in the secret room. At least then I would be safe for the moment. What else could I do? Jump off the side? They would just laugh at my cowardice, and I would die anyway. There was no use hoping for the other sailors to come to my aid. They would just be overpowered. What had I done to deserve their sacrifice?

Nothing.

I bit my lip as they inched closer, and waved my sword in an attempt to keep them at bay. Axe struck out with his long knife, and I blocked him just in time. He was strong, but my reflexes were fast. I blocked every one of his blows, but then Bartholomew and Bones joined in too, so I was fighting three of the beefiest members of my crew.

All at once.

I struggled to hold my own. My arms burned as I was slowly forced backward. A cut appeared on my left forearm, then on my leg. If I had a second sword, things would be different. I managed to slice Bart's cheek and then Bones's stomach, but that just made them angrier.

My heel hit the edge of the boat.

I hated being on the defence. Offence was my specialty—it felt powerful. But now, fear of death overpowered the thrill of the fight.

Blocking their blows became more and more difficult, even though I had the longer sword. I felt a sharp pain as Axe's blade grazed my bicep, cutting through my coat and my undershirt. I was only barely able to stifle my gasp. *Do not show weakness.* If I was going to go down, it would be with bravery.

I put all the strength I had left into my strikes, and I managed to cut each of them multiple times. But finally the weapon was knocked from my hand, and simultaneously, Axe lurched forward and slashed at me with a knife. Overwhelming pain erupted across my abdomen, and I cried out, dropping to my knees.

A couple pirates laughed.

"Aww, did you get a little ouchie?" one mocked. "If you were a *man*, you would still be fighting."

My vision went blurry as tears filled my eyes. I gasped for breath, and all thought escaped me. I pressed my hands to my stomach, feeling warm, wet blood soak through my clothes. I was yanked up by the collar of my jacket, my arms roughly pulled back and tightly tied. My bandana was pulled off and my hair fell down. I smelled dead fish and whiskey in his breath as Axe's face loomed into view.

"Yer not so brave now, are ya?" he taunted. I couldn't meet his eyes, I was trying so hard not to let him see me cry. "Now, where's her hat?" He yelled to the other crew members. "It's all mine, now." He threw me to the ground, and I felt someone pull my boots off and tie rope around my ankles.

"Captain Axe, Sir!" someone called.

"Huh?"

"Since she's no captain no more, she doesn't need that fine coat, does she?"

*Uh, oh.* I had a bad feeling about where this was going.

"Are ya sayin' you wan' her coat, bucko?"

"Sure thing, Cap'n, if you don' wan' it!"

"Can *I* have it Cap'n?" another asked.

I looked at Axe. "Please, no..." but no one seemed to hear me.

My hands were quickly untied and my coat jerked off. I fell back to the deck, with no way of defending myself. I didn't know how bad the cut on my stomach was, but it was still bleeding.

"Let's take her shirt, too," one man sniggered.

They were taking pleasure in humiliating me. I squeezed my eyes shut, silently begging this all to be a bad dream.

"Stop!" someone shouted.

I opened my eyes to see Alexander push his way through the crowd. A glimmer of hope peeked through my agony.

"Look, here's the boy tha' killed Tommy," Bart growled. "Yer either brave or daft for comin' over an' tryin' to ruin our fun."

It seemed that Alexander hadn't planned out what to say next. "Er...I...You shouldn't do that. It's not right to humiliate a woman in such a way."

I wanted to slap him. You couldn't talk to pirates about right and wrong; they'd just laugh at you.

"Are ya choosin' the little wench's side then? Ya want ter get her same fate?" Bart demanded. "Drownin' ain't fun." He chuckled like he'd just made a joke.

Alexander met my eyes for a few moments, his eyes burning hope into me. But then he threw his head back and laughed. "*Her*? You think I'd risk anything for a girl like that?" He looked Bart in the eye. "She's not worth it, sir."

*Not worth it.* The words echoed in my head. *Is that what he's thought all along?* Was he just *playing* the sympathetic, honor-bound sailor, trying to see how best to manipulate me?

Fine.

*It's not like I ever trusted him.* He was just one more piece of evidence that people will always let you down. But rage and betrayal boiled in my stomach like a dangerous potion, hot and volatile.

"Did you hear that, Girly?" Bart cooed gleefully. "You're not worth it."

I squeezed my eyes shut again, and another tear rebelliously escaped my eye. Maybe I had, without meaning to, allowed myself to hope he was different. Was that why I felt this way? There was an ache in my chest that was foreign to me; I didn't know how to name it.

Someone dragged me up again, and my shirt was ripped open. All I had left was the tightly wrapped linen around my chest, and the protection it gave was the only comfort I had. I was starting to see stars, but I struggled against the man holding me. Alexander was nowhere to be seen, but I forced myself not to care.

"Why are you listening to him?!" I screamed. My head spun from being pulled up so fast, and from losing so much blood. "A sea slug would be a better captain than Axe!"

My curses and name-calling did nothing to deter them; instead they returned their own mixtures of profanities and insults. Their harsh words echoed in my head: I was bad luck, I was the reason we couldn't find any good ships. I was the reason Tommy was dead. They blamed everything on me as they bound my hands behind my back so tightly they started to tingle. A large hand reached for my neck and snapped the small chain around it. I watched with hatred in my gaze as they handed the key to their new leader.

They had dragged me near the edge of the boat, but now Axe ordered them to release me. Balancing carefully on bound feet, I threw my shoulders back and kept my chin high. The tear tracks down my cheeks felt cold as they dried. When Axe smiled, his teeth were stained red. Did he expect me to give up? To accept my fate as his slave? Had he forgotten that I was Anne Bonny's daughter?

When he reached for me, I hopped backwards as far as I could with my ankles tied. I jumped again and stumbled, but didn't fall. I didn't need to look behind me to know there was a break in the railing. Axe stepped forward.

Two years of fighting by their sides, and they underestimate my courage?

For one last fleeting moment, I stood on the edge, my senses taking in everything I had missed. It was just past twilight, and the stars were out. The night was too pretty. I was too young. There was treasure yet to be found. I looked around at them all, silently cursing them for the greatness they stole from me.

Then the moment was over; my time had come. I held my breath and jumped.

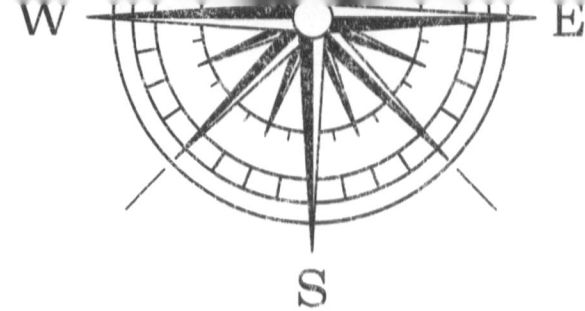

W                                      E

S

## Chapter 8

I PLUNGED INTO THE COLD WATER, then kicked hard up to the surface, gasping for air. I strained against the bonds that held my hands behind my back and my ankles together. The men that used to follow me and fight for me now laughed and waved as they watched me struggle. My ship crept along. Soon they would drift out of reach, and I'd be naught but a corpse drifting downward toward the seabed below.

A wave sent a bucket load of saltwater down my throat, and I coughed and sputtered, trying to stay afloat.

But I knew it was all going to be in vain.

I couldn't balance. My face kept dipping toward the water, and the waves seemed hungry. The salt water stung my fresh wound, the pain almost too intense to bear. I tried to force my hands out of their restraints, but the ropes were too tight. My fingers had lost their feeling. I held my breath and pulled my knees to my chest, trying to get my arms around to my front. I sank deeper. Panic crept in, and I abandoned the effort, kicking frantically toward the surface.

My head broke through the waves and I filled my lungs. I had drifted into dark shadow, the side of the ship within arms length. A glance to my left told me my audience had dwindled, my crew members' necks straining around the aftercastle in an attempt to keep me in view.

I watched my chance of survival wane as my ship continued to glide, its sails full. The stern of the ship came up to meet me.

My head went under again, and my muscles burned with the effort. I kicked and kicked, but I was only able to grab one more breath before the sea pulled me down once more.

Panic clouded my mind. I thrashed about underwater.

*Which way is up?*

Finally I gave in to the urge to breathe. Water filled my mouth and infiltrated my lungs. Spots danced behind my eyelids as hope drifted far out of reach. I thought of my mother and father. *Is this what they felt right before they took their last breath?*

I was no longer Cassandra.

Just primitive fear.

Pain.

My muscles relaxed and I stilled, my thoughts muddled.

I hardly felt the strong arms that wrapped around my waist, and the pain that accompanied it was a distant ache as I was pulled upwards through the water. My head breached the surface, and I coughed and wretched, my mind still hazy as I emptied my lungs of seawater. I was still gagging and sputtering when the realization came: *Alexander*. I could make out his strained face in the moonlight as he gripped a rope.

"This would be a lot easier if you could hold on to me," he groaned quietly as we glided through the water, pulled by the boat.

I said nothing. Sweet relief filled me like the air in my lungs. I hated having to be grateful to him, but I was.

Immensely.

I shivered as the wind whipped my exposed skin, robbing me of any warmth. My hair was plastered to my face. My stomach still burned and stung, but I thanked whatever gods were out there that I was alive.

I'd thought I was gone. My hopes and dreams came rushing back to me, as if from another life. *I will hide no longer. I will reach the treasure as a fearless woman, and prove all the doubters wrong.*

Alexander's arm tightened around me, and I winced as a new wave of pain came. He struggled to pull us back in, but since I was dead weight and he only had one arm, I had no idea how he was going to pull us in and climb up to the gallery.

"I do not forgive you," I breathed. The way he said the words *not worth it* was still fresh in my mind.

"Cass, I just saved your life. And that's the first thing you say to me?" He was incredulous.

*Cass*, my mother's voice called. My throat closed up with grief, but it took me less than a second to push it down and take a breath. I shook my head, trying to forget the pain that name brought. The first weeks were the worst. I'd forget she was gone, and I'd call for her. The nickname she always used for me brought back hints of bitter-sweet memories— ones I wasn't ready to face. "You're not allowed to call me that," I bit out.

"Then what would you like me to call you? Cassandra? Cassie?" Annoyance flitted through his tone.

"Anything but Cass."

"Fine. Now please hush so I can figure this out."

"You had a bad plan. You should've brought a knife."

He grunted, fumbling with my bonds. "It would have made freeing your hands a lot easier."

"It would've made gutting you a lot easier, too." The words were empty of threat and anger; it was a feeble attempt at my old pre-mutiny self.

He laughed without humor. "In that case, I'm glad I forgot one."

We were both very frustrated and cold by the time he got my hands untied. My wrists hurt, but it was nothing compared to the pain in my abdomen. I couldn't tell how deep the cut was, but the agony was overwhelming. I tried to ignore it, and grabbed the rope, pulling myself along until I began to climb vertically, my torso out of the water. I needed to get my feet around the rope, but they were tied, and every flex of my torso was torture. I had nothing but my arms—how was I going to climb all that way? I looked up at the back of my beautiful ship, longing to be up there. The balcony of my cabin was fifteen feet above the water's surface.

"Everything alright?" Alexander said behind me when I had paused.

I glanced at him, then adjusted my hands so that I was facing him. He was still in the water, gripping the rope, but his face was dark, the moon at his back. "On a normal day this would be quite easy for me." I shut my eyes tightly against the pain.

Alexander sucked in a breath. "Oh *God*."

I looked down to see a six inch long gash above my belly button, warm blood running down my stomach and staining my pants. Alexander pulled on the rope, and soon he was right up close to me. "I'll help you."

"I don't want your sympathy."

"Climb on my back, I'll pull us both up."

I made a face. "No. I don't need your help."

I looked up, and climbed hand over hand up the rope until my hands and arms were burning. I grunted, trying to get a little higher. My feet were just barely out of the water, but my hands were starting to slip. I looked down at Alexander, who hadn't moved on his spot on the rope and was still half swimming.

"Try not to fall," he whispered. "We don't want a splash to tell your friends you are alive."

"They are not...my friends," I said through gritted teeth.

"Are you certain you don't want assistance?"

I didn't want to further injure my pride, but my hands were slipping again.

*It would be worse to fall.*

I grudgingly slid down the rope. Avoiding his gaze, I delicately positioned myself on his back, wincing. I wrapped my arms around his neck. The warmth of him seeped into my skin, and I shivered. We rose out of the water as he climbed arm over arm.

I tried to focus on something besides my pain, but the next thing my brain landed on was almost worse—two years I'd spent around tanned, muscled men. Why were *his* arms a magnet for my thoughts? I shook it out of my head, annoyed.

In no time, we were up and over the back railing, crouching underneath the window. I saw movement—light flickering behind the rippled glass. Someone, presumably Axe. I hoped he hadn't found what my key was for, but I had left the box in plain sight. My muscles tensed as I thought about him rummaging through my things. Would he take my compass? I panicked. Would I be able to find it again? Would he throw it overboard?

"Now what?" Alexander whispered.

I blinked. The world spun, and I placed my hands on the wood for support. Then the moment passed, and I was able to answer. "There's a secret room under my cabin. Under the rug, there's a trapdoor."

"We should wait until he goes out or falls asleep."

"No time," I gasped. Everything was spinning again, and spots appeared before my eyes.

Alexander looked at me, and his eyes filled with concern. "What's wrong?"

"I..." I blinked again, trying to stay conscious.

He grabbed my shoulders, and that was the last thing I felt before the world went dark.

———◦◦———

The first thing in my consciousness was pain. *Am I still alive?* I took a difficult breath, constricted by something tightly wrapped around my stomach. *Yes, I must be.* I felt hard floorboards beneath my head and back, and became aware that I was soaked from head to toe. With that realization, everything that had transpired before I'd lost consciousness swooped back to me. I pried open my eyelids and spied Alexander, who was sleeping peacefully with his back against the adjacent wall. I closed my eyes again, wondering what my mother would have done, if her crew had mutinied. Would she have tried to kill them all? Would she have cried when they cut her, screamed at her, and stripped off her clothes? Shame crept into my stomach. She would have remembered her backup plan, surely. If I hadn't been distracted, none of that would have happened. I couldn't stop thinking about that, hating myself.

*If I had remembered.* None. Of. This. Would. Have. Happened.

"How are you feeling?"

I looked up at him. "I feel like I traded spots with Preston."

He laughed without humor, hugging his knees.

I put my hands over the bandage on my stomach. I could hardly breathe, between the bandage and the linen wrapped tightly around my chest. What had Alexander said before the mutiny occurred? Something like, if I hadn't distanced myself so much from them, they would've been more loyal to me. When I first hired them, I thought being a gruff, cold captain would earn their respect. I had thought fear was the best way to keep people in line.

I expected the boy beside me to remind me of that, to rub it in my face, that the mutiny was all my fault. But he did nothing of the sort.

"The knife didn't slice all the layers of your skin, luckily. I hope the wrap is good enough for you; I've never done that before."

I smiled half-heartedly. "Now I may as well be wearing a full corset." He smiled. I gingerly pushed myself up, looking around. "I hate corsets," I added softly.

The ceiling was low, about a yard above Alexander's head as he sat there. The room was square, eight feet by eight feet. Everything was covered in dust. There were swords, guns, bullets, and extra gunpowder in one corner. Another corner housed a couple jars of water and one crate of medical supplies. On a small barrel sat an oil lamp, the only light source in the room. I crossed my arms over my chest and put my hands protectively over my shoulders. They were bare, and so was a strip of my midsection. *And he was right there.* Staring at me.

"Why did you do it?" I asked him. "I managed to go years without getting into anyone's debt. And now, thanks to you, I owe you my *life*." I tried to sound angry, because I didn't know how to express my gratitude without giving myself up to humility.

Anger glinted in his eyes. "Are pirates not allowed to say thank you? Do you know how much I risked to save your selfish, ungrateful neck?"

I opened my mouth to speak, but he plowed on.

"You know what? Maybe you should just get it over with and kill me." He glared at me.

I decided to be honest with myself. It was a good glare. He was quite handsome, despite his split lip and messy hair. Actually, part of it *was* the split lip and messy hair. His loose white shirt was stained with my blood, and one sleeve was ripped and bloody, a deep cut in his forearm. It took me a moment to process what he had just said. "Kill you?"

"My punishment was death if I ever broke my promise."

I was still confused. "What promise did you make to me?"

"Not to kill any more of your men."

"Aye, well, I wish I could, but I owe you my life." I faltered when I registered the weight of his last sentence. "Wait..." I said, my eyes widening. "What did you do while I was out?!"

He looked down, chewing on his lip. "I realized you were right, when you fainted. There wasn't enough time to wait for him to go to sleep. So I climbed through the window. There was a knife nearby, and— and—"

"And what?"

He took a shaky breath. "I stabbed him from behind." He put his face in his hands. "I never thought I was going to become a murderer," he said weakly. "I never meant to kill your navigator. I was so angry, so *grieved*, I couldn't think straight. And now I have *two* black marks on my conscience."

"So Axe is dead?" I asked quietly. If Alexander was so grieved he couldn't think straight the first time he killed somebody, why would he do it a second time?

"Yes."

"He deserved his death."

"*No one* deserves death."

I hummed. "That's debatable."

He sighed as he looked at me, pain filling his eyes. For a second I felt sorry for him. For all his life, he probably only wanted to do the right thing. And that meant being a good, law-abiding citizen. It meant not hurting anyone. It meant living out his life in the same way as everyone else.

My hand drifted to my collarbone, to finger the chain around my neck, but what I expected wasn't there. Suddenly I remembered the map, and my compass.

"Did you see a box on the table? Was it empty?"

He frowned. "A box? I didn't notice it. Why?"

"It's important. I need it. And Axe had the key that goes to it." I got up on my knees, ignoring the pain, and crawled to the trapdoor.

"Where are you going?"

"To get it."

"Let me get it for you."

"Just because I am a woman does not mean I need help doing everything, *Mister* Callaway."

"You're injured, for Christ's sake! Why do you have to be so stubborn? It's like you assume I think less of you for your gender and interpret everything I say in that context."

I turned back to him. "You don't think less of me?"

"I *do* think less of you." He turned his nose up. "You're a pirate. You pride yourself in robbery and deception."

I rolled my eyes at that, suppressing a smile. Turning away again, I reached up and pushed the door open a crack. After ensuring the room was empty, I pushed myself out, ignoring the dizzying shot of pain that tore through me.

Soft pale light streamed in through the windows. Axe lay on his stomach, with two stab wounds in his back, and multiple cuts on his arms. Blood soaked the back of his shirt, and pooled around him. When Alexander said he had stabbed him from behind, I'd imagined a surprise attack, one hit kill. But this was clearly a messy fight. Alexander's split lip and the cut on his bicep now made sense.

I ran past Axe to the table, where my precious box lay open and rummaged through. *Thank the seven seas,* he didn't take my compass. But the map was gone. I searched around the room, jumping every time I heard a noise. The lock on the door was broken, and if someone came in here... that would be very bad for my health. I let out a breath of relief as I spotted it, tucked underneath a chair. I stuffed it in the box and scurried back through the hatch, closing it behind me.

"Did you find what you were looking for?"

I nodded, and showed him the box.

"What's inside?" He leaned forward, interested.

"None of your business."

"Right. Of course." He leaned back against the wall again, disappointed.

We sat in silence, and I gazed at his forearm. It had stopped bleeding, but I crawled over to the medical supplies and rummaged through the crate.

"What are you doing?"

"Your cut. It would be best to clean and cover it." I brandished a small wad of soft linen.

"I'll be fine. It's not bleeding anymore."

"You'll be fine as long as it doesn't get infected and you have to chop it off," I retorted. I gingerly rose and knelt down beside him, wet a towel with cleaning alcohol, then held out one hand.

Alexander decided it best not to argue. He rolled up his sleeve and extended his arm to me. I quietly began by cleaning the skin around it, wiping off the dried blood. I tried to ignore the way Alexander's muscled forearm felt under my fingers. "You have freckles," he said, the surprise in his voice making me glance at him. Then his brow furrowed, as if realizing he'd spoken aloud. "Sorry. I just hadn't noticed before."

I brushed my fingers over my cheek, having forgotten about them myself. "The water must've washed away the grime I smeared on."

He leaned forward slightly, curiosity sparking in his eyes. "You smeared grime on your face?"

"How else would a grown woman fool thirty men? Every detail matters." I shrugged as though it were obvious. "Grime to blur the lines of my face, paint to thicken my brows, blocks in my boots to add height, a hat to cover my hair..."

"A mustache to hide your lips," he said softly.

I nodded, ignoring the subtle flick of his gaze to my mouth. "Even trimmed my lashes."

"You did *what*?"

I couldn't help but laugh at his astonishment. "My lashes," I repeated, brushing a fingertip across their half-grown ends. "They're too long, too thick. At their natural length, they make my eyes look... soft. Feminine. The last thing I needed was to catch the attention of one of my crew. Sacrifices had to be made."

His eyes held mine for a long moment, thoughtful and searching, as if piecing together who I'd been beneath the disguise. Then a smirk broke through his expression. "You missed a detail. You never took the *lady* out of your stride."

I rolled my eyes. "I fooled them for two years, *boy*, so it must've not been *that* obvious." I went back to cleaning his wound.

"Why not your hair? You left it long."

I paused. I would have cut it to shoulder length like most men did long ago—but every time I picked up the scissors, I'd remember the feel of Aunt Mary's fingers through my hair. Then I'd swallow a knot in my throat. *I love your hair*, she'd say. *Don't listen to Jack—never cut it off.* Returning to the present, I shrugged. "I guess I'm just a little bit vain."

A smile graced his lips. "How did you become a pirate captain? Who are you, really?"

My eyes found his, and my heart skipped under his gaze. Soft and intelligent. *He'll surely use the information I give him against me.* I picked up a new cloth, wet it, and pressed it to his cut. He tensed and grimaced, but I continued cleaning it until I was satisfied.

"Or is that something you would like to keep secret?" He raised his eyebrows at me.

I dropped the second cloth and began wrapping thin linen strips around his arm. "My name is... Rackham. My mum used to call me Cass, which is why I don't want you calling me that. It hurts too much. My parents..." I struggled to keep my emotions at bay; numbness was much preferable. I finished wrapping and tucked the end underneath another strap, then scooted away from him.

"Were they killed?"

"Executed."

"I'm... sorry."

"*Are* you? They were pirates. Lawbreakers. Dangerous, just like me." I stuck my fingers underneath the linen straps, trying to loosen them. It was hard to breathe, and it was getting more and more uncomfortable.

"I don't mind a little danger."

The corners of my lips rose. "That I know."

I pulled harder at the strips around my breasts, but it didn't bring me much relief. The bindings helped me pass as a boy, but now they were unnecessary. I needed to unwrap them, but I lacked another garment. My eyes drifted to Alexander. *Oh, this is embarrassing.* "Can I have your shirt?"

"Sorry?"

"I said, can I have your shirt?" I looked him in the eyes and tried to hide my mortification.

A little color rose to his cheeks. "Erm..."

"Oh please, Alexander, don't make me threaten you."

"Fine, fine!" He pulled it over his head, and I tried not to stare at his muscular torso. He tossed it to me. "What do you want it for?"

I turned around so my back was to him, swallowing and shaking the image of his bare chest out of my mind. I needed to get my head together. "Don't look. And if I catch you peeking I will run you through with one of those swords," I told him, pointing to the pile of weapons. I untucked the end of the cloth strip and unwound it, taking a deep breath in, filling my lungs full of air. *Relief.* I threw the cloth strips in a corner with relish. If I were flat chested, the past two years would have been a whole lot pleasanter.

I pulled his shirt on. It was damp and warm, and smelled of saltwater from last night. I took another deep breath and turned back to him. His eyes were indeed closed, so I took my time before letting him know I was done. His lips were full and bow-shaped, his face clear and unmarred. *I'm wearing his shirt, and now he has none.* Flutters filled my stomach, and I sucked in a breath, trying to quell them. *Stop thinking about that. Stop looking at him.* I glared hard at the floor in front of me, until I'd regained control. "You can open your eyes now."

He looked me over. "Cassie, you have stolen my father's livelihood. You have stolen our freedom. And now you have stolen my shirt."

I smirked. "You'd better get used to it. I'm a pirate, after all."

"Have you always been? Did your mother speak properly, is that why you do?"

I stared into his eyes, biting my lip. "It was my father who spoke properly. I don't know how he became a pirate, but my mother was twenty when she left society behind. She ran away with my father because her husband treated her poorly."

"Interesting. And then she had you?" Alexander's voice was so carefully non-judgemental, I was sure he was doing just that.

"A couple years later." This all was trivial. I wouldn't have told him if I thought it could be used against me. "I was born in Cuba, and my mum lived a few years on land to care for me. By the time I could walk and talk, I knew how to fence and fire a gun."

"I would have liked to see a toddler wield a sword."

"I'm sure I was very cute. My father would visit occasionally, and when I was finally old enough he picked us up and I spent the rest of my childhood on my parent's ship."

"Did you like it there?"

"Aye. Those were the best years of my life. I loved the crew, especially my mum's best friend. Aunt Mary, as I called her, was the one who taught me how to do air somersaults and take a man down with naught but a hairpin and a handkerchief."

Alexander raised his eyebrows. "Impressive. Can you teach me?"

I grinned. "To do somersaults in the air? I don't know if you should try. You might hurt yourself."

"I thought you didn't care about me."

"You're right. But *you* probably do."

He chuckled. "Indeed. But if you could learn it, especially so young, then I certainly can."

I smiled mischievously. "You wanna bet?"

He sighed. "Is everything a game to you?"

"It makes life fun. How much will you give me if you break your head?"

He rolled his eyes, then changed the subject. "What happened to your parents?"

I scowled. "I already told you. They were executed."

"What about you? How are you still alive?"

I looked away, afraid he would see through my defenses, through the wall that held all my emotions at bay. "I escaped. Barely."

He leaned forward. "How?"

I didn't answer.

Alexander sat back against the wall again, sighing. "Cassie, you don't have to tell me anything. But sometimes, trusting someone—just one person—can make all the difference. Not everyone's out to hurt you."

"How would I know?" I murmured. "I've been wrong before. And every time, I've lost something."

*Nathaniel.*

His name rose like a ghost from the deep—uninvited, unwelcome, and far too familiar. I could still feel the sting where his hand struck my cheek—the look in his eyes when I told him the truth. The silence after he crumpled to the floor. I hadn't just lost a future that night. I'd lost the illusion that I could ever belong to someone. That anyone would choose me, once they knew who I really was.

I swallowed hard. "I've learned to keep my distance."

"It takes time," he said gently. "And everyone makes mistakes in that area—putting trust in someone they shouldn't. The journey of life is to learn from it, and move on."

I turned to him, shaking my head. "You are an interesting man, Alexander. I've never met anyone like you."

"Was that a compliment I just heard?"

"It wasn't a compliment," I said defensively.

"No? Was it an insult?" He looked like he was about to laugh.

"It was simply an observation."

"Are you certain?"

"I am never *un*certain."

"Alright, Cassie. If you insist."

I hoped he didn't take that comment to heart. It didn't have a deeper meaning in the way he was making it sound.

"So what about you?" I asked casually, wishing to learn more about how he worked. "Where did you grow up? What was your mum like?"

He smiled. "She's intelligent, kind, and gentle. She had a different teaching style when my siblings and I—"

"You have siblings?"

"Yes. I wouldn't be the eldest if my older brother hadn't died just after birth. I have two younger twin sisters and a brother.

"How old are they?"

"My sisters would be..." His brow furrowed as he thought. "Sixteen. And my brother would be eleven by now. I haven't seen them in three years... I wonder how they've changed."

"And how old are you?"

"I'll be nineteen in a few weeks."

I nodded. He was nearly two years older than me.

"Anyhow, my mother never beat us. Her friends would criticize her for it, but we turned out fine."

"My mum never beat me either. My father did, whenever I wasn't harsh enough to enemies or made a mistake that compromised the raid. But that didn't last long. I'm a fast learner."

"Dear God, that's awful. No wonder you're so... you."

I folded my arms. "What's that supposed to mean?"

"No feelings, no emotions. Not caring about anybody."

"I *do* care about people. I... used to," I corrected myself quietly, drawing into myself.

"I'm sorry. I know how it feels to lose someone you care for."

I didn't answer.

"Perhaps you *do* have feelings."

"Do not. I am the same ruthless pirate you first met."

*85*

"Suit yourself," he said, getting up. "I am going to check on Preston and my father. And see if I can nick a biscuit or something. Would you like me to get you anything?"

"Just my boots, thanks." *Thanks?!* Where did that politeness come from? I needed to get my head on straight. Was I a pirate? Or a lady? I watched him quietly ascend into the room above, still shirtless. I decided that maybe, just maybe, I was a bit of both.

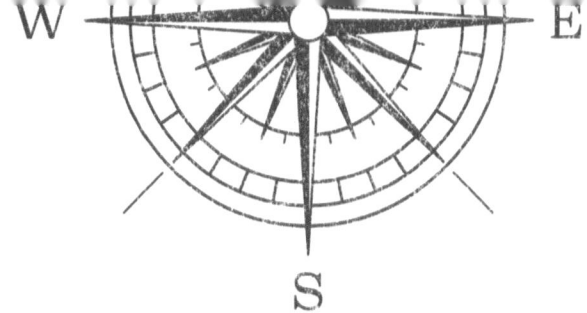

W      E

S

# *Chapter 9*

I STARED UP AT THE CEILING, stretched out on the floor. I tossed up the small roll of bandages and caught it again. I played around with the height, getting it higher and higher until I dropped it.

I watched it roll away across the rough floorboards and sighed. It had been hours since Alexander had left. My eyes were heavy, but pain had chased away all sleep.

*Nights. Warm.* The words swirled around in my head. *What went in between?* A word shorter than both—a connection word, I'd wager. *Nights and warm...something? Nights have warm... Nights are warm...* Even if I knew what this line said, how in the seven seas would it help me find the treasure? *What if nothing written on the map tells me where to sail?* I shook the worry from my head. *It must.*

I picked up the map again and held it above my head, rubbing my thumb over the tightly wound cursive. *The first and third word.* I could barely make it out with the light of a single flame, but there was a little slanted line splitting the first three words from the last three. *That must be the end of a sentence.* Which ruled out 'and' and 'have' for the connecting word. *Nights are warm,* it is, then.

The most useless information I'd ever heard. Maybe it was just the introduction, I thought, my hope feeble. The next line would tell me, 'sail to the southernmost island of the Bahamas' or something.

I began to roll over, but a shooting pain across my abdomen reminded me of my injury. Cursing, I carefully pushed myself up.

If I knew what it was like sitting down here when I designed it, I would have raised the ceiling and added a small porthole. I would have stashed cards or dice!

I needed to get out. Feel the sun on my face and the wind through my hair.

Someone shouted, and my eyes snapped to the ceiling. There was banging. *The door?* My heart rate rose as the sound of heavy boots crossed the floor above me. A moment of silence. A shout of alarm, and the footfalls storming out.

My breaths came quicker. They had found Axe's body. I hoped Alexander and Preston were faring well. If the other pirates would blame anyone for his death, it would be them—or the other sailors we'd brought aboard.

I gently laid myself back down, listening and waiting out the silence. Minutes ticked by. Maybe hours? I couldn't tell.

My stomach rumbled. As long as I didn't make any sudden movements with my torso, I could ignore the pain. Hunger wasn't an issue—I'd gone days without food before. But with nothing to do, no one to talk to?

I hated this feeling. As much as I hated Axe. But he was dead now, Alexander had made sure of that. *Alexander...* I wondered how he was dealing with it. I had always avoided killing people. If I had no other choice, I would make one of my crew do it. It was indirect. I thought that would make me feel less guilty. But Alexander's words kept ringing in my ear. *No one deserves death*. Did my parents deserve death? They had killed many people, but I didn't think so. *Did* Axe deserve his death? Lawmakers and judges execute people for many different reasons. But I had always thought they were too quick to kill. Was I any better? They too, gave the command. They too, turned their backs, too afraid, too *cowardly*, to watch. Perhaps that's what made the difference. They didn't personally know them. They removed themselves, so they didn't have to feel... the pain. Of watching a life be taken. Did it matter what the person did?

I buried my face in my hands, a lump forming in my throat. But maybe... What if this was my chance? To change? I wasn't their captain anymore. I didn't have to be a man to make myself heard. I didn't have to be cruel and mean to get what I wanted. Could it be possible that I hire a new crew as the only female pirate captain on these waters? Would they respect and listen to me?

Then that moment of excitement vanished. Nay. I was only dreaming. They wouldn't listen to me. They couldn't understand. They wouldn't *want* to understand. That was how people worked. People didn't like to change. They were afraid of their world being flipped upside down by a new fact, a new understanding, so they'd shut it out. They'd ignore it. If I was myself, would I ever be more to somebody than a side note? A pretty thing that had no mind of her own? Her only purpose being marriage and good breeding? Sure, some girls liked to stay home and cook and take care of kids.

But not me.

I heard shouts from outside. I strained my ears to listen, but couldn't make out the words that were exchanged.

A shot was fired. I froze—the sound was unmistakable. *Alexander*.

Fear took hold of me, and I scrambled up. *What do I care if he's dead?* A voice inside me scoffed. *I hardly know him.* I clenched my fists, fighting myself. *Oh, I must know.* I couldn't sit down here, wondering if he just breathed his last breath.

My heart was loud in my ears as I stood up on the overturned crate and pressed my hands upward, peeking through the crack and listening intently. This was dangerous. But I couldn't stop myself.

I didn't want to admit it, but I liked talking to Alexander. He respected me, and that was a rare occurrence. *If he was dead...* I lifted the trap door a little higher. I could see the chair and table legs a few feet from me. *It would be because he saved me.* Heart clenching, I risked opening it a little wider, holding my breath. The rug blocked some of my sight.

A loud snore froze me. After a heartbeat, I slowly turned my head and looked up. Bart was sprawled out on my cot, fast asleep, his feet and arms hanging off the sides. I expelled a quiet breath. Then, as silently as I could, I pushed myself up, ignoring the sickening pain from my injury, and crawled out. I gently lowered the hatch and moved the rug back over. Axe's body was nowhere to be seen, but the wood was still stained with his blood. I tiptoed to the cabin door and turned the handle, adrenaline coursing through my veins. I opened it, just a crack, and peered through. I heard Bones's voice and a crack of a whip.

"The cap'n said that if one o' ya doesn't fess up, he'll have ya *all* gutted an' thrown to the sharks!"

"Please, I'm telling you, it wasn't us! You had locked us in the hold, don't you remember?" someone with an English accent argued.

"WELL THEN WHO DID IT?" yelled Bones. "Was it... YOU? Where were YOU after the filthy girl jumped overboard, huh?"

I took in the scene in front of me as the tiny sliver of sight would allow. Bones had gathered the newest sailors, each one restricted by another pirate crew member. The one closest to me was Alexander. I exhaled with relief. None of the sailors had been killed. He was wearing his simple brown jacket, his arms held back by Gabriel, a large pirate who had scars all over his face. Bones leaned in, his face inches from Alexander's.

"I went down to the hold also." Alexander's voice was calm and collected. "I wanted to check on my father and friends. I was not the one who stabbed your large thickheaded friend." Disgust peaked through his tone.

My breath caught in my throat. *Please don't notice, please don't notice.*

He noticed.

"Wait..." Bones stood up, fingering his scruffy beard. "If you were down in the hold, how did ya know he was stabbed?"

I felt slightly ill.

"Well?" Bones demanded, smiling in triumph as realized he had caught the offender.

Alexander glanced sideways, trying to find some-thing to say. "I—I just assumed. I mean, it was holding a bloody knife, so..."

"What?" Bones snapped, taken aback.

Alexander shook his head, gaining confidence. "It was really quite frightening. I don't know if you'll want to hear the story. It might give you nightmares."

I had no idea what kind of story he was making up, but I was impressed with how quickly he thought on his feet. Everyone leaned in, as if drawn by a magnet. They would never turn down a scary story.

Alexander cleared his throat. "Well, after I had gone down to the hold and started speaking to my father, I felt this cold presence. I turned around, and there in front of me was..." He paused for dramatic effect. "A ghost."

A smile crept to my lips. *A ghost story, created on my own ship.*

One pirate scoffed. "No such thing as ghosts."

"Aye, there is!" another one argued. "I saw—"

"Shut up! Let the lad continue." Bones looked back at Alexander, suspicious.

"She was floating a foot above the ground. Her hair was long and dark. Her eyes had lost their beautiful color, and there was a long gash across her translucent stomach. And she was holding a bloody knife. Axe's knife."

*Brilliant man.* He had turned me into a ghost, and sold the story for all it was worth. I watched as they looked nervously at each other, fidgeting. I nearly laughed, letting the door drift a centimeter wider as I pondered his words. *Had he really called my eyes beautiful?* My heart swelled—but then I stamped it out. *It's just one word, idiot. And I don't care what he thinks.*

The pirates whispered amongst themselves.

"Was it really her? Are you sure you saw her right?"

"She's come back to haunt us, just as she said!" Weasel squeaked.

Bones fingered his vest, then twisted the handle of his whip. He seemed to be deciding whether or not to believe Alexander's far-fetched story.

"And," Alexander added, his eyes intense, "She spoke to me. She said that if you ever touched us again, she would kill you in your sleep, just as she did to Axe."

"How come you didn't tell us this before?"

"We thought you would get frightened, since you are all so cowardly," Preston spat. I wondered if he knew I was alive.

The jab at their pride made the men temporarily forget about their other prisoners, and some released them to advance on Preston.

"I could wrestle a shark with my eyes closed, and survive!"

"We're not cowardly, yer cowardly!"

"We'll see about that, tonight, if you don't let us go," warned Alexander.

The pirates hesitated, then backed away.

"Wise choice," Alexander said. He walked confidently towards the nearest hatch, fifteen feet from where I stood. The other sailors followed him, relieved. Alexander bent down, lifted the hatch, and glanced up. Suddenly he hesitated, looking straight at me. I closed the door carefully. *There's no way he saw it was me.*

Resting my forehead on the door, I longed to feel the wind in my hair. I couldn't go out now—I was sure to get caught. I'd have to wait until lights-out. But then what about the lookout? The helmsman? I would have to make sure they didn't see me. Or... I smiled. Alexander had told them I was a ghost—why not use that to my advantage? As long as they didn't fully see me, and it was dark, I could probably pass as a ghost. I smiled wider when I imagined their scared faces when they laid eyes on me.

*Yes*, I decided. *I'll go out tonight.*

Suddenly a hand went around my waist and clamped over my mouth, preventing any noise from escaping. I struggled against my captor, but then I heard a low whisper in my ear.

"*Cassie.* It is I, Alexander."

I relaxed, and his arm unwound from my waist. I turned to him. "What did you do that for?" I mouthed, angry.

"You," he grabbed my wrist and pulled me away from the door, "are not allowed to do that," he hissed, folding the rug back and lifting the trap door. "You could've been caught. Someone could have seen you. *That pirate* could wake up any second." He expelled a breath. "As much as I would love to deflate your enormous ego by saving you a second time, I won't be able to."

I tried to yank out of his grasp. "Don't tell me what I'm not allowed to do. And I wasn't going to get caught."

Bart rolled over and sighed, threatening to tip off the cot. We froze as he smacked his lips and mumbled something. It seemed like an eternity before his breaths evened.

Alexander looked at me pointedly. He put a finger to his lips and then pointed down. *Get in.*

I stepped towards the hatch, reluctant to follow his orders. "How did you get in here?"

"I will tell you once we are safely out of sight."

I rolled my eyes and lowered myself down onto the stool. Bending my head, I walked to the other end, sitting cross-legged. I folded my arms as Alexander followed, fixing the rug, closing the door, and sitting with his back against the wall.

"Well?" I demanded.

He folded his arms to mirror me. "Well what?"

"You were going to tell me how you snuck up on me?" Curiosity had taken hold of me, and there was nothing I could do but satisfy it.

"I didn't specify exactly *when*."

I scoffed angrily. "Yes you did! You said after I went down here!"

He raised an eyebrow, the corners of his mouth pulling upwards in amusement. "I *will* eventually tell you."

"When?" I demanded.

He shrugged. "When I feel like it."

I looked at the ceiling and sighed angrily. "You're such a liar."

"You're more of a liar than me. You are quite mysterious, but then again..." He leaned closer to me. "There's a lot *you* don't know about *me*."

I chewed on my lip. How quickly he caught onto my games, trying to peak my interest and curiosity—manipulate me into giving up more leverage. I unfolded my arms and leaned my head back against the wall, feigning disinterest.

After a few seconds, Alexander changed the subject. "Why were you up there? You know it's dangerous." Then he narrowed his eyes. "You did it *because* it was dangerous, didn't you?"

"Of course not!" I gave an answer that wasn't entirely untrue. "I was hot, cramped, and bored. *And*," I drew the word out, "I'm gut-foundered."

"If you told me earlier, I could have brought you something."

I shrugged, then shifted to another position—but a shooting pain across my abdomen reminded me of something I had to ask. "Do any of your sailor friends know how to stitch people up?"

Alexander's eyes fell to where my cut was, underneath his shirt. "I'll ask Preston. I'm sure he'll know something of the sort."

"I hope so. If I die from an infection, I'll kill..." I trailed off, realizing Axe had already met his fate.

Alexander looked away.

"Sorry," I mumbled.

"He was far from innocent," Alexander finally said, his eyebrows pinching together as his fist clenched. "They all are. My father still refuses to take part in any activities, so they've thrown him in the brig. They're starving him."

I sucked in a breath. "That's awful. If I'd known I couldn't keep them under control and you'd suffer..."

"If you'd never captured me, who would have saved your ass?"

I lifted an eyebrow, still feeling guilty. "I've never heard you swear."

"For you, I made an exception."

I chuckled, then turned serious. "There must be a way to get him food. Preston alone has access to the galley."

"They put a guard on his cell." He sighed. "I'll have to figure something out."

"You will. Tell him..." I hesitated. "Tell him I'm sorry."

Alexander looked at me curiously, then dipped his head in a subtle nod.

"Did you hear where we might be sailing?" I asked.

He shook his head. "Not yet. I'll tell you when I do."

"It would be nice to get off this boat. I don't want to lose it...but I hate being trapped down here."

He nodded in agreement. "Where would you go? What would you do?"

I leaned against the wall and entwined my fingers, thinking. "Ideally, if they dock, I'd find a way to lure them off my ship, then take it back. Then I'd sail away and find a better crew. Maybe I can try a female one instead."

"You really like living at sea *that much*? Are you sure you wouldn't want to try something else?"

"What, you don't like me as a pirate?" I teased.

"I mean, it's boring out here. The only reason I've been a merchant sailor for this long is because of my father. He wants me to stay with him and learn the leadership skills of a captain so that the position can be mine someday. He's proud to work for His Majesty, and so am I, but... I'd rather be making discoveries with the astronomical community."

I pretended to know what that meant. "So you abandon your dreams for the sake of your father's?"

He shook his head. "Discoveries hardly make money. And my father didn't want me to lose my...social standing. People don't realize the relevance of astronomy. They look up at the sky and see twinkling lights."

"And what do you see?"

His eyes glittered with excitement. "I see distant suns, great balls of everlasting fire. I see other planets, too far away for the naked eye to appreciate. I see constellations, stories, calendars, navigation."

I smiled. "That sounds pretty interesting to me. Why can't you study the sky while aboard a ship?"

He sighed. "Telescope technology is expensive. My father won't buy one for me, so until I save up enough coin to buy one for myself, the only ways I can appreciate the sky is with a quadrant or astrolabe. Navigation has a direct use."

"And since a sailor's pay is pittance, you'll take your father's place before you have the extra money to spend on a telescope."

"There are worse things in this world. Like being raided and captured by pirates." He sent me a glare.

I held up my hands. "Aren't we all just trying to survive?"

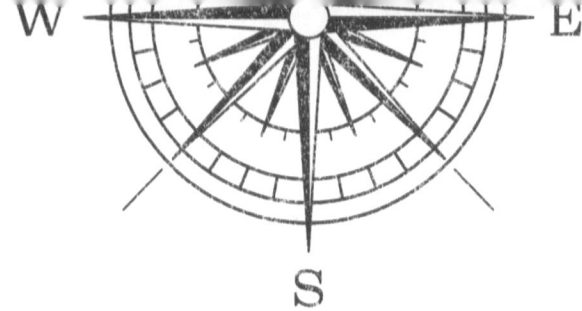

W       E

S

## *Chapter 10*

THE NEXT FEW DAYS couldn't have passed by more slowly. Alexander's visits were few, and he never stayed long. It was daring of him to visit me at all. One night, Preston was the one who entered my little hiding place. I snatched the bread and cheese from his hand and nearly choked myself by swallowing it too quickly.

"How are you faring?"

He pulled out cards as he spoke. "I'm doing fine, I suppose. My bruises are gone and my eye feels better."

"I'm sorry for what happened."

He shrugged. "I've dealt with worse."

I arched an eyebrow. "Really? Do tell."

"I once had to fight off a giant squid while crossing the Atlantic Ocean," he said, splitting the deck and shuffling.

I laughed.

"It's true. We were carrying an important shipment for King George, and it was noonday when we felt the first hit. We heard the loudest thud, felt it in our bones. Then it started rocking, and these bloody huge tentacles started snaking their way up the sides." He used his hands to illustrate.

I shook my head. "That's a bunch of barnacles."

Preston smiled widely. "You don't believe it? Your loss, then. It killed seven of our crew before we managed to get rid of it."

"And how did you get rid of it?"

"I'll tell you. Xander—"

"Xander? What an unusual nickname."

"You're one to talk. Everything about you is unusual. Anyway, before you so rudely interrupted, he distracted it by chopping its tentacles, while I swam deep down and stabbed it in the eye."

"This story seems to be getting more and more fictional. What's next, it swallows the whole ship and spits it back out?"

"Of course not! It didn't like getting stabbed in the eye, so it swam away, leaving us in peace."

I snorted. Even if a giant squid did exist, and attacked a ship, there was no way stabbing it in the eye would help anything. And fish would grow legs before *Preston* would be the one to do it. But I also knew never to judge someone based on appearance. For all I knew, Preston could be a better sword fighter than Alexander. "Thanks for sewing me up, by the way. I don't think I ever thanked you."

He shrugged. "My pleasure." His ears reddened, and he added quickly, "I mean, it wasn't pleasurable—" This time his cheeks turned pink. "You know what I mean!"

I laughed. "Lighten up, sailor. It's a pirate you're talking to."

He gave a small relieved laugh.

"Say, do you know how to read?" I asked him, my tone curious and care-free.

"I do."

I turned around, discreetly opening the lid of my small chest. I grabbed the first two slips of paper that touched my fingers and examined them. I'd marked the ones I'd read with creases, but these were fresh. "I need you to read these to me."

Preston studied them. "Did you copy these from somewhere? What excellent handwriting! You could be the King's scribe."

"Really?" I asked, astonished.

"No. Your handwriting is dreadful."

I glared at him. "Just read the damn thing."

"*Language*, woman! I need a bar of soap! One says 'great' and the other says 'Preston is'." His face filled with surprise. "Preston is great. How insightful! I must agree."

"You are actually the worst."

"Don't blame me! That's what your monstrous handwriting says."

"No, it doesn't!"

"People who are so serious all the time are fun to tease."

I reached for a knife and brandished it at him. "Tell me the blasted words, and don't lie!"

He pouted. "Fine. You have 'clue' and 'seek.' Quite curious words, if I do say so myself. Where did you copy them from?"

"Nothing important," I replied, shrugging. But my heart was *racing*. "It's just something to preoccupy my mind while I rot down here."

"Well, you aren't starting to smell more than you usually do, so that's good."

A laugh bubbled out of me. "Get out of here."

The trapdoor shut. I whipped out the map and laid all the words I'd learned out next to it. Glancing back and forth between them, I organized them chronologically: *Nights. Warm. The. The. Clue. The. Seek.* I tapped a finger to my lips. Likely

*Nights are warm.* On the next line, two lonely *'the'*s. In the third floated *'clue'*. *'Seek'* sat at the end of the fifth.

Plan of action? I'd focus on the third line. I *needed* that clue like I needed breath—it was all I had to hope for. *Why couldn't I have been born to parents who could read?* This was taking ages!

I snatched the deck of cards. The situation I was in was less than desirable. I should have been standing on the prow or at the helm, staring out to the open ocean.

Turning over the top card on the deck, I found an Ace. *People who can read and write hold aces,* I thought bitterly. I fanned the cards out and picked one in the middle. A King. *These are the lucky ones who were born as boys.* I found a Queen at the very bottom of the deck. *Drive. Determination. Daring.* It was the highest card I had, but I'd be damned if I didn't use it to the best of my ability.

I carefully stacked the cards, making a tower. I got it about a foot high when the boat tipped slightly and they tumbled to the floor. I tried again, and achieved one card higher than before, when the boat listed violently, sending my cards to the floor again. I put my hands down to steady myself, as I felt the boat's momentum shift. The ship leaned to port side, sending the swords and crates sliding across the floor. We were turning, I was sure.

*What's going on?* I wondered. I listened hard, but the sounds from above were faint when they reached my ear. Yelling. Surely it was yelling. *Had they found another ship?* Would this be a chance to escape? I crinkled my nose. This was my own ship, damn it! I paid for it with...well, stolen money. Even so!

A distant cannon blast sent my heart pumping. Not loud, but unmistakable. I needed to be out there—that was my forte. I pressed my hand against the curved wall, separated from the battle by a single layer of wood. I jerked backwards, realizing that if the enemy ship was floating on this side of mine—suddenly the wall exploded, a cannonball tearing its way through the side of the ship. I covered my face with my arms, pelted with tiny splinters.

I took a shaky breath and brushed myself off. The cannonball had lodged itself in the opposite wall. Heart pounding, I peeked my head out of the hole. Gone was the horizon, blocked by a massive painted hull with rows of deadly cannons. Sharks swam between the ships, drawn to the scent of blood. Gunshots and screams rang in the air. I pulled my head back in, not wanting to lose it.

Suddenly the trapdoor was thrown open with a *bang*, and Alexander jumped down, a wild look in his eyes.

"What's going on?" I asked excitedly. "How big is the ship that we're attacking? Does it have booty or goods or just people? What flag do they sail under? How many men do they have? Are we outnumbered? Are—"

"Slow down, woman! I can't answer all your questions at once."

"Tell me what's happening!"

"Cassie, I think this is our chance to get off this boat! If they beat your old crew, then—"

"Hold up. You *want* them to win?"

"Yes!" He looked at me like I was crazy. "How else will you get out of here?"

"If we win, and I am the one to lead us to victory..." For the thousandth time, I longed to be a man.

He gave me a look. "You know it's not that simple."

Anger bubbled in my stomach. Who did he think he was? Managing to hold it all in, I huffed, "Fine. Tell me, who's flag do they sail under? Who is their captain?"

"They're English. I'm not certain who their captain is."

Preston leapt down through the hatch, breathless, his eyes bright. "Hey," he said. "Those pirates are getting their arses kicked up there. It's quite marvelous!"

Alexander smiled at that, but I didn't think it was marvelous. What about Johnny? And Wyatt? I couldn't just sit down here, safe, while people were up there, fighting. "I'm going out." I moved for the trapdoor, but Alexander put his arm out.

"No. It's too dangerous. If your crew sees you, God knows what they'll do. They might name you as their captain again so Bart doesn't take all the punishment."

*That* gave me cause to hesitate.

"One more person isn't going to make a difference," Preston pointed out. "They have a bigger ship and way more men. Not to mention quite a few of the pirates are hilariously drunk."

My face hardened. "I thought I solved that problem."

Alexander raised a brow. "They're pirates. What did you expect?"

"Tell them *'I told you so'* for me, will you?" I grumbled. I didn't want to lose this ship—she was like a companion to me. I didn't want it in the hands of the English, nor at the bottom of the sea.

"Cassie, listen to me," Alexander said. "The pirates are destined for the gallows. We can only hope they recognize my father as a friend. If you run out and fight, you'll be counted as one of them, and be captured."

"What're you getting at?"

"Perhaps," he hesitated, "if you waited until the battle calmed down to emerge, and told them you are a captive, then you could get a free ride back to land. You'd need to..."

"Play the damsel in distress?" I finished, wrinkling my nose. It'd been so long since I was treated as inferior, and I never wanted to go back. I shuddered, imagining playing the less able, less smart, less brave. I definitely could—Aunt Mary was an excellent actress and seductress, and taught me a few things.

Instead, I wanted to teach them a lesson they'd never forget. *But is this the best time to do it?*

He crossed his arms. "If you have a better plan, then by all means, speak your mind."

I pursed my lips. "I have *many* other ideas. But yours is..."

"Superior? Finer? Preferable? Exceptional? Of higher quality?" Preston rattled off.

I blinked. "What?"

"I have more, you know."

Alexander rolled his eyes. "Never mind Pres. Are you in or not?"

I nodded. "I guess we'll see how well I do at acting."

"Brilliant. Let's go," he said in his crisp British English, lifting himself out through the hatch. *He'd fit right in.*

I waited for Preston to follow, then knelt and lifted the lid of the little box. Three things were of great importance: the map, my compass, and the little pieces of paper on which I had copied individual words. I unrolled the map and folded it instead, tucking everything in a leather pouch to protect them from the weather. Then I stuffed it in my pants pocket. I grimaced at my outfit—the bloodied rip in the sleeve of Alexander's shirt, my worn, salt-encrusted pants—and wished for the first time for a dress. I crawled over to the pile of weapons and selected a short dagger, for emergencies. Slipping it into my boot, I climbed through the trap door.

Alexander murmured, "When it's safe, we'll go out and tell the whole truth, minus Cassandra. We are...family friends and were giving her passage to England to visit her grandmother, when we were attacked." He lifted a brow at me.

I shrugged. "Got it. Family friends. English grandmother."

"Alexander," his father said sharply, stepping up to join us at the cabin door. "Lying might cost us our lives. If she is discovered—"

"She won't be. I've already risked my neck for her once, so she better not throw it away."

I folded my arms. "You think I would've gotten this far if I hadn't been any good at being someone I'm not?" I turned to Captain Callaway. "How'd you escape the brig?"

He swung his hardened gaze on me. "My son took advantage of the chaos."

I bit the inside of my cheek as I realized my life depended on his willingness to keep my secret. My pride suffering, I clasped my hands and said, "I'm sorry, Captain. I'm sorry you had to suffer. I didn't mean for any of this to happen. But I'm glad you're about to gain your freedom, even if it means I lose my ship."

The captain studied my face—the subtle slant in my brows and relaxed lower lip. He finally gave a curt nod. "You are lucky my son is so compassionate." He sent Alexander a look. "Too compassionate, sometimes."

Alexander's mouth twitched, then he turned back to the door. "She's not like the rest of them," he murmured. "She doesn't deserve to be hanged."

I watched, tense, as he pushed open the door, the creaking drowned out by the noise outside. I was the first one out, hardly noticing Alexander's attempts to stop me as I ducked under slashing swords. I looked around, instinctively reaching for my sword, but it wasn't there. I was unarmed.

Many pirates lay unmoving. The deck was scattered with Redcoats, herding their captives by gunpoint into a pack near the foremast. The metallic scent of blood drifted through the breeze.

It was then that the precariousness of the situation hit me, and my anger vanished. I raked my eyes over the enemy ship, then up to the top of their mainmast.

A flash of indigo below the country's colors.

My vision tunneled. My feet felt unsteady. I was suddenly ten years old, my mother's voice in my ear. *Run!*

This English ship had not been prey. It had been the predator.

*Pirate hunter.*

Fear gave way to an anger so intense, it was as if a wild-fire had spread through my body. I was going to bring this captain to his knees.

I took a steadying breath, pushing everything down. If they suspected even for a moment that Alexander and his friends were pirates as well...that would be the end of the line for them.

So I imagined flowers and dresses. Remembered high tea and corsets.

Tossing my pride overboard like useless cargo, I threw myself to my knees with a relieved wail. "Thank the Lord on High! Who are our saviors? The fearless soldiers who saved us from these devil-possessed pirates!"

I was immediately approached by a young man with silky, white-blond hair. He was dressed similarly to the others, except for the silver trim down the front of his coat. "Miss! We hadn't seen you until now. Up now, and tell me your story. How on earth did you come to be on this pirate ship?"

Standing up, I glanced at the muskets leveled at the three men behind me, then across the ship to my crew. Thank the stars, they hadn't yet noticed me. I met the young man's pale blue-green eyes, strikingly familiar. "Our ship was raided by pirates. They took me and five of the men as prisoners, forcing them to work and fight under pain of death! How awful it was! I would've been subjected to a fate far worse, but Alexander and his friends helped me hide where they couldn't find me." I stuck my bottom lip out and widened my eyes, *praying* he bought it. I wished for my lashes again—they were only partially grown back since I'd last trimmed them.

"It was a miracle you came to our rescue! I hate to imagine what they would've done to me if I was discovered."

He stood a little straighter. "Of course, Miss. We're doing our best to rid these waters of the likes of them. They'll go straight to the gallows, as soon as we get back to land."

"The gallows?" I asked, my pretense faltering. "Won't they get a trial?"

The sailor chuckled. "Yes, but we all know they're guilty."

I scowled.

The Redcoat turned to Alexander and his father. "There were five men captured?"

Captain Callaway quickly made introductions, then pointed across the ship. "Had Benedict and Colin not been under pain of death, they never would have fought their own people."

The six of us were escorted to the side of the ship and up onto the narrow gangplank.

"Did they take your dress?" the soldier said behind me as we walked.

It took me a moment to realize he was addressing me. I shook my head. "No. When the pirates attacked, Captain Callaway told me to exchange it for men's clothes in an attempt to keep me safe. After we were taken prisoner, my disguise didn't work for long."

"It must have been awful frightful for you, to be captured and all. Pirates are despicable, the lot of them."

I bit my tongue and glowered.

Minutes later, my crew was forced across after us. They shuffled along, some dragging their feet and stumbling. I stepped back behind Alexander and the Redcoat, hoping they wouldn't notice me.

"Ghost!" Weasel slurred, lifting a wobbly finger. "She brought this upon us in 'er fury!"

I grinned, but then Bart caught my eye. He lunged, chains clinking, pushing past the Redcoats who were caught by surprise. Alexander stepped forward protectively, but the soldiers managed to restrain him before he reached us. "I'm gonna kill ya," Bart slurred, growling as they forced him down the hatch.

Last in line, Johnny caught my eye and winked. "'Ello, Ghostie."

A smile lifted my lips. He wasn't drunk, nor surprised to see me alive. *I'll get you out of here, Johnny.* A group of Redcoats excitedly hurried past us in the opposite direction. *Keys and a rowboat...at midnight...* I worked to solidify a plan.

The ship had quieted down by the time I came back to the present. *Why haven't we set off?* My head snapped to *The Mirage* as the soldiers burst from the hatch and sprinted across the gangplank, yelling, "Go! Go!"

The order was repeated. The gangplank was stashed away and the ship slowly set off, a strong wind filling the sails. It dawned on me, as I pulled the image of the Redcoats from my memory, that they'd been carrying small barrels. "No, no, no," I murmured, wringing my hands.

"What's wrong?" Alexander asked.

I turned to Blondie, desperate. "No! That's not fair! Stop it!"

He looked at me like I had two heads, but I didn't care. "No! How dare y—" The rest of my sentence was muffled by a hand that clamped over my mouth.

"Cassie." Alexander hissed in my ear. "Control yourself." He released me before it attracted further attention.

KA-BOOM.

I staggered, then watched in despair as an explosion tore a giant gash in the hull of my ship. My ears rang painfully as wood splinters flew. A cheer erupted all around me. Water poured in, the sea sucking *The Mirage* downward like a hungry beast. Soon she would rest on the seafloor, never to be seen again.

I felt a scream of rage building inside me. Why did I have to lose so much? First my parents, then my childhood, my title as captain, my dignity—and now my ship? I clenched my jaw and gripped the railing so hard my knuckles went white. *Losing your temper won't bring your boat back*, I could imagine Mary warning. *Play the long game—act the part*. I drew a shaky, painful breath.

I'd lost another thing I cared about. What else was new? That was my life.

Losing.

"The name's Joshua," Blondie said a little while later. "Joshua Barnet."

I froze. *That name*. A malicious promise curled inside me like an angry snake. I couldn't even look at him when I choked out, "Are you his son?"

"Ahh, so you've heard of my father?"

I forced a smile and finally met his gaze. "Yes."

He nodded proudly. "I am indeed the son of the most daring adventurer and pirate hunter in the world: the honorable Jonathan Barnet." He said the last three words slower, to increase the dramatic effect.

I curled my fists. *Most daring adventurer? The honorable?* God, if I could punch that smug look off his face...

After all these years, I was back on Barnet's ship again. But this time, at least so far, I was not his captive.

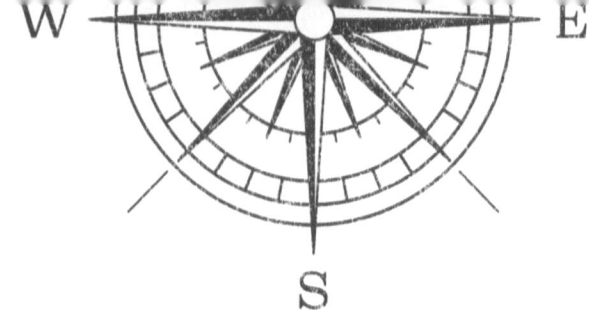

## Chapter 11

I STARED AT THE FOOD laid out in front of me, my mouth watering. It'd been ages since I'd eaten a proper meal.

The room—despite only being occupied by a few people—seemed overcrowded. The long dining table could probably hold most of the crew, but Joshua informed me that they ate at a later time. I dug my fork into the dried meat and soft carrots and stuffed them into my mouth. Both sailors on either side of me, Alexander and Joshua, ate in a more lady-like manner than me, but I felt no shame. Most everyone was quiet except for Alexander and Preston, who were failing at their attempts to keep their conversation and laughter hushed.

I stuffed some more food down my gullet before looking up. Captain Barnet sat at the head of the table, his back upright, with a spotless napkin tucked into the front of his shirt. His cold black eyes roved his guests, and his jaw ticked as his eyes passed over the boys. I glanced away before I risked eye contact. If he recognized me, I would be in trouble. He would lock me away and I would never get my chance to kill him.

"How are you liking your meal?" Joshua inquired.

I looked to my left and put a piece of steak in my mouth. "It's good."

"I hope you are pleased with the change in company."

"I... am," I lied.

"You can call me Josh, if you feel so inclined."

"Josh," I repeated absently. I was frozen, my eyes once again on the captain. He had aged since I last saw him, his neatly trimmed beard streaked with gray. The lines between his eyebrows had grown deeper, and his eyes filled me with hate. They seemed to be trying to tug a memory from my subconscious. The memory I had tried so hard not to let surface. But it grew stronger and stronger, like the spring tide rising up against a seawall. Soon I couldn't block it any longer, and the world in front of me blurred, the memory flooding back to me, vivid as if it happened yesterday.

*My whole body shook uncontrollably. My stomach was rebelling, but I refused to bring shame on pirate blood by emptying its contents all over myself and this cursed deck. An image of our captor swam in my mind, and I fought it. Imagined bringing a pistol up to his head and—*

*BANG.*

*I looked up suddenly, and another of ours collapsed to the deck. Barnet suppressed a smile, a sadistic gleam in his eyes.*

*"Toss them overboard and clean up this mess. Then I want all hands ready to dock!"*

*"Where is he, ye filthy bastard?!" Mum yelled at the captain. "Where's Finn?"*

*I blinked.* Finn?

*"Oh, he's alive. He's receiving an excellent education, which is more than* you *could ever give him. Then he'll come help me rid the world of filth like you."*

*My bewilderment grew. What were they talking about?*

It seemed that all of my mum's loss and grief and hate and rage exited her throat all at once, a sword that meant to pierce his heart straight through. Her howl did nothing but bring a smile to his lips.

He stepped away and began dealing out orders. Not half an hour later, we were marched down the dock and lined up like livestock. I leaned into Mum, trying to gather my courage as I watched a fat man in a big white wig shake hands with the captain.

"Jonathan Barnet," the captain said. "I'm here to hand over these gallows birds. You have the money?" He handed the man a scroll of paper.

"It's a pleasure to meet you, Captain Barnet." He peered at the scroll through his spectacles. "Thirty-one in total, perfect. Just enough space. The public has been starved of a good execution for long enough." He waved at two black carriages with bars for windows. "We have the money just over there."

Mum leaned down and squeezed my hand. She whispered so quietly I hardly heard her. "Cass, listen to me. As soon as I say, ye are goin' to run as far an' fast as ye can. They underestimate ye and didn't chain ye to me, and ye can use that to yer advantage."

"But what about you and father?" I looked at her, worried.

"Don't worry about us. When I say 'go,' run away an' hide an' don't look back. It's yer only chance." She pressed something into my hand, and I looked down. It was her favorite compass. I had the worst feeling inside me, so heavy and sharp it almost took my breath away. Did that mean I wasn't going to see her again? "Keep it close by, an' maybe someday ye will find yer way back home."

"But they're going to kill you. I can't just leave you to die!"

Mum glanced up. Barnet was walking back towards us, two of his crew carrying a big chest between them. "There's no time to think of a different plan. Take this too. If ye find it, ye won't 'ave to depend on a man to save ye from poverty."

"I'll come back for you," I promised, taking the soft roll of parchment and stuffing it down my shirt.

*Mum dove at the man nearest me, stealing his sword and running him through with it, despite her chained wrists. I ducked under the hands of his friend and dove from the brawl, scared for my life—*

An intrusive clinking sound brought me back to the present, and I almost fell out of my chair. My palms were sweaty, my heart was pounding. Everyone had gone silent. Had they noticed? Had I blown my cover? Were they going to lock me away? I looked back and forth, but no one's eyes were on me.

Barnet cleared his throat, and I relaxed, realizing that he had just clinked his glass with his knife. "Once everyone is finished, I will assign night and early morning jobs, and we'll need accommodations for our new guests. I believe we have a few extra hammocks, do we not?"

*Finn.* The name from my memory seemed to haunt me. Who was he, and how had my mother known him?

"We do," Joshua answered.

Barnet nodded. "You will be in charge of getting our guests settled. As for the rest of you," he addressed the quartermaster, "Inform my sailors that they may eat after they clean the weapons and furl the sails."

"But sir, they've been working all day, and they haven't eaten—"

"Who is the captain here?"

"You are, sir." The quartermaster bowed his head. "I mean no disrespect, sir."

"Good. Then you will follow my orders. After they are finished with their rations, they need to wipe the table and wash the dishes. Then pick three for the night watch."

The quartermaster took his dish and left the table, but I stared hard at Barnet. His fancy tricorn hat, his decorated coat, his *stupid* wig—it was like he thought he was better than everyone just because he was rich and he had England's blind support. He was no better than me, he was just a pirate sponsored by the government. A privateer. Someone who hunted people for money, or raided enemy ships. Did he actually believe what he was doing was right?

*He won't be doing it much longer,* I reminded myself. As soon as we were close enough to shore, I would strike. He would go to bed one night and never wake up.

And I would have my revenge. That is what my parents would do, what they would want me to do. They believed in justice. Revenge. Freedom. If there was someone that ruthless and evil hunting *me*, I could never be truly free.

So he needed to go.

Now that I was viewed as a lady, I had the unfortunate advantage of being underestimated. No one on board would be suspicious of me, except for the captain, if he recognized me. All I had to do was act weak and gentle. That wouldn't be too hard, would it?

It wasn't long before night fell upon us, and we stood waiting in the lower deck of the ship while Joshua fetched our hammocks.

Preston bounced on the balls of his feet, turning to Colin and Benedict. "Can you believe how nice this ship is? And the food!"

Benedict, a tall, lanky man with long brown hair tied in a little bun at the base of his neck, shook his head in wonderment. "It was even better than the grub I ate in my hometown. They must've just come from a port."

Colin scratched his chin. "How does he afford all that? How does he get to be so rich and not us?"

"Life isn't fair," Benedict said, shrugging.

I sighed. "No, it isn't. He's essentially a pirate who thinks all other pirates are evil, and the government supports him. He's allowed to sell people into bondage for a boatload of money, while it's against the law for me to steal some food off of a ship. How fair is that?"

"I can see why you don't like him," Alexander told me.

"He sells people into slavery?" Preston asked.

"No." I felt a wave of emotion crash against my chest, but I didn't let it surface. I kept my face hard as stone. "His buyers lock them up for life or hang them. Usually it's the latter."

"But he only does that to people that deserve it," Colin argued.

"People like me?"

Colin shrugged, his gaze leveling at me. "I've no idea what you've done, so who am I to say what you deserve?"

I nodded thoughtfully. "I'd say, if I was religious, I'd be going to Hell. But since I'm not," I smiled smugly, "I can go anywhere I want."

"I don't think it works like that," Preston laughed.

"Here they are," Joshua called, coming back with a tall stack of folded blue canvas. He threw one to each of the men.

I folded my arms. "Where's mine?"

"I'll put it up for you," he replied. "Follow me, there's some extra room down here."

I lifted a lantern off its nail on the wall, then followed, the others close behind me. If Joshua thought I couldn't hang my own hammock, he had *loads* to learn about me.

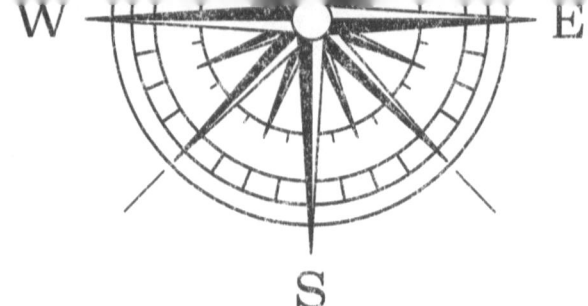

## *Chapter 12*

"REJOICING AND... WARNING."

I stood at the starboard side, Alexander next to me. I creased the pieces and tucked them back into my pocket. It was nearly midday, and we weren't alone. Barnet had men washing the decks, patching the sails, and fixing the holes *The Mirage* had blown into the side of the ship.

I mulled over this new information. The third line read: '*But this clue...a warning.*' I was missing one word. '*Gives*', possibly? I chewed on my lip. '*Rejoicing*' was the second word on the fourth line. I knew nothing of the final line, but there was '*the*' and '*seek*' on the fifth.

Staring off to the horizon, I murmured my thanks. I'd turn my focus to the second line next. Hopefully then I would have a hint for my bearing. I thought about the fifth—what I *sought* was surely the treasure. And I'll be rejoicing once I find it. But what was the clue and warning?

"You *do* realize that giving me one or two at a time isn't going to stop me from sorting out the meaning?" Alexander had his arms crossed and his eyebrows raised. The wind ruffled his hair.

"You'd have to unscramble them, too. And remember them all," I replied. For the millionth time, I wished I could read.

He sighed. "Have I ever given you reason to distrust me?"

"You snuck into my room to kill me once, remember that?" I smirked.

"I wasn't going to kill you," he argued. "I just wanted to force you to let us go. You can't blame a man for wanting his freedom."

"Freedom." I opened my palms and stared at them. "I've spent my whole life chasing it. I thought it meant doing what I wanted, but..."

"You were tapped."

I returned my gaze to him. "Aye. I'm still trapped. Maybe I'll always be."

"That's only because you're hiding. If you changed your ways and lived an honest life—"

"Really?" I cut in. "If I bowed to every written and unwritten rule that dictates your way of life, if I respected the *men* who decide proper behavior for women, if I abandoned the sea for home and hearth—*then* I'd be free?"

He bit the inside of his cheek, a tiny crease forming between his brows. After a moment, he sighed. "No one can imprison you for being a captain. It's what you do with that title that matters. Do you take, or give back? Do you hurt— or protect?"

Guilt stirred in me, but anger surged faster. "Let me open your eyes," I said, my voice cold. "I do what's best for me, because no one else will. Your laws don't help me—they exist for the government, and the government exists for itself. Why should I *give*, when all everyone else does is *take*?"

"That's not true." He shook his head. "There is *kindness*. People care for each other. They give. They sacrifice. The world would collapse if they didn't."

I turned toward the sea, my fingers wrapping tightly around the railing. "You've lived a sheltered life, Alexander Callaway. You haven't seen with your own eyes your government's injustice. You haven't heard natives' stories of England's brutal colonization." The image of Wyatt, barely breathing, surfaced. "You haven't seen the destruction slavery wrecks a man's body and mind."

I let out a heavy breath as I found his eyes. "*You do not know.*"

He finally nodded. "You're right. I don't. *But I want to learn.*"

My eyebrows lifted.

He smirked. "You keep surprising me, Cassandra. I only wish you weren't so cold. I might learn more."

I took my time answering. "There's nothing else to know about me."

"Oh, that is *such* a lie." He shook his head. "I think you'd be the most interesting person on this ocean, if you would just drop your guard."

"If I did, I'd get stabbed in the back." I lifted my chin and eyed him. "I wonder why you don't feel the same."

He turned his head and scoffed like he couldn't believe me. But when he looked back, his eyes were full of concern. "Someone hurt you badly, didn't they?"

I rolled my eyes, hiding the twist in my chest. But his blue eyes stayed on me—clear, patient, impossible to ignore. For a moment, I almost believed he'd understand.

But then my gaze hardened. "No one can hurt me."

He shook his head slowly, disappointment showing on his face. "Whatever you say, Cassandra." He turned to leave.

My arm shot out and my fingers wrapped around his elbow. He looked back, and when I'd realized I touched him, I abruptly let go. My arm fell stiffly by my side.

He raised an eyebrow, and slightly embarrassed, I changed my mind. "How long did it take you to read?"

I could see he was slightly discouraged at the subject change, but he answered my question anyway. "I'm not entirely sure... I was very young. Maybe one or two years to learn the basics?"

"Two years?!" I slumped against the railing. I didn't have that long. I was impatient to find the treasure—I'd waited long enough. *But while I'm stuck here, I may as well learn something.* I cringed. "Can you teach me?"

He looked taken aback. "Teach you?"

"Yes."

"I thought you were too stubborn to want to learn anything."

I swallowed, turning to the sea. The glittering water comforted me as I explained, "That's not how I used to be, you know. I thought that to be a captain, you had to be a certain way. Like my father. It seemed like my crew respected me, at first..."

"And then they mutinied."

I drew patterns on the wood with my finger.

"I'll teach you," he decided.

I smiled. "We'll need a quill and parchment—"

"Leave it to me." I watched as Alexander strode off. It wasn't long before he returned, a frown on his face.

"What happened?"

"Joshua said he wouldn't give us parchment unless *he* was the one to teach you."

I looked heavenward. "You told him?"

"Yes..."

Folding my arms, I explained, "It's much harder to get what you want if you tell a person everything. If you tell them only what they want to hear, they'll be much more... compliant."

"How do I know if you're not just telling me what *I* want to hear?"

I smiled. "I don't want something from you. Yet."

"What about just now? You wanted me to teach you how to read."

I shrugged. "You're easy. All I had to do was ask."

He expelled a breath. "Fine. So what are we going to do now?"

"Thanks to you, I guess I'm learning from him."

"The captain I know wouldn't give up so easily," he said, folding his arms.

I smirked. "There will be some use to it. There's a bit of information I need, so I might as well kill two gulls with one shot."

———•·•———

"**L**et's start with the simple ones." Joshua leaned over me and scratched three letters on the parchment. The black ink bled outwards, blurring the word. He had used too much of it. "This means 'the.'"

"The," I repeated, with a nod of my head. *What're the chances the first word he teaches me is the only one I've known since childhood?* That and, '*Kingston.*' The name of my father's ship had long since been engraved in my mind.

I sat at his desk, which faced the wall. He stood at my back with his arms on either side of me, one hand holding the quill and the other resting on the desk. He was too close for comfort, but if he had feelings for me, it added to my list of unfortunate advantages.

Being a woman, if I played my cards right, I wouldn't be the target for suspicion if Barnet was found dead in his chambers. I imagined his blood on my knife. My heart was numb to this task. Vengeance fueled me.

*But to direct the blame away from Alexander and the rest?* That was the question hovering in the back of my mind as I tried to listen to the captain's idiotic son. *Can I get him to believe me? Blame it on Bart, who snuck out of his cell at night? Hide the keys...*

Joshua wrote another small word directly under the first, this time with the letters slightly farther apart so it was more legible. "Is," he said.

"It's very kind of you to teach me," I said, my voice buttery smooth. "I wasn't able to really learn before, because my parents died, and my uncle believed I didn't need the skill."

"I'm so sorry." His voice was filled with concern.

"Yes," I sighed sadly. "But you know, it was actually a good thing that my ship got captured by those pirates."

He chuckled, as if I reminded him of a small child who was taught to find the silver lining. "And why is that?"

I boiled inside, but I reminded myself I was not who he thought I was. I was a pirate, a seductress, a woman who knew how to get what she wanted. *Build trust first, then ask questions*, Aunt Mary's voice slipped into my head. I kept my tone happy as I replied, "If I hadn't, I would never have landed on your ship. I never would have met you."

He leaned in closer, his lips inches from my ear. "You know, if you need anything... anything at all... just come to me."

"Oh, you are *such* a gentleman. I wish there were more men like you." This was going even better than I expected. Not many men were so easy to wrap around my finger.

"*I* don't wish such a thing." His lips brushed my ear.

*Ew.* "You know," I said, leaning away from him slightly, "now that I think of it, I do need something."

"And what is that?"

Was he trying to make his voice lower? *Pathetic.* Alexander's voice was naturally—I cut that thought off immediately. "I was wondering where we're going."

"Oh." He sounded disappointed. "My father said we're delivering the prisoners at New Providence. Why do you ask?"

"I was wondering how many days we will be at sea. I mean, that delicious food won't last that long, will it?" I giggled.

"You're right. But we have more preserved food as a backup. Are you used to worrying about food? Did you have to take care of younger siblings?"

"Yes," I lied easily. "Just one. My uncle didn't care much for us."

"Ah. I understand how hard it must have been to lose your parents. My mother died during childbirth."

I gave him my condolences, but felt nothing for him. The son of my enemy was also my enemy. "Should we get through a couple more words, then?"

"Oh yes, of course. Then I'll test you."

Once he had a dozen words written, I couldn't recall the first seven. He took another good chunk of time trying to get me to remember them all, and by the time we took a break we were both frustrated.

"Thank you for trying to teach me, Joshua."

"Josh," he corrected.

"Right," I said. "But I'm done for the day. I just—" I put my hand to my head.

"It's all right, I understand."

I stalked out into the short hallway. *Why is reading so difficult?* I wasn't used to things coming easy, but this was ridiculous! Thrusting open the door, I stepped out into the sunlight. The upper deck was large, with a navigation table anchored to the floor and an elegant wooden wheel at the front. Barnet and another sailor were bent over the table. I ambled towards the stairs, taking a subtle peek at the map between them.

"Seven days, I estimate," said the sailor. "We're close."

"Let's make it in six," Barnet answered. He glanced at me, and I quickly looked down and kept walking. "Meanwhile, let my son know he will be in charge of interrogations. I want to know the island on which they all hide. If we take their base out, they'll have nowhere to run."

I took the stairs, curiosity taking hold of me. Was Barnet searching for the biggest, most secret pirate haven in the Caribbean? The very one I'd be headed to once I was free of him?

I jogged to the side of the boat. Slipping my hand into my pocket, I fingered some of the parchment slips, recalling the most recent words Alexander had read for me. *Cool. Creek.* I hadn't dared pull out the map and compare the words to sort them out—so I had to repeat them in my head until I could find a moment when no one was watching.

I lifted my gaze skyward. It had been too long since I climbed the rat lines and rigging of a ship, so I glanced around at the men scattered across the deck, making sure no one was watching. As I hoisted myself up onto the ropes, I felt nostalgia for my younger years, when I'd climb up and stand in the crows nest. When I nearly reached the top, I turned myself around so I was facing the open ocean, holding onto the ropes behind me. The wind blew through my hair, brushing it into my face. The height, the possibility of falling sent a thrill through me, even though I knew I wouldn't. It felt so good to be here, like all the worry in the world couldn't reach me, like I was free of everything. *What would it be like,* I wondered, *without Barnet? Without all my hatred and my burden of vengeance?*

I imagined the wind carrying it away, and I smiled, the truest smile I had shown in forever.

A smile for just me and the sea.

"Oi!"

I looked up. The man in the crow's nest was leaning over the side, and I turned around to look at him better.

"What's ya doin' up here like that? You could fall!"

I was taken aback. "I won't fall." I took one hand off and switched them, so for a moment in between I wasn't holding on at all, and did this a few more times. "See? I'm fine!"

"You're crazy, that's what. I don't even see men doin' that, I tell you."

"Well, I'm no man."

"Ya sure as Hell ain't. One o' the most beautiful ladies I've ever seen."

"Oh." I allowed for a smile, slightly confused and flattered at the same time. I didn't meet very many men that were as frank as him, yet not sleazy or obsessed with women. "Thank you."

He smiled in return. "Well, as long as you don't fall, I won't say nothin'."

"Thanks." I turned back to the sea, but the moment was over.

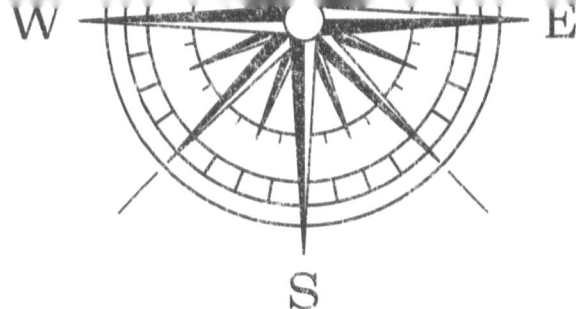

*Chapter 13*

"**D**ID SOMEONE LEND YOU a shirt?" I inquired of Alexander, who was tying a rope to the rail. A loose white shirt had been layered under his brown jacket.

"Are you disappointed?"

I rolled my eyes, resting my arms on the railing.

"How did it go? Did you learn anything?"

"With Joshua? We went over some fifteen words, the easier ones. But I only remember a few of them."

"What's one you know best?"

"In."

"Alright, how do you spell it?"

I scrunched up my face, trying to visualize the word in my head. "A line, a dot," I described, drawing it in the air with my finger. "And then was sort of a—"

"*Dear Lord.*"

I looked to my left, and Alexander was looking up to the sky in exasperation. "What?"

He raised his eyebrows at me. "Did he not teach you the alphabet first? How are you supposed to learn to read without knowing the alphabet?"

"I know some letters," I said defensively. "I know 'a' and 'b' and 'c'."

Alexander sighed, turning around. "Well, that's a start."

"Alexander!"

I looked up. Alexander's father was standing next to Barnet, and there was a heated energy between them, like they'd just finished an argument. The sight of those eyes, that infernal wig, brought the fury back into me. *The beatings my father endured. The noose around his neck.* Vengeance, like a thick boa circling round a circus man's shoulders, was my burden to bear once more.

"Up here, now! The captain of this vessel has a question," he barked.

"Of course, sir." Alexander walked briskly to the stairs and climbed them. I followed, hiding my black heart behind pretty eyes.

When we got to the top, Barnet waved his hand at me. "Not you, Miss. Off with you."

I gritted my teeth. "I'll stay right where I am, thanks."

Barnet stared at me, expressionless. Then he yelled to the sailors on deck, "Somebody come get this girl and bring her below decks. She's getting in the way."

My fists clenched. *If I were a man...*

"Just ask me the question, Captain, there's no need for that," Alexander said. I could hear the slightest, smallest, hint of worry in his voice, like he was afraid I'd lose my temper and push the sailor that would try to restrain me down the stairs. Luckily, Barnet listened to his request.

"When you were on the pirates' ship, did they say anything about an island called Tortuga?"

Just hearing the name brought a warmth to my chest. He'd never find that little gem of paradise. How sorely I missed it. *It won't be long now.*

Alexander shook his head in confusion.

Captain Callaway nodded curtly. "You see? He doesn't know anything. With all due respect, these questions are better aimed at the pirates in your brig."

Barnet ignored him and looked directly at Alexander, his black eyes glittering. "If you're lying, I *will* find out. And when I do..."

"You don't need to threaten him, he's not—"

"Quiet, girl," Barnet snapped, not even looking at me.

I fumed inside. It took all of my willpower to stop myself from wrapping my fingers around his neck.

"She's right, Captain. I'm not lying. I had no idea that island even existed."

Barnet nodded, oddly expressionless. "If you ever hear anything about it, come to me. The pirates that hide there are a dangerous lot. If the world is to become a safe place, we need to rid it of scum like them."

"My son has killed two of them already," Captain Callaway said proudly. I was the only one who noticed Alexander stiffen. "He fought ferociously against them when they took our ship, then killed their *captain* whilst a prisoner on board their boat! He hates pirates as much as you do, sir."

"How on earth did you manage to get away with that?" Barnet's quartermaster exclaimed.

Alexander's voice and face were devoid of expression when he answered, "I blamed it on a ghost."

"And they believed you?" Barnet asked suspiciously.

He looked down. "They're a superstitious bunch."

"You're not going to tell them the story?" his father prodded.

"No need," Barnet interrupted, looking disinterested. "He clearly isn't inclined to tell it. You are dismissed."

I led the way down the stairs, smiling to myself. My old crew, hired in Cuba, probably thought Tortuga was nothing more than a myth. *Ha.* Barnet had no clue I was the only one on board who knew where to find it. He would overlook me like every other man had, and as a result he was doomed to fail. I relished the thought.

Preston came skipping up to us. "Alright, Xander? Cassie?" When we nodded, he pointed a thumb over his shoulder. "That fellow over there told me that Captain Barnet is responsible for the arrest of six notorious pirate captains and their crews. Six! That's like— like—"

"Around forty per crew, multiplied by six... That's two hundred and forty people!" Alexander whistled.

"And he sent them all to the gallows," I said flatly.

"What did he want with you?" Preston asked, elbowing his friend playfully. "Getting special attention from this Captain too? You're not trying too hard, are you Xander?"

Alexander smirked. "No. He wanted to know if I knew where some island was. 'Tortilla,' was it?"

"Tortuga," I corrected him.

He smiled, his eyes dancing with humor.

I rolled my eyes. "Tortuga's the safe haven for anyone escaping authoritarian rule," I explained to Preston, lowering my voice. "It can't be found except by those who already know of its whereabouts."

"And you've been?" Preston whispered back, interested. "Where is it?"

I shrugged. "I dunno."

"You're lying," Alexander murmured, squinting at me.

I lifted a finger to my lips, failing to suppress a subtle smile.

His gaze fell there. "What will you do once you get to the island?"

Smirking, because I knew it would irk him, I replied, "Barter for a sloop, pick up a crew, and raid and plunder to my heart's content."

Alexander's face fell in disappointment, then darkened with a twinge of frustration. "Of course." He turned away, his voice lowering. "Why did I think you could change?"

"Change?" I laughed. "Did you really think that mutiny would deter me? I'll just try again with a different crew. I learned a few lessons, but that doesn't mean I should give up on my dream."

Preston raised his eyebrows slightly. "Your dream is to raid ships?"

"What about when you're older? Wouldn't you ever want to, I don't know, have a family?" Alexander added.

*The last family I had was hanged.* "Never really thought about it," I lied. "What about you?" I quickly turned to Preston. "What do you want to do when you're older?"

The boy thought for a moment. "If I had my druthers, I'd be an Alarm Boy."

"A what?" Alexander said, perplexed.

He gasped. "You must live under a rock. You've never heard of such a crucial job? You go around to people's houses and scream at them until they wake up!"

We all burst out laughing, but my smile melted when a movement above caught my eye. Joshua said something to his father, who nodded curtly, then descended the stairs and opened the hatch a few yards away from us. My curiosity sparked as I watched as the captain's son disappeared down below.

"I don't like him," Alexander murmured. Even though he didn't mean to be heard, I agreed.

"Stay here," I ordered, then quietly followed Joshua down the hatch. I raked my gaze around, but the captain's son had already disappeared. Lantern aloft, I crept toward the bow of the ship, weaving around hammocks hung between beams. I came upon a set of stairs leading down below, and kneeling, I strained my ears.

*Voices.*

One word filtered through my memory: *interrogations.* I tiptoed down the steps, then tucked myself behind a barrel full of shackles and sharp objects. The brig looked similar to the one in my old ship, only larger. Cells lined the walls and brown spots stained the floor, looking suspiciously like dried blood. My crew was separated into each of the cells, three or four in each, but none of them noticed me yet.

Not the same brig as the one I was trapped in long ago. But it still gave me the shivers.

Joshua was standing at the second cell down. He gripped the bars, a mean and intimidating look on his face. "Tell me what you know about the pirates' lair. The island of Tortuga."

Johnny was the one who answered from his relaxed position in his cell. He reclined against the bars separating the cells, his legs crossed and a hat over his eyes. "Mate, we know nothin' o' the sort."

His lazy drawl seemed to get on Joshua's nerves. He shook the bars. "Tell me what you know! I know you know. You're pirates."

"You think all pirates come from Tortuga?" Wyatt asked him from inside the same cell, his accent heavy but decipherable.

"All right," Joshua growled. "I'm tired of your games. It's going to be the easy way or the hard way. Which way do you choose?"

"The easy way," Johnny said. "Obviously. Why would anybody wanna choose the hard way?"

Joshua huffed, not expecting that reply. "Wonderful. Now tell me where they all hide."

Johnny removed his hat and scratched his head. For a moment I was worried he knew and would tell him, but he just said, "I don't know why someone invented the hard way. I mean, who would be daft enough to do that?"

I almost laughed, but Joshua stamped his foot. "My father and I want answers. *Now.* So if you don't answer me, I'll have to resort to less kind measures."

"Listen, laddie, don't waste yer time down here tryin' to integrate us about somethin' we know nothin' about."

Joshua was undeterred, and unlocked the cell, opening the door just enough to walk through. Johnny was yanked up by the collar, and he flailed his arms, off balance. Joshua leaned in so his nose was inches from Johnny's. "Tell me," he said through gritted teeth, "or you're going to get a taste of the cat."

Wyatt stood up and Weasel cowered in the corner. "We're trying to tell you, we don't know nothin'. Now let my friend go."

"You will not order me around, slave." He pulled out a pistol and pointed it at him.

Wyatt's face darkened, and so did mine. "I am no man's slave."

"Tell that to your future master. Now," He threw Johnny to the ground and looked at him. "Tell me or I'll kill your *friend*."

The other pirates were craning their necks to watch. If Joshua was picking on Bart or Weasel, I would've relished watching. But I was afraid for Wyatt's life—and my body tensed, ready to leap forward to his defense. At the last moment, I remembered Aunt Mary. She was guiding me, even in death.

I stood up. "Joshua?" Surprised laced through my timid voice.

The captain's son whirled around. "Miss Cassandra!" His voice lost its harshness as he stepped out of the cell. "What are you doing down here? You shouldn't go sneaking around and eavesdropping like that."

"I'm sorry, Joshua."

"Josh," he corrected again.

"Josh," I repeated, smiling softly. "I was curious where you were going. What are you doing?"

He cleared his throat. "Miss Cassandra, you need to go back up those stairs. You do not need to watch this."

I clenched my jaw, but just as quickly relaxed it and stuck out my bottom lip. "Please, Josh," I whispered, striding forward. "Don't shoot that man." I looked up at him with big pleading eyes, which was the opposite of what I *felt* like doing, but it seemed to do the trick.

He faltered. "What do you suggest, then?"

"I suggest you believe them."

"Believe them? But they're pirates—they don't tell the truth!"

"Then why are you bothering to question them? If you won't believe anything they say anyway?"

"I..." He struggled to find a response.

"I don't think they've ever been to that island. Maybe they're from somewhere else."

He stuffed his gun in its holster with frustration. "Then how am I going to find out where it is? If even pirates don't know about it?"

"I'm sure some pirates know about it. Just not this group."

"What if she knows where it is?" Bart barked from a couple cells down.

I froze. Then I remembered my act and relaxed my posture, tilting my head and raising an eyebrow. "What do you mean? Why would *I* know where it is?"

Joshua chuckled as he locked Johnny and Wyatt's cell. "*Indeed.*"

Bart growled at me, his eyes dancing with murderous light. "The little wench was our captain." He spat on the ground.

Joshua stalked over to stand in front of Bart.

I followed, laughing softly as my heart stuttered with nervousness. "Captain? You're just trying to take the blame off yourselves. How selfish. Perfect for a ugly brat like you." I glared at him. He was *not* winning this fight.

He shook the bars, a snarl on his face. "We mutinied, and all it got *you* was freedom. That's not fair!"

"What a far-fetched story!" I exclaimed. "Me? A captain?" I scoffed, looking at Joshua. "You don't believe this, do you?"

He stroked his puny little beard, the color barely visible against his fair skin. Bart lunged, reaching his arm through the bars, trying to grab me. I leapt backwards and in a burst of protective violence Joshua slammed Bart's elbow into the bars. "Don't you dare touch her!"

The pirate howled, stumbling back and clutching his injured arm. After a few seconds, he recovered his malicious sneer, his gaze landing on me again. "How'd ya survive, anyway?" he growled. "Yer hands an' feet were tied."

Joshua turned to me. "They tried to kill you?"

I nodded, schooling my face into a timid, melancholy expression, and then studied my feet. "They tied me up and were going to force me to...to..." I tried for a sniffle. "I'd rather *die* than be their slave, so I threw myself into the water." I didn't have to fake my shudder.

Joshua looked at the pirates with a murderous gaze.

"She's a lying little wretch! Don't trust her."

"And trust you instead? You're pirates!" Joshua spat.

"She's a pirate, too!" Bones exclaimed.

"How dare you make such accusations!" I huffed, folding my arms.

"I'm gonna kill you," Bart whispered menacingly. "I'm gonna rip your heart out."

"That's enough of that." Joshua took my arm and guided me away. I glanced over my shoulder as we walked. All but Johnny and Wyatt were glaring at me, hatred radiating from their bodies.

I let Joshua lead me up the stairs, sensing he felt an increased need to protect me after my story. I buried my annoyance and frustration at him. *He's a necessary tool.*

I thought about Johnny and Wyatt. Barnet would sell them to some old government official, and they would surely be hanged. Was it worth risking my future to break them out?

The more I thought about it, the more sure I was. *Yes.* I'd free them. There would be a small window of time between docking the boat and unloading the prisoners, when most of the crew would be busy. I would have to steal the key from Joshua—that wouldn't be too hard. It was lucky that Johnny and Wyatt were in the same cell, but I worried about Weasel. I didn't want him to escape, because it would destroy my chance of saving the other two. Weasel would have some other plan in his head, one that involved getting *me* captured while he escaped. *The slimy rat.*

We finally emerged onto the main deck. Alexander leaned against the rail, folding his arms, a playfully grumpy expression on his face. Preston balanced above him, walking along the railing, arms outstretched, his eyes bright with amusement.

"You're going to fall, you know," Alexander told his friend, looking up at him.

"If I do, you can just yell, 'MAN DOWN!!' really loudly."

Some sailors looked up in alarm, ready to rush to the rescue.

"Sorry!" Preston said, raising a hand in apology. "False alarm." He took another step, and lost his balance, his arms flailing rapidly. "Woah!"

At the same moment, Alexander caught sight of me, and I realized Joshua's hand had slipped down my arm, and was now brushing my fingers. I stepped away from him, but Alexander had noticed, and his expression darkened a fraction of a degree.

"Incoming!" Preston yelled, as he fell toward Alexander. The latter barely had time to look up before Preston collided with him, and they landed on the deck in a heap.

I cackled as they disentangled themselves and stood up.

"*Ow*," Alexander groaned, rubbing the side of his head.

Preston beamed. "That was fun! Let's do it again!"

I giggled. "Please. That was the funniest thing I've seen all day."

Alexander grinned. "You laughed. I've never heard you laugh before."

"You've heard me laugh before."

"Not like that."

"What's *that* supposed to mean?" I raised an eyebrow.

"Just that...I was simply saying..."

"He likes your laugh," Preston finished for him, a big smile on his face.

"What?! No, that's not..." Alexander trailed off, unsure of what to say.

I shook my head, amused. "You both are ridiculous."

"Indeed," Joshua spoke up. I flinched—I'd forgotten he was there. "You need some lessons on how to speak to women." He leaned toward Alexander and lowered his voice. "I'm free some of the day if you want advice."

I stifled a laugh. If I were to rank the men by their charm, Joshua would come in near last. That sailor I'd met in the crows nest was better than him!

Alexander glared at him, but Preston just laughed. "Mate, I'll ask the fish first."

"As you know less about women than they do," Alexander added.

Joshua snarled. "You will not talk to the first mate like that. I could report you."

Alexander snorted. "Like I care."

I rolled my eyes at them and left them to sort out their... differing opinions on wooing women. I didn't think I could give them good advice anyway; I wasn't a proper lady, built and honed by society.

I was a pirate captain.

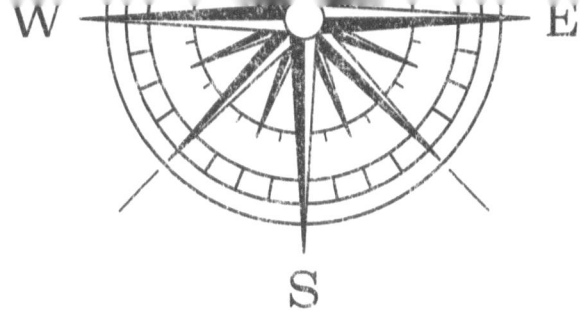

## Chapter 14

THE AIR WAS STILL, and not a ripple disturbed the dark water. The boat subtly rocked, from the steady rising and falling of the water. I rubbed my fingers across the polished wood as I stood and gazed out to the horizon, to the white glittery gleam on the surface of the sea, beautiful ghostly light reflected from the crescent moon. I closed my eyes and breathed in, warm salty air filling my lungs. All was still. The watchman was asleep in the crows nest; the last of the lanterns had long since been blown out. I was alone with the twinkling stars above. As I looked up, I wondered if my parents were up there. I wasn't religious, but it was a comforting thought to think they lived in the stars, watching over me. If only I truly believed it.

The stillness of the water, the calmness of my surroundings, didn't reflect the raging storm inside as I thought about how the captain of this ship had ended them. He sent them all to the gallows. I clenched my jaw, red-hot emotion bubbling and boiling in my stomach. He had killed my family, everyone

I loved; he deserved a worse death than hanging. But I couldn't provide that. All I had was a knife, the one still in my boot.

"You're up late."

I whirled around. Alexander was walking toward me, moonlight reflecting off his dirty-blond hair.

I swallowed. "Couldn't sleep. Why are you up?"

He reached the railing, and I turned around, looking out over the water like him. Our arms brushed, and I fought the instinct to move away. "There was this sailor near me who had the *loudest* snore."

"That's why you couldn't sleep?" I said, raising my eyebrows.

He smiled sideways at me. "I didn't even know someone *could* snore that loudly."

I chuckled.

"It's a beautiful night."

I nodded. "I like it when the sea's like this. It's not very often that it's so calm."

"Do you know what my favorite part is?"

"What?"

"The sky." He stretched his neck to look up, and my eyes caught on his jawline. "Since the moon is only a thin crescent, you can see all the stars."

"Aye." I breathed, then finally got my eyes to gaze heavenward, hating myself for the time it took. "Aunt Mary thought they were the souls of our loved ones."

He looked at me, as if choosing his words carefully. "Do you believe that?"

I took my time answering. "I don't know what to believe. Hers seems far fetched, but your theory—with each star being floating fireballs—seems just as unlikely." I tried to imagine it.

He smiled. "Believe it or not, it's true. Although there's debate whether they're suns just like ours or...something else."

Shrugging, he continued. "I think they're suns. But they're so far away there's no way to prove it."

"What about that one?" I pointed to a brighter star lower in the sky. "Is that one closer to us?"

"That one's a planet. Saturn. And that one's Jupiter." He pointed to another bright speck. "Both have moons. Jupiter actually has four."

"Four moons?" Astounded, I looked at the shining crescent and tried to imagine four of them. I turned back to Alexander and lowered my eyelids. "You're just telling tales."

"I swear I'm not! It takes a fine-tuned telescope to see them."

I let him ramble on about planets and orbits and things I didn't quite understand, until he stopped himself and looked self consciously at me.

"I'm boring you, aren't I?"

I shook my head. "No, keep going. It's calming to listen to you." I quickly added, "Just because it gives me something else to focus on, instead of everything else that's on my mind." I wanted to kick myself. The only way it could've been worse is if I'd stuttered.

He nodded, looking back out to the water. "There's so much the stars haven't taught us yet. Sometimes I wonder if I should have stayed at Cambridge..." His voice trailed off. "But no," he resolved after a moment's hesitation. "That wouldn't have worked."

"Why not?"

"Ever been to London? Seen the state in which most people live?"

I shook my head.

"No words can describe it. I'm luckier than most because of where my father stands, but no one is exempt from the danger of press gangs."

I'd heard of such mobs. They were sent by the King's navy to capture people and force them onto their ships, because Royal Navy sailing conditions were so bad that nobody wanted to volunteer. "But aren't you working for the King anyway?"

He grinned. "My father's a much kinder captain than the ones in the Royal Navy."

"Was going to Cambridge worth it? I mean, you're a sailor now. Don't you feel like you wasted years of your life?"

"Learning? Absolutely not," he scoffed. "Knowledge is treasure. I'm grateful I was able to go to college. Learning about the stars and planets helps me to navigate, and the knowledge will help me if I ever decide to take a different path."

"You don't need a compass to navigate?"

"It certainly helps, but as long as there's a clear sky, like tonight...you can do without."

"This I did not know."

He turned around. "See those seven stars over there? Sort of near the horizon. They're brighter than the others, and form the shape of a cup with a long handle."

It took me a minute to find the stars he was talking about, and counted them again just to be sure. "It looks nothing like a cup."

"Yes, well, that's the best you got for stars. The constellation is called the Big Dipper. And if you follow the direction that the bottom of the cup points, you'll find the North Star. Every other star moves, but not that one. That one stays roughly in the same place, so you can always rely on it."

"Why doesn't it ever move?"

"It's closely aligned with Earth's north pole."

"Thanks to you, my head hurts."

"You asked for it."

"Not really."

He sighed, leaning his back against the rail, his face shadowed.

I heard a huge yawn from the crows nest, and the sailor stuck his head out and looked down at us. "Do you lovebirds want me to strum a song? Ya look like ya need it."

I was grateful for the dark to hide the color that rose to my cheeks.

"No, thank you, Sammy." Alexander didn't seem fazed.

"Ya sure? My fiddle's just over there."

"Go back to sleep," I told him, rolling my eyes and turning back to stare at the moon. It had risen a little farther from the horizon.

We stood in silence for a while, before I asked him quietly, "Do you ever miss the rest of your family?"

He smiled sadly. "Absolutely. I think about them every day. I wish I could write them. I think when we land I'm going to head back to England. I'm tired of boats."

A frost crept into my heart, but I ignored it. "I suppose it would be nice to take a break from living on a ship. But I couldn't stand to be away from the ocean for too long."

Alexander looked down at his folded hands. "What do you like about the ocean?"

I shrugged. "I like all the sea's different moods. I like how you can never predict it. I mean, I like being prepared, but if you always know what to expect, then there's no satisfaction in being prepared, 'cause everything's the same, you know?"

"Yeah." He nodded.

I chewed my lip. "This question is a subject change—"

"Ask away."

"A while ago you said it was no wonder I hated Barnet so much. How did you know? I never told you."

"Easy. Every time you look in his direction you make a face."

Taken aback, I said, "Really? But I thought I had..." I trailed off. I thought I had control over my expressions.

"Oh, well it's really subtle," he assured me. "But I can tell."

"Do you think *he* can tell?"

"Probably not. I don't think anyone else noticed."

I relaxed. "That's good."

Alexander turned to me. "Did he kill your parents?"

I swallowed, then nodded. "He traded them in for money. Shot four of my friends point blank and sent the rest to the gallows."

His eyes filled with sadness and pity. "I'm so sorry."

I shook my head. "He's just going to do it again and again. I must stop him."

"What are you going to do?"

I couldn't tell him what I was going to do; with all his moral integrity he'd try to stop me. But I *could* tell him some of it, so I lowered my voice. "First, I'm going to help Johnny and Wyatt escape."

He leaned in so he could hear me better. "Part of your crew, right?"

"Aye."

"Why not all of them?"

I raised an eyebrow at him. "Aren't you a scholar? A lot of them want to kill me. And the more people I try to break free the harder it will be."

He ignored my jab. "I'll help you."

I was about to reject his offer, but I realized he could be useful, so I smiled. "I'm still working out the details, but we'll need a distraction. I'm going to steal Joshua's keys, and right as we're docking I'm gonna bust them out."

"So you want me to cause a distraction for you to steal the keys?"

"No, not for the keys. I need you and Preston to cause the distraction once we dock, so I can get them off the boat."

He smiled mischievously. "I think we can figure something out."

My heart did a tiny leap and then beat more strongly, but I told myself it was from anticipation to carry out my plan. Not his smile. Not the way his blue eyes gleamed with excitement, or the way his hair caught the moonlight.

I could see so deep into his eyes, but it didn't make me certain of his intentions. Why was his expression so hard to read? With Nathaniel it had been easy; he was a plain boy with plainly shown desires. But with the boy in front of me? I felt like he could've been thinking a million things. He didn't move closer, the way Nathaniel would; he just leaned against the taffrail with a slight smile playing across his lips, his eyes searching mine.

I swallowed, cursing my voice for abandoning me. The effect he had on me was unnerving. Finally I managed to tear my eyes away and mumble, "I... I'm feeling tired. I think I'll go to bed now."

"Good night, Cassandra." His voice was deep and smooth. "Sweet dreams."

Our eyes met, and the smirk he wore said he had some ideas of what I'd be dreaming about.

I rolled my eyes and stepped away, but couldn't stop myself from glancing back as I lifted the hatch. He hadn't moved, his back still against the railing, his eyes on me.

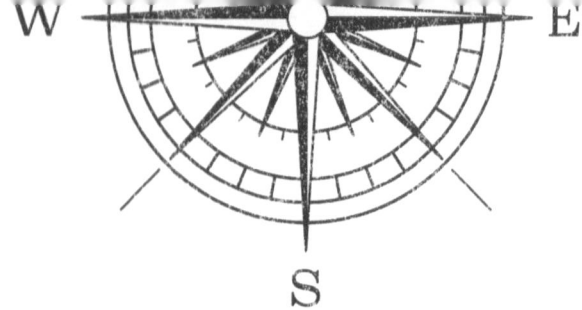

# *Chapter 15*

CRACK.

The whip echoed across the water, and so did the strangled cry of the sailor bound to the mainmast. The first drops of blood dribbled down his bare back.

Barnet gave a nod to the bosun's mate, and the hand raised again. The sailor's back and shoulders tightened in anticipation of the blow.

Joshua hurried over to me. "Miss Cassandra! I told you to go below decks."

"What was the offense?"

"Insubordination. Please, this is not for your eyes to see."

"What a cruel punishment!" I let him lead me to the hatch. That was not the first time I'd seen blood, but the sight of such a harsh punishment delivered for what was likely a disrespectful comment was sickening. I bit my lip, stopping myself from saying, *Does your father take pleasure in watching others suffer?*

I climbed down the ladder and into the dark belly of the ship. I sat against one of the cannons, propping the gunport cover open so I could breathe in fresh sea air. This was quite worse than on deck, I decided. I could hear all the awful sounds just as well—only now I sat alone in the darkness, the grisly sight replaced by imagination.

I scoffed, hugging my knees. My fury and disdain for Barnet and his cotton-headed son grew with each crack of the whip. It seemed to last forever.

When it finally ended, I did not relax. Walking toward the hatch where a beam of light illuminated floating dust, I rolled my head around on my neck. Tight muscles were bringing on a headache. It was the same gory punishment inflicted on my father, day after day.

By the same man.

I hated to remember it. I longed to carve it out of my mind. He made me watch. *He made us all watch.*

I shuddered and lifted my knife in front of my face, my eye reflected in the blade. Soon, I wouldn't look at it and see myself.

I'd look at it and see his blood.

———————

A few hours later, I exited the washroom, fresh from a bath. I wore the same pants, but a new top. Alexander's sopping shirt was draped over my arm, still ripped on the forearm but no longer bloody. My cut was healing nicely. A few more days and I could remove the stitches.

Stepping into the hallway, I ran into my enemy. Taken by surprise, I was barely able to restrain the scorn from my voice when I said, "Hello, Barnet."

He grabbed my arm as I squeezed past him. His grip was like iron. "You will address me as 'Captain' or 'Sir' at all times. Just because you are a *woman* does not mean you are exempt from my leadership." His voice was as cold as his eyes.

I yanked my arm out of his grasp. "Fine, *Captain*." He was not my superior.

He cocked his head slightly and said, "Have we met before?"

My heart skittered with nerves. I shook my head. "No. I think I would recognize your face." I bit back a less-than-kind word to describe it, then left before he could say another word.

I jumped down the stairs three at a time and skidded to a stop next to Alexander, who was practicing a half hitch knot with Preston. The wind blew through my wet hair, cooling me.

"Is that my shirt you have there?" he asked, by way of greeting.

"Aye. Washed it."

"May I have it back?"

"No. I'm keeping it." I flashed him a playful smile.

"Why?"

"Because you want it."

"Who's shirt do you have on now?"

"Joshua's."

He raised an eyebrow. "Why are you wearing *his*?"

I pouted. "Do you know what happens when white linen gets wet?"

His cheeks colored. *What fun it is making him embarrassed.*

Preston snickered. "Xander was hoping you'd come and steal his again."

I snorted.

Above, Barnet emerged from the hallway, with Joshua behind him, dressed like his father today, minus the headpiece.

"Hughes!" Barnet shouted. The strong breeze didn't even rustle his grey wig. It stayed frozen, an ugly waterfall the color of rat fur spilling down his shoulders.

"Here, Captain!" A man in his early forties stepped forward.

"Have you updated the ship's log?"

"The ship's log, sir?"

"Yes, Hughes, the ship's log." Barnet was already impatient. "With a count of the pirates and the goods we have gained."

"No, sir, not yet."

"What are you, trying to shirk your duties? Get to it!"

"I—I can't sir." His voice dropped to a whisper so that all I could make out were mumbles.

Barnet leveled an imperious stare at him. "Speak up, man!"

"The ship's ledger is missing, s-sir." The man's cheeks were pink with shame.

"Missing?" Barnet demanded, his voice no louder than before but filled with fury. By now everyone's attention was on him and Hughes.

"Sir, I woke up this morning and it was gone. I swear, it wasn't my fault. Someone must have stolen it!"

I felt Preston and Alexander's eyes on me. I looked at them and shook my head the tiniest bit. *It wasn't me.*

Barnet's eyes roved around the deck, then landed back on Hughes. "Where is your son?"

"My—my son?"

"Are you going deaf? Bring him here."

The man looked around, silent. A little boy with an elf-ish grin came running down the deck and stopped beside his father, looking up at his captain. I shot a surprised look at Preston and Alexander, for I had not even known he had been on board. The boy was skinny, with flaming red hair, and looked to be about ten or eleven years of age.

"Here, sir!" he squeaked.

Barnet stared at him coldly. "Let down the royal sail. This is a good wind, we need to take advantage of it."

I narrowed my eyes, not bothering to hide the fury written on my face. I knew what he was about.

The little boy looked up at the mast and swallowed. "Y-yes, sir." His voice had gone quiet.

"What was that?" Barnet snapped.

"Yes, sir!"

"Good. Now get to it."

The quartermaster stepped forward. "Captain, sir, are you sure that's a good idea? It's quite high, and the wind—"

"Are you questioning my orders?" Barnet growled.

The sailor shrank away, while the boy stepped up to the rigging. Everyone watched as the little redhead climbed higher and higher. He was past the first sail, then the second. He slipped once, causing my heart to jump into my throat. As I thought about it, I realized why I was so on edge, and the memory came flooding back to me. My job was to trim the first sail, not the... I shielded my eyes as I counted. The fifth sail up. I'd rolled when I fell, but still ended up with an injured ankle and bruises all over. *He* would surely die.

We all held our breath watching the brave child continue. He reached the top gallant sail without an incident. He was almost there, when suddenly he lost his footing, and his leg went through the ladder. He desperately grabbed at a loose rope, and it held him for a second. I tensed, looking around. Nobody was moving. I looked back at the boy. He was beginning to pull himself up, but the knot at the end, stopping it from sliding through the pulley, was beginning to loosen. Somebody had not done their job correctly, and I was not going to stand by and let the boy be at the mercy of fate.

I ran to the side and scrambled up Jacob's ladder, my eyes on him, heart beating wildly. Another second and the knot unraveled. As the rope that so delicately held the boy's life zipped through the pulley, he screamed and made a grab for the ladder, but his fingers only brushed the cord. I thought that was going to be the end of him, but miraculously his ankle tangled in the spider web of ropes, and suspended him there, upside-down. My legs and arms were burning. He had a few more seconds at best.

A few more feet. His boot began to slip. "Help!" he screamed, flailing his arms. His wide, frightened eyes landed on me and I saw a fragile hope dawn in his pale face.

"Don't move!" I yelled at him, swinging my body around to the other side of the rope ladder.

His foot slid out, and I lunged at the same time. Somehow I managed to grab his hand as he fell, but his momentum pulled me down as well. I yelped, but didn't fall. We swung there, one hand holding the ropes and the other gripping the boy's sweaty hand.

"Cassie!" Alexander shouted, fear edging into his voice.

I grunted, trying to keep his fingers from slipping out of mine. "Laddie, I'm going to swing you to the ladder. I won't let go until you have a firm grip on the rope, so don't worry about falling. Savvy?"

He squeaked his understanding.

"One, two..." I started the momentum towards the slanting ladder. "Three!" This swing was harder, and he reached the rope.

"Got it!"

I let go of his hand, and he scurried around to the other side. I grabbed the rung with my other hand, relieving my burning forearm, and hooked my legs around the ladder. I had climbed halfway down by the time the boy's feet touched the deck, and a cheer went up from some of the sailors. I smiled at Alexander, and he let out a weak laugh, relieved.

The little red-head ran to the arms of his father, who hugged him tightly, then looked up gratefully at me. I gave him a two-fingered salute.

"Boy, do you realize that the royal sail is still furled?"

My eyes fell on Barnet, his hands resting on the railing. He met my eyes, furious that I had thwarted him. I stared defiantly back at him, my relief overcome by anger.

The man let go of his son and stood, turning to his captain. "Don't punish my son because you're angry at me," he growled. "If you need someone to unfurl the sails, there are many capable sailors on this deck, including me."

Barnet fixed him with a cold stare. "I suggest you stop worrying about your son and start worrying about finding my log. I'll give you until the end of the day to find and update it. If you don't have it by then, rest assured you'll regret ever losing it." He turned his attention to the cabin boy. "You should never have come down. A sailor that doesn't do his duties is no use to me."

"He's just a boy," I exclaimed. "Besides—"

"You," Barnet pointed his finger at me. "Get down here and don't give me any disrespect."

I narrowed my eyes, and looked up. The sail was fifty feet above me. *Easy.* A pleasurable defiance tingled my limbs as I wrapped my fingers around the next rung up.

"What are you doing?" Joshua called.

"Letting down the sail," I yelled back, climbing quickly now.

"But you don't know how! Come back down!" When I gave no response, he tried again. "I'll do it for you!"

I glimpsed over my shoulder. Joshua started for the stairs, but his father held him back, watching me. Oh, this was so reckless. It might blow my cover. But part of me hated letting anybody stop me. I was finished with playing the helpless side note. My heart beat with wild, rebellious exhilaration as I rose higher and higher into the sky, aware of all the eyes on me.

Finally I reached the desired spar, and carefully swung my legs out on each side, so I was sitting on it. I scooted to the nearest tie, and undid the knot that held the sail. The corner unfurled, and I moved on to the next one and the one after that. I finished the last one, watching with pride as the sail filled with wind, before climbing down on the other side. I didn't wait to reach the bottom of the ladder, instead I jumped, landing in a squat to absorb the impact. I hardly made a noise.

"Show-off," Alexander said.

The wind flipped my damp hair in my face, hiding my proud smile.

"Miss Cassandra!" Barnet glowered down at me from the helm, and my smile melted.

I pushed the hair out of my eyes. "Yes?"

"Up here. Now."

*Uh oh.* I obeyed him this time. Everyone's eyes were on me, but I kept my posture calm and confident as I ascended the stairs.

Joshua joined me in the captain's quarters. I folded my hands as I sat in the chair they offered me and took note of everything in Barnet's room. A cabinet, probably for his clothes. A big bed, a table covered in maps, writings and sections of newspapers pinned to the walls—

"Miss Cassandra."

My eyes snapped to him. I crossed my legs, waiting.

"How did you know how to trim the sails?"

I looked at Joshua. "Really? That's your question?" I sighed. "It's pretty self explanatory. You just undo the ropes tying the canvas up. Easy."

"No, it's not that simple. You must know how to untie the knots, which *isn't* self explanatory."

I waved my hand, like it was no big deal. "Alexander's showed me a few things."

"What's your name?" Barnet asked.

"Cassandra."

"Your *full* name."

"Smith," I said quickly. "My surname is Smith."

"Cassandra Smith."

"Yes."

"What was the name of your ship?"

I thought fast, trying to remember. Captain Callaway had mentioned it once... "The one I was on before I was kidnapped?" I asked, stalling for time.

"Yes."

"The... Britannia." *Whew*. The more details I kept truthful the better, in case he had asked the same question to Alexander or his uptight father. "I needed passage to England to visit my grandmother. Alexander's family and mine have known each other for quite some time, and he and the captain were kind enough to give me passage and protection."

"How long were you aboard the pirate ship? How long ago were you captured?"

I hesitated. "I can't be sure—I was locked away for some time, not knowing day versus night. Could be...two weeks?"

Barnet's stare was unsettling. Finally he said, "There's something you're not telling me."

"Why would I lie to you? *I* have nothing to hide. But you seem threatened by my courage. Are you perhaps the one hiding something?"

He narrowed his eyes.

I tilted my head, feeling rather daring. "Cowardice?"

"*Cowardice*? Watch your mouth, girl," he spat. "I hold your life in my hands. One word from me, and you could be thrown overboard."

"Father!" Joshua exclaimed, horrified.

"However," he continued icily, "since I am a fair captain, I shall give you a second chance. But rest assured, *girl*, the next time you interfere with my orders, you will be punished."

"I understand, sir." It took all of my willpower to say those words. To maintain my composure and hide my vengeful thoughts. *I will kill him. His breaths are numbered.*

Joshua led me out of the room, my hands quaking with rage.

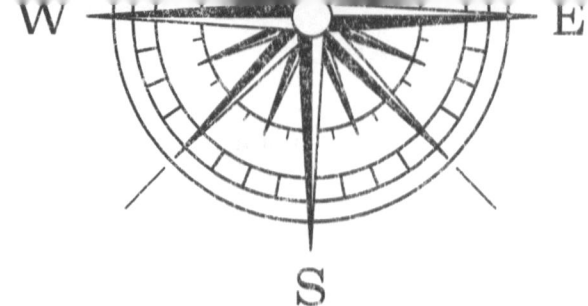

## Chapter 16

I THOUGHT ABOUT THE KNIFE in my boot as I stared at the glittering water, my arms resting on the rail. I imagined the blade sinking into his chest. *I am Cassandra Rackham. This is for my parents.* His eyes would widen in surprise as blood spread across the front of his shirt. He would fall lifeless to the floor. There was a twist in my gut, then cold. I shivered. *Joshua would no longer have a father.* I swallowed and quickly pushed all remorse away. Joshua would be next in line for leadership. It would be easy to manipulate him. Easy to secretly unlock Bart's cell and hang the keys up right back where they were. Offer the suggestion that the vengeful pirate had picked the lock.

"Hello." Alexander pulled up another crate and sat next to me.

I flinched, quickly pushing all thoughts of vengeance aside. This man understood my hatred for Barnet. He'd take one look at my face and realize what I was planning.

Alexander held out his hand. I almost smiled. He knew what I wanted—I no longer had to ask. I placed two unmarred slips of paper on his palm.

He glanced at them. "*Meets*, as in, she meets him for the first time. *Where*, as in, where does her heart lie?"

I nodded, envious of how easily words came to him. Just a glance, and he knew what it said. *Meets. Where.* My fingers itched to draw the map.

His eyes caught on something past me. "What's that—on the horizon?"

I turned, squinting my eyes from the sunlight bouncing off the water. The horizon was a smooth line, unmarred by land or ship. I frowned and turned back to him. "I don't see anything."

"Oh. I must've imagined it."

My eyes dropped to his hands—empty. I scowled. *He thought he could get away with that, did he?* "Give them back."

He bit back a smile. "Give what back?"

I rolled my eyes. "The parchment pieces, idiot. I know what you just tried to do."

"I haven't the faintest idea what you're talking about. I gave them back already—they're in your pocket."

I leaned toward him and whispered, "There's a knife in my boot. Don't make me use it."

He grinned. "You'd *dare* pull a knife on me in front of the entire crew?" He shook his head. "I think not."

I raked my gaze down his shirt, then his pants. *Must I check his pockets?* The idea of touching him made heat rise to my cheeks. I clenched my fists and expelled a breath.

He chuckled, then pulled out the pieces of paper and offered them to me. Relieved, I tucked them away.

"How is your reading going?"

I huffed. "Joshua's infuriating. He's all high and mighty because he's a wealthy captain's son. And he thinks I'm incapable of doing the simplest things just because I'm a woman. I don't know how I'm going to survive three more days on the same ship as him."

He was quiet for a moment. "I thought you fancied him."

I scoffed. "Where did you ever get *that*?"

He shrugged. "Well, you spend half an hour in his room every day—"

"Learning to read!"

"And you took his shirt—"

"What's that got to do with anything?"

"And the other day you were holding hands."

*When did I—oh.* Joshua had slipped his hand into mine while I was distracted watching Preston fall on Alexander. "That was nothing."

Alexander arched an eyebrow. "Are you certain?"

I gave him a sideways smirk. "Are you jealous?"

"Me?" He scoffed. "I think it would be amusingly ironic if you fell for the son of your enemy." He bent down and pulled two items from inside his boot, which he then held out to me.

I looked at the rumpled feather quill and folded sheet of parchment, surprised. "Where did you get that?"

He hesitated.

I smiled widely. "You stole it, didn't you? *Ha ha!*" I clapped my hands. "Congratulations!" I patted him on the back, then murmured, "You are one step closer to becoming a pirate."

"I don't want to be a pirate," he grumbled.

I laughed. "Why not? The freedom doesn't sound good enough? The adventure?"

"It's because I don't want to *lie* and *cheat* to make a living."

"There are just as many people out there who lie and cheat and don't call themselves pirates."

"What, like thieves and lawbreakers?"

"Don't think so lowly of me, Alexander. I'd bet thirty shillings that someone you respect has lied and cheated just as much as me."

"I don't know about that."

"Then let me ask you this: if I stopped lying and cheating, but still sailed under a jolly roger, would you still think lowly of me?"

"I don't think lowly of you."

I hesitated, emotions stumbling over each other. "But I'm a pirate. You hate pirates."

"You're different."

"Different? Why? Because I'm a woman?" Was Alexander like any other man I'd met?

"No, its—"

"Because I'm *pretty*?"

"No! It's because—"

I pouted. "So you *don't* think I'm pretty?" *Not* that I cared what he thought of me—he was always so polished and proper, I couldn't resist the urge to rattle him.

Indeed, he looked mortified as he stumbled over his words. "N–no, that's not what I meant. What I mean to say is—" He glanced nervously at me, saw the smirk on my face, and realization dawned in his eyes. "You're toying with me, aren't you?"

I raised my brows innocently. "What in the seven seas do you mean?"

He folded his arms. "Is this what you do for entertainment? Make wild assumptions and observe how people will react? Come on, Cassandra, lay off."

"Lay off what? I have every right to question whether or not a man finds me pretty."

He stared at me. "You think it's normal for a woman to walk up to a man and, out of the blue, ask if he thinks she's pretty?"

I shrugged. "It's probably not *that* uncommon."

"You know what *is* uncommon? Asking it for the sole purpose of playing with that man's emotions."

I tried to stop my smile, but he saw the amused glint in my eyes.

"Ah," he said. "So that means that you do not care what my answer is, correct?"

I adjusted myself on the crate and leaned on the railing. "That's right."

He leaned closer, staring intently into my eyes. "Are you quite positive?" he said, his voice low and inviting. The wind rustled his hair.

I forced a laugh, looking out to sea. "I am most definitely—"

"You wouldn't be disappointed if I said you aren't? You wouldn't feel"—He put his mouth next to my ear—"elated if I whispered... that you're beautiful?"

I grew flustered, then angry. I pushed him away, my fingers tingling where they touched his chest. "No! I don't care one bit."

He leaned back against the railing. "It's not much fun being on the other side, is it? Just because you can play with people's feelings doesn't mean others can't do it to you."

I stiffened. "*You* don't know what goes on inside my head. I am in total control—"

"You blushed."

"Did not!" But just the fact that he said that made heat rise to my cheeks.

"Control is an illusion, Cassie. That's why people get frightened when it's broken."

"Oh, very wise of you," I scoffed.

"It is natural to feel emotions. There is no shame in responding as any person would to another's words or actions. There is nothing wrong with it."

"But it makes you predictable. It lets people take advantage of you. It makes your lies less believable."

He turned serious. "What if you didn't need to lie anymore? What if you learned to trust?"

"What if I don't want to?"

"Then at least save the lying and distrust for your enemies."

"I do. Believe it or not, I've never lied to you." I paused for a moment, wanting to tease him. "Except for the times that I have." I hid my humored smile.

His eyebrows lowered. "You know what? You can learn to read on your own." He shoved the paper and quill into my hands, stood up, and walked away.

Shocked, I looked at the items in my hands. "Alexander? Alexander, wait!"

He stopped.

"I was joking! Lighten up—the only lies I've told you were out of necessity, before you knew me." He turned back to me, and I took a few steps toward him. "I won't lie to you again. I promise."

He looked doubtful. "How do I know your promises are worth anything?"

I stuck my bottom lip out and rounded my eyes. "Please believe me? I won't break your trust."

Very slowly, Alexander's smile returned.

For a brief moment, I faltered. There was such hope there, such trust. What would he think of me tomorrow morning, when they discovered Barnet had been killed in his sleep? When I robbed Joshua of his heartless father?

My eyes drifted away. *So what if he turns cold?* I'd been alone since I was ten years old. I was used to people leaving.

It was pitch black when I left my hammock. I crept forward, my hands outstretched, until I felt smooth wood underneath my palm. Breathing shallowly, I paused. Indecision, doubt, and fear seemed to claw at me from the darkness, beckoning me back into my hammock. I pressed my back against the wall and then slid down until my bottom hit the floor, the knife clutched to my chest.

I squeezed my eyes shut. Images flashed behind my lids. Blood spurting from a hole in Zach's chest. My friend's bodies tossed into the sea. The sadistic gleam in his eyes as he watched my family suffer.

*For them. For them.*

I jumped up, heart pumping.

Wrapping my fingers around the ladder, I breathed deeply, relishing in the pain and fury that burst from my heart. Heated energy flowed through my limbs, propelling me.

I emerged onto the main deck and lifted my gaze, the half moon like a lantern. No helmsman. Just the watchman to worry about, but Sammy would be looking out to sea, not to the deck. I ascended the second set of stairs, trying to clear my mind and relax my tense muscles. Uncertainty kept creeping back into my mind. A frustrating little voice reminding me that killing him wouldn't bring them back.

I quietly pushed the door open, then walked into the dark hallway. I could hear my own heartbeat as I located the captain's door and placed my hand on the cold latch.

*Unlocked.* Barnet must've trusted his crew.

I tiptoed into his room, closing the door behind me. Barnet's thinning black hair was streaked with gray, and his eyes were closed. My breathing was audible in the tense silence that filled the room. How did this moment come so swiftly? I'd thought about it almost daily since that newspaper depicted my father, strung up by his neck. That drawing gave me a scar that would never fade.

I'd thought I'd be ready past the point of all doubt.

I gripped my knife harder. This was the way. Once he was dead, I wouldn't have to feel that burning hatred every time I looked at him. I could finally let it go.

The moment in the rat lines came back to me. The wind whipping through my hair, that moment of lightness, happiness. I'd let it go for a moment, even while Barnet lived. Would killing him make that lightness permanent?

I raised my arms, held the cold blade close to his throat, my heart beating wildly. He stirred. *This action can't be undone*, that voice inside me cautioned. I looked at his peaceful face. How could he rest well knowing all the horrible things he'd done? All of the people he'd killed? My palms were sweaty, and I gripped the knife tighter.

*Damn it.* How would *I* rest well, knowing I killed him in his sleep? Was murdering him, knowing he had a son who cared for him, any different than him killing my mother?

*He'll never send another to the gallows.*

But what if, when I raked the knife across his throat, instead of releasing all my anger, it added another burden to my shoulders? My thoughts drifted briefly to Alexander. Was it his fault my damn conscience wouldn't leave me alone?

*Barnet has a son.*

I stood up and lifted the knife away, my chest tight, my stomach queasy. I turned around, my hands shaking as I padded towards the door. I gritted my teeth. My decision to walk away would haunt me forever, I was sure.

I took a cleansing breath. In the end, I would know I had a cleaner conscience than the man I despised.

*But don't you worry, Barnet. I'll find a much cleverer way to repay you.*

As I turned the handle, my eye caught sight of a book on the dresser. Curious, I tiptoed over and lifted it closer to study. I quickly flipped through pages filled with ledger lines and scribbled notes, with numbers in the right hand column. Narrowing my eyes, I glanced back at the man I'd almost murdered. Did he steal the ship's ledger from that poor sailor just for a show of power?

Anger bubbled up inside me again, and I tucked the book into my pants as I slipped into the hall. I'd find some subtle way to return it. The wood creaked quietly under my feet as I tiptoed passed Joshua's door. Suddenly I heard movement on the other side. I froze and held my breath, not wanting to announce my presence. Two seconds. Three seconds—nothing. I exhaled and took another step, but immediately I was bathed in soft light.

As Joshua stood in the doorway, a candle aloft, I realized I was still holding my knife in one hand. Too late, I shoved it behind my back and out of sight, dread settling in the pit of my stomach.

He'd already seen it.

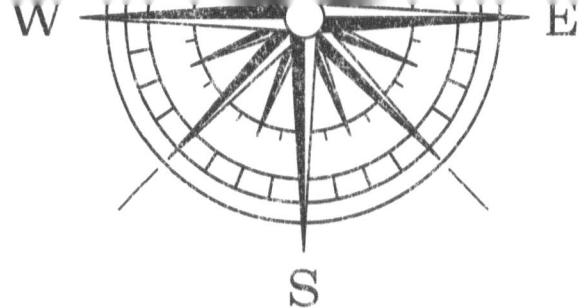

*Chapter 17*

I CURSED SILENTLY as Joshua's eyebrows knitted together in confusion.

"Cassandra? What are you doing here? What is that behind your back?"

I needed to make him uncomfortable to distract him from his own question, so I said the first thing that came to mind. "It's a thing only ladies would care to know."

"What do you mean? I thought I saw—"

"Please don't embarrass me, Joshua." I tried to act flustered.

His cheeks reddened with confusion, but he whispered, "Alright, Cassandra. But please, don't call me Joshua."

I nodded.

He sighed. "Why are you up here, awake at this hour?"

"I was using the head," I said timidly.

"The head? The toilet, you mean?"

"What else would I be using? *Your* head?"

He paused. "Where did you say you were from again?"

Heart pounding, I cleared my throat. "Part of my family lives in England."

He dismissed whatever thought he had. "You need to ask permission before you use our bathroom. My father doesn't fancy people sneaking around near his rooms."

"I wasn't sneaking."

"My father will treat it the same. Now get back to bed, off you go."

The knife felt cold against my wrist as I slipped away, my heart pounding.

———◦•◦———

The weather steadily grew warmer as we sailed closer to New Providence, while Alexander taught me the alphabet. It was now just two days before we were set to land. Two days until we'd go our separate ways, never to see each other again. I rubbed the slip of paper between my thumb and forefinger, hating the ache that crept into my chest. I'd only known him for a few weeks—how had I already grown accustomed to his presence? I closed my eyes. *I won't have a problem leaving him.*

Alexander shifted beside me, staring down at the gray-blue water as it lapped anxiously against the side of the ship. "Days are warm," he murmured. "Nights are cool...where the creek meets...the pool."

My spine stiffened. "What did you say?" I whispered, my voice hoarse.

The side of his mouth curled upward and a gleam shone in his eyes. "It's a riddle."

*It's a riddle.* My heart pounded. "It doesn't say 'pool'."

He tilted his head. "No?"

"None of the slips of paper I gave you said pool," I amended.

He shrugged, looking down to hide his smile. "Creeks often flow into larger bodies of water. If it rhymes, 'pool' makes sense."

I folded my arms and glanced away. I couldn't believe he'd figured that much out. "You got it wrong."

"Did I?"

I reluctantly added, "Partially."

He stepped closer. "Which *part* did I get wrong?"

"You mixed up two words." *Nights are warm, days are cool.*

"Which words?" he pressed.

"Not telling."

He threw his head back and laughed. It was such a lovely sound, I couldn't help but smile.

*Two days.*

My smile faded. I looked back at the water. Took a breath. *Weren't nights usually colder than days?* I would think it meant somewhere inside, where a fire heated the house at night but not during the day—except for the second line: it was by a creek. Neither hint did anything for me—there were millions of creeks with pools on this earth!

I stepped away from him and leapt up onto the rail, gripping the ratlines for support. The sea was aggravated today—waves rocked the boat, and the clouds were so low that the tip of the mainmast almost brushed them. A northeast wind whipped through my hair and clothes, and although it wasn't cold, I shivered, an ominous feeling creeping up through my toes.

A storm was coming.

I glanced over at the helm, where Barnet stood tense; he sensed something too. But this was just the prelude—we could still get some distance out of the sails.

It wasn't long before the sea became furious, the white-capped waves vigorously rocking the ship. I had to struggle to keep my balance as I walked across the deck, shielding my face from the pelting rain. I had been waiting for Barnet's call to furl the sails, but it never came; instead, he was gone from sight, probably taking shelter in his cabin while the rest of us struggled to keep the ship from capsizing. I looked up, my hands shielding my eyes. Sammy was still up in the crows nest, clinging on for dear life. I screamed his name, but the wind swept my voice away. "Why are you still up there?!"

"Can't shirk my duty!" he replied. His shout was no louder than a whisper by the time it reached my ears.

The deck pressed against my boots and the crates along the starboard side slid away from the rail. The large wave rolled under the hull, and I forced myself to stay upright. The rain was making the deck slick and dangerous. I watched most of the sailors race below decks to tie down the cannon and knew we were going to capsize if we didn't face the waves head on.

I glanced up through the pelting rain. Captain Callaway was arguing with one of Barnet's right hand men up near the helm. Their voices were lost to the wind, but I could tell Callaway was exasperated. Alexander and Preston made their way towards me, their hair messy and plastered to their faces. I closed the distance in a few strides. "What's happening? Where is Barnet? Why isn't he out here giving the order to furl the sails?"

Alexander shook his head, mystified. "My father's trying to talk to him, but that man won't let him inside. I think Captain Barnet wants to get to New Providence as soon as possible, and believes we can make it a little longer."

"He's crazy!" I exclaimed. "And his crew are too frightened of him to think for themselves."

"Maybe we could do it ourselves," Preston offered.

"Tie up the sails? Dangerous, but if it works, it might save us." I turned to the few other sailors up on deck and had to yell over the roar of the waves. "Men! All hands to the rigging! Let's furl the sails!"

"But the captain hasn't given the order yet!" one said.

"Do you see him around anywhere? He doesn't know how bad it's gotten! You're the sailors—you know this boat better than him! Can she hold out much longer?"

A wave sent the sea gushing across the deck, the water sweeping into our boots. "No, not for much longer. But the captain won't be very happy..."

"That won't matter if we're all sinking down to Davy Jones! Do you have a death wish, or what?" I walked to each of the ropes attached to the corners of the sails and loosened them as I spoke. "Besides, the longer we wait, the worse the storm will get, and the harder it will be to tie up the sails." The mainmast's sails were soon flapping back and forth, no longer a driving force of the ship.

They couldn't argue with that, so we split up and headed for the shrouds on either side of the ship, our feet slipping as the deck tilted up and down.

I paused at the side and picked up the remaining two loose-coiled ropes, all the others taken by the sailors already climbing up Jacob's ladder. We would need at least eight people, but there were only four sailors, plus Alexander, Preston, and myself. Which meant none of us could afford to stay behind. So I handed the ropes to the two boys next to me, knowing I had the most experience up on the masts. "Tie it around your waist and thighs, in case you fall."

"What about you?" Alexander said, looking up and down the rail. "There's no more ropes."

"I'll be fine."

"Last time you went up there you almost lost your life, and that was on a good day."

"Last time I was saving a small child! I'll be fine if I don't have to worry about anyone else. Hurry! We don't have all day."

Preston followed my orders and started for the ladder, but Alexander shoved the rope back into my arms.

"What are you doing?" I asked, incredulous.

"You should use it."

"Do you really think that *I'm* more likely—"

"I would never forgive myself if I put that on and you fell to your death."

I searched his eyes. *Is there something wrong with your head, boy? If I fell to my death, it would be from my error, not yours.*

I finally shrugged. "Your choice. But don't expect *me* to blame myself for *your* death." I made a couple loops and slipped them around my legs and waist, the ship beneath me pitching and yawing. I wrapped the extra rope around my shoulders as I jumped up to Jacob's ladder, Alexander following my lead. The wind battered us with raindrops as we climbed. We stopped at the mainsail, and I spit hair out of my mouth as I shimmied down the spar towards the other sailors. My stomach tightened and filled with butterflies as I carefully moved along, my hands gripping the slick wood, my feet supported by the single rope running from the swaying mast to the tip of the spar. After we spaced ourselves out evenly, I tied my safety rope around the spar. Each time the mast swayed, my heart beat faster. Whatever movement that was felt down on the deck was magnified up here, and would just grow worse the higher we climbed.

Together, we gathered up the canvas, rolling it up as tight as we could. Alexander reached underneath the spar and grabbed a rope, then wound it around in a spiral so it held the sail from falling back down. I took the rope from him, finished the spiral, and tied it tight. I looked up from my work just in time to see the captain emerge.

His ugly face was contorted as he screamed, "I did not give the order to furl the sails!" His voice was barely audible, but it made the other sailors cower with new fear. "I will not tolerate disobeyers. Get your feet down on this deck now, or it will either be the sea or myself who will take your lives."

I glanced at Alexander on my left, then Preston on my right, and watched in dismay as the four other sailors descended the ladder. *Prisoners of fear.*

"I'll admit this wasn't my best idea!" Preston yelled, squinting through the rain. "I'd rather not be skewered by him!"

I quieted the rage inside me and reminded myself that I could not change the choices of others. "You're probably right. Alexander, let's get down."

Alexander looked at me like I'd grown an extra eyeball. "You're backing down? What's come over you?"

"I don't want Barnet to kill you two just because you stayed up here with me." I gripped the spar, shifting my weight to counter the mast's movement.

"But you can't tie up all the sails by yourself," Alexander argued. "Plus, if you stay up here he'll—"

Lightning tore across the sky, narrowly missing us. Deafening thunder shook my bones.

"Just go," I said fiercely, my heart pounding. Preston started down, but Alexander still hesitated. "Barnet won't kill me. Now hurry!"

Preston's rope was still attached to the spar, so as soon as it went taught I untied it so he could get all the way down. The wind flicked my wet hair across my face, and I wished for a ribbon to tie it back. Alexander took a long look at me, concern in his eyes. He seemed to understand he couldn't change my mind, so he started down, just as Preston landed safely on the deck.

It was noonday, but dark as dusk as I shifted my position on the slippery spar, reaching over to the knot tying me in place. I fought a shiver, urging my fingers to move faster. My inner thighs burned from squeezing the yardarm. I made one last yank on the rope, retightening the knot.

I looked out to sea, spitting wet hair out of my mouth. The waves had suddenly shrunk, and the boat was no longer threatening to capsize. I let out a breath, relieved. But as I squinted through the rain and darkness, I could see even less far than before. And that distance was shrinking.

Fast.

*No, no, no, no.* This was *not* good.

"ROGUE WAVE!" I screamed at the top of my lungs. Sailors' heads turned, and a second later everyone was scrambling.

"Tie yourselves to the boat!" Captain Callaway bellowed. "If you can't find a rope then go below decks!"

"Give me the wheel!" Barnet yelled. "Sailors, to your posts! If you find a rope, use it! Otherwise, stand your ground!"

"We're going to capsize!" one sailor wailed, frantically tying himself to the mast.

Barnet spun the wheel, and the ship turned toward the wave, angled slightly. Alexander was halfway down the ladder—and the wave was approaching fast. "Hurry!" I urged him, making sure all of my knots were tight.

This was going to be a rough ride.

The bow of the ship tilted upward, the wall of water taller than the mainmast itself. The prow rose up, up, up towards the angry sky. Unanchored crates and barrels slid across the deck and splashed into the water. I held on to the spar for dear life, but it was slick with rain.

My hands slipped.

I screamed as gravity took hold, my heart jumping into my throat as I hurtled downward. The rope pulled taut and I gasped in pain—but I fell no further.

The ship rose higher.

I grabbed the rope and pulled myself into a sitting position. Fear struck my heart like lightning, and I searched wildly for Alexander. *Thank the stars*, I found him. He was gripping the rope with two hands, his legs dangling over the stormy sea below. His lips were tight with effort. His sandy hair was dark and messy, but his blue eyes shone in the darkness.

My heart filled with dread. *Don't let go.*

The ship climbed higher, the deck vertical, but we were almost to the crest. He could make it.

But then one hand slipped off. Alexander grimaced as he reached up again, fingers brushing the rope. The ship shuddered, and his remaining hand slipped by two fingers.

Our eyes met. When he saw me floating in midair, the panic left his face, and he flashed me a knowing smirk. I could imagine him saying, *See? I told you you'd need it.*

"Alexander!" I screamed. "Alexander, don't you *dare* let go!"

He looked at me a moment longer, the wind and rain whipping at his sodden clothes. I hated the acceptance on his face as he whispered something that was lost in the wind.

His last three fingers slipped.

"NO!" I sobbed, reaching out as he fell, down, down, down, until the merciless sea swallowed him whole.

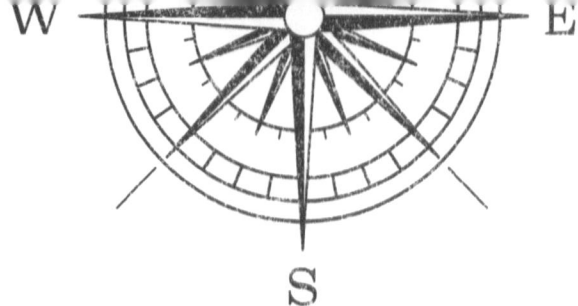

# Chapter 18

**T**HE PROW BROKE THE CREST, showering everyone on board with cold, salty water. Then suddenly we tipped in the opposite direction, the ship racing down the back side of the wave, and I swung forward with frightening speed. My eyes widened as I braced myself for impact, my legs and arms outstretched, ready to catch myself before I hit the mast. My feet hit, but slipped against the wood, spinning me so my shoulder slammed against the mast. I grunted and tried to grab something, but my fingers only brushed the wood as the pendulum continued its course. The ship finally leveled, but that sent me flying back the other way. This time I was ready, and compensated for the slickness of the mast. After I'd steadied myself, I grabbed the rope and pulled myself up, suddenly aware of the tingling numbness in my legs.

*I can still save him*, I thought, hating the hopelessness that was building up inside me. *He isn't gone. He isn't.* I climbed hand over hand until I was back on the spar. I untied my safety rope, cursing. *Why didn't he just take it for himself? Why did he have to be so selfless? So* damn *heroic?*

The rain ran into my eyes and down my face as I hurried down the ladder, but I didn't wipe it away. My throat tightened and my eyes stung; if I was crying, I wanted the rain to disguise it.

"Xander?! Where's Alexander?" His father was frantically untying himself.

I landed on the deck, then wobbled, catching myself on the railing.

"Where is my boy?" he yelled again.

The other sailors were still catching their breath and marveling at the fact that they were alive. Preston was a few feet from me, not bothering to free himself from the railing.

"Cassie?" His voice cracked. "Cassie, where's Xander?"

I swallowed, afraid to speak, unsure if my voice would work. My legs suddenly felt like lead. I shook my head as Captain Callaway approached, holding out his hand to shield his face from the pelting rain. I wished right then that a wave would crash down upon my head and wash me away.

"Cassandra, where is my son? Did he have a rope?"

I swayed on the spot, my vision blurry.

"Cassandra!" He grabbed my shoulders and shook me. "Where is he!"

"He had a rope!" Preston turned toward me, angry. "*You gave him a rope.*" Then his eyes fell on the twisted cord trailing from my waist.

I looked at my feet and choked out, "He's gone. I'm sorry. He's gone."

"No!" Callaway screamed, and ran to the railing. I watched as he leaned out, hopelessly calling his son's name.

Preston furiously tore at the knots tying him to the railing. I knew immediately what he was going to attempt. I raced forward and caught him at the railing, wrapping my arms around his body.

"Stop!" he bellowed, struggling to free himself. "Get off me, filthy pirate! You let him fall!"

"Please," I begged, fighting him. "There's no chance to find him in this storm. You'll drown!"

"That's what *you* deserve! But that's not what *he* deserves!"

I braced my hip against the railing as I wrestled Preston away. The boat rocked violently and we fell to the deck. I ignored the pain zinging up my arm as we wrestled in two inches of ocean water.

"Please!" I yelled as I put him into a lock. I forced him to look at me. Rain dripped off the ends of my hair and onto his face. "He wouldn't want you to go after him! He'd want you to be safe!"

"Don't tell me what he would want," he spat. Furious tears mixed with the raindrops sliding down his cheeks. He stopped struggling against me, and water receded out from under us. "He's been my best friend since we were young. *You* don't know him at all!"

I fought down my rage. "I know. I know, savvy? Just please, don't jump in after him."

His eyes dimmed, swallowed by a crushing sorrow. His head fell back as a raw, guttural sob ripped from his chest. I scrambled away as he keened, each cry splintering into choking gasps. I stumbled and slipped to the bow of the ship, clenched my fists. Trying to block out Preston's angry words and the heartwrenching sound of his sobs.

I promised Alexander I wouldn't blame myself for his death. It *was* his fault. He was an idiot. *A daft, reckless englishman—* I sank to my knees. *Who always did the right thing.*

I wanted him back on the ship so I could punch him and tell him to never do that again. He should have taken it. I should never have let him go up with me. I placed my hands on the deck, felt the cold seawater wash over them. Listened to the *thump-splash, thump-splash* as the boat sailed on over the white-caps.

The image flashed in my mind. Suspended in midair, falling slowly, his arms outstretched, no fear in his expression. His last words ripped away by the wind. I turned my shaking hands palm up, letting the raindrops hit them.

I felt a hand on my shoulder. "It's not safe for you, darling."

My whole body stiffened, and I shook him off. "I don't want to talk to you, Joshua. And *don't* call me darling," I snarled.

"I understand you're grieving, but I'm trying to keep you safe. The storm isn't over—"

I twisted around, my body shaking as I glared at him. "Leave. Me. Alone."

He hesitantly obeyed, afraid of the fire in my eyes. I turned back to the prow, squeezing my eyes shut. My heart swelled with each wave, threatening to burst. *I wrap all my sorrow in a canvas sail. I tie a cannonball to it. I watch it sink below the waves. My chin is raised. My shoulders are back.* Water ran down my face and dripped off the tip of my nose. I tasted salt on my lips, and wished it was just the seawater splashing up over the rail.

Captain Callaway's voice grew hoarse. Eventually he fell silent, but I knew he was still staring off into the storm.

I balled my hands into fists and screamed angrily. *Why?* Why did Alexander have to be like that? Why did I let him come up with me when I knew he had no rope? I was trained for survival at sea. I was an excellent swimmer—I would have survived.

*He won't.*

*No.* No, it wasn't my fault. If that damned hunter had given the order to furl the sails a few minutes earlier, it never would have happened. My nails cut into my palms and I boiled inside.

*Barnet* was responsible for Alexander's death. I should have killed him when I'd had that perfect chance. But that was in the past. I wasn't going to let myself spend all my energy on killing him, because years ago I'd watched the downfall of a fellow pirate who became crazed with revenge. But I felt it in my bones that it would be mine.

Someday.

Someday.

Soon.

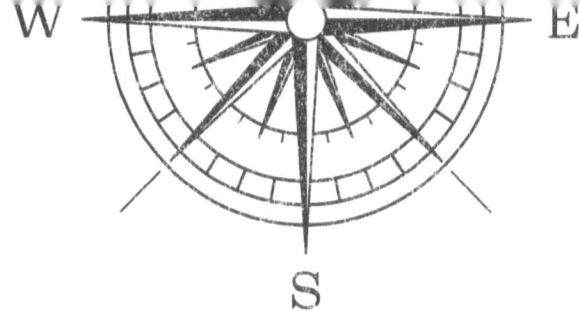

W          E

S

## *Chapter 19*

**"L**AND HO!"

I ran to the edge of the ship. Sure enough, a faint strip of land hovered above the horizon, distorted by mirage. If Barnet would risk the safety of his crew and passengers for the money he would gain from selling his prisoners, then I was going to take the liberty of releasing those prisoners. A wolfish smile crept up on my face, imagining his expression when twenty or so pirates were suddenly set loose on his deck.

I waited until the island filled our view before putting my plan into action. A knot rose in my throat when I thought of the boy who was supposed to help me. Why did it feel like I'd been hollowed out? My eyes roved across the deck, searching for my enemy's son. My gaze paused on Captain Callaway, who was sitting on a crate against the edge of the ship. He was staring into empty space, his eyes bloodshot. He looked a decade older. I swallowed, drawing my gaze from him. I needed to focus, but my mind couldn't help but wonder about Alexander's curly-haired best friend. I hadn't seen him in days.

The knot in my throat grew more painful. *Deep breaths*. I pushed down the guilt and anguish that threatened to come spilling out. Now was not the time for compassion.

I had a job to do.

I located the boy I was looking for, and mentally prepared myself. He stood by the helm, standing like he had power over everyone on board.

"Joshua!" I called quietly, forcing the most natural flirty smile I could manage. I beckoned to him, but didn't wait for him to follow as I made my way to the open hatch. I needed a more private, quiet space, and almost every sailor was on deck. As I walked down the steep steps, I glanced over my shoulder. Joshua was right behind me.

"What is it?" he asked.

I looked around for any other sailors, but saw none. "It's just that...we're almost there. Is this the last time I'll see you?" I stepped closer, looking up into his eyes. The last time I glimpsed the key, he had put it into his left pocket. I hoped it was still there, otherwise I would have to resort to less inconspicuous measures.

"Your place is not on this ship, and I won't leave my father." He reached up and touched my face, and although I squirmed inside, I let him. I needed to check his pocket without him noticing, so I waited for an embrace.

"So this is goodbye?" I said quietly, sadly.

"I'm afraid so, Cassandra. But not for quite a few minutes," he added, a smile creeping up on his lips as he leaned closer.

"Oh, but it's not enough," I whispered, reaching with my left hand and fingering the tips of his hair. He took it as an invitation to grab my waist and pull me closer, and as he began to close the gap between our lips, I reached with my free hand into his pocket, my fingers moving delicately so he didn't realize what I was doing. *Rats*. I retracted my hand, my spirits falling. The thought of kissing him made me sick, so I turned my head away like I was embarrassed. His kiss landed on my cheek. I took my hand from his shoulder and patted his other pocket, hoping that it would be there, but no such luck. Joshua pulled away and brushed my hair behind my ear.

"What is it?" he asked.

"What is what?" I had to think fast. He was right here, and the key was nowhere to be found. I didn't have time to search his quarters, but there was one last option. My last resort, for good reason. But it would have to do. He was about to speak, but I cut him off. "One moment," I said, lifting my knee so I could reach inside my boot without bending over. I whipped my knife out and held it beneath his chin, so he could feel the cold metal on his skin and know I was serious. His eyes widened and he stumbled backward in surprise, but I advanced, pressing his back up against a wooden support.

"What are you doing?" he exclaimed. "How—who do you think you *are*?"

I couldn't help smiling. I wanted to tell him *so* badly, to see the surprise and fear on his face when he heard my name. But I just threatened, "keep your voice down, or you'll never find out." I removed the sword from his scabbard. "I'll be keeping this. I'm really sorry for the inconvenience, but the easy way didn't work, so now you get this."

Hurt confusion crossed over his face, but I didn't care. "What do you mean? Was that all an act?"

"Tell me where you put the key to the prisoner's cells."

"Never."

"I want the key, and you want your life. So let's make a trade."

"You won't kill me."

I narrowed my eyes. "You don't know me. You have no idea what I'm capable of."

"Well, I'd lose my life either way, so I'd rather choose the more honorable option."

"What do you mean?" I asked, taken aback.

"If my father found out that I gave you the key and he lost the fortune he was going to gain from them, he'd kill me."

"But you're his son!"

He couldn't meet my eyes. "He needs to be able to trust the men who work for him."

"So he threatened you with death? That *does* sound like him."

He shrugged. "It's just how he operates."

I wondered how he'd come to terms with that. My father was tough on me, but not *that* tough. "Oh, well he doesn't have to know. I'm going to make it *very* clear to him who really was responsible for the loss of his prisoners." I pressed the knife harder to his throat, making him wince. "I don't have all day, and there's no need for you to die just for the sake of a silly key."

He gritted his teeth. "It's not a *silly key*." He hesitated for a half second more before slowly reaching underneath his collar and lifting the key from around his neck.

I exhaled with relief as my fingers closed around it. "You're going to walk with me to the brig, and don't try anything funny, because I can throw this knife pretty good." I walked directly behind him, touching the blade to his spine as we marched down to the brig.

"Hello, sir," the lone guard said to him, and then nodded politely to me. But I didn't wait for his eyes to land on my weapon; I struck out, disarming him with Joshua's sword, and hitting him over the head with the pommel. Joshua made a move for safety, but I stopped him, and once again he had a cold blade pressed against his throat. I looked around at the prisoners, my former crew, as they stared back at me.

"Now you can see," Bart growled from a couple cells down. "She was the one lying, not me."

We both looked at him. "You really were their captain?" Joshua asked, his voice strangled. "You were lying the whole time?"

"It's what I do to survive," I told him. "Would you lie to save your life?"

He growled. "You wouldn't have to lie if you hadn't become a pirate in the first place!"

"Everyone lies. Pirates are just the ones who get fingers pointed at them." I turned my attention to the men in the cells. "We're docking in a few minutes. When we do, you all will be loaded into boxes like livestock and taken to prison. After that, you will be given an unfair trial and most certainly be found guilty. I hope you all know what comes next." I paused to let the words settle in, watching their grim expressions as they sat helpless, silent. I needed them to be desperate enough to agree to my terms. "I want you to know that I am sorry for your fate. Even after all you did to me, I still would not choose this for you."

Bart and a few others growled, disbelieving. "Surely you did not come down here just to tell us that?" one asked.

"Nay. I came down here to tell you that I am your last hope." To further accentuate my point, I dragged Joshua closer to Johnny and Wyatt's cell and shoved the key into the lock, and there was a soft *click* as it disengaged. "Johnny, Wyatt, Weasel, I am in need of your assistance. If you do as I ask, I will free you. Do we have an accord?" I waited for their agreement, then warned, "The upper deck is filled with Red Coats. If you go racing up the stairs, you'll surely die." I pulled the door open and waited until they filed out before I shoved Joshua inside, slamming the door shut and locking it.

"Hey!" he yelled. "What are you doing?!"

"Hold your tongue or I'll cut it out." I smiled when he quieted. It felt good ordering him around.

I addressed the three pirates standing in front of me, knowing the rest of the crew were listening as if their lives depended on it, which they did. "Your goal is simple: escape the ship without getting caught or killed. Create as much chaos and havoc as possible. Ruin Jonathan Barnet's day. Destroy his ship on your way out, but don't kill *any* of the crew members. If you want to be angry at someone, it should be the captain and *only* the captain. His crew follows orders out of fear."

Johnny flashed me a devilish grin. "Aye, aye."

Weasel and Wyatt hesitated, so I smiled and cocked a hip. "Did you not expect me to ask you to do something so fun?" Wyatt returned my smile, and I handed him Joshua's sword as a sign of trust. He took it gently, his eyes full of wonder at the intricately designed hilt, inlaid with the finest gold, and the perfectly crafted blade, three feet in length. I wanted it for myself, but for some reason I felt like Wyatt should be the one to wield it.

"I want that," Weasel whined. "Why does *he* get to have it?"

"You cannot give my sword to him!" Joshua shook the bars, angry. "He's a black man! He lacks honor and refinement and—"

"A black man once risked his life to save mine. All the honor *you* have comes from nice clothes and a full belly," I shot back, my blood boiling. "What did I say about keeping your mouth shut, you miserable coward?" I walked to the unconscious sailor, removed his gun, and handed it to Johnny. "Can I trust you to injure, not kill?"

"Aye."

I turned around and looked into the rest of the cells. "What about you all? Who thinks they can follow this last order I'm giving you? Who wants to escape before it's too late?" Hands raised into the air, but Bart's was last to go up. Anxiety crept into me. I could easily picture him coming straight for my neck as soon as his cell was unlocked. So it was his cell that I saved for last, and I stood there, unsure if I should take away the one thing that was stopping him from trying to hurt me. But how could I let the other man sharing his cell die for the sake of my fear? "How do I know revenge will not get in the way of your promise?" I asked him.

"You don't."

I nodded. "I see. Well, I wasn't the one who killed Axe. The man who did that is dead now, so you don't have to worry about him." My throat grew tight when I thought about it, so I pushed Alexander from my mind. "The only thing you have to be angry at me for is not caring enough about your needs, as captain. But I am no longer your captain, you and your friend made sure of that. So I think we're even."

Bart thought that over. "Who killed Axe? How did he die?"

I didn't want to tell him. He didn't deserve to know. Luckily another solution came as Johnny held the pistol out to me. I looked at him in confusion.

"I'll find another one in a minute. You can 'ave that. I wouldn't trus' Bart if I was you, either. Unlock tha' door, would ya? We're runnin' outta time."

"Right. Thanks," I added, unlocking the door. "Out with you, out with you." I didn't wait another second before yelling, "All right, crew! We've spent enough time dilly-dallying! Go up the stairs and make sure we've arrived at the dock before you go charging out. But first, to the armory with you!"

"Rahh!" they yelled excitedly, before charging up the stairs.

I looked at Joshua's angry face one more time, dropping the key at my feet. "If you can reach it, it's yours," I taunted, walking away and removing the lantern from the wall on my way out. I took my time up the steps, wanting to enjoy every moment of this. This is what made pirating so fun, besides the gold and silver and other spoils. It was rubbing your success in the faces of your enemies.

I stopped short when I got to the top, ignoring Joshua's cries for help, a brilliant plan taking shape in my mind. My body pulsed with new excitement as I raced past the hammocks to the bow of the ship. A couple bodies littered the ground, but when I inspected them, they were still breathing. *They'll have one heck of a headache when they wake, that's for sure.* As I passed the stairs up to the main deck, I saw that the pirates were crowded around it, lying in wait for the opportune moment to pounce. I heard sailors up above shouting to one another as they made ready to anchor.

I continued on, knowing time wasn't on my side, and held the lamp low to the ground, searching for a sign of a trap door. Finally I found it: nestled in a corner, a small brass handle was screwed to the floor. I yanked it open and jumped through, landing softly on the last level of the ship. It was cooler down here, and I could tell that it was below the water line. The safest spot for storing the most dangerous substance on the ship. The only light came from the single candle I held, encased by glass. But not for long. It shone upon many small barrels, stacked atop one another. I set the lantern down and walked to the nearest one, prying the cork out with my knife. The gray-black powder glittered as I tipped it over and dragged the barrel backwards, forming a trail across the wood.

A fuse.

This was better, I decided. Better than killing him. I would take down his legacy, and he would be able to do nothing but watch as it crumbled before his eyes. I stepped over to the end of the fuse, then opened the little glass door that protected the gunpowder from the open flame, and carefully pulled out the candle. It was about one and a half inches wide and two inches tall, and I guessed it would burn for almost an hour before there was no more wax left. I scooped the gunpowder into a pile, then pushed the candle into it, twisting it back and forth until the flame was level with the top. It reminded me of a tiny volcano—like Tortuga. As soon as the candle became shorter than the piled gunpowder around it, the powder would slide toward the flame, lighting the fuse. And then it would be a few more seconds before—BOOM.

Revenge would be mine.

At least, I hoped. The candle idea was the best I could do without a mile long fuse.

I rushed up the stairs, the beautiful sounds of a skirmish sending my blood pumping.

The ship had indeed made it into the harbor, but the pirates had interrupted the docking. The wind was blowing us farther from our dock and closer to the next ship. But that was the least of Barnet's problems—pirates were everywhere, hacking away the fresh paint on the rails with axes, dumping barrels overboard, cutting ropes and screaming like maniacs as they battled the sailors.

I dodged and weaved my way towards the edge of the ship, then spotted Barnet on the opposite side, nose to nose with Callaway. I guess he assumed *he* had something to do with all his prisoners escaping. I huffed. I wasn't about to let somebody else take all the credit, so I jumped up on the rail and grabbed hold of the rope ladder. "Hey Barnet!" I screamed. He looked over, and half of the sailors and pirates stopped to look at me. "Carry on," I told them, before looking back to Barnet. "He wasn't the one who caused you all this trouble. So let him go."

"Then who did it?" he yelled, furious.

Below me, the sailors were beginning to overpower the pirates, as they outnumbered them four to three. One sailor caught a pirate off guard and stabbed him with his bayonet. He fell, and as blood pooled around him his comrades jumped ship, some landing in the water and swimming towards the dock, others leaping past me into the neighboring ship and scurrying towards safety. I only had a few more seconds before the chaos ended and I was singled out, so I had to cut my speech short. "Who did it?" I repeated. "The only daughter of Anne Bonny and Calico Jack, that's who. But don't worry, Barnet. I'm not done, yet. This is only the beginning. Next time we meet, you'll be wishing you had never made an enemy out of me." I didn't wait to see his reaction before I jumped into the sloop and ran onto the dock, two more pirates following my lead.

As we raced away from the water, I heard Barnet scream, "AFTER THEM!"

⸺◦◦◦⸺

I kicked little pebbles as I shuffled down the street, my head bent low, the cap pulled down over my eyes and my hands stuffed in my pockets. The solid earth felt odd under my feet, like my body expected the ground to rock. *Sea legs weren't meant for land.*

I tried to ignore the sounds of crying children and begging mothers. I had nothing to offer them besides the clothes off my own back. The streets were damp with excrement and the air was clogged with a foul smell. Chickens and orphaned children alike wandered aimlessly around, scavenging for any edible substance. I couldn't see glittering water from where I stood, but I knew the harbor was close. Once in a while the cool sea breeze would blow between the leaning houses, lifting the odor for a moment, but it would fall back down again like a thick, transparent fog. *And Alexander wondered why I like it better at sea?*

*186*

As swift as that thought came, a choking misery grasped me. An image of his body floating down to the sea floor forced its way into my mind, nearly bringing me to my knees. Why did I have to lose so much? What was I doing wrong?

Tears threatened to fall, but I clenched my fists. *I won't blame myself.* It was Barnet's fault for keeping the sails up too long. It was Alexander's fault for refusing the safety rope! I nursed my anger, a welcome relief. He thought honor was more important than self-preservation, did he? Well look where that got him.

"E-excuse me, ma'am." The voice ahead of me was a hoarse whisper.

I looked up to see an old man with a scraggly, thinning beard holding out his bony hands. He sat cross-legged, leaning against the side of a house.

"Anything you can spare?"

I shook my head. "Sorry." I turned out my pockets to prove it to him. "If I had anything I'd give it to you."

His hands fell disappointedly, and I walked on, noticing the many wanted posters tacked to the sides of buildings. I searched for someone I recognized, but didn't find anyone. *They must be petty thieves*, I thought, *accused of stealing bread.* The threat of pirates was shrinking, but old Governor Rogers still focused his attention on lawbreakers instead of the starvation that was threatening so many of his citizens' existence. I remembered the stories my mum would tell me, that before King George sent him to straighten this place out, it was a place like other pirate-ruled islands: wild and free, stocked with enough pigs and chickens to feed everyone that stopped by for a few merry drink-filled weeks.

A *BOOM* sent the windows rattling and my heart jumping, and I sprinted towards the disturbance, excitedly eyeing the smoke billowing into the sky from behind the creaking structures. I raced down an alleyway and skidded to a halt as a lovely chaotic scene unfolded in front of me. I crouched behind a cart of hay, gleefully sniggering to myself.

The last of the powder kegs went off, sending another *boom* rolling away across the water, and the mainmast creaked and whined as it tipped over, snapping lines and shrouds before it crashed down onto the deck of the neighboring boat, crunching both rails and sending shards of wood shooting in all directions. My eyes landed on Barnet's flags, now hanging lifelessly from the downed mainmast. One was the red ensign. The other was his personal signature: a thin indigo flag, with seven white slash marks like a bear had taken its claws to it. I tilted my head, recalling the first time I'd laid eyes on that flag. At the time it only had two slashes. My heart sank. *Pirate ships he'd captured?*

The sailors were yelling and running off the ship, whose bow was sinking perilously toward the water. Barnet was on the deck, holding one hand to his face and screaming furiously at everyone in close proximity. His son was pulling him toward safety, and as they stumbled closer I noticed blood dripping down Barnet's wrist and chin. I smiled smugly, hoping it was excruciating.

The water beneath the ship bubbled and churned as it pulled the hull deeper, and the waves now lapped over the deck. Before long, only the tip of the standing mast pierced the water's surface, and Barnet and his crew stood staring at it, defeated. I allowed myself another smile before pulling my hat down and slipping into the shadows.

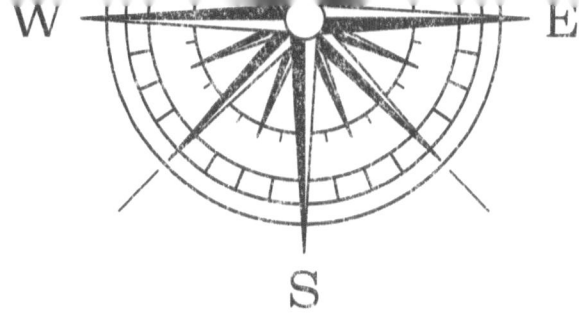

## Chapter 20

HUOH, HUOH, HUOH!
  I groaned deliriously, the familiar sound grating on my ears. I opened my eyelids a crack and lazily swatted the air.

*Huoh, huoh, huoh!*

The bird perched above me hopped closer, so it was directly above my head. "Go away," I told it angrily. The night chill still lingered in the air, as the sun peeked above the horizon, bathing everything in a soft pink light. It was too early to face all of my problems. Why couldn't I have remained unconscious for a couple hours longer?

*Huoh, huoh!*

I groaned again, shutting my eyes and adjusting my weight on the hay I had fallen asleep on. What did I do to deserve *this* for a wake up call? Suddenly my face was covered in warm, thick liquid, and I bolted upright.

"UGH!" I tried not to gag as it dribbled down my face, inching toward my lips. I heard a flapping as the seagull took flight. "YOU STUPID BIRD!" I screamed, fumbling for my pistol. Squinting with one eye, I took the shot, but in my disoriented anger the gull escaped with its pitiful life. I threw down the useless hunk of metal and wiped off as much poo as I could, before resuming my tirade. "Filthy, disgusting—piece of—of—TRASH!! Arg!!" I stamped my feet, getting several looks from early passersby, then stalked around the side of the building and toward the water, hardly aware of anything around me, looking through my eyelashes. I laid at the edge of the retaining wall and reached my hands into the water. I scrubbed my face with the cool salty water for a solid five minutes, before sitting up and dangling my legs over the side. The soles of my boots skimmed the water as I looked out to the sea, watching the sun slowly rise, listening to the street behind me slowly come alive. A boat, a little black dot, grew steadily bigger as it closed the distance to the port.

My anger slowly gave way to a painful ache deep in my gut. It wasn't fair that good people died so easily. It wasn't fair that Captain Callaway had to lose his oldest son, and Preston his closest friend. *Alexander.* How could I blame him? He was one of the few people I had ever met that didn't have an ulterior motive. He only ever had good intentions. He was so different from me—when he looked at people, he would notice the good in them first. *When I meet new people, all I can see is...all the ways they could possibly hurt me.* Maybe that was why I had survived this long, but he didn't die because of his haste to trust. He died because... I didn't want to, but I thought back to the storm. His eyes, so calm and knowing, as if he had already accepted the possibility of death long before he actually fell. If he'd had that rope, he wouldn't have died. But if I hadn't had that rope...*I* probably would have died.

Twice he saved my life, and now I'd never be able to repay him.

My stomach tightened and a heated ball of emotion rose to my throat. I lifted my knees and hugged them tightly, trying to quench it before a tear escaped my eye. *Deep breath. Deep breath. Don't feel. Focus on something else.* The clatter of horse-drawn carriages on the cobblestone streets. The sound of voices, young and old, happy and annoyed. Horses neighed. Fishermen called to each other as they finished their rounds and brought their boats into the dock.

I closed my eyes, but immediately opened them again, because I couldn't stand seeing his face in my mind, his hair plastered to one side, his lips moving silently as he formed words I would never hear. I choked back a sob. I shouldn't be feeling this way. I only knew him for a few weeks. Was that enough time for me to care? After all that effort I put in to *not* care about him, to dislike him...it was all in vain. When I'd banished this overwhelming grief all those years ago, I thought it would never come back.

I wiped my eyes with the back of my hand, then looked out at the water. It was a calm day, the waves lapping against the stone underneath me. I inhaled, then let it out slowly, trying to clear my mind. To focus on the water. But I couldn't think about it without remembering it killed him.

I jumped up and started along the seawall toward the harbor, my hands opening and closing. In a section of water between docks, the tip of a mast still pierced the surface of the water. I tried to smile, but the sight didn't bring me the satisfaction that it should've.

Eventually I arrived at the busiest part of the harbor. Men bustled past carrying lobster crates, fishermen bundled up their nets from their early morning catch. I watched the fishing boat I was observing earlier make its way to the docks. It was a small boat, crewed by four men. I don't know why I was compelled to stop at the dock they'd anchored at, but I did. I watched them work—three of them looked similar: weathered, with long scruffy beards and shoulders hunched with age. But the fourth—I couldn't quite get a good look at the fourth. The others kept moving and blocking my view, but I couldn't shake the feeling that the man should be familiar. Finally, with his back to me, he shook hands with the fishermen and stepped off the boat.

My breath was gone. The ground beneath me felt unsteady, and everything around me became silent and dim.

Except him.

He smiled when he noticed me, but I couldn't smile back. I was dizzy. I wasn't sure what was worse—the sadness, almost grief, when he was gone, or the burning mixture of emotions I felt watching him walk toward me.

Alive.

How was it possible?

When Alexander stopped ten feet from me, I saw he had lost his tidy, clean-shaven sailor-boy look. His clothes were dirty and a little tattered, and his hair was messy and windblown. He was tanner, his nose and cheekbones peeling from sun damage.

But I couldn't look away.

I tried to find words, to say something, but when I opened my mouth no sound came out.

"Hello, Cassandra Rackham," he said quietly. The words were too formal.

"You're alive," I stammered.

He scuffed his boot on the wood beneath him, hands folded behind his back. "Yes." He smirked. "Are you angry that I couldn't stay dead?"

It was like something snapped inside me, and all the weight and wretchedness I had been carrying inside dissipated in one angry scream, startling him. "Why?! Why didn't you just take the rope? It would have saved all of us a whole lot of grief."

It took him a second to find words. "Cassandra," he whispered, then took a breath. "I was extraordinarily lucky. You would have died!"

"I would have rather taken the risk," I said angrily. "You have lots of people who care for you." My voice caught in my throat. "There's no one alive to grieve *my* death."

His expression filled with compassion, and his eyes deepened. "No one? You don't think *I* would have grieved for you?"

"You were really being selfish." I pretended like I hadn't heard his last statement. Pretended like it hadn't struck me to the core.

"Selfish?" Alexander now looked at me like I was ridiculous. "How?"

"When someone dies, who's hurt more: them or the people left behind?"

Alexander was quiet for a moment. Then he took a few steps toward me. "I'm sorry I caused you to grieve. But please understand this: I would never have forgiven myself if I took the rope and watched *you* fall into the sea."

I swallowed. "I do. I *do* understand that." I looked down and whispered, "More than you think."

"Well, I'm here now," he said quietly, stepping closer.

I looked up again, into his eyes. *No.* I remembered all too well what happened the last time I let someone in. *But he knows me*, part of me pleaded. Would that make any difference?

I narrowed my eyes and jabbed a finger to his chest. "If you ever, *ever*, do that again—"

"Wouldn't dream of it," he said with a sideways smile, as he grabbed my hand and lifted my finger away.

I felt a spark zip from where our hands touched down to the bottom of my belly. Alarmed, I removed it from his grasp and folded my arms, trying to act like I had always been. Trying to act like I had been fine. "Good. Now, let's go find your father and get you cleaned up." I swallowed, searching for something to complain about. "You smell of fish."

———

We found them at a shop that, according to Alexander, was called "Harris and Burton's Naval Supplies and Rentals." They were waiting in line to buy tickets for the next ferry, most likely back to England. An old man stood behind the counter, with half-moon spectacles and a wig. He held a clipboard and a quill, his assistant collecting money from each customer.

I glanced down at my tattered pants, stained shirt, and muddy boots, knowing we were out of place among the few well-dressed people in the room. I caught a few people glancing at me, disgust written in the subtle wrinkling of their noses.

"Preston!" I called softly. "Captain Callaway."

They turned, and their muted expressions morphed into shock, then relief as they beheld the boy next to me. Preston rushed forward with a joyful exclamation and nearly knocked Alexander over with the force of his hug.

"My son! My son!" Callaway cried out, sinking to his knees. "Are you truly here or is this another dream to torment me?"

"I'm here. I'm here." Alexander knelt and embraced his father tightly, his voice cracking with emotion.

Callaway's body was wracked with sobs. His son held him until his breathing calmed.

"I'm alive," Alexander repeated softly.

I stepped back and leaned against the wall behind me. Everyone in the store had frozen, staring in wonder and bewilderment at the scene unfolding before them. An older lady dabbed at her eyes with a white handkerchief. My heart ached for a reason I couldn't quite pinpoint. I felt alone, standing off to the side, watching them shed tears of joy and love for each other. Why did seeing them so happy make me feel empty inside?

The three men finally rose, Callaway wiping his eyes. "This was surely God's hand. Oh, Lord, I thank you! What a miracle you have given us!" He turned to his son and took him by the shoulders. "My son, clearly you were put on this earth for a purpose."

"How did you survive?" Preston asked eagerly, bouncing on the balls of his feet. "How did you make it back here?"

Alexander shook his head, disbelieving. "I won't take too much credit for it. It was mostly luck."

"Well, tell us what happened!"

I leaned forward in interest, curiosity replacing my loneliness.

"Once I fell in, I thought I was done for, but Captain Barnet's ship had lost a barrel or two before I fell, and so I grabbed one and held on for dear life. It felt like forever until the storm calmed down, but a while after it did, some fishermen found me and were willing to take me here."

Stepping toward them, I looked at Alexander and nodded thoughtfully. "I'm impressed. You're tougher than I thought you were."

"Of course he's tough. He's my son," Callaway said proudly. Alexander beamed at that.

I smiled. "I will say, though, if you ever tell that story again, you shouldn't skip on the scary details. And you should definitely take the credit."

"Yes, man, add some embellishments! You almost died! This is a story you're going to tell for years!" Preston added.

"Here, here!" I raised an imaginary glass. "These kinds of stories are great for boring sea trips."

He laughed.

The old man at the counter cleared his throat loudly. "*Madam*, here are your tickets."

"Oh!" The woman tore her eyes away from us and turned back to the salesman. "Thank you. Good day."

"Next!" He eyed me unkindly, announcing to the room, "And if you aren't here to buy anything, kindly exit the premises." He turned to his assistant and muttered something.

"I'm glad I'll be buying three tickets instead of two," Alexander's father said happily as he walked up to the counter, Preston following close behind.

Alexander looked like he wanted to say something, then decided against it. Instead, he looked at me, melancholy. "You don't want to come with us, do you?"

I shook my head, then said under my breath, "I'm headed for Tortuga." I hesitated, wishing my heart weren't so heavy. I thought of the riddle, and how much I still didn't know. *Nights are warm, days are cool, where the creek meets the pool...clue... warning...rejoicing...* and finally, *seek*. "I need your help with one last thing. I didn't want to learn to read just for its own sake."

Alexander raised a brow. "Color me surprised."

I smiled half-heartedly at his sarcasm, anxious thoughts coursing through my head. *What if he was faking and he didn't really care? What if once I showed him, he'd want the treasure all to himself?* I took a deep breath, clearing my mind. It was worth the risk. "You must swear never to tell anyone what I'm about to show you."

"I swear."

I glanced around the room, which was empty except for us, the two men behind the counter, and a third sitting on a waiting bench, all but his large forehead and receding hairline hidden behind a copy of the local newspaper. He wore lustrous black boots and a fraying brown piece of cloth draped about his shoulders and around his chest. I frowned. He was certainly not there when we'd arrived, but I hadn't noticed him come in.

I turned back to Alexander, knowing the stranger was too engrossed in the news to overhear me. I took a deep breath, pulling the leather pouch out of my pocket and extracting the old, crinkled parchment. There was water damage on one edge from the rainwater that had seeped through the opening of the pouch, but the map was largely unscathed. "I need you to read this for me."

Alexander's eyes went wide as he gingerly held the map out in front of him. "Woah," he breathed. "How old *is* this?"

I shrugged. "No idea."

He rubbed the paper in between his fingers. "Could be from over a hundred years ago. It feels like it's made of linen, which explains why it's lasted this long. And the way the map is drawn hints—"

"Alexander," I scolded, amused that he was more interested in the historical significance than the information it held. "What does it say?"

"Yes, sorry. It's just—*wow.*" He cleared his throat and pointed to each of the words as he read them:

*Nights are warm, days are cool,*
*Where the creek meets the pool.*
*But this clue brings a warning:*
*All rejoicing will turn to mourning*
*When the fortune you seek*
*Becomes your greatest misfortune.*

"Read it again," I told him breathlessly. He obeyed, and I repeated it word for word in my head. My heart pounded excitedly. Somewhere there was a place where the nights were warmer than days. The treasure was buried at the point where a small river meets a pond. My limbs tingled with anticipation. The clue warned of a danger, but didn't specify what. *How would the great treasure that was buried become a threat to me?* I remembered watching men quarrel over coins, and how my mother taught me to target people who flaunted their wealth. Understanding sunk in. *Great wealth paints a target on your back.*

Well, I wasn't an idiot. I didn't need an old piece of paper to tell me not to brag about my treasure. I thought back through the entire riddle, looking for any other hidden clues, but found none.

I huffed, folding the map and slipping it into my pocket. "The map isn't any help yet, but I was hoping at least the writing would give me some clue as to *where on earth this is.*"

"That piece of paper is a treasure in and of itself," he murmured.

I shot him a look.

He rolled his eyes and returned his focus to the problem at hand. "Perhaps we're missing something."

I faltered. "*We?* Aren't you...returning to England with your father?"

He swallowed, fidgeting with his sleeve. "That would please him. He's planning to return, find his ship, and continue his merchant business. I don't mind helping him, but... it seems like an endless cycle. You know—back and forth, carrying goods for other people. Before you captured our ship..." He swallowed. "I was dying, slowly."

"So you're glad I captured your ship?" I asked, surprised.

"Absolutely not. I hate pirates and I always will. A friend of mine will never come home because of your cook." Anger flashed across his features. He took a breath and looked me in the eye. "Be that as it may, unexpected events and near-death experiences tend to open the eyes. And I, for one, value knowledge greatly. Therefore, I will not regret my time aboard a pirate ship, nor my fall into the sea."

I stared at him, intrigued. "How wise."

"Is that sarcasm I hear?"

I laughed. "Certainly not! So what, your near-death experience convinced you to re-think your life? You want to go treasure-hunting with me?" I meant that last question as a joke, but Alexander looked down.

"What am I thinking?" He scoffed. "I can't leave Preston. My father would never approve. Besides, if I go, I might never see them again."

"One, Preston would kill you if you didn't let him in on the fun. And two, of course you'll see your father again! Just go to your family home and wait for him there." Then I realized what I'd just said. *Did I just encourage him to come with me?* Had I gone mad?!

Alexander was quiet while he thought.

"If you don't want to leave him, you don't have to. You could go back to living how you were before, a quiet life on the seas. Pretend your ship was never robbed. Pretend you never beat a pirate captain in a swordfight." The smile I got was worth the difficulty admitting it. What started as an attempt to reverse what I had said a moment ago ended up sounding *more* convincing, in a counter-intuitive kind of way. I couldn't help myself from continuing. "Pretend you never fell off that ship and fooled us all into thinking that you'd died. Pretend you never met me." The last sentence left me in a whisper. I don't know why it didn't come as easily as the others. I don't know why I said *any* of that, but I felt like he needed it. To make him realize that he couldn't forget. No matter how hard he'd try, he wouldn't be able to banish it from his mind.

He searched my face, his eyes a fathomless blue. "No," he murmured. "That's not possible."

I didn't know how I would have replied, or if he would have said something more, but just then Captain Callaway and Preston walked back toward us, holding tickets.

"Good news!" Callaway exclaimed. "We got them for a discount, since we work for the King."

"Oh, good," Alexander said half-heartedly.

He looked back at me, something intense in his eyes, but I offered no encouragement. Instead, I tilted my head ever so slightly, in a way that said, *Is this something you want bad enough?* I learned early on that if I wanted something, I needed to be strong enough to get it. I didn't get any encouragement to stand up to my father, intimidating and fierce as he was. I didn't get any support when I wanted to say what was on my mind. But doing so anyway made me stronger.

Preston held Alexander's ticket out to him, but he kept his hand at his side and cleared his throat. "Listen, I... I don't want to go back to England. Not yet."

"Pardon?" His father said, taken aback.

"What on earth do you mean?" Preston asked.

"I don't want to go back to England yet," Alexander spoke a little more strongly, looking at his father. "I've always done as you asked. I came along each voyage because I wanted to help *you*. Because *you* needed me. I don't mind being at sea, but nothing ever happens." Alexander was rushing his words now. "We go back and forth and give most of what we earn to the ship owners and the King."

Preston frowned. Captain Callaway narrowed his eyes and looked between Alexander and me. "What has she been telling you? Has she gotten into your head? Remember who you are, boy! Your duty is to the King. We give to the King because he protects us." He reached out and gripped his son's shoulders.

"Apparently not enough," I muttered under my breath.

"What if I don't like the King?" Alexander retorted, eyes widening when he realized what he'd just said.

His father gasped. "You can't say such things!"

Resolved, Alexander shook his father's hands off his shoulders. "Father, the Royal Crown takes and takes. Working for the King has only given us social status. The salary you receive is only enough to feed our family, upkeep our home, and keep you paying your rent to the ship owners. You've no other choice but to keep working. Think about what we could do with more money! Mum could use the extra money to publish her book. We'd be able to afford a tutor for Jane and Hannah, and Owen could go to university."

Callaway growled at me. "What have you done, getting into his head? He was a respectful boy and a good, law-abiding citizen before *you* came along."

I held my chin high. "I didn't do anything, Old Salt. This was all him."

"I just want to be free, Father. If I pursue this—if it pays off—it could change our lives—our family won't ever have to worry about money again. Please, Father, you must understand. It's just one journey. I'm not going to become a pirate. I've no intention of engaging in criminal activities, I promise."

His father clenched his jaw. "If you run around with *her* type, you become her type."

"*My* type?" I growled. "You, Old Salt, shouldn't be talking. I swear—"

Alexander flashed me a look like, *let me handle this*, so I reluctantly backed off. This was his fight, after all.

"There's nothing wrong with her, Father. She's a good person."

"No, I'm not," I scoffed. "But *he* is," I told Callaway, pointing my thumb at his son. "You should know that, being his father. Nothing *I* do will change who he is."

"It seems to me like you've already done that," Callaway snapped.

"Can we take a little pause here?" Preston interjected with a finger raised.

"What?" Alexander and his father demanded in unison, both a little high strung.

"What do you mean by 'if it pays off'? Did I miss something?"

Before I could stop him, Alexander whispered something in his friend's ear, and the latter perked up instantly, his face full of wonder and excitement.

Preston turned to me. "Is it true?"

I rolled my eyes. "Keep the secret, will you?"

"Certainly." Preston elbowed Alexander. "Say, when you're a rich man and captain of your own ship, Abraham won't have anything left to lord over you. Miss Emma would start following you around like a lost puppy again."

My jaw tightened for a moment. I took a quick breath and looked away, pretending to be distracted by something else. *Miss Emma?* I wondered, forcing my gaze back to the boys so neither would notice my sudden discomfort.

Alexander's expression had closed down. "She didn't follow me around like a *lost puppy*. And it's been three years. Emma has probably married Abraham already."

"Come on, mate. Don't give up hope so easily."

He raised a brow. "I'm not blind. If she loved me, a little extra money and status wouldn't have mattered. What she loved was the attention I gave her."

"Didn't you tell me she was teary when you said goodbye, and gave her word she'd wait for you?"

Alexander looked troubled.

The odd feeling that had taken hold of me worsened, then morphed into anger. I hadn't even met the girl, and I hated her.

*No way would I let* my *treasure benefit* her. I clasped my fingers together, inhaling through my nose to calm myself. *No need for all this emotion. I don't care who Alexander does or doesn't like.*

I really didn't care.

"Alexander," Captain Callaway said sternly, his voice lowered. "If you take part in piracy, you'll have no hope of marrying an esteemed girl like her."

Alexander took his father by the shoulder and led him out of earshot. I strained to listen, but didn't dare creep forward. *An esteemed girl like her.* Anger filled me once again. *What made her so esteemed, huh? Being born to the right parents? Wearing frilly hats?*

Preston leaned over and whispered, "How much do you bet that the Captain says yes?"

I thought it over, putting all thoughts of *Emma* out of my mind. "I think Alexander's going to come with me no matter what his dear father says."

Preston seemed to be doubtful, and then he sighed. "I hate to see them argue."

"Does it happen often?"

He shook his head. "Nay. Xander usually listens. But he does have his stubborn side...that's when things get messy."

I nodded.

Preston cleared his throat. "Listen... I'm sorry for what I said before, about it being your fault that Xander died. I was grieving and it felt better to blame you."

I slapped Preston on the back, and he seemed surprised by the action. "Don't worry about it, sailor. You acted like anyone else would've."

Alexander and his father argued for a few minutes, keeping their voices hushed. I caught a few faint phrases related to how I was a "bad influence." Callaway turned his head to glare at me, but Alexander put his hands on his shoulders, and his angry gaze left me. As I watched them, Callaway's shoulders slumped in defeat, and Alexander pulled him into a hug.

"That went better than I expected," Preston said brightly.

When Alexander's father stepped back from the embrace, his jaw was set, and he nodded once to something his son said. Then they strode back to us and Callaway looked at Preston. "I assume you're going with them?"

He patted the sides of his pants happily. "I go wherever he goes, sir."

Callaway nodded tiredly. "Very well. I'll...return your tickets, then."

"I'll see you at our family home, Father," Alexander promised. "If we succeed, I won't be gone long."

I could see sadness in the old captain's eyes, and I felt a twinge of sympathy, even when he grabbed my arm and pulled me aside.

"I kept your dirty secret from Captain Barnet, risking my own life and my family's well-being, and this is how you repay me? By persuading my boys to play with fire?" he demanded, his voice low. "By taking them away from me and convincing them that their own king abuses his power?"

I shrugged my arm out of his grasp and took a deep breath. "Thanks for taking the risk to keep my secret. I could be...I could be waiting to dance the hempen jig as we speak. So you have my thanks." I pressed my hands together in prayer and shook them. "And your king *does* abuse his power. You're blind if you don't see that!"

He glared at me and opened his mouth to say something, but decided against it. He stepped back, his arms folded tightly across his chest. "You better not get them into trouble," he growled.

"I'll do my best," I said, a smile spreading across my face. "But no promises." I backed away until I was near the boys, then gave him a little salute. "May the wind be at your back, Old Salt. Godspeed."

Although I'd never admit this aloud, I was glad I wasn't leaving this island alone.

———•◦•———

A little while later, we were making our way through the crowded streets, back toward the harbor. Houses and shops rose up on either side of the narrow, messy cobblestone street, and since there were no sidewalks, people and horse-drawn carriages mingled as they made their way toward their destinations. I spied a young black-haired man bumping into an older one, and as he continued walking I saw him slip a leather wallet into his pocket. I smiled to myself. *Not bad.* A newspaper boy was flocked by curious people as he shouted this morning's headline into the air. "Pirates at large! They could be coming for you!" I wondered if I was mentioned somewhere there. I doubted I'd get as much credit as I deserved. There probably wasn't even a decent price on my head.

I hummed quietly as we walked, looking around at all the people trapped in the society they've created. Men strolled down the streets, leading silent women in long poofy dresses. They weren't really silent, of course. They talked and laughed airily every so often, but I knew that their lightheartedness was just a facade. How could anyone be happy when all they could talk about was the latest fashion and their husbands and the weather? How could they be happy with everyone trying to shush them up when they tried to insert themselves into a political conversation? I shook my head sadly.

"So where are we headed?" Preston asked. Then he gasped. "The secret pirate lair?"

*205*

"Don't announce it to the whole town," I answered, "But aye."

"How will we get there? We don't have any money!"

I sent them a look. "If you think that's a problem, you don't know what you've gotten yourselves into."

As we approached the street corner, a girl burst out of a rickety building with a sagging roof. The door bounced off the side of the house with a *bang* as she stormed into the street, narrowly avoiding getting trampled by horses as she looked over her shoulder.

"I hate that boy!" she yelled. "He's not even a man! He's a pig!"

An older woman emerged and glanced nervously up and down the street, her eyes landing on us for a moment before turning back to the girl. "You're making a scene," she hissed. "Come back in and we'll talk about it."

I kept walking, slowly approaching her.

Alexander tugged on my arm, silently telling me to continue and stay out of their conversation, but something held me there. "Go on without me," I whispered, but he didn't move.

The girl huffed, blowing a stray piece of caramel-brown hair out of her face. She was small and slight, with pale skin, upturned green eyes, and bow shaped lips. She squared her shoulders, a defiant look in her eyes. "No! I'm sick of your long speeches about how it's for my own good. You and father just want money so you can pay off his debts!" She stepped out of the way of another carriage, but kept her distance from the woman I assumed could only be her mother.

"Judith!" She sighed loudly and put a hand to her forehead. "You have almost twenty years. It's high time you get married. You don't want to be the old maid of the town, do you?"

Preston stepped closer to her and muttered under his breath, "I think your mother might be the pig here."

Judith stifled a laugh, but I exclaimed, "Old maid? At nineteen?!"

"Exactly, mother. I'm still young. Can't I have a few more years to myself?"

"You've had more than enough. And *you*," she snapped at me. "This is none of your business."

Alexander grabbed my hand. "Cassie, I agree, we should go. Apologies, ma'am," he added.

I yanked my hand out of his grasp and turned back to Judith, lowering my voice. "I agree with you, Judith. You shouldn't have to marry anyone you don't want to. I'm actually starting a…" I hesitated. "A society, of sorts, where women can be free to do and say what they want. If you're interested, meet us at the harbor before nightfall today." If there was any girl looking for freedom, I would welcome them aboard…the ship I was about to steal. I doubted she'd actually take me up on the offer, but it was worth a shot.

I turned away from her, and the three of us kept walking, leaving her to deal with her possessive mother. Before we got to the harbor, I had one more stop to make.

The market.

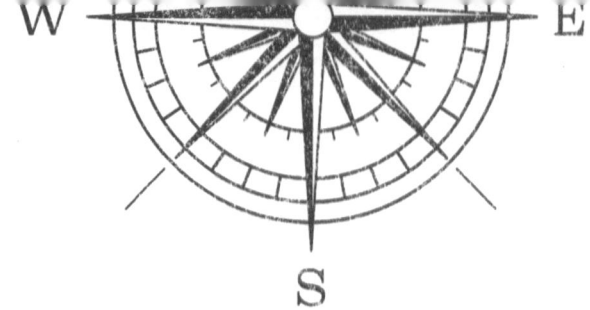

# Chapter 21

"**R**un!" I called breathlessly, a sack draped over my shoulder.

Together we raced down the street, the two of them holding bags like mine, full of precious food that would be crucial to our journey. I just wished we already had a ship to jump onto, but that wasn't in our cards.

"Thieves! Those three are thieves! Someone grab them and make them pay!" the angry shop owner yelled.

I risked a glance behind me. The two constables, dressed in matching black uniforms, raced after us, waving their batons and yelling, "Get back here, scoundrels!"

I laughed, dodging carts and carriages and unsuspecting people.

Someone tried to grab Preston, but he ducked and whacked the man with his sack. "Tell me again how we're going to get out of this?" he wheezed.

I snatched a shawl off of an old woman's back as I ran. "Find easy disguises, and as soon as we round that corner, put them on and hand your bags to me."

Preston swiped a tricorne from the top of a wealthy-looking man's head, and he joined the chase, too.

"You're terrible at this," I panted.

"How was I supposed to know he'd run after us?!"

"Run faster!" Alexander yelled.

We were slowly losing them, and for the first time I was grateful for the crowded streets. I spotted a horse-drawn cart of hay parked on the corner, and I slapped its rear as I passed, yelling, "Giddy-up!" It careened into the miniature mob of angry men, sending them diving out of harm's way and giving me enough time to pull the two boys into a narrow alleyway. We walked a few strides to a pile of crates and collapsed behind them. The buildings on either side of us were a little more than two arms lengths apart, casting deep shadows on the path between them and creating a sense of claustrophobia. Regardless, I was grateful for the cover.

"I think we lost them," Preston whispered.

"Shhh," I said, listening until the angry shouts dissipated. Then I smiled. "That was fun!"

Alexander shook his head. "You and I have a different idea of fun."

"I can't believe we got away with that!" Preston yell-whispered.

I stood up and draped the shawl over my head and shoulders. "Hand me your bags. We need to look as different from when we stole this stuff as possible. Preston, I don't think it's a good idea to wear that."

He frowned as he removed it from his head. "Why not?"

"It doesn't blend in," I explained.

"Excuse me," said a small voice from behind me.

I whipped around to see two little children, a girl of about ten and a smaller boy lurking behind her. Their faces were smeared with dirt and ragged clothes hung off their thin frames. They were both barefoot.

"We're hungry," the girl spoke again, pointing a small finger at the burlap sacks I was holding. "We haven't eaten in two days. Can we have some?"

"Where are your parents?" Preston asked.

"Gone," the little boy whispered, peeking out from behind his sister.

"They couldn't afford to keep us, so they left us on someone's doorstep," the girl elaborated. "But those people couldn't take care of us either."

"Oh. That's horrible." Preston answered, putting a hand to his mouth.

I slipped the bags off my shoulder and set them on the ground, flooded with memories of hopelessness and desperation a hungry belly brought. *Of course I was going to give them food.* I didn't even care if we ran a little short on our voyage.

"It's not strange," the little girl said. "I have a lot of friends who live on the streets with us. Some of them...don't make it." She hung her head, but perked right back up again when I opened one bag. I grabbed a lime, a loaf of bread, two biscuits, and a rather large slab of dried, salted meat. The two kids looked at the food in their arms like it was made of gold.

"Thank you," the girl said, her eyes sparkling with tears.

I smiled warmly. "That lime is sour, but make sure you eat it, savvy? It'll help stop some sicknesses." *Like scurvy.* I shuddered. The effects were hideous and lamentable, especially since a charming smile could get me what I wanted.

They nodded eagerly, stuffing their mouths with bread as they walked away, a new spring in their steps.

I turned to Alexander and began to speak, but he cut me off, a curious look in his eyes. "Where did that come from?"

"What?"

"You just—" he gestured to the children as they turned the corner and were lost in the crowded street. "You were compassionate. And not only that, you were *generous*. Where did that cold, self-serving captain go?"

I stared back the way they went. "I used to be her. Same age. Didn't have anyone to care for, though. I just wish...I could do more for her. When you're a beggar like that, you see no way out. No hope. The best you can do is keep surviving." I turned back to them, picked up a sack, and threw it over my shoulder. "Ever since Rogers got control of this island and pushed out all the pirates, the poor got kicked aside. The newcomers manipulated and swindled them, and now many are like them: beggars."

"It wasn't like this before Governor Rogers?" Alexander asked, picking up the other two burlap sacks.

I shook my head. "Nowhere near as bad. See, the seventy or so people on this island helped each other. They cooked together and ate together and laughed together. Now there's too many people to do that."

"Overpopulation does lead to starvation," Preston commented. "And that only happened once he became governor?"

"Aye. People from England finally felt like it was safe to come over." I tugged the shawl tighter around me and stooped over like an old woman. Wishing I had a cane, I murmured, "Come on, you two. Let's get out of here."

We made it to the harbor without getting spotted, which was a relief. The constables probably thought the pursuance wasn't worth it. They didn't get paid enough to chase after three teenagers stealing food.

We stood in the shadows, watching the harbor. There were guards on the bigger boats, so I ruled those out. "We'll need a rather small boat, but a fast one. It can't be a Jolly boat, of course. Those don't have sails. A cutter could work... or a small clipper." I pointed to a ship about twenty-five feet in length, with a narrow hull and tall sails. "They're slightly more difficult to handle, but they're really fast."

"Looks like there's a few people on it," Alexander pointed out.

"Aye. If they don't clear out by nightfall we'll have to go for that cutter." It floated by the far right edge of the harbor, fifteen feet long, with two small sails and an oar on each side for extra speed. A single frayed rope attached it to the dock, and no one stood to guard it. I was a little surprised, since cutters were usually great boats. This one had a few rips in the sails, but as long as there wasn't a leak, it would get us to Tortuga. All we had to do was wait until nightfall and steal it.

Easy.

———◦•◦———

A little bell rang as we pushed the old wooden door inwards, and the sound of guffaws and booming voices reached our ears. It was suppertime and crowded inside the bar, and there were overturned chairs and wet spots dotting the floor. One man stood behind the counter, his face almost completely covered by a black, bushy beard. I felt eyes following me as we weaved between tables, and when I glanced around I caught sight of a man with pale gray eyes and a simple tricorn. I was seized with the feeling I should know him. My gaze dropped to the floor and I noticed excessively polished boots, as black as midnight.

"You pay up front," the barman growled even before we got there.

I pursed my lips. My pockets were empty. I looked around and spotted a betting game going on between two men in the back corner of the room, a pile of coins on the table. "Be right back."

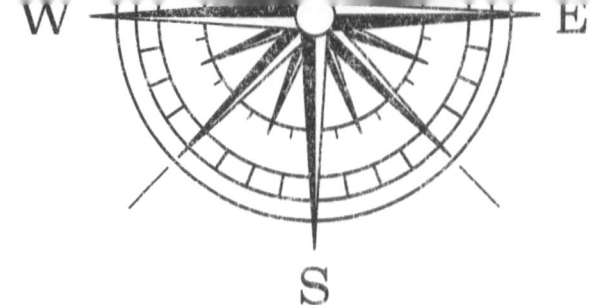

# Chapter 22

WE WAITED AT THE HARBOR until the sun painted color across the sky. Wyatt stood protectively over Johnny, who had slumped unconscious from too much drink. We'd found both of them in the tavern, and I'd invited them along. As soon as they heard my description of Tortuga, they were hooked.

I hoped the girl would show—I wanted her to be free, like I was. Not bound to a man she hated.

The harbor was mostly deserted, besides the few guards idling on or around the bigger ships. A cool breeze swept up from the water as the sun hovered just above the horizon, the sky turning pink and gold. I stepped out from the shadows and casually strode towards the abandoned cutter, Alexander and Preston following my lead. Wyatt and Johnny stayed put, hidden for now.

"What are we doing now?" Alexander whispered.

"If Judith's going to show, she should be here soon. We'll wait a few more minutes before setting out on that." I gestured toward the little boat.

Alexander snorted. "*Threadbare*—a fitting name."

I laughed.

Preston pointed toward the street. "There she is."

I followed his gaze. The girl hurried across the street, glancing behind her every few feet. Surprised, I stepped forward. "You came."

She shrugged elegantly, her silky hair hanging down to her elbows. Like the first time we'd met her, she wore a simple brown dress and stained white apron. "I was curious. You said you were... starting a society? So I'm..."

Preston chuckled knowingly. "The first one to join? Far from it, my friend. We're so popular, we already have over a hundred members."

A look of confusion settled over her face. "But..."

Alexander cleared his throat. "He's jesting."

I rolled my eyes. "Aye. It's just us. My name's Cassandra. Our *society*...well, it's not exactly..."

"We're looking for tough men and women to join our crew," Alexander told her.

"Crew? Is that why we met at the harbor?"

"Aye," I said.

Judith raised her eyebrow a fraction of an inch, her eyes falling to Johnny. "And why would I want to join your crew?"

"The pay is either really good or terrible," Preston said matter-of-factly.

Judith gave a small laugh, unamused. "What's that supposed to mean?"

"I'll explain later," I told her, hoping she wouldn't be too closed-minded. "First, I need to know a few things. Do you have any skills that would be useful to us?"

She shuffled her feet. "Well, I can sew. And cook..."

I pursed my lips.

"You can't tell me you're surprised by that, Cassie," Preston said.

"I know. I was just hoping...never mind. Do you have any passions? Any dreams?"

Judith hesitated. "Well, yes, but they don't have anything to do with sailing."

I smiled. "Well, I'm glad society hasn't beaten them out of you yet."

She chuckled darkly. "Believe me, everyone I live with has tried. I...want to become an actress." An excited gleam appeared in her eyes. "But not just that, I want to write *my own* plays. And I want to travel the world and perform in different places." Her shoulders slumped as reality settled back in. "I suppose I just...don't want to be another ordinary girl in an ordinary tenement that nobody cares about."

"Judith?" I said, smiling. "We have a lot in common."

"You want to be an actress too?"

"No, but I want to be free to be who I am and do what I want."

Judith nodded eagerly. "And make a difference in the world."

"I can't promise you that you'll become a famous actress, but I *can* promise you freedom. If you join us, you will be able to travel the world. And maybe get rich along the way."

Alexander nodded. "But before you agree, I need to warn you. One: you will have to leave your family behind. You won't see them again for many months. Two: nothing's guaranteed. Three: there may be multiple times where you will find yourself in great peril. There's even a small chance of death."

I looked at him and put my hands on my hips. "Are you *trying* to scare her away?"

Alexander folded his arms. "She needs to know exactly what she's getting herself into."

I nodded, conceding the point. "We'll teach you what you need to know to survive on these waters, but in times of crisis, you can never be certain it'll be enough."

Judith tucked a strand of hair behind her ear. "I didn't know sailing could be so dangerous."

I met Alexander's eyes. I had a feeling if I told her the truth, she wouldn't want to come along. He nodded curtly. "Judith...you'll need to know how to swordfight, work with sails, fire cannons, shoot a gun, and take down a man twice your size." I could see the gears turning inside her head until it dawned on her.

Her eyes widened and she took a small step back. "You're not...p-pirates, are you?"

The boys beside me shook their heads and relief filled her eyes.

"*They* aren't," I told her. "But I am."

Judith pointed to me, then to them. "You're a pirate...and they aren't pirates... But pirates are killers!"

I put a finger to my lips. "*Shhh*. We're not killers. Some are, but most of us are just misunderstood. We're just like you, except we have freedom. If you don't want to come with us, fine. As long as you don't talk to anyone about our conversation."

She was quiet for a moment. "Well, aren't pirates liars? How do I know you're not lying to me?"

Alexander folded his arms. "She's not lying."

"How do you know she's not lying?" Judith argued.

"I can tell." He looked at me.

"No you can't," I scoffed. I was an expert at lying. I had *years* of practice. No one I'd ever met could tell when I was lying, so it wasn't possible for him, a man—*boy*—I'd only known for a month to be able to. *He was probably just saying it to convince her,* I told myself.

"First of all, I beg to differ. Second, you're not really helping our case."

I looked down. "Right."

Judith turned to Alexander. "Why are you helping her, then?"

"For the money, of course," I said.

Alexander shook his head, his eyes searching mine, as if willing me to understand something I couldn't see. "Not only for the money."

*What is he thinking?* "Why else, then?"

He held my gaze a little longer before dropping it and shaking his head.

Preston cleared his throat. "Alright, so...are you in or out?"

Judith bit her lip. "I'm not afraid of danger, I just..."

"Can't leave without me?" The call came from the other side of the street.

I stiffened. A young man emerged from behind a house, and I narrowed my eyes as he sauntered toward us. His clothes were rags, but he carried himself as if he owned the entire town. I recognized his messy, short, jet-black hair, but not his face. My heart pounded. *How many other people had been eavesdropping on us?*

Judith whipped around. "Jacob! I didn't know you were listening."

He smiled wolfishly, reaching her. "You should know by now, Starlet, I'm always looking to do things I shouldn't, and *you—*" He grabbed her hand, twirled her around once, and dipped her. "—have found the jackpot."

"Is this the pig you were talking about earlier?" Preston asked.

Judith laughed as he let her up. "No."

"I'd wager," I murmured, "that he's the reason she didn't want to get married." I scrutinized him, trying to remember where I'd seen him. It was recent, I was sure.

Jacob gasped dramatically. "Did Porky propose? We're his lines memorized? I bet his mother put him up to it."

Judith scoffed. "Likely."

"Did you at least keep the ring? It could pay for..." He leaned in and whispered something in her ear.

Judith shook her head. "I threw it back at him."

He smiled. "Shame. I guess that means we'll have to team up with some pirates, then. Where's your ship?"

I pointed my thumb behind me. "For now, it's the one with the idiotic name." I hadn't planned on recruiting many more men to my crew. Too many of them felt superior to women. And none of them were really what they seemed. They might be charming and sweet on the outside, but a woman could never know if they'll become possessive and controlling once she was bound to him. I hoped for Judith's sake that Jacob wasn't one of those men. "What makes you think I'll let you aboard, just because you're Judith's *beau*? What do you have that I want?"

He cocked his head. "What do you mean?"

I stepped toward him. "Who are you? What can you do?"

"I..." He broke eye contact. "Sword fighting." He looked back at me, fidgeting with the hem of his shirt. "I can sword fight. And I can—"

I held my hand out to silence him. "You're terrible at lying."

He looked sheepish. "What?"

"Busted," Judith whispered.

"Aye." I nodded, folding my arms. "Now, would you like to tell me who you really are, or shall I guess?"

He tilted his head, intrigued. "Guess."

*Alright*, I thought, stepping back and looking him over. "You've lost your parents or aren't attached to them. You either have an alcohol problem or you work at a bar—my guess is the latter. You're in love but you're too poor for her father's tastes, so you've been trying...other ways to earn more money. Nothing too risky, but pickpocketing can be lucrative if you're good at it," I said pointedly.

"Pickpocketing?" Judith gasped.

"I—I didn't—" He ran a hand through his hair. I guess my statement took the wind out of his sails. "How did you know?" He rounded on me. "You almost got it spot on. How?"

"Hey, mate. No shame," Preston told him. "We've all done things we're not proud of. I, for one, have eaten so many apple betties that I threw up all over Xander's father."

We were all quiet for a moment. "Aye..." I cleared my throat. "Thanks for sharing."

Preston laughed. "Anytime, my friend. Anytime."

I assessed Jacob as the world grew steadily darker around us. "When you spend your life being hunted, and you live your life hunting for ways to make your life better, it's useful to notice things. And use it to your own advantage. For example, the way you were eager to jump aboard a pirate ship with your bonnie lass tells me that your relationship with your family is rocky or nonexistent and you don't want to leave her side. Your clothes smell of rum, which was why I guessed—"

"I work at a bar."

"Exactly. I'm glad you don't have a drinking problem."

"Why? I thought pirates—"

I stuck my chin out and glared at him. "Only careless pirates drink."

"Stop interrupting," Alexander said. "I want to hear how you knew he was a pickpocket."

I smiled and shrugged. "Easy. I saw you when we were in town, on the street by the bank. I will say, you did a smooth job taking it, but you could've been more discreet when you slipped it into your pocket."

"I guess... thank you?" It sounded like a question.

"No!" Judith exclaimed. "*Not* thank you! Jacob, you don't need money to be worthy of me. I love you." She reached for his hand.

He pulled away. "But we won't be able to be together if I'm so poor."

"Yes we can. We can if we go with them."

He thought for a moment, then looked at me, Preston, and Alexander in turn. "Tell your captain that I don't have any special skills, besides pickpocketing I guess, but I will be willing to follow orders and work hard if it means we can get away from here."

Alexander looked at me. "I think, once we get to Tortuga, you're going to need an outfit that looks slightly more... captainy."

Jacob looked back and forth between us, but he recovered from his surprise quickly, and the corners of his lips slowly lifted as he said, "A female captain. I like that."

I nodded curtly. "Good. For your sake," I added. "You'd regret it if you said otherwise. Now, we need to get going before we attract any unwanted attention. I've been here for one day and people are already on the lookout for me."

Jacob turned to the girl beside him. "What do you say, Starlet? Shall we run away together?"

He made it sound so...romantic. *Ha.* They were in for a big surprise. She smiled broadly. "Absolutely."

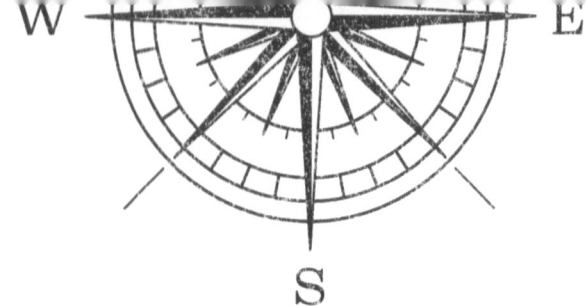

## Chapter 23

I LOOKED AROUND THE CUTTER, taking stock. "Is there anything of value on this ship?" I asked. "Any tools? Extra rope? Patches for the sails?"

They shuffled around, looking under the benches. Judith held up a coiled rope and Preston showed me a dirty old blanket, but that was it.

"Secret compartments?" I tried.

Alexander pried open a rather large compartment underneath a seat on the port side. *Perfect*. I tossed him the sack nearest to me and pointed to the other two. "Put the food in there," I told him. "But we're missing the most necessary thing." I hopped out of the boat.

"Water," Alexander realized. "Where do we get water?"

I pointed to the other ships. "That clipper will probably have enough. Alexander and Wyatt, you come with me. The rest of you stay in the boat. Get ready to push off as soon as we get back."

"What about me?" Preston asked. "You need as much muscle as you can get!"

The corners of my mouth tugged up. "Stay."

We silently walked past a few dark docks before I found the ship I wanted, my eyes wide, hoping nothing would get the jump on me. I could feel the two men close behind me as we crept down the dock and neared our target ship. The main mast stood twenty-five feet tall, and the hull was deep, set with eight hatches for cannons. Likely for defense, not offense. Lanterns hung from each mast, warning thieves like me that there was a watchman on board.

We crept up the gang plank and paused at the rail. There were two men, both with muskets leaning against them. One man was slumped against a crate, his head slowly falling toward his chest and then jerking back up again. The other was younger, as far as I could tell, and leaned against the mast, watching his companion struggle to stay awake.

"I'll wake you when I'm too tired," he whispered. "Besides, nothing ever happens around here."

The other nodded, laid his musket on the ground and followed it, using his hat for a pillow. I thought about my options. I was no match for a rifle, but we could use distraction. I ran through some possible scenarios before I picked the best one. "Stay here," I breathed. "Wait for my signal."

"What are you going to do?" Alexander asked.

I put a finger to my lips. "Just watch. And stay out of sight." I rolled my neck and shook out my hands, then stood up. I was no longer the daughter of two pirate legends, but instead an innocent girl who'd lost her way. My shoulders hunched in a self-conscious manner, and I called timidly, "Sir?"

His head jerked toward me and the grip on his musket tightened. "What are you doing here?"

I glanced at his partner, who hadn't stirred. I hoped our conversation would be hushed enough that he wouldn't wake.

"I'm so sorry, sir. I've lost my way. I'm not from around here, and my parents said they would meet me outside the boat shop but I don't know where that is. I saw the lights on your boat and I thought you could help me," I added.

He relaxed a little, obviously not seeing me as a threat. "The boat shop? You mean *Harris and Burton's*?"

"I think so," I said, stepping closer. *If I could just get my hands on that gun...*

"Well, you see that street, the one on the right closest to us..."

I wasn't listening to what he said as I stepped closer. He was at arms length from me now. He faltered when he realized this, and apparently wasn't sure how to react. "Does it ever get boring, just standing on a ship that's not even moving?" I asked him quietly. "Have you ever had to use this?" I brushed my fingertips across the barrel.

He hesitated a fraction of a second before answering, and I knew the lie was coming before I heard it. "Once."

I gasped, looking up at him with big doe eyes, thankful my lashes had grown out by now. "Really?"

He nodded, pleased at my response. "But that's not a story your ears should hear."

"Oh. Alright." I pretended to be disappointed. "You must be very brave. Is it..." I hesitated, keeping to character. "Is it heavy?"

"My musket?"

"Yes. Is it hard to hold?"

"Not for a man like me." He puffed out his chest ever so slightly.

"Can I try holding it? I want to see how heavy it is. My father won't let me near his," I explained.

He hesitated, then held it out to me. What harm could it do, handing a loaded musket to a harmless girl?

*Sorry, mate. That was a mistake.*

I promptly clonked him on the head with the butt of the rifle, hard enough to knock him out. I caught him as he crumpled, and laid him quietly next to his friend. I confiscated the other's musket before hissing, "We're clear—let's go."

Alexander and Wyatt emerged from behind the rail, the former trying to hide the fact that he was impressed. I told them to go below decks while I stood at the top of the stairs as a lookout. I leaned on one of the muskets while I waited, listening to the small waves lapping the sides of the boat. I turned my gaze heavenwards. The first stars were beginning to show their timid, twinkling faces. It would be a peaceful moment if I didn't have two guards threatening to wake up at any moment. Finally Alexander and Wyatt appeared at the bottom of the stairs and began making their way up, their breath heavy with the fifty gallon load they were carrying. I waited for them to set it down. "What took you so long?"

Alexander ignored my comment. "How many will we need? How long's the journey?"

"I'd say one. Two if we wanted to be on the safe side, but I'm not sure if we can fit it."

"How long will it take to get there?" Wyatt asked.

I tilted my head, thinking. "I'm not quite sure. I've never traveled there from this direction." I pulled out my compass and squinted at it, wondering if the captain's quarters had a map.

"You're saying that you made us steal food, a boat, and sneak onto a guarded ship to get water and you *don't even know how to get there*?" Alexander asked, annoyance and frustration filling his voice.

I huffed. "Not true. Go get another barrel while I fetch something."

"You mean *steal* something," he muttered as I climbed the stairs, holding a lantern in one hand.

I pushed through the door behind the helm. I knew where we were going, roughly. But a map would help. It wouldn't have Tortuga on it, but I could fill it in. Not physically, of course—I wouldn't dare draw it out in case it fell into the wrong hands.

I located the captain's door and pushed through it. The light from my lamp filled the room with a dim glow, banishing the dark. After ruffling through a few drawers, I grabbed what I was looking for and headed out.

The men weren't back yet, so I sat cross legged on the deck and placed the lantern and map in front of me. I pulled out my compass and traced my finger along the path we would take, calculating. The fastest route would take us southeast, down between the east tip of Cuba and an unnamed isle at the end of a long chain of islands. There, just a few miles north of Hispaniola, lay the island we were headed for.

The sound of labored breathing greeted me before I saw their faces, and I waited while they heaved the barrel over the last stair. "Oh good, you made it." I stood up and folded the map. "Let's go."

They picked up the barrel again and followed me to the gangplank and down the dark dock. "Don't trip," I warned them quietly, holding a doused lamp. We'd need it on the journey, but until we made it out of the harbor I wanted to be as discreet as possible. We made it to the others and loaded the barrel into the boat without incident, and I thanked our lucky stars. "Where are you going?" I asked Alexander as he started to climb back out of the boat.

"There's one more," he reminded me.

I waved my hand. "We don't need it."

It was difficult to see his expression in the dark, but annoyance was apparent in his voice when he whispered, "You made us carry that barrel through the entire ship and up a flight of stairs for nothing?"

I grabbed his wrist and pulled him back in, a smile on my face. "Not for nothing, surly boots. T'was character building," I teased, untying the boat and pushing off. Moonlight glinted off his teeth as he grinned, folding those strong arms and shaking his head.

"Everyone comfortable? It's going to be a long couple of days if you've never been at sea," I told them. They nodded in understanding. "Judith, Jacob—if you're going to be a part of this crew, you're going to need to learn to carry your own weight. This," I indicated to the sail that was folded and tied against the mast, "is the mainsail. Pull *this* and *this* to unfurl it." Judith obeyed, and I caught the boom and lowered it into its resting position, forcing everyone near the back of the boat to shift slightly toward the sides. The sail filled with the cool night breeze, and our little boat sped off. I smiled, perching by the rudder and resting my hand on the tiller.

Preston looked behind us at the shrinking masts of docked ships. Squinting, he whispered, "I think I see someone."

I looked back. "What?" I said sharply, straining my eyes in the dark.

"Never mind. I just saw movement. But it was probably nothing."

I nodded. "We're fine," I assured him. There was no one around when we left. I closed my eyes, breathing in the fresh sea air. Now that we were away from the harbor, dead fish and rotting things didn't plague the breeze. "You all should try to get some rest. I'll wake you if I'm too tired to steer." I lit the lantern again, placed it beside me, and pulled out my mum's compass. If she were here, I'd feel better. She would know what to do with the uncomfortable feeling in my gut, like our easy escape was too good to be true. I looked between the map and the navigation device. The arrow pointed toward me, which meant we were on the right course. I just had to stay awake to keep us that way.

"You should get some sleep," I told Alexander when he came and sat next to me a while later.

"Couldn't," he said simply.

I pulled out the map and tapped the empty sea above Hispaniola. "Tortuga's southeast of us. We'll be at sea for four or five days, depending on the wind." When he said nothing, I continued. "I didn't realize we'd have so many mouths to feed, so we'll have to ration."

"We'll be fine. Don't worry."

"I'm not."

"Then what are you worrying about?"

I hesitated. "I don't know. I just have a bad feeling. Like, nothing went wrong as we were leaving. Things usually go wrong. And who was on the dock when we left?"

"There's no point in worrying about what you can't control. Save your thoughts for what lies ahead."

"We can't have anyone following us," I murmured, hardly hearing him, as I stared off at the dark island that was shrinking behind us.

"We'll be able to be sure once it's light."

"Aye."

"How is your wound?" he asked me.

My hand went to my stomach. It was still tender, but it was healing nicely. "It never got infected, luckily."

"I'm glad."

A comfortable silence fell between us. The little lamp cast a soft glow over Alexander's features, and for the first time, I allowed myself to savor the way he made my stomach flutter. The way his full lips curved gently downward when he was lost in thought. The wind tousled his hair across his eyes, never quite long enough to be tied back and tamed.

From the moment I met him, I was afraid he'd distract me, worried he'd use his good looks to his advantage. Deep in the world of piracy, looks like those could get you a long way. It made it easier to manipulate people. But never, not once, had he tried to control me in any way. Did he simply not realize he was gorgeous?

Alexander's lips curved up in a teasing smile. "What?"

"Sorry?" I leaned back, alarmed that he'd noticed anything.

"You were staring at me."

"Was I?" A little heat rose to my cheeks, and I looked away. "I have a lot on my mind. Excuse me for seeming a little stressed."

He chuckled. "You didn't look stressed."

I inhaled quickly, my heart starting to pound. *Quick! Distract!* "I didn't kill him," I whispered. "I came close, and I should've, but I didn't. I kept thinking about what you said, how nobody deserves to die. But then *you* almost died because of his madness, and I could've stopped it if I'd killed him when I had the chance. He *does* deserve it. He's the one person who deserves it."

"Who...who are you talking about? Barnet?"

I nodded.

"He's a bad man, for a multitude of reasons that, since meeting him, my eyes have been opened to. But you made the right choice. Even if he does deserve death, you shouldn't be the one to seal his fate. You don't deserve such a black mark on your conscience. It will only weigh you down."

"It would add to the few I already have," I confessed. "But you're right. Killing him would be less satisfactory than making him watch all that he holds dear crumble to pieces."

"Is that why you helped all the pirates escape?"

"And sank his ship," I added with a wicked smile. "The explosion was bloody epic."

He chuckled. "I wish I would have been there to see it."

We were quiet for a few more minutes, until I whispered, "It was partly my father's fault you know. That we were captured." I bit my lip, unsure why I said it.

Alexander must've been surprised at this sudden confession, but he said nothing.

I took a deep breath, looking forward. "He and most of the men got stewed. Too drunk to think straight, much less fight. It was me, my mum, Aunt Mary, and Will against Barnet's entire crew." I shook my head sadly. "We were no match."

"I'm...sorry." He didn't ask for more of the story, like he was afraid if he pushed at all I would close up.

Maybe this was what I'd needed all along—his steady presence, the safety it brought. The story I'd carried alone for years spilled out, unburdening me at last.

"Your life's story," he commented, when I'd finished the tale of my miraculous escape, "even so far, would make a most intriguing novel."

"You think so?"

"Indeed. I'd wager you'd bring sympathy toward pirates, turning them into real people with honest emotions instead of the frightening myth they are now."

"Except no one would publish it, because I'm a woman. And I would never publish under another man's name."

"There have been female authors. My mother's one!"

"Really?" I raised a brow. "Didn't you say she needed more money in order to *self* publish?"

"But it's only because she doesn't like to use other publishers."

"And why's that?"

He faltered. "Because publishers didn't want to give her much royalty, and because...they wouldn't let her unless she had a signature from my father."

"Exactly my point. We get treated so unfairly." I yawned widely. I was glad I had somebody to talk to, to keep me awake.

"If I could change it, I would."

"You're the only man I've ever heard say that."

"How many men have you met?"

"Quite enough."

"I'm sure there are more men like me."

"Nay." I shook my head. "There are not. I've traveled far and wide, Alexander. No man has ever been able to beat me in a swordfight, and you...you did." I shot a smirk at him.

He laughed, the sound deep and lovely. "No wonder you looked so shocked."

I turned my gaze back to the prow. "Aye. But that's not all. No one's been so quick to forgive. No one's been so honest and trusting and *selfless*. You've spent three years on the open ocean, just because you wanted to help your old man." I looked at him. His blue eyes held mine there, and I couldn't look away. "I couldn't be more different from you. Why don't you hate me?" I whispered.

He didn't answer. Just kept his gaze locked on mine.

"Tell me," I pressed.

"I can't," he finally said. "I can't hate you. There was a while when I tried..." He laughed softly, then shook his head. "I couldn't do it for long."

"Why?" I breathed. His face was close enough for me to see the gold flecks in his irises, and at that moment they were more valuable than the finest, rarest metal.

"I don't know," he murmured, slowly, hesitantly leaning closer. His gaze flicked down to my lips and up again.

Suddenly my heart was seized by cold trepidation, and as if shaken out of a trance, I looked away. Years ago, I had promised myself I would never make such a mistake again. It was a path with too many twists and turns that not even the best navigator could predict. Anxious thoughts raced through my head. *What if he only came along for the treasure? To help his family maybe, but also to convince that* girl *to marry him? Emma.* A sour taste filled my mouth. Was he just using me to get what he wanted?

I glanced down at my compass for something to do and adjusted the tiller to keep on course. I was aware of him next to me, no longer leaning forward, but I was afraid to see his expression. Nay, not afraid. There was no reason to fear! Frustration came instead. Why did I feel this way? Why did I care about his feelings? That was never supposed to happen. I glanced at him. He was facing forward, eyes angled slightly down, but I couldn't read his expression. I didn't want the silence to stretch on forever, so I took a deep breath and murmured, "Want to hear a story?"

He looked at me, and tilted his head questioningly. "I would."

"One fateful day, a young girl lost her parents," I began. "Having nowhere else to go, she took to the streets." My throat constricted painfully. I rubbed my knuckles, transforming the memory into a sea tale so I could separate from it. "One morning, a handsomely dressed boy passed her after stepping out of his carriage. Although she was beneath his notice, she watched him until he disappeared into a shop. Known to some as an addle pate, he seemed like an angel in her eyes. He was her chance. Any desperate, bold girl would try to catch his attention. But although she was desperate, she wasn't foolish. She followed him home—"

"A little creepy, perhaps?"

I chuckled. "Aye. But no one caught her, so who was to judge? She spent the next few weeks learning his habits and his family's dynamics. Then she took the biggest risk she'd taken since her parents died." I hesitated, knowing Alexander wouldn't approve of this next part. I looked him in the eyes.

"She hid herself in lies. Made herself anew. And then—accidentally—bumped into him. He was smitten.

"Of course, she had to keep track of all these lies about running away from her family and needed a place to stay, and that was exhausting. Add that to corsets and heavy petticoats, sitting idle and silent all the time...it was a life she never would've chosen for herself. But it was better than a hungry belly, ya know?"

Alexander nodded, captivated. "What came next?"

I shrugged. "It would've continued like that until she died. She got used to it, and even let herself—" I swallowed. "Love. But the night before her wedding day, everything changed. She'd let herself trust him too much. She told him her true parentage...who she used to be. He hit her for keeping such a terrible secret." I laughed softly, scornfully.

Alexander was leaning forward. "What was her secret?"

I eyed him. "You'd make a terrible detective."

He chuckled, and as he gazed at me, his eyes deepened. "She was a pirate."

I looked down. Alexander knew that my story was not fiction, but I continued. "Hitting her didn't work out too well for him. She realized, after she'd knocked him out, that it was over. She couldn't save the marriage—but she didn't want to. She realized she'd traded freedom for safety. So she stole as much of their jewelry as she could carry and ran away."

Alexander was silent for a time. "He didn't deserve you."

I sighed. Now that I'd said all that aloud, it seemed silly for me to still be hurt by what a man did nearly three years ago. But emotions weren't rational, and no matter how hard I tried to keep them buried, they would always pop back up again. Now that I'd confessed, would they finally dissipate?

"He probably stopped thinking about me a week later," I speculated, my voice turning hard. "But every hardship I've encountered has made me stronger."

"I think that one hurt you more than it helped you." Alexander's eyes shone with empathy.

I glanced at him. "Don't look at me like that. I was taught a valuable lesson, adding to the others that help me survive."

"Maybe they help you survive," he whispered. "But they sure don't help you live."

Alexander's words echoed in my head as my heavy eyelids drifted shut. The world dissolved into dreams—of him, the sea, and moonlight. Then everything blurred, and the ocean and sky became violent. I watched, helpless, his lips moving silently as his figure slipped from the mast, falling toward the churning black water below.

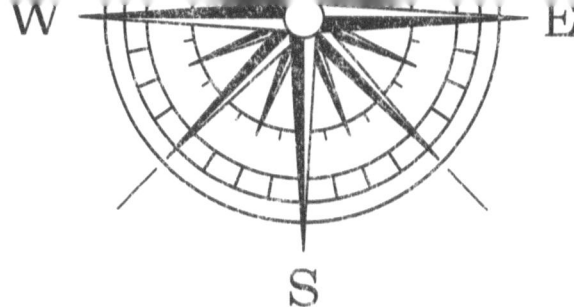

# Chapter 24

"**No!**" I GASPED, sitting bolt upright. Pain shot through the side of my neck, and I groaned as I massaged the kink and looked around. The water was glittering with the newly risen sun, off the port side. A strong breeze filled the patched mainsail and ruffled my hair. Johnny was finally awake, and was picking his nails with his pocket knife. Judith and Jacob were sitting in the shade of the sail, excitedly whispering to each other.

"Nightmare?" a voice beside me said.

I whipped my head around and winced, as another burning sensation flared up towards the back of my head. Alexander was sitting where I had last seen him, his hand on the tiller, looking a little weary. I shoved my hand into my pocket and pulled out my compass, dread filling me. *I fell asleep on the job. How far have we traveled the wrong way?* But when I looked down, we were still headed south. I exhaled, relaxing. Then I turned back to him and rubbed my eyes. "You kept us on course?"

"Aye," he replied, smiling tiredly. "The stars guided me."

I grinned. "You just spoke like a propper sea-ripened pirate."

"It's the sleep deprivation," he said, pointing to his head. "It's messing with my brain."

"Ahh, I see," I said, still smiling playfully. "You still sound like a brit, though."

"Would you rather I didn't?"

Chuckling, I said, "God, no. Your accent is downright seductive." My face warmed. *Did that just come out of my mouth?* Before looking back at him, I explained, "You'll need it on this pirate island to bargain for lower prices."

He laughed. I grabbed the tiller, unable to meet his eyes. "I've got it from here. Go nap. Take the shady spot behind the sail."

He hesitated, then succumbed to his physical needs. "Thank you," he yawned, ducking underneath the boom and lying down. Jacob threw him a blanket, and he crumpled it up and used it for a pillow.

"You deserve it," I breathed, my heart warm. I sat peacefully, listening to Preston and Wyatt debate the value of the latter's new sword. Every so often I checked our heading, and then did a sweep of the horizon, wishing for a spyglass. Someone could be floating out there, following us, and I'd be none the wiser.

On the seventh time I turned around that day, my eyes caught a little brown dot on the horizon, behind us. No bigger than a flea, my hope was that my eyes were playing tricks on me. But I knew better than to rely on that. My jaw tightened with angst as I turned back around. "Johnny, Wyatt!" I barked.

"Aye, Captain?"

"I need you at the oars. There's a ship behind us that we need to lose."

"You think it's the person at the dock?" Preston asked.

"Could be. Whatever the case, we can't have anyone following us. Jacob, double time on the baling. Preston, tighten those sails."

"Yes, ma'am!"

After an hour or two, I could no longer see the boat behind me, but I didn't fully relax. I made everyone take a turn rowing, even Judith. She needed to build strength for what was ahead of her.

The next few days passed by in almost the same way, with Alexander, Preston, and I taking turns at the tiller. Our supply of food and water slowly diminished, and by the fourth morning we'd completely run out and everyone's spirits were low. But soon the air turned misty, blurring the horizon, and my anticipation grew.

"How much longer?" Preston groaned. His gaze fell downward as his belly rumbled. "There, there," he patted it. "I'll fill you up with lots of stew and pudding soon enough. And maybe some apple betties..."

I looked around at the dense fog that had settled around our little boat, so thick that I could not spy the front of the boat from where I was perched by the rudder. Judith wrapped her arms around herself, shivering with unease. A smile took hold of my face. It had been so long since I'd last been here.

"Is this a good thing or a bad thing?" Alexander asked, looking around and seeing nothing but gray.

"It's good," I assured him. "It means we're close. I have no idea why this island's always wrapped in fog, but it's partly why nobody knows it exists. Sailors think the area's haunted, so they keep out. Whoever's at the bow," I called forward, "keep an eye out for spires that stick out of the water, and old shipwrecks. We don't want a hole in our boat."

We glided along, the boat bouncing up and down with each small wave. I guided us around jagged spikes and mast tips that stuck out of the water, trusting my crew to call out a warning every time they saw one appear in front of us. After half an hour, the fog began to thin, the sun resumed shining, and soon the island loomed into view before us. We were still quite some distance away, but I could make out the unbreachable walls and the immense gates that protected the harbor. The whole island was a fortress, shaped like a crescent moon, the tips connected by a towering stone barricade. My heart raced in my chest to see the sheer magnitude and greatness of it. Suddenly I remembered the warning that my father shared with me when he first took me here, and I leapt up. "We need a flag."

"We have a flag," Jacob said.

I looked up, and indeed we did—a British ensign. I put my hands to my head, alarmed. "Not that flag! That's not the message we want to be sending to a load of pirates!"

"Can't we just tell them we're pirates too? And we stole this boat?" Preston asked.

"Not if they blast us out of the water first," I retorted. "The guards are very protective over the island. If they see anything they don't like, their cannons will be able to sink a ship almost a mile away."

Alexander whistled. "Then what kind of flag do we need?"

"Each flag sends a message," I explained, mostly for the newcomers' benefit. "Obviously each country has their own flag, but there's more. Skull and Crossbones screams pirate, yellow warns of disease, red threatens 'no quarter' if the opposing ship puts up a fight, and white asks for a truce."

"So we need a white flag," Alexander said.

"Aye. Or a Jolly Roger, or anything that will tell them we're on their side. But I think white's our only option at the moment."

"We don't have any other flag besides the British one," Preston noticed, looking around. His eyes landed on Alexander, and with a grin, he threw an arm around his best friend's shoulders. "Oi, mate, I know exactly what you're thinking. You want to save us from disaster and dazzle a certain young lady by heroically offering the shirt off your back. We all appreciate the offer, especially Cassandra over there."

Alexander gave Preston a hard shove and sent him sprawling into Jacob and Judith. The latter gave a surprised squeak as she was knocked off the bench. I chuckled, hoping my warm cheeks weren't visibly pink. In Preston's teasing, I had become unwitting collateral.

"No, thank you," Alexander grumbled.

"Is it because of *Miss Emma*?" I meant it to come out casually, but my voice turned hard when I spoke her name.

He stared at me for a moment, his gaze hard to decipher. Then in one smooth motion, he grabbed the hem of his shirt and pulled it over his head.

Judith squeaked, averting her eyes from his perfectly toned muscles.

I laughed at her reaction, eager to release the tension that had built inside of me. Alexander tossed his shirt to me. I yanked my gaze away from him and said, "You'd better get used to it, Judith, because I'm not giving it back to him."

"You're not?" he called as I began to climb the mast. "Can't I get it back once we dock?"

"Only if you beat me in a swordfight," I challenged from the top, my cheeks still warm. "But I'm going to find you a superior getup once we reach the island, so you won't need it." I cut the British flag down with my knife, then tied his shirt in its place. Satisfied, I shimmied down and dropped into the boat.

Alexander shook his head. "Pirates."

"**S**tate yer name an' yer purpose," the man at the gate yelled down to us. He stood atop one of the two castle towers that sat on either side of the iron gates.

"Cassandra Rackham, daughter of Calico Jack and Anne Bonny," I shouted back. "Here to pick up a ship and crew."

"Ya know the code?"

"Aye," I told him. The code was Tortuga's version of laws, except they were more like common courtesy, guidelines for heated arguments.

He hit some sort of lever, and a moment later I was listening to the grinding of gears as the gates began to retract, pulling into each of the towers.

"Many thanks." I saluted him as our boat sailed past.

We gazed in awe at the island towering above us as we glided closer. Houses and shops of all different styles crisscrossed their way up the gradually sloped sides of the mountain. Dense, tropical forest stretched its fingers around the town and up toward Raven Peak. The glittering obsidian and hardened lava flows that decorated the summit with sparkling designs gave it its humble name. Everything about this place was beautiful and untamed, from the glistening turquoise waters to the dark volcanic tunnels that snaked through the island, many yet to be discovered.

"Welcome to Tortuga," I announced, hoping the island had the same effect on them as it had on me. "The island where you can be anyone, do anything, and say anything—and you'll belong."

"It's beautiful," Judith breathed.

"Is that a volcano?" Preston asked, astonished.

"Aye, but not to worry—it's been asleep for many decades," I assured him, my eyes roving over the ships we passed. They were from every corner of the world, anchored here and there in the shallow waters.

In no time, we were secured to a dock and walking toward the sandy shore. The breeze carried music and laughter through the trees, filling my heart with joy and excitement. *How much has the town grown since I've been here?*

"Welcome!" A man with baggy pants waved as he approached us. "Do you need someone to watch your boat?"

I looked back at the cutter, making my decision and asking if he was looking to buy. After a bit of bargaining, we waited in the shade of palm trees for him to return with his money. I sighed. "What a terrible deal."

Alexander reclined in the sand, his hands behind his head, staring up at the leaves and sky overhead. "Eight hundred guineas? Given you sold him a stolen boat, I thought it was just fine."

I stared hard at the palm fronds above me, refusing to let my eyes drift sideways towards his bare chest. "Aye, but the problem is, we won't be able to steal a boat here—we'll have to bargain for one. And this is barely enough to buy a dinghy."

"Have any regrets?" Preston asked the two lovers.

"None yet. This is better than I ever dreamed." Judith admitted.

"It feels so much more relaxed out here." Jacob commented. "I think I'm going to like it. I fantasized about being a pirate when I was a young boy, but I never thought I'd actually be one."

"You never told me that," Judith said.

"I never told anyone," he replied. "People always told me they were bad men. I never wanted to be evil, but I dreamed about treasure-hunting." He chuckled, shaking his head.

"Well then, you're in luck, my friend," I murmured under my breath.

After the man returned and the sack of money was in my hands, I gave a handful of the coins to my wonder-filled crew. "Let's explore my favorite town in the world."

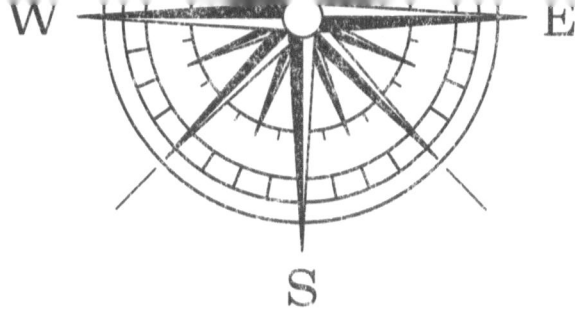

## Chapter 25

OUR FEET SPRAYED fine, glittering white sand as we trudged up the beach and along the edge of the forest until we came to a break in the trees. I could see a narrow pathway that led straight back a hundred yards before it disappeared. The earthy smell drifted up to my nostrils as we walked along the forest floor, parrots cawing and squawking in the distance. Finally a black cliff rose up fifty feet and the pathway veered sharply right, a narrow ridge chiseled right into the stone. It snaked back and forth, rough volcanic rock on the straight edges and stairs on the bends.

"Great whale turds, this is dangerous!" Preston mumbled clutching the side of the cliff with his fingers.

I coughed out a laugh. *Never heard that one before.* Sweat was slinking its way down my spine by the time we were standing on top and looking up at the town. Music and laughter intertwined with clucking hens and salesmens' calls to create a charming symphony. Colorful buildings and restaurants lined the streets, and open-air spice markets and fruit stands sent sweet fragrances to my nose. Jewelers stood at their carts of necklaces and earrings and shouted friendly greetings to anyone that passed. Chickens roamed the dirt roads.

Judith's gaze was full of wonder, her jaw slack with amazement.

Preston shot forward with his arms out, veering after a chicken. "Food!" The squawking bird gave a valiant effort to escape, but a moment later Preston sauntered back to us with it tucked under his arm.

"Those are someone's chickens, you know," Alexander pointed out, his eyes full of mirth.

"I doubt they'd notice one's missing," I said, chuckling.

After stroking its feathers a couple times, Preston patted it on the head. "Don't worry, little chicky. I wasn't actually going to eat you. I'm saving room for a cow." He tossed it away, the chicken squawking and frantically flapping its wings.

Alexander frowned thoughtfully as his gaze traveled up the road.

"What're you thinking?" I asked him.

"This place is more organized and safe than I expected it to be. I thought you said they have no laws."

I tilted my head. "Not exactly. There's a code you heard the guard at the gate mention. And there's an elected king—kind of like a captain—who takes complaints from villagers and does his best to manage the island. But people are mostly self-led and self-made."

Alexander nodded. "I suppose it works for a small population. No wonder you try to hide this place from the world."

I shrugged, and we continued making our way up the road. "This is where we'll spend the night," I announced as we came to an inn. "You can find somewhere to spend your payment, but the food's cheaper here, and I need to catch up on the latest news, so I'm staying. But fair warning: stay in pairs and be wary of sellers trying to swindle you."

"Aye," Johnny agreed. "Always bargain for a lower price, s'what I say."

Judith and Jacob immediately left to explore.

"You coming?" Wyatt asked Johnny.

He shook his head. "I'm goin' to buy meself a drink."

"Come on brother, don't you want to spend it on something better?"

"Bah. Nothin' sounds better to me right now. Go on without me." He eagerly pushed through the doors, his pockets jingling with unspent gold.

"I'll go with you," Preston offered. "I want to find myself a bakery!" He turned to Alexander. "You coming?"

He hesitated.

"Go on, have some fun," I said. "Get yourself a new shirt if you want."

"But if I go, you'll be alone. Trouble flocks to you like gulls to a boat. What will you do if I'm not there to bail you out?"

I rolled my eyes. "I'll be *fine*. I'm not going to cause trouble."

He arched a brow, not convinced in the slightest, and turned to his friend. "Stay safe?"

Preston saluted. "You too, mate. I'll see you later!"

A band of lutes, lyres, and fiddles played a jolly tune from the corner of the tavern. The air was filled with delicious smells, which drifted from the kitchen in the back of the room. My stomach ached with hunger, and I looked around for a table to sit at. It was lunchtime, and the room was filled with chatting people.

"I should have gone to buy a shirt first," Alexander murmured.

"Nonsense. There's plenty of people without their shirts. Look, over there." I pointed to a man stumbling over to the counter.

Alexander looked at me incredulously. "The drunkard?"

The corners of my lips twitched up in amusement. "How about there?"

"That's a child. A *child*," he repeated, a disgruntled frown on his lips. "There are no *respectable* men in this establishment lacking shirts."

We walked up to the counter. "No one's staring at you," I informed him, before addressing the woman at the counter. "Two orders."

Her eyes traced up Alexander's torso before landing back on me. "Would you like to try today's special? The octopus is excellent."

Alexander sent me a pointed look, crossing his arms over his chest. I fought the urge to laugh. "No. Pork, bread, and cheese will do."

"Of course. Find a table and we'll send it over once it's ready. Anything to drink?"

"Just water." We found a free table, and before I reached the nearest chair, Alexander pulled it out for me. I paused, staring at him questioningly.

"Don't overthink it," he told me. "I'd do this for anyone."

I sank into it, weakened by the aroma drifting from the food around us. "How very polite of you." I set the heavy bag of coins on the ground.

He came around and took up a chair opposite me. "What can I say? Solid earth brings out the gentleman in me."

I grinned. "What are you going to buy with your share?"

He pulled a coin from his pocket and flipped it between his fingers. "A shirt, first and foremost. And a sword. Maybe some new boots. What about you?"

"Definitely a sword. I'd like to buy a whole new outfit, but I have to save the money to bargain for a new boat." I frowned, troubled. "I have to hire more people, too—I don't know how I'm going to afford all that."

"Then why did you give us money to spend?"

I raised a brow at him. "Why d'ya think? You're part of my crew. I...didn't want to mess up again." I was afraid he'd say something snarky about that, but I shouldn't have worried.

He reached into his pocket. "You can have my gold."

"Keep it. Besides, I'm still going to run short."

"Perhaps we'll get lucky. Maybe someone will give us a boat for cheap."

I crossed my fingers. "That's what I'm hoping for. A stroke of good old-fashioned luck."

"Here's your waters," the waitress said, as she set the glasses down on the table. Her pretty eyes lingered on the man across from me, and I felt a spark of something hot and uncomfortable in my chest. "Your food will be ready shortly."

Alexander thanked her and picked up his glass. Grateful that she'd gone, my eyes roved around the room as I brought the cup to my lips. The cold water felt soothing as it slipped down my throat. Then my gaze landed on someone, and the liquid went up my nose. I set my glass down, choking.

"You alright?" Alexander chuckled.

I squeezed my eyes against the burning in my nose. When it dissipated, I looked back up, wiping my mouth with my sleeve. I spotted her again, across the room, sitting against the wall with only her drink as company. I gripped the table, suddenly unsteady. *It's not possible.*

"Cassie?" Alexander repeated, looking carefully at me. "What's wrong? You look like you've seen a ghost."

"I have," I whispered, my voice hoarse.

*It can't be her, can it?*

*Don't be foolish. She's dead. Don't get your hopes up.*

*But what if she is?*

*Your eyes are playing tricks on you.*

*I think I'd recognize my own mother.*

The chair grated on the stone floor as I pushed it back and rose unsteadily.

"Cassie? Where are you going?"

I could hardly hear him as I made my way around the tables. The closer I was, the more sure I became. *It has to be her.* Pain squeezed my heart like it was a wineskin. *That's my father's favorite bandana.* And even though there were a few gray streaks, she still had that same strawberry-blond hair.

I swallowed. "Mum?" I asked timidly.

She hardly glanced up at me for more than a moment, and took another swig out of the old mug before mumbling something incomprehensible.

"Mum?" My voice broke. "Mum, it's me, it's Cass." I leaned over and touched her shoulder.

She grabbed the collar of my shirt and pulled me closer, the stench of rum in her breath. "He took everythin' from me," she spat, her Irish accent strong. "He took my dearest friend. He took my husband. He took my life. My beauty. He– he–" Tears spilled out of her eyes. "He took my children," she wailed, pushing me away. "My beautiful children." She buried her head in her arms.

"Mum, please–" I knew the man she was referring to, but couldn't she see I was right here?

"Stop callin' me mum! Can't you see I'm not a mother anymore!? Whoever ye are, I don't care. Go away," she yelled, her speech slurred.

I felt like a knife had slid between my ribs. *How could she?* Anger overtook the sting of her rejection. It had been seven years, but *I'd* recognized *her.* "Anne Bonny," I said firmly, remembering that drink was affecting her mind, "Look at me." I forced her head up. "I know who you are. I know what you've done and I know what you've lost. You raised me, taught me, loved me, and saved me. Don't you remember?" I pleaded. "Please remember," I whispered, taking her head in my hands. "I'm your daughter, Mum. It's Cass."

It was then that she focused on me, really saw me. "Cass? *Oh Cass.*" She stood up and almost knocked me over with the force of her embrace. I breathed a great sigh of relief as tears welled up in my eyes. My heart swelled. She released me and held the sides of my face, staring at me, soaking it in, as if she only had a few more seconds and wanted to memorize my face. "Is this all another dream?"

I let out a half-laugh, half sob. I couldn't help the tears streaming down my face. "No. It's real. You're alive!"

"It's been so long," she moaned softly. "I thought I'd never see ye again." She brought her forehead to mine, her cheeks glistening.

My chest burned with emotion. "How did you survive?"

Her laugh was bitter. "That's a very long story, a memory I don' care to dwell in."

Suddenly I became aware of the shirtless presence in the corner of my vision. He was staring slightly open-mouthed a few feet away, and I met his eyes. "Alexander, this is my—"

"Mother," he finished, clearing his throat. He smiled, the shock leaving his face, and extended his hand in greeting. "I can see that. It's a pleasure to meet you."

*Even on a pirate island, his Cambridge habits never fail him.*

"Gah. Cass, who is this boy?" Anne stepped back, disgusted, but then lost her balance and crashed into the table.

I reached out to catch her, but wasn't fast enough. Her mug tipped over and amber liquid spilled out, dripping down the cracks in the wood. Supporting herself, she picked it back up and held it above her head, the last few drops falling onto her tongue.

"Shame, that." She set it back down and remembered what she was doing. "Now listen here, Cass."

"He's my friend and ally," I interrupted. "Why are you so..." I struggled to find the right adjective.

Anne gripped my shoulders. "Men are not to be trusted. They ruin everything. If yer father hadn't gotten drunk—"

"I know, mum, I've spent long enough thinking about it. But men aren't the problem, *rum* is."

"No! It's both." She pointed a finger at Alexander, accusing. "Ye stay away from my daughter. An' why are ye standin' 'ere without a scrap o' cotton on yer chest? Are ye tryin' to seduce her?"

"No!" he exclaimed.

"Mum!" I cried, exasperated. "Seriously! Leave him alone." I huffed, deciding to forget she said that. "What happened to you? I thought you swore never to drink. Now look at yourself! Barnet didn't take away your beauty, you did! By drinking this garbage!" I grabbed her arm. "Come on, let's get you out of here."

"No! I'm not goin'." She reached for her empty cup. "My life's over. I'm stayin' here." She choked. "Ye don't need me anymore."

I tugged at her arm. "I *do* need you! Please—come—on—" I grunted as I tried to pull her backwards with me.

"No!" she shouted. "Stop tryin' to help me."

She gave me a hard shove, and I lost my balance, but Alexander caught me before I fell and placed me back on my feet. I growled as I smoothed out my shirt. "Fine," I spat. "Stay here like a sea slug and waste away your life. I'm not going to sit here and waste mine while I could be out there finding treasure!" I spun on my heel, pushing past Alexander as I stormed out of the tavern.

My face was flushed with anger and hurt. Nothing made sense. I'd finally found her, and all she wanted was to stay there and drink?! I kicked a stone and it flew into the air, before skidding across the ground and coming to a halt. I needed her. Couldn't she see that? I screamed angrily at a large wheelbarrow full of hay that sat a little ways off from the side of the inn, but, of course, I elicited no response. Frustrated, I shoved it over, spilling the hay onto the uneven ground. Unsatisfied, I stomped off, frustration and betrayal gnawing at my insides.

She was my mother. She was supposed to be there for me. *Who loves a drink more than her own daughter?* I found myself in front of a little stone retaining wall not far from the inn. Beyond it was a steep hill hidden by dark foliage. I sat down heavily and dangled my feet over the side, clenching my fists into tight balls.

Alexander found me not long after.

"Don't," I warned him, seething. "I might do something I'll regret."

"You won't hurt me," he said quietly, sitting next to me on the wall.

"*Don't* underestimate me," I gritted out.

"I am not," he said simply. "I know what you're capable of. I also know the lines you refuse to cross, despite your impulses."

I fumed, itching to punch him. Punch *something*. "Go away. I want to be alone."

"If I were in your shoes, I would feel devastated as well."

"I'm not sad! I'm angry. Go away. If you came over to make me feel better, you're doing a rotten job."

He was quiet for a few moments. "Tell me how you're really feeling."

"I don't want to talk about *feelings*," I said through gritted teeth. I consoled myself by imagining shoving him off the wall and watching him tumble down the hill.

"Alright," is all he said.

A few more minutes passed in silence. Breathing heavily, I swung my legs, my heels hitting the stone over and over. Finally I said, "Look, if you're not going to say anything, why are you still here?"

"If you really want me to leave, then I'll leave." His voice was low and calming.

I said nothing for a while. "She's not—" I took a breath and let it out slowly. "She's not supposed to be like this. She *wasn't* like this. She was smart, and strong, and... *sober*." I laughed sadly, pulling my knees to my chest. "She loved me."

"She still loves you."

I shook my head. "She's not Anne anymore, not the Anne I knew. She's an old drunkard. She doesn't care about me anymore."

"She must've never gotten over her grief. And she made a costly choice to turn to alcohol, but that doesn't mean she's lost her love for you. As soon as she sleeps it off, she'll be reasonable."

"After all these years, I've finally found her," I whispered. "But I feel...like I haven't really *found* her."

"I understand."

"Do you?" I said sharply, turning to look at him.

He gazed at me, not frightened by my hard stare. "I can't pretend I've been in your situation, because I have not. But I have lost some things, Cassie. Some people I've loved. I'm not entirely in the dark."

Guilt crept into my heart.

"I know how you must be feeling," he continued. "To finally have something that you've been missing for a very

long time, only to discover that it wasn't what you needed...
It must be devastating."

I looked forward again and nodded numbly.

"Heartbreaking," he added softly. "Is it heartbreaking?"

"Yes," I finally whispered.

"I don't think you should give up on her, Cass. *Cassie*," he corrected himself quickly.

"You can call me Cass. If you want," I added softly.

"Cass," he whispered.

I looked up at him. It was odd hearing that name come from someone other than my mother, but I liked the way he said it. It was somehow...different when it came from his lips.

"You shouldn't give up just yet. Give it a day—she'll realize how lucky she is that you've found her."

I looked at my hands. "I hope you're right. I hope she remembers who she is." I pushed myself up and cleared my throat, anxiety filling me as I remembered what I'd left behind in the bar. "Besides, the longer we spend out here, the more time it gives them to steal our gold."

"No need to fret," he said, getting up and lifting the bag out for me to see. "I brought it with me."

I sighed in relief. "Thank God. Come on, I've got a mother to save."

"Now you sound like yourself."

The doors banged inwards as I marched through the tavern once more. She was at the same table, her mug apparently refilled, because she took another swig. "Mother. Listen to me." Anne looked up at me, bags under her eyes and skin slightly sagging. Her depression and rum had taken its toll. "I needed you all of those years, and you took care of me. Now, you need me. It's my turn now, mum. I can help you if you let me," I pleaded. "Do you really want Barnet to win? Because he only really wins if you give up. I don't know how you escaped, but you did it. And that means *he didn't win*. But it's no difference to him whether you live the rest of your life like this, or you really did die. Either way, you're out of his sight and out of his mind. Right now, *he's winning*."

I paused, waiting for a reaction. When nothing came, I plowed on. "Once, you were the infamous Anne Bonny, the one who could kill three men with one shot. Now, they've forgotten. It's high time you remind them of who you are."

"When did ye learn to give such rousin' words?" She went to take another gulp, but I intercepted it and pried it out of her grasp. I upended it on the floor, and she reached out, whimpering.

"Who are you, Anne Bonny? Who *are* you?"

"Yer wasting your time. Ye can't help me."

"No!" I grabbed her by her dirty shirt collar. "You are a pirate. You are a brilliant woman who can best nearly any foe. And most importantly, you are my mother, and I'm *not* giving up on you." I reached into my pocket and pulled out her compass and pressed it into her palm. "I've found my way home, mum. Now you need to find yours."

Eyes wide, she stared at the item in her hand and swallowed. "Ye still 'ave this?"

"Of course I do. I never forgot about you."

She met my eyes, her pale blue-green ones softening. "Neither did I." She handed the compass back to me, sighing. "Yer not goin' to let me alone until I agree with you, eh? Alrigh'. What's yer brilliant plan?"

254

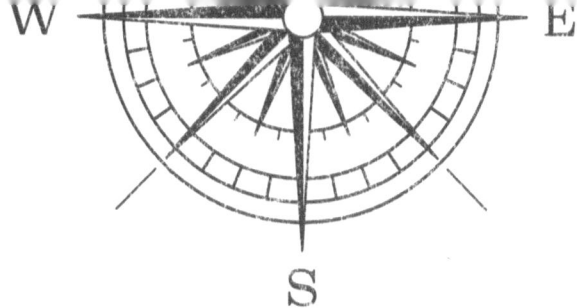

S

*Chapter 26*

**"Y**E MEAN TO TELL ME, ye were *on his ship*, within arms reach of 'im, and ye didn't slit 'is throat?!" she exclaimed angrily. "Ye had the chance to avenge yer family an' ye didn't think to take it?"

I sat on the bed and kicked off my boots. It was only after the rest of my crew returned and settled into their rooms that I began telling my mother my story. She listened quietly until I got to the part about the dreaded pirate hunter. "That's not entirely true," I said defensively, dispelling a wisp of shame. "I sunk his ship and released his precious prisoners so they could cause havoc in the town. And I already told you, I didn't just let him walk away unscathed! I *did* cause him bodily harm, just...not the fatal type."

"But you were there! Ye were there an' ye looked in his eyes an' ye still let 'im walk away?" She grabbed my shoulders. "Do ye not remember how cruel 'e is? Do ye not remember what 'e did to us?"

"Of course I remember," I snapped. "But you must understand. I was in a...very delicate situation."

"A delicate situation, ye say?" She sat on the bed next to me, and the mattress sagged a little. "What kind o' delicate situation?"

I stared at my boots, knowing she had an eyebrow raised in disbelief. She wouldn't believe there was a situation where killing him would prevent me from escaping. She knew what I was capable of at the age of ten, and she probably could guess how much better I've gotten since then. There was no point in hiding the truth from her. "Look, mum. I thought about it. I thought about it a lot. But when the opportunity presented itself, I...couldn't." I hung my head. "I don't know what stopped me. I guess I thought that I wouldn't be any better than him if I killed him in his sleep."

"O' course ye would be better than 'im," Anne said, her voice losing most of its harshness. "You would've stopped 'im from killin' so many more people."

"But what would that make me? It's not honorable at all to kill a man when he's sleeping. Besides, not everyone on that ship hated him. Some of his sailors looked up to him, and his son *loved* him. I couldn't take that away."

"Son?" she asked sharply.

"Yeah..." I tilted my head. Her eyes went unfocused. "What's the matter?"

"Nothin'." She shook her head to clear it, then met my eyes again, suspicion in her gaze. "That sailor boy seems nice."

I was caught off guard by the sudden change in subject. "Come again?"

She leaned closer, narrowing her eyes at me, searching for something in my face. "Has 'e gotten into yer head?"

"What? No!"

"Is that why ye were unable to end Barnet's life? Is that sailor all about mercy an' forgiveness? Has 'e been wooin' ye with that fine torso of 'is? That why 'is shirt's missin'?"

"Mother, calm down!" I exclaimed, burying my burning face in my hands. "He has not been *wooing* me. And he's not the reason I couldn't kill Barnet. He was just helping me. We needed his shirt for a white flag to get us past the gates."

"Why did 'e decide to help ye?"

I paused. "I don't know."

"Did ye offer 'im money?"

"Sort of."

"An' how much help has 'e actually been?"

I didn't really know why, but I felt the need to defend him. "Loads of help. He started teaching me to read while we were on Barnet's ship—"

"So 'e *has* gotten into yer head."

"What?"

"Why else would ye want to learn how to read?"

"To know what the map says! Obviously!"

Anne froze, then tilted her head. "The map?" And then all at once the excited gleam that I'd known and loved for years returned to her eyes, and she leaned forward eagerly. "The one I gave ye all those years ago? Ye still 'ave it?"

I smiled, pleased to see her finally motivated. "Of course."

"Well, where is it?"

I slipped the old, soft paper out of my pocket and unfolded it for her to see, trying to recall the poem Xander—*when had I started thinking of him as Xander?*—read to me. I squinted at the words, only a few of which I could read, until it came back to me, and then I whispered it to her.

"Are ye sure that's all it says?"

"Aye."

"That's hardly a clue." She rubbed her temples frustratedly. "There are a million pools or ponds or lakes that 'ave creeks running to 'em."

I thought for a moment, massaging my jaw. "It sounds like whoever buried the gold must've had a rough time with it. Maybe they were being hunted? Otherwise, why would they bury the gold instead of spend it?"

"I dunno, but that don't matter. The clue doesn't 'ave any hint on where in the world this piece o' land is."

"It's almost like...we're missing something. What if this is only part of it? What if there's another clue out there that tells us where we're supposed to go?"

She rubbed two fingers across her chapped lips. "Aye. Aye, yer prolly right. I believe yer father had a hidden compartment somewhere on *The Kingston*, but 'e never told me where it was or what was in it."

"Never?" I raised my eyebrows, intrigued. "Didn't you look for it?"

"Sometimes. But he didn't want me doin' that. Besides, I was busy enough lookin' fer other opportunities, if ye catch my drift."

A secret compartment? The answer could be there, on that boat, but it was miles away. "Do you think it's still in the cove?" I smacked my forehead with the palm of my hand. "I shouldn't have sold that boat—"

"You mean *The Kingston*?" she asked, surprised. "Nay, it's 'ere."

I stared at her in shock. "What?"

"*The Kingston*'s here," she repeated, as if I should've known this already. "An old friend o' Mary found an' repaired it. But we'll have to bargain for it."

My eyes widened as I shot off the bed in excitement. "Well, what are we waiting for? Let's go!"

"Furl yer sails a lil', Cass. She'll never recognize me in this state. Besides, it's gettin' dark. We should wait til mornin'."

I *yearned* to go see our old ship. But since she was the only way I was going to do so, I had to wait until she was ready. I sighed. "I suppose we have the time."

---

The next day, I was up with the sun. Sitting up from my cot, I stretched my arms over my head. Orange light streamed through the window, and songbirds sang a beautiful melody. I sprang up and ran over to Anne, who had the bedsheets pulled over her head. "Come on, mum. Let's go see your friend," I said enthusiastically, shaking her.

She groaned and rolled over in her bed. "Have ye gone mad? It's too early. If yer lookin' fer somethin' to do, go bathe yerself. That's a clean towel next to the wash bin," she mumbled. "Ye'll have to fetch some water."

I looked over at the corner of the room. Indeed, there was a graying towel folded on the floor, but the tub was dusty.

My arms ached by the time I poured the last pail of stove-heated water in the basin. The work was worth it, though, because the soap smelled wonderful—a mix of coconut and sweet vanilla. As I lounged with closed eyes, resting my head against the wood, I felt all of the anxiety I'd been carrying drift away in the warm water.

"How is it?" Anne asked after a while, still buried in the blankets.

"Glorious," I responded.

"You gonna let yer mother 'ave a turn before the water gets cold?"

I grinned. "You *do* need it." I stood up, letting the water run off me, before wrapping the towel around me and exiting the tub.

Rising, she nodded to the chest at the foot of her bed. "Grab some fresh clothes."

I padded over to it and lifted the heavy lid. It was filled to the brim with simple dresses, corsets, trousers and baggy linen shirts.

I examined each item. A dress wouldn't do—too restricting. I tapped my fingernail on the floor of the chest, and it occurred to me that it was much shallower on the inside than on the outside. Curious, I grabbed all of the clothes and dumped them on the floor, then stared at the bottom of the chest.

"Smart, that's my girl. There's a latch concealed in the corner," she murmured.

I looked over at her, feeling warm pride spread through me. The sudsy water made her hair look darker and longer, and it flowed around her shoulders and danced in the water. She seemed younger today; her skin was less saggy and her eyes were brighter. Her full lips—ones I had inherited—parted in an encouraging smile.

"Go on. The latch."

"Right," I muttered. I ran my fingers along the smooth wood until they hit a crease, and I used my nail to pull it up until it acted as a sort of handle. I gave it a tug, and the false bottom lifted free. I set the board on the ground, looking down in amazement. "This is Aunt Mary's favorite outfit," I breathed. "And her sword." I lifted the expertly crafted weapon reverently.

"Aye. Haven't seen it since before we were captured."

"I miss her, Mum." I closed my eyes and kissed the hilt.

"So do I, child. I miss her dearly."

I placed the sword back in the box, and my throat tightened. "What became of her? Was she hanged?"

"We were both imprisoned after we told the judge we were pregnant, but she died o' gaol fever before we could escape."

My heart constricted. "That's awful. May she rest in peace," I whispered as I picked up the wooden board again.

"What're ye doin'?"

"Putting it back."

"Ye aren't goin' to wear it?"

"Me?" I exclaimed, a little shocked.

"Yes, *ye*. Yer her height, and she'd want ye to wear it."

"But..." I didn't know what to say. When I was a little girl, I always admired Mary's outfits. Sometimes I'd steal items of her clothing and try them on myself, and when she'd catch me, she'd tickle me. The memory made me smile.

"It would just be gatherin' dust, otherwise. Don't let such fine attire go to waste." She scrubbed her scalp with the fresh-smelling soap before dipping her head under the water.

*What a fine point*, I thought. I pulled on black leggings and her loose white shirt, the neckline so wide it slipped down off my shoulders.

"It's supposed to be like that," Anne explained. "It makes it easier to seduce men."

I rolled my eyes. "I'm not going to be *seducing men* any time soon."

"What about that sailor ye had with ye yesterday?"

"Mother!" I said, slightly embarrassed but relieved she was sounding more like herself. "He's just a friend. *Friend*, mum! There will never be a need to *seduce* him."

She gave me a playful smile. "As long as 'e doesn't get into yer head, yer free to get into *his*."

"He already has someone waiting for him back home," I mumbled. I couldn't let myself hope Emma had already married Abraham.

"Ahh, all the more fun!"

I rolled my eyes again, before grabbing the next few items in the chest. A black corset with ties in the front and a long, brown, elegant waistcoat fashioned for women, with a black collar and matching black leather cuffs. I hesitated.

"What, ye don't like corsets?" Anne said, lifting herself out of the tub, grabbing my discarded towel and wrapping it around herself.

"Let's just say... I haven't had a very good experience with them."

"Come now, try it on. This was the only one Mary would wear. Maybe ye'll 'ave some better luck."

I reluctantly tried it on, slipping the laces through the holes and pulling. It was a tad uncomfortable, and forced my back even straighter than it was before, but nothing I couldn't get used to. Satisfied, I donned the waistcoat and knee-high black leather boots.

I stepped in place, testing out the two-inch heels. "Feels like I'm a new woman." I tied the waistcoat closed with a wide belt, which held the sheath for my new sword. The large clasp was decorated with pure, shining gold.

"Ye know what Mary used to say. Ye look nice, ye feel nice. And ye look *fantastic*."

I smiled at her, bigger than I had in a long time. *I have a mother. She's alive and well and finally happy. At least...until she remembers her loss*, I thought sadly. I'd have to keep her away from the rum.

"What's wrong?" she asked.

"Nothing," I said quickly, looking into the chest once more. "I'm missing one last thing." I picked up Mary's beautiful tricorn hat and turned it over in my hands. It was navy blue and a little worn, but I liked it all the same. It held a secret I'd been wanting to know since I was a child. Every piece of this outfit had its own story. After all, Mary wasn't inclined to spend honest gold. She would tell me those stories when I asked for them, but never the one I wanted to hear most. I would ask again and again, but she would just laugh and say, "When you're older, my little Sea Queen. When you're older."

"I'm older now, Aunt Mary," I whispered.

"What's that?" Mum asked.

I perked up hopefully. "Do you remember the story I always wanted to hear when I was younger? The one Aunt Mary would never tell me?"

Anne dropped to the floor and fingered one of the wadded dresses, chuckling. "Ye were so cute, ye know, when ye wanted something." She decided to go with some trousers and a simple shirt, and quickly pulled those on.

"So? You know it?" I watched her expectantly as she squeezed more water out of her hair and picked up an overcoat not unlike mine.

"Aye, o' course I know it. That belonged to a high standin' Naval officer some time ago. Mary needed information on when the next shipment o' gold was leavin' the harbor, so she worked 'er magic on 'im. Not with that outfit, I'm afraid." I don't know why, but I relaxed a little. "Anyway," she continued, "once she got what she was looking for, she knocked 'im out, stripped 'im, and tied 'im to the window."

I sputtered. "Naked?"

"Aye." She nodded eagerly, a humorous glint in her eyes. "Stark naked. She made sure 'e was nice and secure, so 'e couldn't escape until the town woke an' somebody came to get 'im." She laughed. "His dignity an' good reputation? Flew right out that same window."

I laughed and cringed, imagining it. "I can see why she saved that story for when I was older."

She pulled on her boots, sighing. "Mary would 'ave told it better. It was the only time ye would sit still, remember? When ye were listening to 'er stories." She chuckled. "I was always on the edge o' my seat, even when I'd already heard the tale before." Her smile faded and a darker look filled her eyes as she whispered, "I'll never hear 'em again."

"Would you like this hat?" I asked her, holding it out and hoping to distract her.

"Ye don't want it?"

"I think Mary would want you to have something to remember her by. Besides, you'd look good in it. I think I'll buy myself a new one."

She shrugged like it was nothing, but took it gingerly, unsure of herself. After a few moments, she pressed it onto her head and walked to the small mirror above the wash bin. She nodded in satisfaction. "I think I'll try that khol pencil."

As she traced her upper lid, she explained, "It makes yer eyes look bigger an' fiercer. Mary used to wear it, remember?"

I nodded, swallowing. "Can you do some on me, too?"

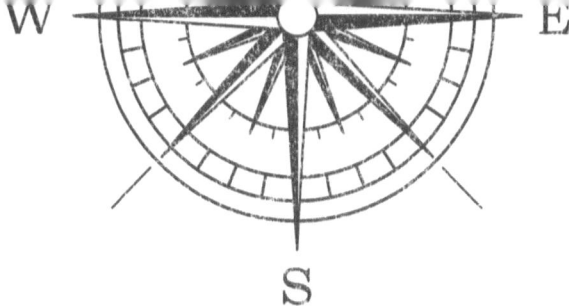

## Chapter 27

"**H**EY, CREW," I SAID, feeling powerful in my new boots as I walked toward them. They sat around a table, talking and sipping their drinks. My mother walked next to me, her lucky old bandana around her wrist. Preston had a wide brimmed hat with a big feather covering his curly brown hair. When he saw me, he stood up and bowed, making a big show of sweeping the air with his hat as he took it off.

I laughed. "I like it," I told him, and he smiled and placed it back on his head, touching the feather to make sure it was still in place. Anne and I took the last two empty chairs, and Wyatt slid a glass of water to me.

"Thanks," I said, before finally letting myself look at Xander. His eyes traveled up and down my new attire, a faint smile on his lips. I tried not to notice how good he looked: he'd washed up, and wore a simple linen shirt. His hair was wild and tousled in all the right ways. I could just imagine running my fingers through—I stopped the thought in its tracks. *Seven seas*, my mother was right. When had he gotten into my head?

I turned to Jacob, who seemed to have gotten himself a makeover. "Did you spend every coin you had?" I teased.

Jacob smirked, leaning his chair back on two legs. He wore a brown leather vest with gold buckles, but left it unclasped. His white undershirt had a hood, and the sleeves had been torn off, baring his arms. He wore a red bandana, silver cuffs covering his forearms, and a black baldric, which held no pistols.

"Do you know what that's for?" I pointed to the baldric.

"Yeah. It holds the sword holder." He stood up to show me.

I snorted. "It's called a scabbard, and that kind of baldric isn't supposed to hold your sword—it's for pistols. You should put your scabbard on your belt."

He looked down. "Oh. I'll fix that."

"I like your getup, though. You've definitely achieved *the look*. Did you get new boots?"

He put his foot on the chair to show me, and I stood up to get a better look. They were black, with big gold buckles. I nodded, trying not to laugh. "You need to take this man shopping." I pointed to Alexander.

"Me?" Xander asked, surprised.

"Yes, you. You look like a lost sailor who shipwrecked on a pirate island." I sat back down, smirking.

"Don't worry, Captain." Jacob winked. "I'll make sure he looks as striking as I do."

I laughed, but Xander folded his arms and scowled. "I don't need help shopping for clothes. What makes you think that Jake should be giving fashion advice? Look at him! Nothing matches."

"You shouldn't be criticizing *my* clothes, mate. The captain here seems unable to take her eyes off them."

Xander's mouth twitched. "Shut up," he said, annoyed.

"Or maybe," Jake lowered his voice and leaned closer to him, "It's not my clothes that she can't take her eyes off of."

Alexander elbowed him. "I said, *shut up*."

Judith gave her beau a whack on his thigh, which made him laugh. "Stop teasing him," she ordered.

"I love it when you hit me," he responded, not a drop of sarcasm in his voice.

I sat down in front of my eggs and toast, biting my lip. I finally had a solid plan—with news of *The Kingston*, and the clue hidden on it, the treasure was no longer a distant dream.

It was time to tell them.

I took a deep breath, nerves fluttering in my stomach. "In my possession is a *very* old treasure map. There aren't enough landmarks for me to make out where we should sail, but there's a riddle." I recited it from memory: "*Nights are warm, days are cool / Where the creek meets the pool. / But this clue brings a warning: / All rejoicing will turn to mourning / When the fortune you seek / Becomes your greatest misfortune.*" I let that sink in.

Jake drew a dramatic breath, his eyes lighting up. "We'll be rich!"

"You had this back before you were mutinied against?" Wyatt asked in his thick East African accent. "And you didn't tell us?"

I fidgeted with the hem of my sleeve. "It would have been no use, since I had no heading and none of us could read. And there weren't many I could trust."

"But you trust us?" Johnny asked.

"Aye. All of you." I looked around at them all before continuing. "My mother and I believe that there's a clue hidden on my father's ship. It's docked here in Tortuga. We find it, get our heading, bargain for the galleon, and set sail."

Johnny tapped his fork on his plate, leaning back in his chair. "How much is the treasure worth?"

I bit my lip. "I don't know. But hopefully quite a lot. After all, gaining a valuable treasure could paint quite a big target on your back, and based on what the riddle says..."

Alexander leaned forward. "When the fortune you seek becomes your greatest misfortune."

"How do we know it isn't talking about some trap set to protect it?" Johnny argued.

I nodded curtly. "We will have to be prepared for anything. What do you say? You wanna find this treasure?"

They eagerly agreed, so I turned to my mum. "I'd say it's high time I was back on *The Kingston*. How do we find it?"

※

The scent of fish, jasmine, and gunpowder filled the warm breeze as Anne led us up the road. The town oozed wealth, but it was the kind of wealth that didn't, to some extent, discriminate. It didn't matter what their skin color was or where they came from: if someone wanted to start a little shop, they could start a shop. If they wanted to share their home country's unique food with the town, they could open a restaurant. That's why the streets were lined with colorful buildings, from old Japanese tea houses to African jewelry stands and everything in between.

We stopped at a little hut with flowering vines snaking their way up the sides. It sat on the very edge of town, half hidden by trees. Anne stepped forward and rapped her knuckles hard on the door. We stood there, waiting, and when I was about to propose the possibility that no one was home, the door creaked inwards, just enough for the person on the inside to see out but not enough for us to see in.

"Robin?" Anne said. "It's me. Anne. Ye remember?"

The door opened wider, and there before us stood a woman about my height, with pin-straight, midnight black hair that flowed around her thin shoulders and stopped at her hips. She was younger than my mother; I would guess she would be Mary's age if she were still with us. She had beautiful downturned eyes, a fathomless green, and thin lips. She wore a simple green dress and nothing to cover her feet, so I couldn't help but notice her thick, dirt-filled toenails.

"It's been a while," she said, leaning against the door jam. "What do you want?"

"Why do ye assume I want somethin'?"

"You always want something when you come to visit me."

"That's not true," Anne responded, a little defensive.

Robin just raised an eyebrow, then looked at all of us one by one before returning her gaze to my mum. "Well, since it appears that you have taken my advice and took a bath, I'll listen to what you have to say."

"I found her," Anne blurted. "I finally found 'er." She took my arm and pulled me forward. "Cass, meet Robin."

"Cassandra," Robin's face lit up in happy surprise, and she embraced me. "Mary told me all about you the last time she was here. She stepped back, melancholy. "It's been so long since I've seen her," she addressed my mum wearily, before looking at me again. "You're grown up. Mary had said you were only a little girl. Has it been that long since she died?" Her eyes lost focus.

Not wishing to dwell on loss, I cut to the point. "Robin, Anne told me that you found *The Kingston* and brought it back to be repaired."

"Did she now?" Robin put her hands on her hips. "So this is why you came up here?"

Anne waved it off. "It's just a small favor."

"Small favor?" She folded her arms. "It's almost a three-mile hike. *Small favor*," she scoffed.

"Please?" Alexander asked. "We really need your help."

Robin scrutinized him. "You've got yourself a girl?"

"Pardon me?" he asked, taken aback.

"A girl," she repeated, with the same tone as *duh*. "Yeh have a girl?"

He cleared his throat, obviously uncomfortable. "Not at the moment. Why do you ask?"

Amused, I fought down my grin.

Robin turned inside her hut and bent down, then stood up with a pair of boots in her hands, which she slipped on. "It wouldn't take much effort to get one, is all I'm sayin'." She winked at me, before closing the door behind her.

I stepped back, and then my face hardened. *Absolutely not.*

"So why do you need this ship?" Robin asked us as she walked back through the path towards the main road.

"Because we don't 'ave one," Anne responded, following her.

She scoffed. "You're going to need a better reason than that if you're going to convince her to hand it over."

"Her?" I asked. "Weren't you the one who fixed it?"

"Darlin', I'm much too poor to fix and keep a *galleon*, especially when I'm not using it."

"Then who has the ship?"

"A young woman by the name of Naomi." We turned right onto the dirt road, and the steepness of the mountain combined with the warm air brought droplets of sweat to my forehead.

"Where are we going?" Preston asked.

"You'll see," she said simply.

"Isn't this the way towards the King's mansion?" I remembered from my last trip here.

Judith gasped. "Is she the queen?"

Robin chuckled. "No, but she acts like it. She inherited most of her wealth from her grandfather, a privateer who grew rich in the Anglo-Dutch wars. She runs a little school of sorts, where she teaches the few children on this island how to fight and what-not."

"Do you think she could teach us?" Jake asked, gesturing to himself and Judith.

"I'll teach you as soon as we get our ship back," I promised. "We'll probably have lots of time on the trip."

"Do you think we'll actually have to fight?" Judith murmured nervously.

I pretended not to hear her. There was no definite answer for that, and I didn't want her to worry.

We rounded a bend, and the King's stone mansion loomed into view. It was no castle—too modest for that, and rightly so. Though the townsfolk treated him as a superior, he was no monarch to be worshipped, and his rule lasted only until the next election. The treasury, hidden underground near the mansion, had fascinated me as a child. I'd once searched for its secret entrance, rumored to be embedded in the obsidian of the mountain's peak.

As we approached the gates, Robin veered left, and took us on a narrow path through dense forest. We ducked under vines and hopped over fallen trees, until we stopped where the black rock formed a towering wall in front of us, covered in vines.

I drew in a breath as Robin pulled back the sheet of vines, revealing a dark tunnel leading deep into the mountain. "Woah," I breathed.

"Hold," Robin ordered no one in particular.

Wyatt took hold of the vines while Robin stepped inside, lifting a torch from its sconce. She knelt, struck two stones—a dull gray and a shiny silver—until a spark ignited the torch, casting dancing light on the walls. Standing, she smiled at her success. "Follow me."

Robin led us down the sloping tunnel, which forked several times. I memorized the turns—right, right, left, right—in case I needed to return alone. The passage seemed endless, winding deeper with every step. Left. Right. Faintly, I heard running water, and soon we emerged into a massive cavern.

A glowing pool of water stretched as far as I could see, curving around the stone walls and out of sight. Luminescent algae sent rippling blue patterns dancing across the high ceiling, mystical and unlike anything I'd ever seen. Torches blazed along the walls, and tunnels branched off in every direction.

But what caught my eye the most, what drew the breath from my lungs, was what floated in the water not far from where we stood: my father's impressive ship, the one he cared for and loved so much. The mainmast stood over eighty feet in height, but still far from scraping the ceiling. It was freshly painted, but the name on the stern still read *The Kingston* in golden letters. It was even more beautiful than when I had last seen it; this Naomi lady did a fine job.

"I see you've brought some company," a musical female voice spoke from somewhere up above, her voice echoing softly around the cavern. "Are they new students?"

We lifted our eyes to see her standing on a balcony jutting from the cave wall. She descended the stairs, her deep magenta dress and silk cape trailing behind her. As she approached, I took note of everything about her: the confident way she held her shoulders, her timeless beauty, her Indian heritage. The front half of her long, dark hair was pinned back with a golden clasp, and her painted lips matched the deep red-pink of her embroidered dress, which had capped sleeves and revealed a thin strip of her midriff. Golden jewelry adorned her ears, neck, and wrists, and she moved with such grace I could've sworn she was floating. Stopping before us, she smiled warmly and bowed her head. "*Bienvenue.*"

"Huh?" Jake asked.

"Welcome," she repeated, in English this time.

"How are you today, Naomi?" Robin asked, stepping forward and giving her a quick embrace.

"Wonderful. I just received the shipment of silk I ordered from China, so I'm in a very good mood. And Frieda's getting better with a pistol. She can shoot a bullseye from over twenty-five feet away."

I whistled. "Impressive!"

"So glad to hear it," Robin said. "Where are the students?"

"Training," Naomi answered. "Would you like to watch?"

She led us around the water's edge, but my gaze could not be torn from the ship. *I'll get you out of here*, I thought. I wondered how much money she'd want. I doubted I had enough. The sack I carried could probably pay for the masts, maybe the sails, if Naomi was feeling generous.

We entered another tunnel, guided by torches anchored along the walls. "So, what are your names? You all must be from out of town, since I've never seen your faces."

"I'm not, but the rest of 'em are," Anne informed her, just before we emerged into a smaller room than the last—but just as breathtaking. A gaping hole in the opposite wall gave a magnificent view of the jungle, and beyond that, a sparkling blue ocean. My jaw dropped open. *Had we really journeyed straight through the entire mountain?*

The room held seven sweaty children, their constant motion a whirlwind of energy. An older one—my age, I'd wager—dangled from a rope attached to the ceiling, his bare arms toned and glistening as he put one hand over the other, so far above the ground he'd surely break his legs if he fell. Some of the younger children carried large rocks as they raced from one end of the room to the other. A pair was wrestling ferociously on a straw mat tacked to the ground. The youngest one, a little boy of about five years, was the first to notice us. He put down his rock and, after staring at us for a moment, he halted the girl who was passing him and whispered something. One by one they stopped and stared.

"*Salut*, children," Naomi smiled at them. "Nice work. You are all looking very strong."

"*Merci,* madame," they said in less-than-perfect unison.

Suddenly two girls ran into the room from a tunnel on the other side. They were obviously twins, but not exactly identical, and looked to be a little younger than I. One girl clutched her upper arm and the other stood anxiously beside her, holding a sword at her side. They both had dark brown hair, held back in a thick braid. Their deep brown eyes shone with innocence, and they had a smattering of freckles across their noses. Like most of the children here, the sun had kissed them, giving their skin a beautiful tan look that most assuredly wouldn't be appreciated in the western world. The philosophy of European ladies was, *oh, handsome sir! Look how pale and pretty I am, because I've never worked a day in my life! Please protect me, the delicate flower that I am!*

"Jade cut me," the girl holding her arm sniffled. She released her hand and held it up, showing us her bloody fingers.

"I didn't mean to!" the other girl burst out. "It slipped."

"Jade, Emerald," Naomi said sternly, stepping around the others and inspecting her arm. "What did I tell you about using wooden swords? They'll keep you safe until you have developed more control."

"We thought we were good enough," Jade pouted. "Fighting with wooden swords is no fun. They don't have that *balance*. They don't feel right in your palm, like real ones do." She waved the long blade in the air, cutting down an invisible enemy.

Naomi grabbed her hand and pried the sword out of her grasp. "Run along to the infirmary and fetch some bandages. Hurry, now."

Jade sent a curious look our way, but then scampered back the way she had come.

"Class, I'd like you to meet our new guests." She looked at us expectantly. "Won't you introduce yourselves?"

"My name's Cassandra Rackham. This is my mother, Anne Bonny, and that's my crew." As I introduced the rest of them, they nodded or raised a hand in greeting.

"Pleased to meet you." Her eyes scanned over me quickly. "You don't look like the typical new student."

I shook my head. "I'm afraid I'm here for a different purpose."

She nodded, like she expected that. "Are *any* of you here to learn from me?"

Judith and Jake glanced at me. *There'd be another time for that, mates.* "No," I replied. "But I'm sure you're a very good teacher. We need something slightly more...tangible."

"Have you been to Arca-tic?" the smallest boy piped up.

"He means the Arctic," an older girl with white-blond hair clarified.

I chuckled, squatting down to his level. "No, but I've been to other places, like the Americas."

"I want to see the big white beasts," the boy proclaimed, spreading his arms as far as they could go to show me their size. "Are they real?"

"Polar bears?" Xander said. "Yes, of course they're real."

"Have you seen them?" The boy's eyes widened.

Xander shook his head. "No, but I've read about them."

The small child's shoulders sagged in disappointment. "Reading's no fun."

Naomi ruffled his hair. "Don't say that, Aaron. It's only hard until you get good at it."

"Aaron," I repeated, still eye level with the little boy. "Good, strong name you got there, young man."

He smiled and buried his face in Naomi's cape. She laughed lightly and picked him up. "How many rocks did you carry?"

He held up all his fingers.

"I did forty repetitions," challenged another young boy a few years older than him.

"Well, I did seventy-hundred!" Aaron retorted.

"It doesn't matter how many you did, as long as you did your best," Naomi instructed, setting Aaron down.

Just then, Jade returned with a wad of gauze and a bottle of clear liquid, which she handed to her teacher. As Naomi began to clean and wrap Emerald's wound, I looked around at all the other kids. Jade and Emerald were sitting side by side, whispering to each other. But wait—Emerald was standing up, having her arm bandaged, and Jade was standing next to her. I looked back and forth between the pair on the ground and the pair standing up, until it registered.

"You're quadruplets," I said, astonished.

"There are four of us, yes," one on the ground said happily. "It makes it easier to surprise our enemies. Or be double spies."

"Quadruple spies," the other one giggled.

"I'm Ruby," she said, standing up and holding out her hand.

"And I'm Pearl," the other one said, copying her sister.

I stepped forward to shake their hands.

"You're all named after precious stones," Judith pointed out.

"Aye," Ruby agreed, lifting her chin. "We're destined to find buried treasure."

"And be super rich," Pearl added matter-of-factly.

I laughed. "I like your high hopes. So who are the rest of you?" I looked at the other students.

"The name's Charles," the oldest boy said, finally dropping down from the rope. He had a round face, intense, dark eyes, and silky black hair tied at the nape of his neck. He stood tall and confidently, crossing his muscular arms over his chest. All the students here were visibly strong, even the littlest children. I wondered if some of the older ones would have any desire to join us, because a crew of seven wouldn't be enough to sail a ship the size of *The Kingston*.

"Children," Naomi announced, "I want you to pair up and practice the seven defenses. Once you're done with that, run through all the kicks that you know. I'll be giving our *invités* a little tour."

"*Je comprends*, madame," Sarah answered in perfect French.

Naomi took us through the next tunnel and up a long flight of slippery stone steps. The next room was circular, lit mostly with torches, but natural light streamed through an archway leading to another room. The one in which we stood was filled with boxes and tables covered in colorful fabric. Crude manikins stood about the place, some half dressed and others bare. A large spindle sat against a wall. A woman in her late twenties bent over a table in the center of the room, holding a piece of cloth in one hand and a needle in the other.

"Hello, Frieda," Naomi called. "*Comment ça va?*"

"*Comme ci, comme ça*," she muttered. "*Cette robe est difficile.* Silk is hard to work with."

"Ah, *je sais*. But I'm sure it's nothing you can't handle."

Freida smiled at the compliment, then looked up from her work and removed her glasses. "*Qui sont-ils?*"

It took me a moment to pick that last phrase apart, but I took it to mean, *Who are they?* There had been a French speaker aboard *The Kingston* when I was little, so I'd picked up a bit of the language.

"Travelers. They need my help for something, but haven't yet disclosed it." Naomi picked up a folded piece of sky blue cloth from inside an open crate and held it next to Judith's cheek.

She stepped back. "What are you doing?"

"Seeing what color works best with your skin tone," she explained. "This blue won't work. And certainly not beige." She tossed the cloth back where it came from and put a finger to her lips.

"I don't need..." Judith began.

"Hush, darling," Naomi interrupted. "It'll be my gift to you. I make it my personal responsibility to make sure all those in my house are properly cared for. You're next, *monsieur*," she warned Xander. After a moment's thought, she decided, "Navy blue with white laces. I have *just* the dress."

"Why?" I asked her, suspicious. "Why are you just *giving* us things?" I had enough experience to know there was always a reason behind such actions.

"They who give have all things; they who withhold have nothing."

"Is that your motto?" Preston asked.

She smiled. "It's a proverb, from my home country."

"She's full of 'em," Frieda told us.

"What a great thing to live by," Johnny said. "I love me some free stuff." He reached for some green silk, but Wyatt smacked his hand away.

"Have you no manners?" he muttered into Johnny's ear.

Naomi smiled softly. "This is why I spend my time teaching instead of traveling. Many of the children you met came from nothing. The quadruplets are orphans. Since I am privileged to have had a grandfather with money and connections, I have power to help people. I give the youngsters something they can protect themselves with, something they can use to become profitable. They learn from books down at the schoolhouse, but they learn practical skills from me."

Just from listening to her, I could guess why Naomi was more admired than the king. When I had first heard Robin say she acted like royalty, I thought she meant snotty and cold. But the woman that stood in front of me was a born leader.

Naomi glided towards a large wardrobe and threw open the tall wooden doors. Inside, dozens of different dresses of all different shapes and sizes hung from a metal pole that ran across the top of the wardrobe. After searching for a few minutes, she pulled off a dark blue dress with white lace on the ends of the sleeves and matching white laces that cinched up the front.

"I think it would look gorgeous on you," Frieda assessed.

"It's beautiful," Judith breathed, her eyes wide with longing, as she took the dress gently in her hands.

"I'm glad you like it," Naomi smiled. "It might need a little tailoring, but I think it'll fit. Now...for the rest of you." She tapped a finger to her lips, surveying us. "I know I said you were next, young man, but Cassandra's just a quick fix."

I raised an eyebrow. "Quick fix? I do not need—"

She put a hand on my arm. "I didn't mean to offend you, *mademoiselle*. I just meant you could do with some accessories." She guided me to the archway where daylight seeped out of. My hand tightened around my sack of coins. Her generosity was unusual, even for Tortuga, and it was unsettling. *Who would just give away things?* There had to be a price.

There was always a price.

Against one wall was a large bed, and I realized this must be her room. There was a large skylight above, covered in thick warped glass to stop the rain from ruining everything inside. There was a gold framed, full-length mirror against the opposite wall, and a large dresser next to it. A beautiful handmade rug covered most of the floor.

"So you're the leader of that little group," Naomi phrased it as a statement, rather than a question.

"Aye."

"You're young for a captain. Why did you end up coming to Tortuga?" She walked to the dresser and pulled open the first drawer.

I hesitated. "I needed a better ship. And a bigger crew."

She fished out a pair of big gold hoops, and held them up for me to see. "You like them?"

I nodded, eyeing the simple pieces of jewelry.

"They go well with your outfit," she agreed. "Here, put them in."

I took them in my free hand and put them in my ears, then glanced at the mirror, angling my head in different ways.

"What's that you got there?" Naomi nodded at the bag I carried. When I didn't answer, she said, "Gold, hmm? Running low on it, myself."

"Aye?" I said, lifting a brow. "Is that why you're pampering us? To get us to trust you?"

"How crafty that would be—but no. I've always treated my guests this way." She turned her back to me as she walked to the other side of the room, toward another wardrobe. "See, I was always generous. I didn't make my students or their parents pay for my services. I fed the children that could not feed themselves, and gave much needed aid to travelers like yourself. But the funds that I inherited..." She paused at the cabinet, turning her head. "Are not without limit."

"Why are you telling me this? What do you want?"

She opened the doors, and the back wall of the cupboard was covered in hooks, on which hung different kinds of hats, mostly tricorns and wide brimmed ones, which were best for sailing. "The question is, what do *you* want?"

"I want my father's ship. The one I grew up on. The one I lost when a pirate hunter caught us unawares." I paused, then spoke my last sentence slowly, to make sure she heard every word. "The one floating just downstairs, in that glowing pool of yours."

She glanced at me, then turned back to her hats, running her hands across the many rows. "I should really sell these," she muttered. She selected a beautiful black tricorn with thin, delicate, gold trimming. "No captain is without her hat. This matches your belt and boots."

I narrowed my eyes. "Did you hear what I..."

She held the hat out. "What you said? *Oui, tous les mots.* Every word. Now, would you like this hat, or should I give it to someone else?"

I snatched it out of her grasp and stuffed it on my head, before I remembered my manners. "Thank you."

She smiled. "My pleasure." Then she turned to face the exit. "Frieda!" she called.

Frieda came running and skidded to a halt right next to me. "Yes, madame?"

"Tomorrow morning, take these down to the market." She gestured to the hats. "See if you can make a nice profit for me, will you?"

"*Oui*, madame. Of course." She bowed her head quickly.

"But leave the two at the top. I like them."

Naomi sent her back to my crew before turning to me once more. "You must understand, under the present circumstances..." She grimaced, as if it pained her to speak the words. "I can't just let you take the ship. It's worth a fortune after all the money I've put into it—"

"Thank you for that, by the way. It means a lot to me and my mother." I hoped to appeal to her soft heart.

She gave me a small, strained smile. "And to Robin. But the trouble is, I need more funds to keep everything I have created from dying. I need to sell that ship."

I pursed my lips. I'd hoped her generosity would extend to the ship, but that's where my luck ended. She wouldn't accept the sack of coins I held, as it was only a fraction of what she would earn from selling it. I needed a new plan.

"I think I know a way for both of us to get what we want."

She cocked her head. "Do tell."

"I will. But first, I need to search our—the ship. Only then will I know if we can help each other."

She thought it over. "Show me what you find, and I will allow you to search for it."

"Fine. *If* we find it." I hurried through the archway to find Frieda measuring Xander's arms.

"A nice dark red color would look excellent on you," she told him, stowing away her tape measure.

I chuckled.

Alexander shot me a look, like, *why did you leave me with her?* "May I put my arms down now?" he asked her.

"Oh, yes!"

I looked around the room. "Where's Judith?"

"Right here," Judith called, stepping out from behind a changing screen and discarding her faded brown dress on the nearest table. She looked like a new woman, her new dress prompting her to stand taller and put her shoulders back.

"Come on, crew," I said. "We have a ship to search."

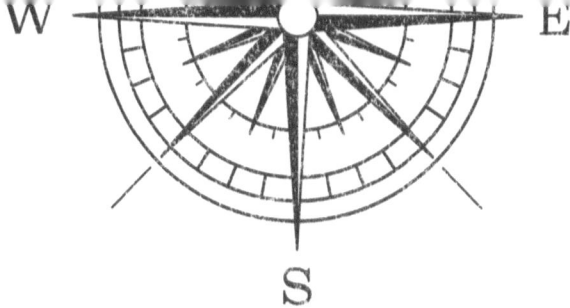

## *Chapter 28*

WE TOOK A ROWBOAT out to *The Kingston*. The water glowed as we glided through it, listening to the steady *plink* of droplets falling from the stalactites far above and sending tiny ripples across the water's surface. Alexander pulled on the oars. My eyes roved over the impressive piece of work, soaking it in. The sails were furled, but even so, I could see Naomi had dyed them a deep, royal blue, which matched the freshly painted hull and the top of the taffrail. Pale gold coated the railing balusters and the masts, and trimmed the edges of the gun ports. Two rows of cannons stuck out on either side, in addition to the weaponry on the main deck: crossbows and swivel guns were mounted every ten feet, with cannons placed between them. *This galleon is fit for a king*, I thought, and a suffocating doubt swept over me. How was I, poor and lacking, supposed to get my hands on such an art piece?

As I hoisted myself up over the side of the ship, I left my worries in the rowboat. People were relying on my leadership. There was no room for doubt.

After everyone was gathered on deck, I gave my instructions. "The clue's likely to be another piece of map, or an object with an inscription carved on it. It'll probably be hidden in a secret compartment, but it could be anywhere on the ship."

"So be thorough," my mum added. "Tap on walls an' see if they're hollow. Listen fer loose boards when ye step. It could be anywhere, so it'd be best if we split up."

"Aye, aye!" Preston gave an exaggerated salute, pulling a smile to my lips.

Towards the stern of the ship, twin staircases flanked a set of glass-paned double doors. Alexander slipped through the doors and into the hallway beyond, but Anne and I, a single thought on our minds, raced up the stairs, past the helm, and through the captain cabin's door.

Looking around brought back so many memories. Many-paned windows lined the back wall and some of the sides, sending eerie blue light dancing across the ceiling. The room was wider than it was deep. A glass door at the back led to the quarter galley, a deck that wrapped around the rear of the boat. Nostalgic, I remembered a clear night, when my parents brought me out there to watch the sky. My little nine year old eyes opened as wide as they could be, wanting to be the first person to spot the next star that streaked across the sky. Closing my eyes, I fell deeper into the memory—my father's warmth as I leaned back against his chest, trusting the strong arms around me to keep me secure as I dangled my legs off the railing. I opened my eyes, my heart squeezing painfully.

A queen-sized bed sat in the corner, a desk sat adjacent, complete with drawers and a mirror. I lit the lantern that hung beside the door, and it cast light on the rest of the objects in the room. A bookshelf, a wardrobe, and a big chest all sat against one wall. A beautiful rug covered the wood floor, and as I turned on the spot, taking it all in, I remembered the covert trapdoor in the corner that led down to the map room below.

"Oh, how I've missed this place," Anne murmured, sitting down in the bed.

"Naomi cleaned it up," I noted. The shelves were no longer cluttered with nicknacks—instead lined with books. I walked to the wardrobe, half expecting to see my father's old clothes inside, but it was empty. I checked the chest, with the same result. "Cleaned it *out*, too," I said, my voice turning hard. I longed to run my fingers across my father's favorite coat. And what happened to that rusty, no-good spyglass he refused to trade for another? I hurriedly wiped at a tear before it had a chance to fall and gritted my teeth. "Is there anything of value left in here?"

Anne stood up abruptly and walked to the opposite corner, where she ran her fingers along the vertical wood planks that lined the wall.

"What are you doing?" I asked.

She didn't reply, but I received my answer as she stopped, removed a section of the plank, and reached her arm inside. She turned around and leaned against the wall, sighing with relief as she clutched something to her chest.

I cocked my head, curious. "I thought you said you didn't know where Jack's secret compartment was."

She opened her hands, and I realized it was her good luck charm from long ago: a small feather, with a string and colorful wooden beads attached to it. "Yer father thought I needed me own little hidin' place, so 'e showed me this."

I nodded. "Do you know of any more hiding spots?"

"Nay, but let's 'ave a look around. It looks like Naomi didn't search the room very good, so there's a solid chance she 'asn't already found what we're lookin' fer."

We spent the next quarter of an hour combing the cabin, wrapping our knuckles along the walls, testing floorboards, looking for hidden buttons or handles, and checking for false bottoms in the desk drawers. My heart jumped when my fingers hit a crack in the back of the wardrobe, but it turned out to be nothing.

"Have you found anything yet?" I murmured.

"Nothin'," she replied wearily, pulling out books to check the back of the bookshelf.

I looked around for anything I hadn't searched yet, and my eyes landed on the bed. I cursed myself for not thinking of it earlier, and dropped to my hands and knees, gazing underneath. "I'll need a light," I concluded.

"What's that?" Anne gave up on the bookshelf and came over to me as I reached under the bed, feeling the cracks in the wood under my fingertips. "Let's move it."

After a few shoves, we managed to move the heavy bed frame aside. The floor beneath looked no different, but when I took a few steps over where it had rested before, I heard a *creak*.

I instantly dropped to my knees. My heart thumped with excitement as we pried two loose boards up—but then it sank all the way to my stomach as we stared down into the compartment beneath.

Nothing but dusty rum bottles.

I stood up and kicked the board, swearing. "This is where he would have hid it." I removed my hat and ran a hand through my hair.

"Not fer certain," she countered, placing the boards back where they belonged and standing up.

"What?" I demanded. "You know something I don't?"

"No," she said simply. "I just know yer father. He woulda had more'n two hidden compartments aboard 'is ship. An' under the bed woulda been a wee bit too obvious. If anyone were to raid 'is ship, 'is room might be the first place to look."

I nodded. It made sense, but *couldn't she have said that earlier?* "Where should we check next, then?"

"I'm sure the chart room won't take long to search." She walked to the corner of the room, and opened up a hatch that led down below.

I followed her down the ladder and found someone already there.

"You found anything yet, sailor?" I couldn't help the hope that creeped into my voice.

Alexander shook his head, but I told myself I'd expected so as I gazed at my new surroundings. The map room was much smaller, with a table and four chairs surrounding it. There were still numerous maps pinned to the walls, as well as newspaper clippings from long ago. Alexander caught me staring at one with a crude drawing of Blackbeard's severed head on a bowsprit.

"Printed in February of 1719," Alexander said, stepping forward. "Blackbeard beheaded by..." He quickly scanned it. "A Highlander under Lieutenant Robert Maynard."

"They say his body swam three times around the ship before being claimed by the sea," I murmured, tearing my eyes away from the blood dripping out of the old pirate's neck.

Alexander scoffed. "A load of horse dung."

"On these waters, nothing is for certain."

"He could've swam seven times 'round, fer all we know," Anne said playfully.

I turned my attention to a barrel that sat in the corner of the room, and started for it as Alexander said, "It's nothing interesting. Just a chip log."

He hadn't been lying. A long rope with knots in it was wound on a reel, the other end attached to a piece of wood shaped like a quarter circle. The tool was used to tell the speed of the ship.

"There's nothing here," Alexander told me. "You may as well move on to a different room." He left without another word.

We scoured the remaining rooms on this level: the first mate's cabin, the quartermaster's cabin, and finally the infirmary, all without any luck. The rooms were mostly bare, with just a few items on display as if Naomi was planning to showcase the ship to potential buyers. That worried me, but if all went well, I could bargain with her and save *The Kingston* from being lost to some nitwit.

Disheartened, we walked down the narrow hallway and out the double doors, finding only Alexander out on deck. He was crouched near the bow of the ship, running his hands along some of the boards. A glowing lantern sat beside him.

My mother and I ventured down below, and together with my crew, we searched every level. Every room. Every barrel, every box, every nook and cranny we could find. There were no more secret compartments. Down here, the ship resembled an ordinary vessel. As I left the hold, which was lined with cells on one side and empty barrels on the other, I wished this ship wasn't so large.

As I made my way back through the ship, movement caught my eye. I turned my head and peered through the darkness down the hall, but whatever it was had already disappeared. Half a second later, Preston and Jacob nearly plowed me over as they raced past me, yelling, "Get it, get it!"

I watched with utter bewilderment as they skidded into another room and slammed the door. I was tempted to follow and see what the ruckus was, but I remembered my task. As captain, I had to stay focused. Besides, I was sure they'd bring it to my attention later.

As I neared the ladder, Judith appeared beside me. "No luck, Captain. None of us have found anything."

"Very well," I sighed, climbing up. "There's still a chance it's on the main deck."

"Listen... I know this is off topic, but is there a printing office in town?"

The question took me by surprise, and I turned to look at her as she ascended the last two steps of the ladder. "A printing office? Like...for books?"

She nodded, then held up the journal she'd bought with her share of the gold. "I've filled about a quarter of this, and I'm wondering if there's a way I could publish a book. I don't mind putting it under Jacob's name," she said quickly.

"Jacob's name? Why in the seven seas would you do that?"

"Well...it's often very difficult to get someone to publish for a woman," she explained. "Sometimes people don't allow it."

"That's ridiculous," I said. "You should try it here in Tortuga. I'm sure there's a printing press somewhere in town. And if they deny you, I'll slit their throats."

Judith's eyes went wide. "Oh no," she said, appalled. "Pray, don't do such a thing."

I clapped a hand on her shoulder, stopping myself from laughing. "Don't worry. I'll take the blame so it won't ruin your peaceful reputation."

Judith's eyebrows knit together, concerned, and she clutched the notebook to her chest. I left her standing there, wondering how I was going to make a fighter out of her.

Johnny and Wyatt had already joined Alexander on deck, and while the former two were deliberately searching, running their hands along the railing and pacing back and forth across the deck, Alexander was relaxing on a crate, leaning against the taffrail and engrossed in a book. I tried not to notice the way some strands of his hair fell in his face, or the way the candlelight lit up his features.

"Are you slacking, sailor?" I demanded as I strode up to him. "What's that?"

"Hmm?" He barely looked up from the small, old, leather-bound book in his hands. "Oh, this?" he said, finally registering my presence. He flipped a page. "It seems to be the journal of a man named Francais Drake, an English sailor in the 1500s. It's really quite interesting, actually." He went back to reading.

"Where'd you find it? The bookshelf in the captain's cabin?"

"The mast, actually."

I was taken aback. "The mast?" I repeated. "Like, *in* the mast?!"

He nodded like it was no big deal, and turned another page.

"Does it say anything interesting?" I asked, getting excited.

"Lots of things," he replied vaguely.

"Who was this Drake?"

"I already told you: a sailor."

"Why'd he keep the journal?"

"For a crucial, even *paramount* reason."

I pressed my hands to the side of my head and dug my nails into my hair. "*What* reason?"

"I guess you'd have to read it to find out." His voice was low and inviting, meant to spike my curiosity.

"Alexander!" I exclaimed.

"Yes, Your Highness?" He finally looked up, a playful grin on his face.

I folded my arms. "Tell me."

"*Je ne peux pas.*"

He said something else in his beautiful French—the educated man he was, I wasn't surprised he was fluent in a second language—but I could only pick out "ta bouche"—*your mouth.* Which made no sense...unless he wasn't talking about the book at all.

Warmth rose to my cheeks. "Don't use your French on me, sailor. Tell me in English!"

"*Pourquoi?*" He said, his voice as smooth as silk and his eyes shining with false innocence.

I narrowed my gaze. If he was going to use French to tease me, I'd have to brush up on it. "Are you toying with me?"

"Of course not!" His British accent was annoyingly alluring. "I would never keep important information *just* out of reach of my captain's fingertips."

I snatched the book out of his hands and looked at it myself. My eyes grazed down the delicate, yellow, wrinkled page, but I couldn't read a single word.

"Do you realize...it's upside-down?"

I glanced up to see his amused smirk, and flipped the book over, annoyance bubbling in my stomach. *This man!* Why did he have to be like this? The cursive was much too messy, but I pretended to be able to read it. Xander leaned back with his arms resting on the railing, clearly enjoying this. I glared at him.

"Make any progress?"

"Tell me what it says."

He laughed. "Well, I don't know. Nothing interesting so far. You'll have to let me read it more so I can find out."

"You mean you were just bluffing that entire time?!" I threw the book at him, and he managed to catch it before it hit the grin off his face.

"Careful, careful, it's a two century old artifact we have here!"

I plopped down on the crate next to him, trying to maintain my annoyance while he read a few more pages. My eyes drifted from the book, tracing along his jawline and down to his full lips. But even as I realized what I was doing, I couldn't stop. *Damn it, Cassandra. Get your wits together.*

Xander glanced sideways at me, and I quickly narrowed my eyes again, folding my arms in a threatening way. He went back to reading, a few moments later he leaned forward, his interest caught.

"What?" I demanded, then softened my voice. "Pray tell me this time."

"As you wish. But only because you asked nicely." He chuckled before continuing, his finger on the page. "He writes here that he was planning an attack on a town called Nombre de Dios..."

"An attack?" I said eagerly. "What for?"

"Erm... it was where the Spanish were temporarily moving their gold—"

"Gold?" I scooted closer to him, accidentally letting our shoulders brush in my excitement.

"Gee, Cass, you're never going to let me finish." But he smiled anyway.

"Sorry, sorry, keep going!" I gushed, possessed by an excitement I hadn't felt in a long while.

Johnny, Wyatt, and Judith crept closer to listen in, and the boy beside me gently turned another yellowed page, his eyes scanning down it. He flipped a couple more, then found what he was looking for. "It looks like he and his men ended up capturing the town and its loot. But..." His eyes scanned down the page. "The Spanish sent backup and Drake was injured in the ensuing fight. It says here:

'My comrades decided to flee when they saw I was bleeding profusely from the wound. They carried me back to my ship, but unfortunately the gold was left behind in their hurry to escape. Words cannot express my disappointment. We lost men—'

Let's see... He goes on to talk about all the effort that went into it, etcetera, etcetera..."

My heart sank. If he lost the gold, then it couldn't have been the next clue. If there was no treasure, there would be no map. "Did they ever get it back?" I asked.

He was quiet for a moment, focused. I tried to stay patient as he flipped a couple more pages.

"No. He stayed in the area trying to raid more Spanish ships, with little to no luck."

I heaved a sigh, suddenly drained. I slid off the barrel and sulked over to the stairs, sitting heavily down upon them. What were we going to do now? I had never let my hopes get so high as a moment ago, but now everything came crashing down.

Alexander flipped to the back of the journal, and I watched his face as he scanned the last page. I watched as his eyes widened, his lips parting as he drew in a quick breath. But I didn't let my hopes jump again as he found my eyes.

"Do you have an ancestor named Matthais Rackham?" He asked me, as if the answer would make everything make sense.

I had a sarcastic comment on the way, but just then my mum stuck her head out of the hatch and said, "Matthais Rackham?"

"Yes," Xander replied, standing up. "Drake gave his journal, *this* journal, to his most trusted companion, Matthais *Rackham*, so that, and I quote, 'he may have some better fortune than I.'"

*Fortune.* The gears in my head started turning.

"That was Jack's last name," Anne said, lifting herself out of the hatch and stepping toward him, interested. "Where'd ye find that journal?"

He told her, and she walked over to the mast and felt for the notch. Soon a tiny compartment opened, just big enough for the book. "Matthais Rackham," she repeated, then shook her head. "Name don't ring a bell. But if he's yer ancestor," she told me, "that explains how Jack ended up with it. But 'e couldn't read, so I guess 'e stashed it away here until 'e could find a trusty translator."

"Fortune," I emphasized, standing up and walking over toward them.

"It means good luck," Alexander informed me.

"No," I insisted. "The map said, 'All rejoicing will turn to mourning when the *fortune* you seek becomes your greatest misfortune.'"

"He's talking about the treasure," Judith said, her eyes alight.

"But Drake lost the gold," I said, thinking back, my heart sinking once more. "It must be a coincidence."

"Lost the gold?" Anne demanded.

I relayed the story to her, and she started pacing, her index finger resting on her chin. "Does it say anythin' else? Did 'e get some other treasure an' bury it?"

"I haven't finished reading," Xander told her.

"Well, get to work, boy!"

Xander rolled his eyes and returned them to the scribbled writing.

I heard laughter coming from down below and turned my head in time to see the last two members of my crew pushing a barrel through the hatch. Once they were both standing on the deck, holding the lid down, they looked up at all of us, recognizing that something had happened.

"What'd we miss?" Preston said breathlessly.

"What's in the barrel?" I returned.

"A vile creature," Jacob said, his voice full of warning.

A great deal of scratching and high-pitched whining came from within. I tried to imagine a creature that would make that sound, but I came up dry.

"Would you like to see?" Preston said happily.

"Absolutely!" Alexander said eagerly, leaving a finger between the pages as he shut the journal.

"I don't think we should let it out," Jacob argued, flipping his hair out of his eyes. "*You* know how hard it was to catch that thing!" he said to Preston.

"I know, but it would be so funny to see it run around on deck!"

Jacob nodded thoughtfully. "We'd have to close the hatches, and block the stairs."

"What kind of creature is it?" Judith asked timidly. "Will it eat us?"

I couldn't help but laugh, it was such a ridiculous statement. The barrel was small, about half the size of a normal one. There was no way a creature that small could ever eat someone.

"Don't fret, Starlet, I will protect you," Jacob reassured her with a dramatic hand to his chest.

"Ready?" Preston asked him. "Three, two, one—"

They removed the lid and kicked the barrel over, and there was a flash of gray as the skinniest cat I'd ever seen raced out and around the deck, its tail straight up.

Preston laughed with delight. I chuckled, and Jacob lunged for the stairs.

"Get the other one!" he yelled, and Alexander rushed past me to the other flight, sending the cat in the opposite direction.

"How in the name of Henry Avery did that thing get on here?" I asked, bewildered.

"I dunno, but it'd be great target practice," Anne said, whipping out her pistol and cocking it back.

"No!" Judith cried, stepping in front of my mother with her arms spread protectively.

Anne sighed, pouting. "Fine. See if ye can calm it down. Jacob an' Pedro—"

"Preston," he corrected. "How on earth did you confuse *Preston* with *Pedro*?"

She waved him off. "We were in the midst o' figurin' out the location o' the treasure when ye two interrupted. That boy—" she pointed to Alexander— "found a lovely journal that'll give us some answers."

The boy's eyes widened at Xander. "Really?" Preston said, bounding over to his best friend. "What've you found? What's it say?"

"I'm getting there," he told him. "Haven't found anything useful except that it was gifted to Cass's ancestor." He looked at me. "Can I see the map?"

"The map? Why do you need it?"

"Trust me," he challenged.

I hesitated. *Fine.* Challenge accepted. I pulled it out from beneath my waistcoat and handed it to him.

He unfolded it and held it next to the open journal in his other hand. "See the length of the tails in the p's?" He pointed to a word in the book, and then in the riddle. "And the slant of the general writing—it matches in both cases. The o's, in addition, are all written with a little hook on top. The cursive is nearly identical," he concluded. "Written by the same man."

"Which means he *did* end up finding treasure!" I exclaimed joyfully.

He nodded smartly, holding out the book to me. "Correct. Now if you'll hold this for me, I'll take a closer look at the map."

I held the old journal in my hands, shifting my weight back and forth in excitement. I looked at the bottom right corner where his finger tapped on the crinkly old paper.

"See the scale bar?" He used his fingers to measure the width of the strip of land. "Approximately forty kilometers. There's a lake there, and a couple of small islands off the coast.

The village has a name that looks Spanish. Or Portuguese..."
He tapped a finger against his chin.

I smiled. I could easily imagine him strolling through a fancy college, carrying all his books.

"We're looking for somewhere along the coast of South America," he concluded.

I traded him the journal for the map. My finger found the red X, and I wondered what treasures lay beneath it.

Alexander flipped to the back of the journal again. We were all silent and waiting, except for the cat, who was pathetically meowing in Judith's arms. As Xander continued reading, anticipation pumped through my veins.

The clock ticked by.

"Just a minute... I think this is it!" he finally announced.

I leaned in, and everyone gathered 'round.

He cleared his throat. "We took as much as we could carry, but the jungle was dense, so we were left with no other choice than to bury the rest of the loot, consisting of about nineteen tons of gold, silver, and other valuables."

*Nineteen tons?* My mind swirled with imaginations: piles of gold coins, long lost royal crowns, silver bars, necklaces weighed down with gems, treasure chests filled with solid gold chalices. My heart beat faster with anticipation.

"Keep readin'," Anne ordered. "We need to know where 'e went to find this gold, where 'e buried it."

Preston sat beside him on the next step, reading over his shoulder, as Alexander flipped back a couple more pages, read some, and then repeated that action.

Finally, Alexander looked up, directly into my eyes. "The Spanish Main. East coast of the Isthmus of Panama."

# Chapter 29

JONATHAN BARNET WAITED expectantly. When the bird came, he caught it easily. The pigeon was used to this routine, and put up no fight. The little paper he unrolled from its leg was small, the writing even tinier. "Docked in Tortuga," it read. "Still no suspicions. Rackham's here for a reason. Haven't found out what. More updates to come."

Barnet nodded to himself, unsatisfied. On his way back inside, he dropped the slip of parchment in the brazier. No one was to know of his plans for the island. It was time to harvest his golden goose.

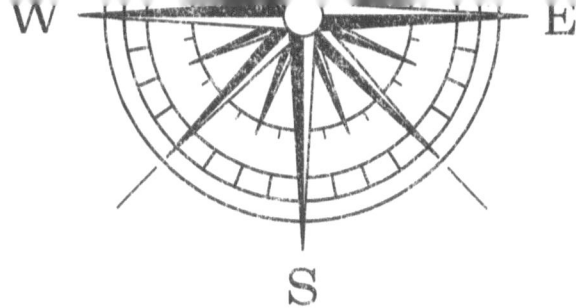

# Chapter 30

I FOUND MYSELF in the town's biggest tavern. Preston had lured Alexander, Judith, Jake, and I with the promise of the best custard in the Caribbean—a celebration of a hard day's work.

We'd shown Naomi the journal—told her everything—and come to an agreement. She'd receive twenty-five percent of the plunder, in exchange for *The Kingston*, and I could divide up the rest of the treasure as I saw fit. She put together the rest of the crew, and we'd spent the entire day getting the ship ready to sail—loading her down with food and supplies.

The room was filled with sweaty, merry people, dancing along to the fiddles and lyres that played a lively tune from the corner of the room. I spied Johnny a few tables down, closer to the bar. I held the spoon to my lips and slurped the sweet, ice-cold French custard. It was the best thing I had ever tasted, and my eyes rolled up with delight.

"Glorious," Alexander murmured from his seat next to me as he dug into his own bowl.

"Told you it was good," Preston said, a big grin on his face. "They freeze it with salt and ice from up north. When I first came here, I was surprised they had it. So far, the only other place I've found ice cream is in France." He had ordered lemon custard, a trifle, a cocoplum scone, and a piece of fruitcake for his supper.

"Can we bring some of this on the trip?" Judith asked.

"There's no way," I scoffed. "We can hardly keep fruit fresh for a few days, let alone frozen cream."

"I think I'll pack some fruitcake, though. It can last a good week," Preston said.

"Are you kidding me?" Alexander chuckled. "That stuff could last for *years*."

I laughed. "Maybe we should start to pack it instead of hardtack."

Judith motioned to all the sweets in front of Preston. "You're going to get sick, you know."

"Naw," he replied, before stuffing his mouth full once again. He slapped Xander's wandering fingers away from his scone, and Xander laughed. It was such a care-free, cheerful sound that my heart leapt.

Hearing a gasp, I looked up to see Johnny perched atop his table, surrounded by curious townspeople. "'S true," he continued, his speech slurred by all the rum he'd consumed. He lifted the mug to his lips and took another gulp. "Nineteen tons o' gold. I'll be richer dan yer chocolate mousse." He tried to snag the dessert out of a man's hand, but he missed and almost toppled off of the table.

The chair legs grated loudly against the floor as I stood up, my eyes narrowed. I strode over to him as another man asked, "Is the trip over going to be very long?"

Johnny shook his head, his drink sloshing against the sides as he adjusted himself. "Naw, 's only in Pa—"

I dragged him off the table and yanked the mug out of his grasp as Alexander announced, "Trying to impress the ladies with your fabricated tales again, are we, Johnny?"

A few of the onlookers chuckled and turned away, no longer interested.

But I was fuming. Before Alexander could guide him away, I hissed in Johnny's ear, "What do you think you're doing?! You want to put a target on our backs?"

Johnny reached his arms behind him to feel his own back. "There ain't one on me," he slurred.

Alexander shook his head in bewilderment and pulled him toward our table. I glanced over my shoulder and spotted the man that had asked about the trip. I faltered. His pale gray irises were too familiar, his forehead excessively large. Our eyes locked for a second before I turned away, my heart hammering.

My mind whirled with unanswered questions. In the bar on New Providence Island, had I seen the same man? Had we been followed? I pulled out a chair for Johnny and sat down in mine, risking a glance over at the table we had just left, but I couldn't find the man. *His shoes.* Did he have the same shoes as the man in *Harris and Burton's*? Had he been hiding behind his newspaper and eavesdropping while Alexander read the riddle? The thought sent anxiety through me like a lightning bolt. I fanned my face, the room suddenly becoming too warm for me to bear.

"Everything will be fine," Alexander assured me.

"We need to go," I told him, yanking Johnny up once again and dragging him with me by the collar of his shirt.

"But you haven't even finished your ice cream!" Preston said. He crammed the last of his scone into his mouth and washed it down with his melted custard.

Alexander left some coins on the table and everyone pushed their way through the crowded room and out into the evening air. I waited until we were out of earshot of anyone nearby before saying, "That man. I've seen him before. I think he's been following us." I rubbed my knuckles worriedly.

"Are you certain?" Xander asked.

"'Course 'e has," Johnny mumbled, swaying as he walked. "'E was so impressed by my—by my—my storytelling." He giggled.

"Shut your—arghhh!" I clenched my fists, barely restraining myself from punching him. "You are banned from alcohol. Usually, it's your choice what you do on land, but you've just lost that privilege. Thanks to you, we may have a gold digger on our heels."

"A gold digger?" Preston asked, surprised.

"Aye," I huffed. "Some sneaky landlubber who thinks he can weasel his way to riches if he follows the *experienced* pirates. Whatever the case, we need to leave the island immediately. Thanks to *Mister Tipsy*, our tail knows how much gold we're going to find and possibly where to find it. He might've even heard the riddle."

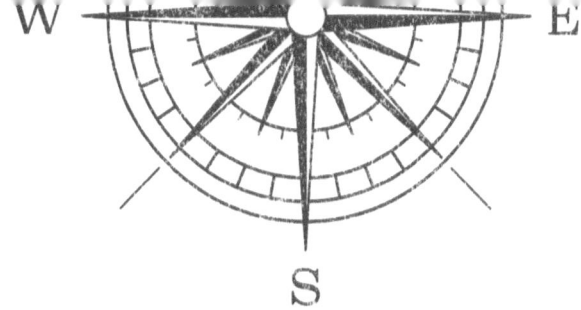

W · E

S

# Chapter 31

T HREE DAYS LATER, *The Kingston* and her crew were finally ready for the voyage. *Three days.* We'd cut the preparation short, working long hours to get her ready to sail, but I still felt like ants had infested my boots. Whenever I wasn't working, I was pacing. Was that gold digger alone? *Wouldn't he ask to join us, then, to get a share of the treasure?* He couldn't possibly imagine he could steal it all on his lonesome. But if he was a spy—who was he spying for? Were they loyal to the Pirate King, or an outsider?

I was anxious to weigh anchor, but Naomi insisted the new members would get tonight to say goodbye to their families. The following dawn, we'd set sail.

I stood in my quarters staring at the impressive array of outfits hung up in my wardrobe. Naomi had outdone herself. I didn't think I needed half of these, especially because a few were actual *dresses.* When would I ever need a dress on a ship?

Powerless until tomorrow, I sulked out of my room, needing a fix for my boredom. Halfway down the steps, I spotted

Alexander moving towards one of the hatches, a bundle of swords in his arms. Suddenly I was tumbling down the last of the stairs. I only had time to realize that I'd tripped over my own feet before I hit the main deck, rolling to absorb the impact. I layed on the ground, groaning. Not because it was painful, but because it was the most embarrassing thing I had done since making him give me his shirt. *Congratulations, Alexander. You get to witness all of Cassandra's mortifying moments. Can I die now?*

I heard the clatter of weapons as Alexander set down the bundle and strided towards me. He stopped at my head and bent over with his hands on his knees, eyebrows knitting together with concern.

*Holy seas*, Freida was right. He *did* look good in red. The open V-neck of his shirt showed part of his chest and two handsome flintlock pistols were tucked into a black baldric across his torso. His hair was cropped shorter and his blue eyes sparkled with amusement.

I pointed upwards at him, my cheeks flushed. "If anyone finds out about what just happened, I *will* demote you."

He laughed. "What could have caused such a tumble, I wonder?" He grabbed my hand, stepped around me, and hoisted me back on my feet. *Oh dear.* He smelled lovely. Campfire smoke and new leather and a fresh salty sea breeze.

I swallowed. "Your makeover," I managed, deciding to cut my misery short and own it. I stepped back and returned a smirk. "I was surprised you'd ever accept one. I thought you preferred looking like a poor, lost sailor."

"I figured since I'm now technically illegal, I might as well dress the part."

I grinned. "You'd look good on the Wanted posters." That made him frown, but I just laughed, picking up the bundle of weapons and placing them back in his arms. "I'm only joking.

With all the gold we'll be finding, we'll be set for decades. You may never even have to raid a ship."

He smiled again. "My family... they won't have to worry about money anymore."

I nodded, then motioned to the swords in his arms. "This reminds me, I need to stock my quarters with more weapons. The ratio of clothing to steel is far too skewed."

———◦✦◦———

My entire sleepy-eyed crew was gathered on the main deck of *The Kingston*. It was just before dawn, but from inside the cave, there was no indication of the hour. I folded my arms, my gaze traveling across a group of about forty. Naomi had traded her fancy dress for colorful, flowy pants and a silk shawl. My gaze snagged on Alexander—in the same outfit as the day prior. My stomach fluttered, but I ripped my eyes away from him and cleared my throat.

I took a moment to appoint positions—Alexander as the sailing master, Anne as my first mate, and a couple other important ones—and then clapped my hands. "Raise the Jolly Roger! All hands make sail! It's high time we get underway!"

A cheer went up and everyone rushed to their positions. I went to stand by the mainmast to watch the Jolly Roger being hoisted up, but I spied something that didn't belong on the black flag. "Halt!" I commanded, before reaching up and inspecting it. "What is *that*?!" I exclaimed. To the left of the skull was a little painted magenta heart. I wrinkled my nose.

Judith stepped up beside me and shrugged shyly. "It needed some warmth to it."

"Warmth?!"

Xander chuckled. "It's cute."

I stamped my foot. "When were we ever going for *cute*? Someone hand me some black paint."

"Come now, Cassandra, no one else is going to notice. Let her keep it."

I glared at him, then huffed. "Fine. But no more painting my flag, *Miss*." I turned my glare to her.

She nodded quickly. "Yes, ma'am."

"Captain," I corrected her. "Now run off and be helpful while we finish getting this flag in the air."

## Chapter 32

THE MORNING SUN was just peeking out from behind the horizon by the time the two warships confronted the fog. His spy had informed him of the population size and strength of the protective walls. His man-o-wars had enough artillery to take down the cannons and gates, and enough men to capture or kill every man, woman, or child who stood up against him. Up until four days ago, his officers weren't aware he knew where the pirate island was. They just thought he was lucky to find all of those pirate sloops. Really, he had been ingenious. He'd placed a spy on the island that would inform him of each ship's destination, and all he had to do was intercept them.

But like every man on this earth, he was growing old. A sprawling mansion on the rolling grass hills of his home country sounded increasingly appealing. So did the handsome reward the King would grant him for the seizure of the entire pirate lair. And once he had taken the island, he'd blockade the only harbor and hunt for Rackham and her treasure map.

Barnet stood on the bow of his ship as it headed into the wall of dense vapor. Suddenly his lookout cried, "Sail, ho! Off the port side!"

Barnet turned his gaze sharply left, and spotted a dark set of sails near the horizon. He lifted his spyglass to his eye and studied the ship. A black flag—he could just make out the skull and crossbones. He clenched his jaw and moved his lens downward to the name: *The Kingston*.

It was Rackham.

The girl had somehow obtained her dead father's wrecked ship. Frustration boiled inside of him, because he was forced to make a choice: take the island or take the treasure.

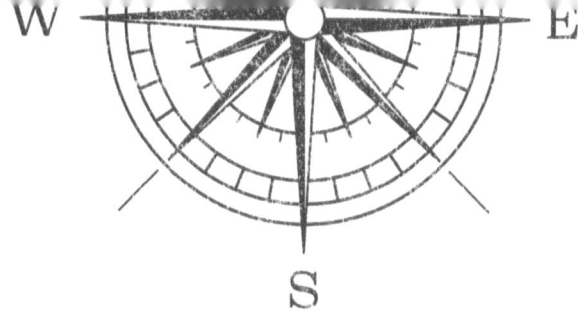

*Chapter 33*

THE CREW WAS GATHERED around a long table in the mess hall, which was located next to the kitchen, near the bow of the boat. Of course, the table couldn't fit everyone, so many had pulled up crates and barrels for makeshift chairs. Circular ports provided a view of the glittering waves as we sailed away from the pirate haven. The table was heaped with fresh breakfast food—some of the last we'd see for a fortnight—in celebration of our departure. I sat at the head of the table, in a jolly mood as my teeth sank into a ripe mango, juice dribbling down my chin.

"Here, Cuddles!" Judith called in a high-pitched voice, leaning over until she disappeared beneath the table. "Cuddles, I have your breakfast!" Finally the aging gray cat streaked out of the corner and over to its new owner, lapping up the milk she had offered.

I scoffed. "You're ridiculous. I can't believe—why in the seven seas would you name it *Cuddles?*"

She shrugged. "The name just... called to me."

"You know what name calls to *me*?" Preston chuckled. "Beastie. Here, Beastie!" he sang.

"I still think it'd be more useful as target practice," Anne said. "It's eating our food."

Judith shot a stink eye at my mother. "No disrespect, Quartermaster, but Cuddles is a living soul, just as worthy as you or I. If *you* would like to be used as target practice, then by all means, shoot my cat."

My jaw dropped. Was I hearing things, or did Judith just issue a threat?

"Feisty," Jake grinned.

I chuckled. "I'm proud of your progress, Judith, but no threatening my Quartermaster."

"She threatened me first," Judith retorted.

"I threatened no one!" Anne exclaimed.

I rolled my eyes. "Shut your gobs, you two. Save it for after breakfast."

Judith glanced down. "Oh! He's licked his plate dry. He must be still hungry. Preston, would you mind fetching the milk pail in the kitchen?" She scooped the cat up and coddled it.

Preston, the gentleman he was, left his plate of eggs and toast and walked through the galley door. "I'll do it for Beastie!"

"His name is *Cuddles*," Judith insisted. It resisted her snuggles and attempted to reach for her meal.

"Get that away from the table," I ordered.

Judith reluctantly set it down when a crash from the kitchen sent it scampering away, its hair standing on end. Another crash and a yelp sounded from the galley.

"Is everything all right in there?" Xander called.

"Do milk jugs usually have eyes?" Preston responded.

Xander pushed himself up and left the mess hall, looking to see what the matter was. Both boys returned, each holding two girls by the arm.

I blinked. "You're not supposed to be here."

Naomi stood up. "Children," she spoke fiercely, causing the girls to cower a little. Then she took a deep breath, calming her voice to a stern manner. "I told you you could not come. Why did you disobey me?"

"We couldn't stay," Emerald argued.

Ruby nodded. "You were going to leave us!"

"And you were hunting for treasure," Jade added.

Pearl brightened. "Will we get to use swords?"

"Hopefully not," I told them, irritated. "Why did you stow away? Now we have *five* extra mouths to feed."

"Not to mention more children to look after," Anne added dourly.

"We're not children!" Jade protested, jerking her arm out of Xander's grasp. "We can be valuable members of the crew."

"We'll help you sail!" Ruby said earnestly.

I looked up again, into their determined brown eyes. "How old are you?"

"Fifteen," they answered.

I nodded slowly.

"You can't be much older than us," Pearl noted pointedly, her chin held high.

"I'm old enough. Since you're inexperienced and are the youngest of our crew, you can be our powder monkeys in times of battle. You'll be expected to do as much work as anyone else on board, and you shall refer to me as 'captain.' Savvy?"

"Yes, Captain," they nodded.

"Now pull up some crates and have a seat. You need a good breakfast for your work today."

I finished my meal early and went to switch out the helms-man so he could fuel up as well. I climbed through the opening at the top of the stairs, and a gust of wind fluttered through my hair. I smiled, striding toward the side of the ship and leaning out over the rail. All that was left of Tortuga was a tiny gray smudge of fog in the distance, and two ships lingering beside it. I frowned. From here, an average pirate sloop would appear only as a speck. These were... I raised my spyglass to my eye and gazed through it. *Holy seas.* English-built man-o-wars: frigates, the second fastest warships out there. How in the name of Henry Avery did someone manage to seize *two*? Any pirate with a drop of sanity would steer clear of such a ship—it just had too many cannons. A broadside from one would decimate an average sloop. I raised the glass higher, and my heart sputtered.

British flags.

The man-o-wars had British flags. The blood drained from my face and my hands turned clammy. And the flag-ship... There was no mistaking the banner that fluttered just below the nation's colors, a strip of canvas with forked ends like the tongue of a serpent. Indigo, with seven white slash marks. My knees weakened and I reached out to the rail for support. *How? How had he found Tortuga so quickly?*

I took a shaky breath to calm myself as I counted the white slash marks again. *Embarrassed about the last ship you captured, eh? Didn't want to count it to your record?*

I stuffed the spyglass back into my pocket and turned on the spot, my mind whirring. How in the seven seas did Barnet get his hands on two British man-o-wars?! Who had informed him of Tortuga's location? With a sinking stomach, I remembered the man that had been following me since New Providence. Did he have something to do with this? If he worked for Barnet, how would he communicate with him while on Tortuga? Everything had happened in such quick succession—it seemed only a fortnight ago that Barnet was demanding the pirate haven location from my old crew. Then I sank his blasted ship. *And somehow he obtains two man-o-wars and appears at the edge of the fog bank?* Plans of this magnitude take time to set into motion. *Something's not adding up.*

But one thing was for certain: Tortuga was in trouble. Did they have enough defenses to fend off two warships of that size? Dread settled in the pit of my stomach as I climbed the companionway to the helm. *Nay.* Tortuga was a small town. If they were caught unawares and the man-o-wars somehow got into the harbor, the men on those ships would most certainly overpower them.

"I'll take the helm, Patterson. Report to the mess hall for your meal."

"Aye, Captain."

I gripped the handles tightly, taking a little comfort in the texture of the polished wood. I stood alone, the weight of worry pressing on my shoulders, while the rest of the crew celebrated down below. *Is this my fault? Should I turn back to defend them?* If we fought bravely, we could possibly take down one frigate before they sank us. I shook my head, guilt pressing down on my heart. Going back would be suicide. And the treasure would stay buried, never to be found.

Tears threatened to come to my eyes, but I stayed the course. Tortuga was my home, and I was abandoning it to the mercy of my greatest enemy. *How could I?* Anger bubbled up in my stomach. Barnet had taken nearly everything from me.

I clenched my jaw. *He will not now take my home.*

I tied a rope to the wheel to keep it in place and marched to the side of the boat. Once more, I lifted the spyglass to my eye and peered through it, gazing back at the fog. It had grown considerably smaller, but the odd thing was...the man-o-wars had not. I studied them more closely, and even though they were far away, it was clear that the ship's bows were now pointed toward me. I lowered the glass, taken aback. That meant...the ships were traveling away from the island.

I thought harder. Did the fog scare them away? Perhaps they thought they had come to the wrong place. Or did they decide they needed backup? And then it hit me like a cannon shot: Barnet was after *us*. He must've recognized this ship—or seen the name. I chewed my lip. *Or...Barnet was just informed of our departure*. Things started clicking into place.

There was never a golddigger. There was only Jonathan Barnet's spy.

Was the slimy, hypocritical captain after *my* treasure?

A few minutes later, I raised the spyglass again, and it confirmed my suspicions. Barnet's two ships hadn't changed direction, although we'd gained a little more distance between us.

I walked back to the helm and removed the rope. I had a new potential disaster on my hands: *The Kingston* couldn't fend off two man-o-wars if they closed in for an attack. I considered my options. I could lead him on a wild goose chase, but we would eventually run out of food. I could abandon the treasure all together and pick a different month to hunt for it. I could try to lose him. A well-built galleon like *The Kingston* could outrun such ships.

*Aye.* That would be the option I would take. I had waited too long for this treasure and I wasn't in the mood for another set back. But outrunning them came with another problem: depending on how far we got ahead, Barnet might catch up while we were on land, trapping us.

I thought long and hard about our situation, and soon I heard my crew coming up from below decks. I took one last look over the side. Barnet's ships hardly seemed to have moved. Tortuga and the fog that surrounded it was hardly visible, and the ships were hovering near the horizon. I narrowed my eyes. Had he changed his mind and headed back? I imagined myself in his shoes. If I knew that he was following us, I might head in another direction. So if I were him, I'd want the element of surprise. I'd stay mostly out of sight, until I needed to check the bearing again.

Well, easier for us.

I turned to my crew, who were gathered on deck, and decided to keep the information from them for the time being. I didn't want them to worry until I'd figured out a plan. "Harwood! Crows nest," I shouted. "Hop to it, now. Davies, Fetherston, and you lot"—I gestured in their general direction—"Unfurl the rest of the sails! We can get a little more out of this wind."

There was a chorus of "Aye, aye!"s and men scrambled up the rigging to let the sails down. The ship lurched forward at a faster pace. If Barnet wanted to follow us, I wouldn't make it easy for him.

———◦•◦———

I fiddled with the divider in my hands as I sat at the square chart table. Two small metal rods were connected at one end by a little screw, making two legs of a triangle. I placed the pointed ends on the map in front of me. The tool was used to measure nautical distance, but Alexander had figured the distance a long time ago. Now I just made it walk back and forth across the parchment, my mind grasping at solutions.

I heard the door open and looked up to see my sailing master's form in the doorway. He looked as fetching as ever, but my heart was elsewhere, weighed down with hopeless thoughts of failure, bloodshed, and the hangman's noose. One road was a dead end. The other was cowardice.

"I've been searching for you."

I sighed, returning my gaze to the maps. "Whatever for?"

"You've been out of sorts since you left breakfast." He walked over and took the chair next to me.

"I'm fine."

He took the divider from my hands and slid the map over to himself. "Thought I already helped you with this."

I didn't answer.

"You can trust me, remember? I've done the measurements. We're on the right course."

"I know."

"Are you looking forward to finding the treasure?"

I glanced at him. He was smiling, but I didn't have the strength to return the gesture. "Aye. It will make us all rich." But my voice lacked the enthusiasm that phrase should have brought.

"Are you certain you are well?"

I was quiet for a moment. No one else knew that Barnet was tailing us. Would the information cause him to lose sleep? I doubted he could help if I told him, but it was becoming a difficult burden to bear alone.

"You're anxious. What is it?" he prodded gently.

I turned my head to look at him solemnly. "We're being pursued."

His brow furrowed. "By whom?"

I swallowed hard. "British ships. Barnet."

"Are you sure?"

"As sure as I am that you're next to me."

He was quiet for a moment, and then determination filled his eyes. "We'll fight him. We won't let him win."

I put my elbows on the table and my face in my hands. "Alexander, he's brought two heavily armed frigates. One hundred and twenty cannons between the two of them. Probably close to three hundred men."

He whistled.

"There's no way we'll come out on top. It'll be a slaughter."

"How would he know about the treasure? How did he find our whereabouts?"

"He must have a spy. And I think I know who it is."

"The man you spotted on Tortuga? The man who was following us?"

I nodded.

"But why did Barnet want to know where Tortuga was if he already had a spy there?"

I frowned. "Good question."

"And isn't he all about honor and ridding the world of pirates? Why would he rather chase after us if he had a whole pirate island he could imprison?"

I gritted my teeth. "Because he's a blasted hypocrite. A proud, black hearted, greedy little—"

"We could lead him elsewhere," Alexander suggested, interrupting my tirade.

I shook my head. "I don't want to abandon the treasure now. After all this time and effort? I shall not."

"We could turn around and chase him down. If we timed it right, we could attack in the night and surprise him."

I ran the situation out in my mind and sighed. "That wouldn't work."

"We could strike a deal with him once we reach the island. If I tell him of my father—"

I laughed without humor. "You forget who we're dealing with. You forget what you've become. As long as you're with me, he won't see you as a diplomat and honest sailor. The day you decided to sail with me to Tortuga was the day you became an outlaw."

He looked down, and I could tell it pained him to hear. Oddly, I didn't think he ever truly accepted it. It was a wonder he chose to sail with me in the first place, if he so strongly despised piracy.

He locked his gaze on me once again. "Well then, what are you going to do?" He said it like he was issuing a challenge—or maybe he was tired of me refusing his ideas.

I stared at him. "I don't know."

"Cass, knowing you, you'll think of something. It'll work out, one way or another." He stood up, determined. "I'll alert the crew. We'll train them harder—"

"No."

"Pardon?"

I rubbed my knuckles. "I don't want them to worry until I have a plan. We need to keep their hopes up and their motivation high. Can I trust you to speak of this to no one?"

"We need them to be battle ready," he argued.

"Then we'll make them battle ready. But I don't want to fight him if I can help it. We'd lose too many lives."

He chewed on that. Reluctantly he said, "Aye, Captain. I'll keep my mouth shut for now. But you better think of a more suitable plan soon, because I do not want them to be caught unawares if Barnet decides to attack us before we reach land."

I knew he was displeased with my decision, but I was grateful he'd respect my wishes anyway. I watched as he strode to the door and disappeared into the hall, a piece of me wishing he would stay.

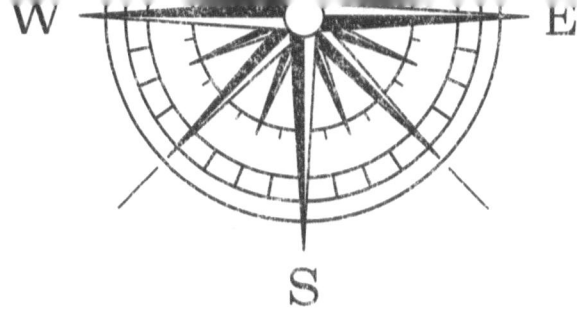

W E

S

*Chapter 34*

THAT NIGHT, MY WIRED BRAIN would not shut off. I laid in bed for hours, long past the time I should have been asleep. As captain, it was my responsibility for the safety and well-being of my crew. And many of them were...friends. Maybe someday, if we survived long enough, I'd consider them family. Had I really come that far as to believe that I could trust them? To my astonishment, I felt comfortable with that notion. They really were people I could trust.

But that meant if they died, a piece of me would die as well. I had brought them along—it would be my fault if they were harmed.

I pushed myself out of bed, deciding I needed something to take my mind off my troubles. I'd take a few laps around the main deck. Hopefully the night breeze would provide some manner of comfort.

I took one step, and the board underneath my foot creaked loudly. The last step of the lower deck's stairs made the same sound... when I was little, I'd learned to skip it. My eyes flitted around the room, memories flooding back to me. Mum telling me stories of old pirate adventures. Mary teaching me tricks. Father guiding my pistol. Those were good times, when we were all together. We'd play the most amusing games...

Suddenly I had the perfect way to distract myself.

I slipped out of my cabin door and out to the quarterdeck. We sat silently in the water, having dropped canvas late that evening. The wheel was tied with a rope, and the drift anchor was down, floating somewhere beneath us. The only person out here was Preston, taking his turn as the night watchman. He'd get a chance to sleep during the day, and Judith would take over the cooking.

I tiptoed down the stairs and stared out over the water. Barnet was there somewhere, floating just behind the horizon. If he had no plans of catching us before we reached our destination, there was no need to overwork the crew by having them sail the ship at night. Besides, it gave us more time to prepare. More time for me to come up with a foolproof plan that somehow got us the treasure *and* got us out alive. I turned and headed for the hatch. After all, a game couldn't be played alone.

I passed all the rows of hammocks quietly, and arrived near the back of the ship, where four small rooms were located, two on each side. When my father was captain, they were reserved for the higher ranks of the crew, but I gave them to my favorite people.

I treaded lightly down the narrow hallway and turned to a door on my right. After carefully lifting the latch, I tiptoed into the room. I lit the candle on the nightstand, so it cast a warm flickering light about the place. There were two sets of bunk beds against opposite walls, Preston's cot empty.

My gaze slid down to the boy in the bottom bunk. Alexander was sleeping on his stomach, his head turned to the side. Drake's journal rested on the nightstand next to him—he'd probably been reading it before he fell asleep. His expression was peaceful as he breathed softly, and it almost made me not want to interrupt his slumber. But my worries were not the company I needed. I crept forward and knelt beside him, hesitating before reaching out and shaking him lightly.

"Alexander," I softly whispered. "Wake up." I shook his shoulder once more.

His eyelashes opened just a crack, and when he registered my presence, he rolled over on his back and rubbed his eyes with one hand. "What is it?"

I opened my mouth to reply, but he abruptly pushed himself up. "Has Barnet snuck up on us?"

"Shhh," I commanded, putting a finger to my lips. "No. Everything's fine, besides the fact that I haven't figured out a solution."

He collapsed back onto the bed, and mumbled, "Were you watching me sleep?"

"What?" I was taken aback, my cheeks warming. "No!"

The corners of his lips rose despite his tired state. "Then why are you in my room?"

"I wanted to invite you to play a game."

He closed his eyes. "A game? In the middle of the night? You woke me up in the middle of the night to play a game?"

A tiny laugh escaped me. Was that a tad bit of frustration I detected in his voice? "It's called Dare or Dive."

He rolled over on his stomach and buried his face in his pillow. "I'm too fatigued."

"Did I hear 'Dare or Dive'?" a voice spoke from the other side of the room.

I looked over my shoulder to see Jake staring at me from the other bunk. Turning back to Xander, I leaned over until my lips nearly brushed his ear. "Alright, then. Me and Jake will go have some fun. Have a wonderful time *sleeping*."

Before I had time to back away, he turned his head—and suddenly his lips were a mere inch away. I froze, unable to breathe. He shifted himself onto one elbow so his lips grazed my ear instead. "You're so manipulative," he murmured.

I stepped back and struggled to gather myself, the edge of my ear tingling where his lips had touched it. "Pirate," I reminded him, managing to put a wicked little grin on my face.

Xander pushed himself up and swung his feet to the floor, his white cotton shirt twisted so a strip of his stomach was showing. His eyes met mine, and he slow-smiled.

Heart pounding, I backed up through the doorway and fled, knowing the boys would follow.

---

By the time we—including Judith and a very enthusiastic Preston—retired to our bunks, half of us were sopping wet, Alexander had little braids in his hair (which he couldn't remove until the following night), and Jake had the crew angry with him for running amidships and belting out "It's a Pirate's Life For Me."

That little game must've done some good, because I woke the next morning feeling lighter. When we got the ship sailing again, I stayed by the helmsman, gazing through my spyglass at the blue horizon behind us. Occasionally I could spy a little dot, who I knew was Barnet, but often the horizon was empty. I glanced up in the direction of the crows nest, wondering if our lookout would spot him.

As I closed my spyglass and returned it to my pocket, an idea struck me. It was so simple, so *brilliant*, I stood rooted to the spot. Why hadn't I thought of it before?

I turned and marched through my cabin door, suddenly filled with a buzzing energy. *Nineteen tons of gold...* I paced back and forth, mindlessly unloading and reloading a pistol as I went, my mind running through all the possibilities. *How long would it take a crew of forty to hike through the jungle with that much treasure? Now, if I had two hundred, three hundred men for the job...* I chewed my lip. If a single thing went wrong, lives could be lost. But if I planned it carefully enough, it could work out perfectly.

I put the pistol away and laid down on the bed, my back to a mound of pillows. I pulled out a little knife. I tossed it up, watching it spin once, twice, before reaching out and snatching it out of the air. *Barnet's not going to expect me to willingly give up the treasure.* I tossed it up again. *Now, if I had the right amount of leverage...* The rhythm of the knife kept my body calm while my mind worked through each and every detail.

I heard a knock on the door. "Enter," I called, sending the knife spinning in the air again. I glanced over at the man standing in the doorway, but my eyes caught on the sight of him longer than they should've, for a sharp pain erupted on the outer edge of my palm. "Damn it, Alexander!" I grumbled, holding my wrist. I kicked the knife away. "You distracted me."

"Apologies, Captain." He shut the door behind him and stepped forward. "I see that Barnet's keeping his distance. For now."

I pushed myself up and eyed him. He'd donned a blue-black shirt, and carried no weapons. "I like your hair," I chuckled. I wiped away the blood welling up on the side of my hand and winced.

"Has anything come to you?" he prompted, ignoring my comment and bleeding hand.

I leaned back on the pillows and motioned him closer. "I have an idea." I took a deep breath. "We let Barnet catch us."

He raised a brow, but waited for me to continue.

"We lead him into the forest." I made a walking motion with my fingers. "He catches us, and I trade the map for our freedoms. We scurry back to *The Kingston* and sail far enough away that it seems like we're leaving. But as soon as Barnet loads most of the treasure onto his ship, we surprise attack them and take the ship!" I clapped my hands, making him flinch. I sat forward and held up my finger before he could comment. "Now, if Barnet takes the map by force, that's the end of it for us. But, if I announce that I've memorized the map while it burns to cinders before his eyes... I can bargain."

He looked horrified. "We're speaking of a two-century old treasure map, and you want to *burn* it? It's a priceless piece of history—"

"Not priceless. *Nineteen tons of gold*," I reminded him. "Would you rather lose your bargaining power and dance the hempen jig?"

He folded his arms, displeased. "So you'll use your own life as leverage. Then he'll capture you and force you to lead him to the treasure."

"Destroying the map will buy me time," I countered. "Then I'll redraw it for him, so that I can hike down to the shore with you. That is, if Barnet keeps his word..."

"He will. He's a man of the Crown."

I wasn't so sure.

Xander thought some more. "If you're going to redraw the map anyway, we might as well make another copy now, so the original can be kept safe."

The corners of my lips lifted in spite of myself. What man cared as much for the parchment as the treasure it led to? "Keep the original, if you so desire."

His eyes widened. "You're not serious?"

I rolled my eyes. "Of course I'm serious. I know you want it."

His grin was ear to ear, and so warm it made my heart melt, despite the anxiety of the topic at hand. His gaze drifted. "Owen would love to see it..."

"Your brother?" I guessed.

He smiled.

I groaned, collapsing back onto the pillows.

"What's bothering you?"

"We need it to look authentic. Judith loves acting, but no one else really knows how. Especially if they felt like their lives were in danger. If Barnet suspects—"

"You're saying we keep them in the dark." Alexander frowned, scowling slightly. He obviously didn't like it. "What if someone gets hurt?"

"Then they would have gotten hurt anyway even if I *did* tell them about it."

"Not necessarily."

"Then I'll make sure it doesn't happen. I'll destroy the map before there's any fighting."

"What about your mother?"

"What about her?" I felt a slight twinge of guilt as I said that.

"She'd want to know."

"Anne's vengeful, and Barnet knows that. Don't you think it would look suspicious if she didn't try to kill him?"

Alexander still looked deeply troubled. "There are so many things that could go wrong."

I closed my eyes. "I know." If my mother succeeded in killing her mortal enemy at the wrong time, the plan would fail. If I didn't gain enough leverage against Barnet soon enough, he could kill *her*. It felt like everything was teetering on a swordpoint. But at the same time, what choice did I have? This was my only chance to find the treasure.

I had to take it.

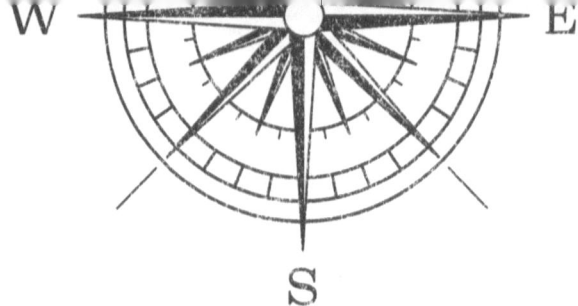

# *Chapter 35*

CLANG. THE SWORDS RANG as they clashed against each other. I stepped back, easily blocking Jake's thrust. "Good. Now, quicker. Don't worry about hurting me."

He paused, his sword dipping down as he wiped sweat off his upper lip. After almost a half hour of practicing, he was starting to tire. All the pirating novices were on the main deck, practicing as well. I was aware of Alexander a little ways away, instructing Judith.

"Again!" I insisted, raising my sword to strike Jake.

He caught the blow, his arms shaking a little.

"If you disarm me, you can rest," I told him.

"But I'll never disarm you," he panted, our swords meeting once again. "You're too good."

"If you think like that, you'll never defeat your attacker. I'll give you five minutes to knock the sword from my hand. Make use of the two disarming maneuvers I taught you. Fail, and you'll take that barrel over there and haul it up the stairs five times."

He nodded, attacking me with new vigor. Once five minutes was up, I left him to do his punishment while I walked around the deck, observing the other pairs of duelers. Naomi, dressed colorfully as always, stood nearby, instructing the quadruplets. Much to their delight, we hadn't loaded any wooden swords aboard, so they got to practice with real ones.

A little while later, I stood with my hips against the railing, watching Alexander with Judith. Something about the way he held his sword made the memory of our duel come rushing back to me. I shook my head, wondering how he'd outmaneuvered me.

"You're doing a fine job as an instructor," I complimented him when he finally made his way toward me.

He smiled, leaning against the taffrail with me. He had rolled up his sleeves and partly opened the front of his shirt. His skin glistened with sweat. "Thanks. You too."

I glanced up at the few sailors above us, who were adjusting the sails. They had to receive almost constant attention for the most efficient sailing. My mother was standing beside the helmsman, her hands behind her back, observing the crew as they worked. *A fine quartermaster.* I looked back at Xander and raised a brow. "Have you taught her the move you used on me?" I tried not to sound like I desperately wanted to learn it myself.

"The move that would've earned me my freedom, if you'd fought fairly?" He gave me a little sideways smirk, which I returned. "No. So far, it's still my secret."

"Teach me."

He leaned in. "Now, why would I lose the only upper hand I have over you?"

I knew he was teasing, but it still made me a little annoyed. "Oh, come on, Alexander. I'm your captain." I folded my arms and gave him an intimidating glare.

The corners of his lips lifted in an amused smile. "There *is* a possibility that I'll teach you, but..." his voice trailed off.

"But what?" I demanded.

He shrugged, still smiling that smile of his. "I see nothing in it for me."

I rolled my eyes and punched him in the shoulder. "You're not allowed to use my words against me." I had said the same thing to him when he'd asked for his freedom back on *The Mirage*.

He laughed. "Fine." And then, as if coming to a difficult decision, he added, "Perhaps in a few years."

I sighed exasperatedly. What would I have to say to make him teach me? I couldn't force him. I tried to recall how he'd responded all those weeks ago, when I'd told him I would let him go in a couple of years. I folded my arms again. "That's not going to work."

He leaned toward me and challenged, "Well, what are you going to do about it?"

"Hmm... I could just politely ask," I said, my voice buttery smooth. Then I gave him a wicked grin. "Or I could fight you."

Preston came skipping over, apparently having eavesdropped. "Asking would be easier," he informed me. "Just do this:" He knelt on one knee and dramatically held his sword, pointing down, out in front of him, as if presenting it to Xander. "Alexander Callaway, would you take me, Cassandra... er...what's your surname?" he murmured out of the corner of his mouth.

"Rackham," I said, bewildered.

Preston looked back to Alexander, who was looking like he was trying not to laugh. "Would you take me, Cassandra Rackham, to be your student in the fine art of fencing?"

Alexander couldn't hold it in any more, and burst out laughing.

I snorted. "I would rather yodel."

Preston grinned widely. "Let's make it a dare, then."

A *dare*?! There was no way I would ever kneel before Alexander and say *that*. I would die of embarrassment.

Preston leaned over the side of the boat, inspecting the water. "Yup! I think there are some sharks trailing us." He turned back to me and clapped his hands. "I guess you'll have to take it, then. Everyone! Gather round as the captain—"

I shoved my hat into Xander's hands. I didn't think about the sharks—or anything, really. I just knew I wasn't about to embarrass myself in front of the whole crew. I took a flying leap and vaulted over the side of the boat.

*Splash.* The cool water was a relief from the sweltering heat of the day. I pumped my arms, and when I breached the surface, I looked up to see my crew members gawking at me. I smirked at them, and realized belatedly that the boat was still moving. Jumping overboard was probably not the smartest idea. *But better than the alternative.* Charles tossed me a rope, and I grabbed it as a small shark glided up next to me, about three and a half feet long. Somebody shouted. My heartbeat quickened as I reached out and felt its rough sandpaper skin underneath my fingertips. It swam away, disappointed I hadn't been small enough to eat.

My crew hoisted me out of the water, and when my feet hit the deck, I looked around at them all as I squeezed the water from my hair. Shock and concern (and maybe a little admiration) was written all over their faces. I laughed. "How refreshing." I took my hat back from Alexander, who raised his eyebrows at me.

Beside him, Preston asked, "You'd rather be shark dinner than ask him to help you? That way would have worked, you know."

I rolled my eyes, a smile on my lips. "They're usually docile. That kind, anyway." I took a seat on an overturned crate and poured the water out of my boots. Although I sounded calm, my heart was pumping excitedly from the close encounter.

"Usually?" Alexander asked, concerned.

I grinned up at him as I slipped my boot back on.

He shook his head, unbelieving. "You are crazy."

I laughed. "That's what you love about me." I turned back to the rest of my crew to hide my burning cheeks. I'd tossed it out like it meant nothing, but it was like I was suddenly hanging one-handed from the rigging, my heart beating ferociously. "Back to work!" I ordered, so I didn't have to look at him. "What are you standing around for! Keep practicing!"

They scrambled to get back to their duties, either as sailors or students.

"I'll show you how I disarmed you," Alexander said behind me.

Surprised, I turned. "You will?"

He smirked and said, "If you stop being so reckless."

"No promises." I winked.

He smiled slowly. Held out his hand like a gentleman. I took it before another part of me had the chance to tell me to stop, and for a second, I found it hard to breathe. I didn't need help off that crate. What was I doing?

He pulled his sword out of its sheath. "The move I used on you is called the *prise de fer* technique. French origins. It requires precision, speed, and the element of surprise to catch your opponent off guard. We'll start by engaging in a civil swordfight, where I will demonstrate the move. Then I'll break it down for you." He stepped back and bowed, again like a gentleman. "Are you ready to begin?"

I bowed awkwardly, not used to the motion. "I was born ready."

One arm behind his back, he jumped forward, thrusting his sword. I caught it easily with mine, then countered. We danced around the deck, aware that a few people had halted their practicing to watch. He swiped at my leg, and I caught it just in time.

He *tsk*ed. "I'm losing my only advantage over you. I shouldn't teach you this."

I smiled as I feigned to one side and then attacked the other way. Sweat ran down my neck and mixed with my sea-water-soaked clothes. We were well-matched, and I *loved* it. I advanced, pushing him back.

"Don't worry, Cassandra. I'll find another."

"I doubt it." I grinned.

Alexander's blade met mine in a clash that sent a shiver up my arm. Before I could react, he shifted his wrist in a fluid, deliberate motion. His sword slid along the length of mine, maintaining pressure. Our blades remained locked, steel scraping in a sharp, metallic whisper as he guided my blade downward and across in a swift arc. My muscles tensed, remembering this.

With a sudden, masterful twist, Alexander's wrist flicked, sending a jolt of force through my sword. My fingers faltered as the pressure on my hilt shifted unpredictably. The sword flew from my grasp, clattering to the floor. It had happened so quickly, I was left stunned, my breath caught between admiration and irritation.

He smiled, victorious. "I love it when I win. On second thought, maybe I should keep this little trick to myself."

I scowled, picking up my sword. "I'll learn to counter it eventually."

"You're right. Besides, what other opportunity will *I* get to teach *you*?"

I pursed my lips, and he laughed at my expression. "Alright, alright. Here we go." He stepped forward and demonstrated the move in slow motion, until the point where the sword would fall from my grasp.

I nodded my understanding.

"The key," Alexander said, demonstrating again, "is to keep control of the blade whilst shifting the pressure subtly. Watch my wrist; it's all in the movement. You draw your opponent in, let them believe they're holding strong, and then twist—not with force, but with finesse. The blade slips from their grasp before they even know what's happened."

I mimicked his motion, my eyes narrowing in concentration. This time, I felt the shift of power in my wrist, the promise of control, and I knew I was close.

"Perfect," Alexander said. "Again."

We practiced for a good while, until Alexander stepped back, his sword raised, and said, "*En garde.*"

*Alright, then. Time to put this skill to the test.*

We were once again dancing around each other, swords clashing, while I searched for an opportunity to use what he'd taught me. I forced him backwards until his back hit the rail. The moment I caught his sword with mine, I knew it was time. His eyes told me that he knew it as well.

I didn't hesitate.

Our swords glided in an arc through the air, steel hissing like angry snakes. *More pressure.* Then I twisted, and the blade dropped from his hand. I panted, a pleased smile forming on my lips.

Alexander's eyes sparkled with pride as he murmured, "Well done." His voice was warm, low enough that it sent a shiver down my spine. Before I could respond, his hands found my waist, steady and confident, pressing gently to guide me back. My breath hitched, heart pounding so fiercely I wondered if he could feel it through the fabric of my tunic. Time seemed to pause for that fleeting moment, every nerve in my body attuned to his touch.

With a deft movement, Alexander released me and shifted his focus—scooped the toe of his boot under the blade of his fallen sword and tossed it into the air. In one smooth motion, he caught it, the weight of the weapon settling perfectly into his grasp. A roguish grin spread across his face.

"You, sir..." I swallowed, "make a very, *very* good pirate."

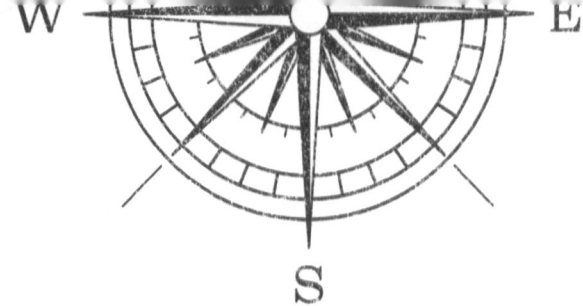

## Chapter 36

THAT MORNING, ALL FOUR CHAIRS at the chart room table were occupied. Alexander sat with perfect posture to my left. Anne lounged in her chair across from him, and I couldn't help but notice the glares she sent his way every time he spoke. Preston sat cross legged, fidgeting with a little sparrow he'd made out of folded parchment. We were two and a half day's sail from land, by Alexander's estimates. I held a meeting like this at least every other day, so I could keep track of the happenings on the ship.

"What's the food status, Preston?" I asked. "Do we need to ration?"

"Nope—we're all good on that front. We have enough water as well, as long as we don't spend more than two days on land."

I nodded, pleased. To Anne, I asked, "Do we have enough axes, shovels, and cutlasses? We're going to have to do a lot of bushwhacking."

"Aye. I think we 'ave enough."

"We're going to want to bring all the compasses we have, Cass," Alexander added. "And assign people to smaller groups, each group having a compass, in case someone falls behind. And it would be wise to bring something to put the map in, so it can be protected from rain."

Anne narrowed her eyes, but I nodded. "Good point. Mum, see to it that that happens before we arrive."

She stiffly nodded.

"If there's nothing else you need to bring to my attention, you're free to go," I told the boys.

When they had left, my mum grumbled, "Why does he call ye 'Cass,' anyway?"

I looked at her, surprised. "You call me 'Cass.'"

"I'm yer mother," she said, in a tone that indicated I should have already come to this conclusion. "*I* was the one who gave ye that nickname. Even yer father didn't dare use it!"

"So? It's probably just easier for him to say 'Cass' instead of 'Cassie' or 'Cassandra.' It's nothing."

That was the wrong thing to say.

"Nothing?" Anne's eyes were alight with frustration and something like...hurt. "How can ye say that? No one but *I* has ever called ye that. Did'ya let yer ex-fiancé call ye that?" she demanded.

I looked down. "No." Before she could respond, I added, "But that was because I thought you were dead. I was grieving. I didn't let Alexander call me that until I found out that you were alive." I reached out and touched her shoulder. "You mean the world to me, Mum. I love that you call me 'Cass.' I like that nickname. Can't you allow someone else to call me that too?"

She harrumphed. "Why that *boy*?"

"What do you mean, *that boy*?"

"He's the only other one who calls ye the nickname I gave ye. Sometimes he don't even call ye 'captain'!" she cried indignantly. "How can ye stand fer it?"

For some reason I felt a strong desire to defend him. "He calls me 'captain' when he's following orders! Calm down about this, mum. Just because he's a boy doesn't mean you need to hate him so much."

She ignored the entire last half of my statement, growling, "And do ye talk a lot with him when you ain't givin' orders? Does he call ye captain *then*?"

I looked at the ceiling and sighed exasperatedly. "What does it matter?"

She was silent for a beat, and then she said sourly, "Ye fancy him."

My head snapped to her, my eyes widening. "I most certainly do *not*." I hoped she didn't notice the pink that had most assuredly risen to my cheeks.

*She did, blast it.* I hated showing my embarrassment. It always compounded my mortification.

"If ye didn't like 'im, ye wouldn't get embarrassed when I told ya that. Ye wouldn't feel the need to defend 'im. An' quite frankly, if ye didn't fancy 'im then 'e wouldn't be here at all."

"That's not true," I insisted. "He... he came here of his own volition."

"But would ya have let 'im?"

"There's such a thing as gray area, mother. I'm allowed to not hate a boy but not fancy him either. He's my *friend*."

She looked me over for a beat, unconvinced. "Well, let 'im stay that way. I'm tryin' to help ye, Cassandra. He'll just be an anchor. Women are better off without men. I learned that the hard way."

*What if, sometimes, I need an anchor?* Instead I said, "But didn't you love Jack? Didn't he bring you freedom?" I knew she blamed my father for their capture, but my father wasn't a bad man. He just made mistakes. A lot of them. But I still loved him, and I was not ready to believe my mother never did.

*Please, I beg you, tell me you miss him as much as I do.*

"He did," Anne muttered after a small hesitation, a faraway look filling her eyes. "He did bring me some good things." She reached out and squeezed my hand, her eyes crinkling with a smile. "Like you."

I returned a smile, warming at the compliment. "I'm so glad I found you."

"So am I, Cass." She stood up and stretched. "Shall we head to the main deck? It's a wee bit too stuffy 'n here fer my likin'."

I nodded, my heart aching. *You did love him. I know you did. Didn't you?* I followed her out into the midmorning sunlight, to find Naomi chatting with Charles as he re-tied a rope around a cleat.

"How is everything?" I asked them.

"*Très bien*," Naomi answered, smiling.

Suddenly Johnny shouted from the crows nest: "Cap'n!"

I looked up, my heart thudding.

"There's no shade up here! Sun's beatin' me down!"

*Barnet.* He must've appeared again on the horizon. I'd entrusted Johnny with my plan. He was eager to prove himself after his last mistake, so I sent him up to the crows nest to keep me updated on our enemy's position. "Would you rather swab the deck?" I shouted back.

"Naw."

That was our code. I searched the deck for Alexander, wondering if he'd told his best friend about the danger that was looming on the horizon. I found him with his back to me. *And his shirt off.* The muscles across his shoulders and back flexed as he and Preston pulled on the ropes. His tan skin glistened with sweat. I swallowed with difficulty. Finished tying the rope down, he spun and looked up at the sail, intuitively gauging the wind speeds and canvas like the experienced sailor he was. As his chin lowered, he caught sight of me.

I abruptly turned to Charles, my heart leaping like some ridiculous dolphin. I stepped forward to stand next to him at the railing. The sight of Xander was burned into my mind, the way a bright spot danced in my vision if I stared at the sun. I could still see his piercing gaze, feel it heating me to my core. "Tell me—" I cleared my throat, heat rising to my cheeks from the sound of my own breathless voice. Gathering my composure, I tried again. "Tell me, Charles, how are you?"

"I'm eager to see land once again," he said, looking out to the sea ahead.

"What're you going to do with your share of the treasure?"

Charles pondered. "I will bring it back to my family. My success will restore their honor."

I cocked my head. "How was it lost?"

He hung his head, a stray piece of black hair escaping his hair tie. "My grandfather's mistake cost their ship's raid and his captain's life."

"And you're expected to make up for it?"

He shrugged. "We are all connected. Even little decisions can ripple, affecting not only our next choices but generations to come. I choose to bear this burden so that my future children may have a clean slate."

I frowned, pondering this. *Is honor so tangible?*

———⊙•⊙———

Robin played a jolly tune on the fiddle while the rest of us huddled in small groups, some playing dice and some cards. I sat next to Alexander, keeping the grin from my lips for the time being. When my turn came around again, I layed down my hand, letting the smile take over my face. "Sorry, boys."

Many of them groaned, especially Johnny, who'd been convinced of his victory. He slid two coins to me, and I collected them with a smirk. Winning two coins was trivial with the treasure ahead, but winning the game was what brought the smirk to my lips. I touched my hat with a two-fingered salute. "Night, gents. I'm heading to bed. Good luck to you all."

Xander caught my gaze, his eyes glittering. "Next time I'll beat you. Better watch out."

A smirk spread over my face, but when I ascended the stairs and poked my head out of the hatch, it disappeared. My mum stood at the edge of the ship, staring at the moon, which was low in the sky and spread a trail of silvery white light out across the water. I planted two feet on the deck, taking silent breaths, and watched her silhouette lift a bottle to her lips and gulp. I took a few soundless steps toward her.

"Oh, Mary," she muttered. "What would ya think o' me now?"

I froze. Sorrow filled my heart. I could almost forgive the drink in her hand. But drinking wasn't going to help her, so I stepped up beside her and put my head on her shoulder and one arm around her waist.

She looked at me, surprised. Then she turned her head back to the water, gloom taking over her face once again.

"I loved her too, mum." I gently pried the bottle from her grasp. She put up some resistance, but eventually gave in. "Tell me some stories."

She sighed, then was quiet for a moment while she thought. "I met 'er when I came aboard yer father's ship. She was beautiful, even under her disguise. It wasn't long before I figured out 'er secret. After all, I was also a woman. She was the fiercest—" Her voice cracked with emotion. "—bravest woman I ever met."

I took her hand, hoping remembering this story wasn't hurting her further.

"We grew so close, yer father became jealous."

"Jealous?" I asked, surprised.

She nodded, then laughed weakly. It sounded as if she'd been crying. "My, yer father could be blind sometimes. He threatened to kill 'er if I didn't distance myself from 'er. So I told 'im she was no man. Mary... Mary was angry with me, for spillin' her secret. But it ended up fine, because they still respected us some. Kept their hands off.

"Mary killed plenty o' fellers. Almost died when we tried to take a Spanish treasure ship. Bad idea, that was." Her voice gradually became stronger, even though she paused to sniffle. "We had to pull out before our ship sank. I dare say it was humblin'. We lost quite a few men. That was two or three months before ye were born," she added.

We spent a few minutes silent, listening to the water lapping against the side of the boat. The breeze was light, and we had taken down most of the sails, save the mainsail. Finally Anne spoke up. "She was there when ye were born, ye know."

I turned to her. "Really?"

She nodded solemnly. "She was there when yer father wasn't. She could've easily left me for a while like 'e did. But Mary...she stood by my side an' helped me give birth to ye. An' helped me care o' ye when ye were just a wee little lass. She'd leave for a time, but she'd always come back." Her voice broke. "She loved me."

I blinked. Mum reached for the bottle in my hand, and I didn't even try to stop her. The way Anne said it made it sound different from sisterly love. More than friendship. "So... so... Mary loved you and you loved Jack?"

"No," Mum said, almost fiercely. "Er...sort o'." She ran a hand down her face and sighed. "It's too complicated fer anyone to understand."

"Did..." I started, my voice soft. "Did you love Mary?"

My mother swallowed.

Suddenly it made sense that she was so much more distraught over losing Mary than my father. I traced circles with my finger on the railing as I chewed on that. "But you had a husband. And then you ran away with Jack, and—didn't you love him?"

Anne raised the bottle once again, and I snatched it away before it reached her mouth. "*Mum*," I urged, my chest tight.

She still refused to meet my eyes. "Ye don't know how shameful it is," she finally whispered. "Ye—ye probably don't even love me anymore."

When she confessed her love for Mary, I thought nothing else could surprise me more, but that last sentence *really* caught me off guard. I almost laughed. Instead, I dropped the grog overboard and pulled her into a hug. "Mum, we're pirates. *Pirates*, for stars' sake! This is why we chose this life, isn't it? So we can be free from the chains of society?"

She sighed, brushing a strand of hair out of my face. "How'd I get so lucky to 'ave a daughter like ye?" She turned back to the sea, chewing her lip. "Part o' me will always belong to Jack."

I raised my eyebrows. "You loved them both?"

"Aye. My heart'll always be split. What'd ya do with my grog?"

I stared at the moonlit water, wondering what it would be like to love two people at once. I didn't love *anyone* in that way. ...*Did I?* Stunned, I was suddenly unsure of the answer. The sight of Alexander's beautiful blue eyes filled my mind—the gold flecks I had noticed the last time we had stood so close. I found myself wishing to study them longer.

I turned back to Mum and took her hand. "Come on, let's get you to bed."

"Don't wanna go to bed."

"You need your rest if you're going to sleep this off." I led her through the door of the aftercastle and down the hall. Once she was reluctantly settled in her bed, I wished her good night and crept back out into the moonlight, closing the door behind me.

"Cassandra."

I whirled around, and Alexander stepped out from beneath the companionway. The little lantern that hung above us near the helm shed little light on his features. "Were you waiting for me?" I asked quietly, looking up at him.

"I was wondering why you went through there instead of up the stairs. Was that your mother with you?"

I nodded solemnly. "Mum never got over the death of Jack and Mary. Mary especially."

Xander tilted his head a little to the side, looking compassionate. "I wish I could do something to help her, but she doesn't seem to like me much."

"My mum?" I asked, grimacing.

"She keeps glaring at me—I get the feeling she doesn't want me around. Can't imagine what that's all about; I've never done anything wrong."

I pursed my lips. "It's not what you've *done*. It's..."

"It's what?"

I shrugged, deciding to tell him the blatant truth. "The simplest version is that you're a boy."

"What?!" he exclaimed.

I put a finger to my lips and shushed him. "Keep your voice down."

It was a couple seconds before he spoke again. "Do you share the same sentiment?"

I raised an eyebrow. "Do I send you rude glares?"

"You used to."

I laughed lightly, recalling. It seemed like so long ago. "You're right. I didn't like you very much. Even after I bested you in a sword fight." I smirked, making light of it.

He scoffed, then allowed a small smile to settle on his lips. He took a step forward. "And how do you feel about me now?"

I was thrown off balance by the question. "I—You're a sailor worth his salt." I managed, stammering a bit. "And an excellent swordfighter."

Alexander leaned ever so slightly closer, his voice low. "That didn't exactly answer my question, Cassandra."

He was so very close—my heart hammered at the proximity. He smelled faintly of coconut soap and seawater, but I resisted the pull and took a small step back. "I don't exactly *have* an answer, Alexander."

He took another step forward, his eyes bright. "I thought you always had an answer. I thought you said you were *always* sure."

My voice dropped to a whisper as I looked up at him. "Not with you. Somehow you're different."

"Different how?" he pressed.

A little frustration burned through me—a welcome change. My voice hardened as I told him, "I dunno, savvy? You just are. Or maybe you aren't—maybe I'm just tired. Good night, *Mister* Callaway," I said pointedly, pushing past him and muttering, "I need my beauty sleep."

"Since when did you care about your beauty sleep?" There was a little amusement in his pleasant accent when he called after me.

I ignored him and hurried up the companionway, my mind whirring with mixed emotions. And my heart—I didn't even want to start sorting out the tangled mess in my heart.

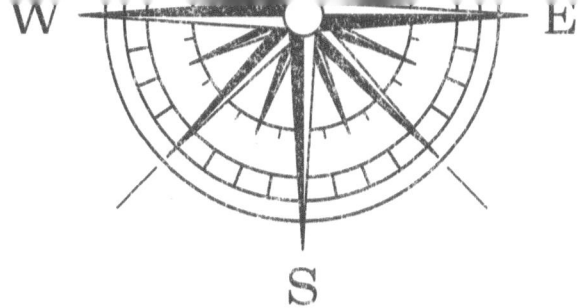

## *Chapter 37*

"**L** AND HO!"
A cheer rippled through my crew. As we neared the long strip of land that connected the Americas, dense jungle and white sand beaches came into view. There were two coves about two hundred yards apart: one that had a very narrow mouth and was completely shielded by trees, and another that provided less shelter. I ordered my crew to head toward the second one. The beach was deeper here, and the nearest bit of jungle was sparser, little huts wedged between trees. I hoped the villagers would be friendly.

I glanced up at the helm, where Alexander stood steering our ship. The wind ruffled his hair, and he leaned against the wheel, relaxed.

We entered the cove and dropped anchor and canvas, then piled in the longboats and rowed to shore. I left four crew members to watch the ship, and took all the supplies we would need for the journey, including some gifts for the villagers, a torch, and, as Alexander suggested, multiple compasses.

As we hiked up the beach, two men and an older woman emerged from one of the huts. They were dark skinned, humbly dressed. We stopped before them, and I debated what to do. A kind gesture to one culture might turn out to be a threat to another. I played it safe and bowed my head. "Greetings," I said.

They turned and spoke amongst themselves, in a tongue I'd never heard. One of the men left and disappeared into yet another hut. The remaining two just stared at us unabashedly. I shifted my feet uncomfortably. Finally the man returned, with another in tow. The new man bowed his head in greeting, and spoke in English.

"Who are you?" he asked, his voice deep and rich.

"We are but humble travelers. We come from a small island not too far from here," I told him, noticing some fathers, mothers, and children emerging from their huts and creeping forward to peer at us.

He relayed my message to the others, then spoke to me again. "We saw your ship approach. We have heard about your kind. If you have come to claim the land we have lived on for generations, I advise you to leave now." He flicked his hand toward our ship.

I shook my head. "That is not why we have come. May we speak to your leader?" I tensed, hoping I hadn't made a big mistake and their leader was standing in front of me.

Luckily, they didn't seem to take offense, and instead argued with each other. Finally they turned back to us. "Follow me," the man told me.

But when the rest of my crew tried to follow, the man stopped and held out his hand. "Her only."

I turned back to my crew and nodded, letting them know I'd be fine.

"Cass—" Alexander started.

"I can handle myself," I informed him, giving him a smirk. Then I turned and followed the man through the woods and into the largest of the huts. It had a fire pit in the center and a hole in the roof to let out the smoke. There was a dirt floor and benches along the walls covered in animal fur. The other huts were circular, but this one was more rectangular.

At the far end, there was a large seat, where the chief himself sat. He had colorful bead necklaces and eagle feathers in his black hair, which was half pulled back in a long braid. A wooden staff rested against the arm of his carved chair. Next to him stood a more humbly dressed man, frowning skeptically.

When we approached, I bowed to him politely, and placed the tools and a small iron cooking pot on the floor as an offering.

The chief spoke, and the man standing next to him translated. "Who you and where you from?" His accent was rich, and if I hadn't been exposed to so many languages growing up, I might have struggled understanding.

"My name is Cassandra, and I come with my...friends and family from a small island not far from here. I mean you no harm. I seek only shelter for the night."

I waited for him to translate, then to reply.

"May happiness find you, Cassandra. My name Chief Ademir. We welcome peaceful people. If you hide nothing, you may stay the night. What plans have you?"

"I am grateful, Chief Ademir. We have come..." I decided to tell him some of the truth. "We've come for a treasure chest hidden somewhere deep in your forest. If you would let us pass, I'd appreciate it greatly."

When the translator finished, the chief held up his hand and spoke. Instead of translating, the other man argued. The chief shook his head. Finally, looking a little annoyed, the translator spoke to me this time. "This not *our* land. Earth is gift, for us to live and not abuse. You pass on one condition:

do not touch any of the plants or animals that live here. They are sacred."

I nodded, relieved. "We will not."

"Good. Chief sends one of our own to guide and observe. He come back safely, we will not harm you. Break promise, and you die."

The translator glared at me, and the Chief remained peaceful. I wondered if his translator added that threat in there himself, but I nodded. It would be helpful to have a guide, but that added an extra problem: if Barnet caught up to us, there could be no guarantee that I could keep him or her safe.

A little while later, my crew mingled with the villagers. There were two other people who knew English, so we tried our best to communicate with the others. That night, supper was a meat and vegetable stew that was cooked over a fire in the biggest iron pot I'd ever seen. We sat cross legged in the sand under a starry sky, my mother directly to my left, and my crew and the villagers were scattered here and there around the fire.

I slurped my soup. "I wonder what form the treasure will take," I said to my crew.

"Likely Spanish coins and silver bars," Alexander responded.

"The map says we should enter the forest a little ways to the left of the village," I announced.

"Shhh," Anne leaned over to me, her eyebrows furrowed. "Don't ye say it so loud."

I laughed. "What, do you think they're going to come after us and steal the gold?"

"Ye never know who ye can't trust," my mum chastised quietly.

*That's what I'm betting on.*

We woke just after dawn, packed our things, and headed out, guided by a cheerful man named Gallardo. I'd pocketed a pistol. In my satchel was a drained rum bottle, a small unlit torch, two stones, and a water canteen. I wouldn't need anything else.

I checked my crew over. The quadruplets were vibrating with energy. Preston was laughing and teasing his friend about his hair. I watched Alexander run his fingers through it, taming it from a rough sleep. *It's probably so soft.*

I jerked my head and turned away. Naomi rubbed her hands together, nodding to me. She'd be the wealthiest of all of us. I tried not to feel slided. *The Kingston* was mine, after all.

"Alright, crew! We'll take it nice and easy up through the jungle, so we can save our strength for the load we'll be carrying down."

A cheer erupted.

"And be on your guard for wild beasts," I added.

Before we left the water's sight, I checked over my shoulder. My eyes widened when I spotted Barnet's two warships, not an hour's sail away. My heart hammered. How had he gained so much on us? *He must have sweep oars.*

Alexander caught my eye when I turned back. He was the only other person who'd noticed. Everyone else was in a joyful fervor about what lay ahead. He forced a smile through a clenched jaw. "It will work," he whispered encouragingly.

"It better," I breathed. I thought about the villagers. How Barnet would question them. *Would they be safe?* I raised my voice. "All right, crew! Onward!"

They cheered, following me, Gallardo, and Alexander into the jungle. As we hiked, it got denser and steeper. The air was so damp it felt like we were walking through a cloud. Scarlet macaws flew overhead, sending streaks of red and yellow through the jungle. Monkeys of all different shapes and sizes swung on the branches. A few toucans croaked at us from high in the trees. I saw animals I've never seen before, and I would have enjoyed it had I not been under the stress of impending doom. Everything had to be timed just right. I used my cutlass to cut the bigger branches out of our way, earning glares from our guide.

"How else are we supposed to hike through this?"

Gallardo said nothing.

It was slow moving, and each root and rock seemed to grow slipperier as we climbed. Sweat and humidity soaked through my clothes, and I had to shed my overcoat so I wouldn't overheat. I was sure Barnet was going to have an easy time catching up to us, since we were clearing the path. *And dropping clothes to mark the way.* Alexander rolled up his sleeves, exposing his muscled forearms.

"The morning rain is about to descend upon us," Gallardo said happily.

"It rains *every* morning?" Preston said, aghast.

"Yes, and as it comes down it takes the fog with it."

"Thank heavens," Alexander panted, as he lifted himself up a boulder.

We heard it before we felt it: a pattering on the leaves above, as a few drops made their way through the branches. Then came a roar, and a half second later, we were soaked. But we kept on stumbling uphill, our hair plastered to our faces. Then the rain stopped as suddenly as it started, and the air cleared up.

We paused for a few minutes to breathe and squeeze the water from our clothes. I knelt and removed the cover off the top of the torch and used flint and steel to light it. Anne asked why I was lighting it so early, but I ignored her. Barnet should be entering the forest right about now. I needed to be as ready as possible. After a few minutes, we stood back up and started moving our tired feet again.

I looked up, but I could no longer tell where the sun was, thanks to the high, thick canopy. It had to have been almost two hours since we started. I pulled the map out of the rum bottle that had been keeping it safe, and looked between it and my compass. "Let's make our way a little more to the right. And remember, everyone, it's fine to take it slow, because we're going to have a hard haul down, if we're lucky."

A few people chuckled.

"Nights are warm, days are cool. Where the creek meets the pool," Alexander rattled off, even though I'd folded the map back up. "But this clue brings a warning: all rejoicing will turn to mourning, when the fortune you seek becomes your greatest misfortune."

"It *has* become my greatest misfortune," I realized, despairing. I dropped my voice to a whisper, gripping the torch tightly. "This might very well end us all dead."

"Drake was being pursued, as well," Alexander said softly.

"Was he?" I asked, surprised.

Alexander nodded. "That's why he had to bury most of it. His crew couldn't carry it all fast enough, and he knew they'd get caught by the Spanish guards. Even though he escaped, he lost two good friends during the fight with the mule train, which they had intercepted as it made its way across Panama."

"How do you know all this?"

"I read the journal."

"The whole thing?"

He nodded.

I laughed. "I suppose I shouldn't be surprised."

"Knowledge is the greatest treasure of all. Reading is also a great way to pass the time."

"Tell me more. Maybe it will make me hate this hike less." I wasn't used to this kind of exercise, and my legs were burning.

"Well, the last four lines of the riddle tell of his grieving. His new friend, fellow captain and French pirate Guillaume le Testu fell gravely ill from an infected wound whilst they were making their escape, and they failed to save him."

"You sound like you're teaching a history lesson," I teased. His perfect accented English would fit right in with a handful of posh school teachers—at least, what I imagined them to be. "You could be a professor at—where was it you went?"

"Cambridge," he reminded me, with a sideways smile.

"You're definitely an interesting sort of man."

"What do you mean?"

"You're all proper and righteous and educated, but then you leave your dear old pa to go adventuring and law-breaking with a woman you only met because she'd pillaged your ship and kidnapped you." I cocked my head at him, curious.

Alexander put a hand on a tree and paused. "When you put it that way, I suppose it does sound a bit unconventional."

"Only a bit," I scoffed, my tone sarcastic. After a few more steps of silence, I said, "So what of the first two lines?"

"Well obviously it's next to a stream," Alexander pointed out. "But not the one on the map. He must have purpose-fully excluded it from his drawing in case it fell into the wrong hands."

"How do you cool a place down during the day? I mean besides the breeze, but the same breeze can't heat the place up during the night. It just doesn't make sense."

Preston came up beside us. "There could be an old magic hag guarding the place."

I chuckled, then looked at Alexander, hoping he had any ideas.

He thought for a moment. "He could be referring to…" He shook his head. "Never mind."

"Go on," I urged.

"Well, I've read that in harsh climates, like the desert, many animals live underground, since the earth insulates them from the harsh cold or intense heat."

I raised my eyebrows. "Could that be the case here?"

Alexander furrowed his brow. I watched him while he thought, warmth flickering in my chest. There was something endearing about the way he wore that expression. I shook my head. *Focus, Rackham.*

"It's quite possible," he speculated. "Although it's more likely that the temperature would be the same, day or night, since the ground is only an insulator."

"Gallardo, are there any such places? Any underground caves?" Preston asked.

Gallardo's expression shifted as shadows crossed his face. "I've heard stories," he said, his voice low, "of rivers and caves running deep under the earth. But my people, we do not go near them. There, evil spirits lie in wait, hungry. It is where the earth swallows the unworthy."

We were quiet for a few moments, feeling the weight of his words. I wasn't superstitious, but imagining the earth swallowing someone gave me the spooks.

Preston spoke up. "The springs probably erode the dirt underground, until it's so thin that even the slightest pressure could cause the forest floor to collapse in on itself, creating a small sinkhole."

I whistled. "We'd better tread lightly, then."

Suddenly a gunshot rang out, sending birds flying and monkeys squawking. My heart dropped out of my chest as an imperious voice rang out, "SURRENDER OR SHE DIES!"

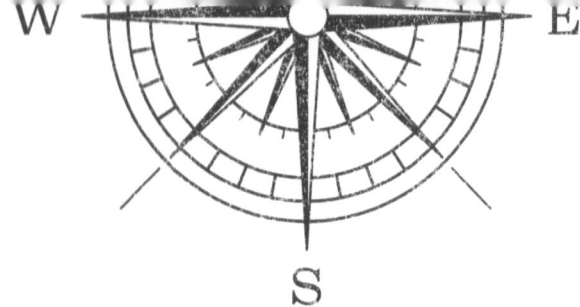

# Chapter 38

"**R**UBY!" SOMEONE CRIED.
 I whipped around as gasps of shock rippled through my crew. "Make way!" I snapped.

Everyone stumbled to either side of the path, save the graceful Indian princess, her body ridged with fury. Past her, Barnet held a frightened Ruby, a pistol pressed to her temple. "How dare you touch her!" Naomi snarled. I couldn't see her expression, but her words were filled with malice.

*Who had let Ruby fall behind?* I thought furiously. The plan had gone astray before it even started.

Guilt crept into my lungs. *I led them into this, and now we're all going to pay.*

I studied the leather patch over Barnet's left eye, the ends of an ugly scar peeking out from the edge on either side.

*That was my doing.*

I remembered kneeling on the deck of his ship, the rain cascading down my face, my heart ripped in two after Alexander fell. I remembered my promise—I'd see the pirate hunter brought to his knees, his life in ruins. He dared to steal my treasure and threaten my crew?

*He's about to lose more than an eye.*

I watched his crew bound uphill on either side of us, surrounding us. Everyone tensed, reaching for their weapons. We were outnumbered four to one.

"Hand over the map," Barnet demanded, looking past Naomi to me. When I didn't respond, he assumed my shock. "Oh, *indeed.* I am well informed. We shall see whether it truly is nineteen tons."

I faked my surprise. *When we return to Tortuga, that spy will be sorry indeed.*

"Now where is it?" he growled.

My eyes narrowed, reaching into my satchel with my free hand.

"It's to your left!" Preston called.

Barnet snapped his head in that direction, then looked back at him. "Don't try to fool me, boy."

Preston cackled. "You don't see it because you're half blind, Captain Cyclops!" I nearly smiled—that boy could bring humor to nearly any situation.

Barnet snarled.

I pulled out the map, the torch burning in my other hand. A branch cracked behind me—someone creeping up, probably to snatch the map away if I didn't comply. Or maybe put a gun to my head. *I will* not *lose my leverage.* "You want the map, Barnet? The only other copy is in my mind. And if you harm any of my crew, I'll die before I let you have it."

His eyes widened, tracking the map as it fell. I dropped the torch on top of it. "NO!" Barnet screamed as it burst into flames, the ink and parchment devoured like a wave wiping out sandy footprints. "*What have you done?*"

"Hopefully saved my crew," I muttered, burying my hatred for him and pulling out a pencil and a small piece of parchment. "If you let us go and give us your honest word that none of my crew will be harmed, I'll redraw it for you. If any of them receive so much as a scratch, I will make it my life's mission to see that you *never* find that gold."

Barnet's face contorted and he raised a pistol at me, giving Ruby an opportunity. She broke free of his grasp and scrambled over to Naomi and her sisters' waiting arms.

Barnet was too furious to care. He took three steps forward, and I boldly matched them.

"How do I know you'll keep your word, *filthy pirate*?" he practically spat.

"We might be pirates, but it is still beneficial for us to keep our promises, *Barnet*."

He considered. "Do you have any other terms?"

I released a breath, relieved. "Let us all go free, unharmed—immediately, without hesitation. Give us twenty five percent of the plunder. Once we leave the island, you cannot pursue us. Ever."

Barnet slowly walked up the path, his pistol still trained on me, and two burly sailors walked behind him, brandishing muskets. I glanced at my mother, who was a few paces uphill from her mortal enemy. Anne looked more murderous than I had ever seen her. *Please*, I prayed. *Not yet*.

Barnet's eyes finally glanced her way, and he faltered. "You are supposed to be dead," he sneered.

Anne's hand found the hilt of her cutlass. "And *ye* soon will be."

"My final bargain," I interrupted, my heart thudding. "Release us and let us walk down to the beach, unguarded and unrestrained. No pursuing us. You..." I sighed heavily, running a hand down my face for the sake of my act. "Fifteen percent of the plunder, and we'll call it even. It's my map, after all."

Barnet looked back at me and laughed. "You are fooling yourself. How do you think you are in a position to bargain? We outnumber you five to one."

I glared, pointing to my head. "I still have the map."

"And I have your lives," he snarled.

I clenched my fists. "Five percent."

"Zero. The only thing you will ever deserve is the noose."

"Fine, keep the filthy treasure!" I yelled. "Just let us go."

Barnet looked faintly taken aback. "Giving up the treasure? What kind of pirate are you?"

"You already said you wouldn't give us any, idiot! Besides—unlike you, I care more for the welfare of my crew than the treasure." As soon as I said those words, guilt swept through me. I had knowingly risked their lives coming here. Knowingly put them in harm's way—for the treasure. But what was I supposed to do? Give up? They wouldn't respect me for that. And it was only a matter of time before we had to face Barnet. *Why not do it now?*

Joshua stepped out of the crowd and stood beside his father. He had a bruise on his cheek and shadows under his eyes. "So you expect us to follow whatever you're going to draw, trusting that it will lead us to nineteen tons of treasure, and let you waltz off with your crew?"

I nodded. "Aye. I'll be true to my word." I raised my voice, speaking partly to Barnet's crew. "Now, I know the crew you hired are good, honest men, so I assume they expect you to be a man of your word, also." I hoped the pressure from some one hundred-seventy men would be enough to force Barnet to keep his word. Holding out my hand, I asked, "Do we have an accord?"

Barnet lowered his pistol and walked forward to shake my hand, leaving his bodyguards with Joshua. His grip was like steel and his eyes like ice. Hesitantly, I sat down cross-legged on the damp earth and began to trace the pencil over the parchment, hating the vulnerable feeling that came from my enemy standing over me.

A mighty roar shattered the tense air, and my head jerked up, panic seizing me. Anne, eyes blazing and cutlass drawn, jumped forward to drive her sword into Barnet's back—but not fast enough. Barnet spun and deflected the blow with the barrel of his pistol. Stepping back, he aimed, and the resulting *crack* of the gunshot rippled through the air, followed immediately by a loud *pang*. A scream tore from my throat, certain I'd just witnessed my mother's death. But upright she remained, unyielding, sweeping her blade at him once more. One of Barnet's bodyguards crumpled to the ground, lifeless. My mother had survived by the sheerest of luck—the shot had ricocheted off of her cutlass.

Barnet's face twisted in fury. He tossed his empty pistol aside and drew his rapier, catching my mum's strike just before it severed his head. Behind him, the remaining bodyguard raised his musket, while Barnet's crew surged forward, seizing my crewmates and pressing knives against their throats. All at once, skirmishes erupted down the line, chaos spilling like wildfire.

Joshua drew his sword. "Father!" he yelled.

"Get back!" Barnet screamed. "She's mine."

I scrambled up. I needed to stop this. *But how?*

"That's not yer son," Anne realized, gazing at Joshua.

That was all the distraction Barnet needed. He disarmed her, ripping the sword out of her hand and sending her to the ground. I stuffed the unfinished drawing down my shirt and drew my pistol with shaking hands.

Barnet stood over my mother, rapier poised above her heart. "You should have died seven years ago, but I guess I'll have to finish the job myself."

Instead of pointing the weapon at him, I leveled the muzzle at my own head and screamed at the top of my lungs, "NOT ONE DROP OF BLOOD FROM MY CREW, OR I WILL NEVER FINISH!"

Eyes swiveled to me. Barnet cocked his head.

"Cass," Alexander said, shocked.

I swallowed, meeting his eyes. Then I turned back to Barnet, my jaw set. "I'm not afraid to die. And if I do, you'll never find that treasure." I surveyed the damage that had already been done. Charles clutched his side, blood staining his fingers, but he nodded bravely to me. As far as I could see, no one else had been severely hurt. "You want nineteen tons of gold and silver? Tell your men to stand down, and I will do the same for mine. Then you will wait patiently while I finish drawing the map," I commanded. After a hesitation, Barnet raised his fingers and his crew stepped back.

When I was finished, I reluctantly held the parchment out in front of me. The moment it was in his possession, Barnet flicked his wrist. "Round them up."

Before I could protest, I was roughly grabbed from behind and my wrists were bound together. I struggled against the men holding me, but it was no use. I was searched, but I'd left my sword on *The Kingston*. The only weapon they found was my pistol.

My mum was a beast. Before they could confiscate all her weapons, she pulled a dagger out of nowhere and stabbed a man in the gut. He hunched over, stumbling backwards.

"Surrender, woman!" Barnet said, thoroughly annoyed. He didn't give a second glance to the man who'd fallen. "You are already defeated."

Anne fought off another sailor, and kicked him away. "Surrender? I've not yet begun to fight!"

He ignored her, examining the map I'd drawn for him.

I grimaced, wanting nothing other than to throw these men off me, but I knew the inevitable outcome. Fighting would only waste my strength.

Eventually my mum was restrained. I was forced onto my bottom and tied to a giant tree, between her and Preston. I growled. "This was not part of our agreement. You said you would let us go free!"

"You're going back on your word, father?" Joshua asked, shifting his feet nervously.

I stared at him, shocked. Was he standing up for us?

"Do you care about them?" Barnet snapped.

"I—I care about your word. Your honor."

Barnet gestured to us. "These are pirates. A man's word means nothing to them."

"They trusted yours."

"I will eventually release them. This is just an added precaution." Barnet put an arm around Joshua's shoulders, who seemed surprised by the action. "We're about to become two of the richest men in the world. Do you really want them to get in the way of that?" Turning and leaving Joshua looking torn, he pointed to someone. "Bring that man forward, but keep him restrained."

I strained my neck to see who he had pointed at, but I couldn't turn my head far enough. I waited until two of Barnet's men brought him into my view.

My breath left me. *Alexander.*

Barnet made Alexander face me. "He will be brought along for the journey. If you lead me astray with this map and I do not find the treasure, he will die a very agonizing death, and I will make you watch." His black eyes seethed evil.

*360*

"No!" I shouted, struggling with my bonds. The spare knife in the back of my corset—if I could only reach it—"You wretched liar! You said we could all go free and no one would be harmed."

"Take me instead!" Preston begged, struggling against his bonds.

"If everything is as you say, he will be returned to you safe and sound." Barnet studied me closely, inspecting for a change in my expression. When I said nothing, just glared at him, he judged, "So either you have drawn the map correctly, or you don't care about his life. Seeing your previous actions, I take it it's the former."

Feeling frustratingly helpless, I locked eyes with Alexander. "Whatever you do, don't die," I whispered, hopefully communicating more than just those words to him. He knew the plan. *Could we still make it work, even after it had gone devastatingly astray?*

Alexander nodded once, knowing he had to tell Barnet about the riddle—and what it meant. He looked as fierce and brave as when I'd first laid eyes on him, and it gave me strength.

Barnet picked three guards to stay and watch us before he commanded his crew to head out. The procession slowly snaked its way up the gradual incline, with Barnet and Alexander at the front. I turned back to see Joshua hesitating at the rear. The huge group was still filing into a line, so Joshua had some time before he was left behind.

"Did'ye ever know yer mother, boy?" Anne asked him.

He furrowed his brows slightly. "She died during childbirth."

"*Ha.* What a lie. He never loved ye like 'e should've, did 'e?"

"He did," Joshua said, defensive. "He is simply... burdened by great responsibility."

I scoffed, then looked at my mother. She was staring at him longingly. And then I began to connect the pieces. Her words from long ago came back to me, bouncing around in my mind like echoes in a cave.

*"Where is he, ye filthy bastard?! Where's Finn?"*

*He took my children. My beautiful children.*

*That's not yer son...*

How had I not seen it before?

Joshua had my mother's eyes. I was going to be sick. *What had Barnet done?* I searched for any of the monster's features in Joshua's face, but found none. He bore no resemblance to my father, either. What...? *Oh.* Anne had been married before Jack swept her off her feet. I took a shaky breath, relieved beyond words.

"Hello, half-brother."

He looked at me, confusion written all over his face. "Excuse me?" He slowly backed up the path, behind the last of the crew members picking their way through the undergrowth.

"Barnet's not yer father," Anne spat. "Ye were meant to be somethin' more. 'E turned ye into a stiff-necked military man, only made to follow orders."

Joshua's eyes widened. "Barnet *is* my father."

"You look nothing like him," I pointed out. "You're adopted."

"Stolen," Anne corrected, emotion filling her voice.

"Lies!" Joshua turned away. "You're pirates. You expect me to believe you?"

I could feel my mum becoming anxious as Joshua walked away. "I'm yer mother!" she called desperately, straining against her bonds. "I named ye Finn! Boy, ye have pirate blood in yer veins."

My mother's son just ran faster, until he was swallowed by the jungle.

I made a face. "He almost kissed me once. *Yuck.*"

Anne just hung her head. I didn't even receive a smile from Preston, who no doubt would've found that hilarious had his best friend not been taken hostage.

"They won't hurt him, will they?" he asked, his voice tight.

"I don't think so," I reassured him, unable to do the same for myself. Alexander was alone amidst over one hundred-seventy enemies. And I was in no position to save him. I hated myself for not anticipating Barnet's cheap move, but I hated the bastard more for it. I tried to reach my knife again, but my hands were bound too tight. I was able to touch the end of the handle, but couldn't get a grip on it. I couldn't reach the one in my boot, either.

But I wouldn't stop trying. *Never.* We had to escape, and it had to be soon. While they were busy finding the treasure.

Trying to formulate a plan, I watched the three guards walk up and down the path, puffing out their chests and pausing now and then to stare threateningly at someone. One red-haired man had a rum belly and thick, chunky arms. The other two had twigs for legs, their uniform pants baggy.

"Did ye really give 'im the true location o' the treasure?" Anne asked through clenched teeth.

I swallowed. "Yes." I couldn't tell her my plan now, for fear that the guards would overhear. So I would have to deal with her anger. *She'll understand later.*

She growled. "I told ye that *boy* would get in the way. Because of 'im, we've lost the treasure. We could 'ave been rich!"

"You're blaming *him*?" I asked, aghast. A retort was about to leave my mouth when—

*Meow.*

I paused, not sure of what I heard. But there it was again: a weak *meow*, coming from somewhere nearby. The guards turned on the spot, searching for whatever was making the noise.

"Cuddles!" Judith exclaimed excitedly. "I knew you'd come save us!"

*How in the seven seas–*

"Who?" one guard asked, anxiously looking around.

There was movement through the undergrowth, and I spotted the little old furball, crouched. When the guards' backs were turned, Cuddles crept out toward its adoring owner. One of the skinny guards spun on the spot, saw the old cat, and jumped back. "Werewolf!" he cried, fumbling for his musket.

The cat hissed.

"That's not a werewolf, idiot," the other told him. "That's a *cat*. Save your bullets. That thing's not going to help them escape."

"Rarrrrr!" the beefy red-haired soldier growled, running at Cuddles. "Scram!"

The old thing tore off down the path, its hair standing on end.

"Great," I said, my voice flat. "Now we've lost the cat."

"Good riddance," Mum huffed.

"Cuddles!" Judith whined.

"Shut up, girl." The red-haired guard jabbed her with the butt of his musket.

"*Casse-toi!*" Naomi told him angrily, causing some of her students to share surprised and smug looks. "Get away from her, you *tête de noeud*."

The guard turned to her, smiling in a way that made me sick. "Feisty, darling. Care to share what those pretty words meant?"

"You are *une vache espagnole*."

"Here, here!" Preston announced, then turned to whisper to me. "Let's all insult them at once—until they can't stand us any longer and will let us go!"

"Or shoot us," I muttered. But at this point, I was willing to try anything. "Have any good ones?"

"More than you'd like to know." Preston smirked before clearing his throat. "Excuse me! Yes, over here. No, just the man with the big nose. Sorry, I can't point. My arms are tied, see."

"What?" the guard snapped.

"Your face would make onions cry."

I laughed.

The man's face turned red with anger, but he turned away without saying a word.

"Ooo hoo hoo! You're sure a hard one to crack," Preston said, shaking his head like he was disappointed. "Hey brown hair! Your teeth are so bad, you could eat an apple through a fence."

The young man self consciously brought his hand up to his mouth and turned to his friend. "Are my—"

"No, you idiot! He's just trying to get under your skin."

"I've seen hardtack with more muscle than the two of you combined."

"Shut it!" they both yelled.

"Are all of your insults centered around food?" I questioned.

One of the quadruplets—I could never tell who—finally caught on. "Hey fanny-face! You have enough oil in your hair to light the lanterns in Port Royal for a week!"

I grinned and called to the red-haired guard. "If your brain was made of gunpowder, there wouldn't be enough to blow your hat off."

Preston cackled gleefully. "And you're fatter than an over-stuffed cherry pie!"

It went on like that, until all three of them were too peppered with insults to know who to scream at.

"Enough!"

We all fell silent. It was a new voice—*Joshua!* Or Finn. Or whatever his name was now. "Hello, brother from another father!" I called, rubbing it in. "Come to join in the fun?"

He pointedly ignored me. "You men are relieved. My father needs a few extra hands."

They looked confused, because, I mean, how could three extra men be of that much assistance? *Especially these poor incompetent fellows.* But they were so fed up with our verbal abuse that they didn't argue. As they hurried up the path, Preston mimicked an evil laugh.

"Tell me more," Finn finally said, his voice so low I could barely catch his words. He was staring hard at the ground.

My mother took a shaky breath. I could see a fragile hope in her eyes. "Barnet captured us twice, but the first time we were able to escape. But not ye. I wasn't able to save ye, and I'll never forgive myself fer that. Ye were only a babe! Barnet kept ye out o' spite. To rub 'is victory in my face, fer the next time 'e caught us." She spat on the ground.

"I... I don't believe you. There's no proof."

"Is that spot on yer lower back still there? Right along yer spine. It used to show up whenever ye got cold, an' fade to almost nuttin' when ye were warm an' happy."

He opened his mouth, but no sound came out. He reached behind his back. Swallowed.

Anne nodded. "Aye."

Finn took a shaky breath. "My fa—the captain isn't going to let you go. I think he'll send you all to the gallows, if the governor doesn't offer a pardon to you first. I came back to... help him keep his word."

"You're letting us go?" I was shocked.

In answer, he knelt beside me and used his sword to cut through my bonds.

Our eyes met, and something passed between us. "Thank you, Josh," I whispered. "I'm in your debt." When he nodded solemnly, I smirked and added, "Half-brother." His face darkened and he stood up. I slipped the knife out of my corset and helped cut Preston's bonds, while Finn released my mother. *Our* mother.

I handed Preston the knife from my boot so we could speed the process up. One by one, my crew members stood.

Johnny rubbed his wrists. "Ow. Those buggers made 'em tight."

"That was nothing," Wyatt said, his voice serious.

"You think you're tougher than me, mate?"

"Yes," Wyatt replied, without hesitation.

Johnny stared at him for a second—then shrugged. "You're prolly right."

I swung my gaze back to my half-brother. "What will Barnet do when he discovers you released us?"

Finn swallowed. "I'll be fine."

"You won't go back to him, will ye?" Anne asked.

He shrugged. "Perhaps. Perhaps not." He turned, and once again, we watched as the forest swallowed him.

Anne took a step forward, but I held her back. "He'll find his own way."

She looked at me, longing in her eyes, but she relented. "Alright. What should we do now?"

"Head back down. Quickly."

Preston grabbed my arm. "What about Alexander?"

"We're not leaving this island without him. I'll kill a hundred of them if I have to," I swore. "But we need to wait for the opportune moment."

He held up a finger. "Panama is an isthmus, not an island. But I'm glad to hear you'd lay down your life for him."

"I didn't say *that*," I argued.

He gave me his classic Preston grin. "Oh come on, we both know it. You fancy him." He wiggled his eyebrows—and received a punch to the stomach.

"Next time, I'll aim lower," I warned him.

"Yep," he wheezed. "You definitely fancy him."

I blew a strand of hair out of my face and stalked away. Charles was leaning against some roots of a giant tree, looking pale. "Medic!" I called, anxious. "Where's Dan?"

"I'm here!" he stepped through the crowd.

"Take care of him! We need to get out of this jungle as fast as possible."

Dan nodded, then made quick work of bandaging Charles's wound. "I'll have to stitch you up when we get back," he told him, helping him to his feet.

Charles nodded, and we were off. It wasn't nearly as slow going as the uphill climb, and we were back on the sand in under an hour. Barnet's two giant ships were anchored a few hundred yards down the coast, and so were the many long-boats he used to get ashore. We said goodbye to Gallardo, and watched as our guide took off down the sand, toward the safety of his village.

"Everyone to the longboats!" I commanded. My overcoat and headscarf that I had discarded along the path were now draped over my arm.

I ran toward them, but Anne yelled, "Just like that? We're gonna *leave*? After all we've done to get here?!"

I stopped and turned.

"We need to ambush 'em! We need to do *somethin'*! I thought ye were better than runnin' away."

"We're not running away," I said through gritted teeth. "And an ambush wouldn't work. There are too many of them and not enough of us."

"Then we'll figure out somethin' else!"

"*Trust me.* We're not leaving yet."

She hesitated, studying me. A gleam appeared in her eyes. "Ye have a plan, don't ye?"

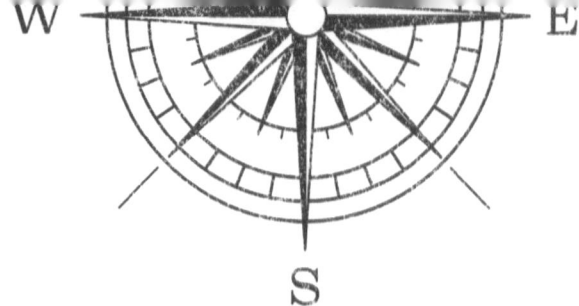

Chapter 39

"**P**REPARE TO DROP anchor!"

We had sailed into the neighboring cove, sheltered nearly on all sides by trees and steep cliffs. *Let Barnet think we fled with our tail between our legs.*

We took the longboats to shore. From there, a group of us hiked left up the steep beach, then through the thin strip of forest until we could see the other cove. *The perfect place to see and not be seen,* I thought as I raised my spyglass, focusing on the few souls that loitered on the decks of the enemy ships. But I couldn't count on that small number—most were probably below decks.

"The lookouts would be staring off at the ocean, and the rest of 'em will be watching the forest, waiting for the gold to be brought down." Robin came up beside Anne and I.

"Aye. How will we row the longboats to their ship without them noticing?" I wondered.

"We could swim for it," Anne suggested.

Robin scratched her head. "Or we could wait until it's dark."

I shook my head. "Too long. They'll have gotten all the treasure by then."

"We could do the white flag approach."

An idea caught hold in my mind. "It's a new crew, right? And there's so many of them. They likely won't know each other too well. We'll row towards them from the shore, pretending we're on their side."

"I think that scheme could do with a distraction," Preston piped up.

"Do tell."

"Cuddles can be the distraction!" Judith exclaimed, cradling the aging cat a few feet away.

I rolled my eyes. She was ridiculous.

"*We* split up," Preston proposed. "Half of us sail *The Kingston* around the corner, and draw their attention and fire."

"Brilliant—as long as you don't put too many holes in my ship. Mum, would you have the honor of temporary captain while I take my group through the forest?"

She smiled, giving me a salute. "Aye, aye."

We relaxed in the shade, watching the comings and goings of the enemy sailors, while half my crew got *The Kingston* ready—awaiting my signal. Finally, we saw movement on the beach.

I tensed, searching for him as the first of Barnet's crew stumbled out of the jungle. *Please be alive. Please be alive.*

Finally he appeared, forced along by a hunk of a sailor, his arms tied behind his back. *Alexander.*

I gripped a tree branch for support. *If Barnet had killed him*—I took a shaky breath, banishing that fear.

He was unharmed.

Then came the bulk of Barnet's men: three or four men to a chest, a few carrying bulging sacks, and the rest weighed down with an assortment of cups and jewelry. Soon all the men arrived—no sign of Finn—and the treasure was laid out on the beach. *Piles and piles of jewelry and coins.* "How much is that, I wonder?"

Behind me, Naomi stood up. "Spyglass, *s'il te plait*," she sang.

I handed her it, and she surveyed the beach. "I wager between seven and eight tons." She lowered the spyglass and looked at me. "If the total is somewhere around nineteen, they'll probably need one or two more trips."

I pursed my lips. "What's more likely? One or two?"

She tilted her head. "Probably two."

This was a very risky gamble. We could take the ship right after they loaded the first trip or the second. If I chose the first, we'd leave the majority of the treasure with Barnet. If I chose the second, it was possible that they would not go back for a third, and we wouldn't get any treasure at all.

In the end, the pirate's blood in me won. I decided to risk it.

I watched Barnet's men ferry the treasure over to his flagship, which was the closest frigate to us. I counted about thirty men on deck while the gold was being loaded, which meant that either Barnet didn't carry nearly as many men as the ship could hold, or he trusted the men on his own ship much more, and took only a fraction of the men from the other.

Back on shore, Alexander was sitting on the sand, tied to a palm tree. *Convenient.* We'd just swing by and pick him up.

Once Barnet's men disappeared into the jungle, we bided our time.

Waiting.

Watching.

I twirled my knife between my fingers, trying to pass the time. More than once I walked back down to the beach, where my crew sat relaxing and playing games in the shade. On the second trip down, I took a longboat with a few others back to *The Kingston* to gather weapons. Arriving in my room, I strapped two baldrics across my chest, all business. I left my corset and coat on the bed. Pouring gunpowder into a pair of pistols, I swept my gaze around the room, hoping it wouldn't be the last time I set foot in my father's room.

Hoping these hours weren't my last.

———⋗•⋖———

**B**arnet's crew finally reemerged for the second time, looking exhausted after their long trek. Most of them collapsed onto the sand, but I heard the captain's shouts for them to get off their arses and load the treasure into the longboats. I scoffed. He knew nothing of his men's suffering.

When the gold was loaded and the empty longboats were dragged onto the shore once again, I ran down to the beach and clapped my hands once.

"Gather 'round, crew. It's time." They snapped to attention. "Our first gamble paid off. Barnet is taking his third and final trip up to the treasure site. He has left his flagship, loaded with the treasure, virtually unguarded."

"Not counting the other frigate full of sailors who want our necks," someone said, provoking a few nervous chuckles.

"Aye," I said, with a slight narrowing of my eyes. "He thinks he's all set. Yet *we* have the element of surprise." I looked around at them all. "This is our moment. This is what we have been waiting for our whole lives. We will thwart Barnet right in front of his eyes!"

"Eye, singular," Preston corrected with a grin. "He looks more pirate than the rest of us combined."

People laughed.

"We'll split into two groups," I announced, gesturing for my crew to split up. "Anne will take a little more than half and sail *The Kingston* around the bend, drawing the flagship's fire. There will be a few minutes until his other ship organizes, weighs anchor, and is able to sail around his flagship to fire on you. Take advantage of it. I will take the rest of you. Arm yourself with the weapons in the longboat." My crew rustled with excitement. I clapped my hands twice, my heart racing. "Step lively now! Time isn't on our side."

After a collective cheer, I led my group along the edge of the forest, out of sight. Just as we burst through the trees, cannons boomed. *The Kingston*, gorgeous royal blue sails full, was still a good hundred yards away from the opposing ship. A blood red flag raised, whipping in the wind—*no quarter given*. Of course, we weren't *really* going to kill everyone on board if they put up a fight. But intimidation worked wonders.

*We need to get over there, fast.* Without us, mine would be outnumbered once they climbed aboard. With us, we could take them.

"Good golly," said the lone guard, staring off at the battling ships. He didn't even notice me sneaking up behind him until I clocked him over the head with the pommel of my sword.

"Cass," Alexander said, relieved. "You escaped."

"*You* didn't," I replied, smiling as I knelt beside him. I scanned his body, looking for any injuries. His shirt was so dirty, it had gone from white to brown. What in the seven seas had happened? "They didn't hurt you, did they?" I reached out to touch his face, but panicked and brought my hand back. *What was I doing?*

More importantly, what was it about him that made me second-guess myself?

It was as if his gorgeous blue eyes were unraveling me. My stomach warmed like a slow-burning furnace. Never—not once—had my heart seized up and then beat so wildly.

Frayed nerves, I concluded. *This close to a battle, nerves get frayed.* Holding my knife in one hand, I reached behind him and felt for the ropes around his wrists. I paused, confused. They were already loose.

Alexander's unbound hand grabbed mine and pulled me in, so close I was nearly leaning on him. He smelled earthy. I had to drop the knife and put that hand against the bark next to his head to steady myself. He gave me a slow smile, and the gold flecks in his eyes sparkled.

"You didn't tell me you already untied yourself!" I laughed, annoyingly twitterpated.

His thumb slowly caressed my palm, sending pleasurable tingles through my fingers. "I was waiting for you to save me. Took you long enough."

*Holy seas.* His low, smooth British accent had never been more attractive. I couldn't breathe.

"What, so I can repay my debt?" We were inches apart, and I couldn't stop myself from glancing down at his mouth.

"You'll have to do it once more."

He pushed himself up a little farther, and the gap between us closed completely. It was like a whole shower of fireworks went off inside me at once. Nothing else mattered except for the taste of his lips.

Soft, and teasing.

"Ha! I knew it!" cackled Robin from somewhere behind us.

We broke apart, and I rolled over onto the sand beside him. Mortified, I realized she was referring to *us*.

"Took you long enough, boy," she teased. "Hurry up, you two. Time's a wastin'!"

I touched my lips, wondering how that had happened.

Aye. Definitely my frayed nerves.

I pushed myself up, forcing my gaze ahead and reminding myself why I was here. *That second delay might've cost a life.* Alexander followed me into the last longboat, splashing through the water while he pushed us off.

"Hurry!" I urged. "They're almost boarding."

"That's not *our* fault," Robin reminded me, grinning ear to ear. "You lovebirds were the bottleneck."

My cheeks warmed. "Shut your gob."

Booming cannons still filled the air, along with the maniac screams of the other half of my crew. I warmed with pride. They were definitely an excellent distraction. We had taken three of the longboats, even though we could have easily fit in two. There would be less for Barnet's crew, and it would be beneficial to be spread out in case they started firing on us. Just as grappling hooks were starting to pull the ships together, we glided into the frigate's shadow. Muskets fired, and I prayed that none of my own were killed by the shots. Silently, we clambered up the gun ports, pausing at the top to peek through the rails. I looked sideways, and Alexander met my eyes. He nodded, a fiery determination in his eyes. I remembered when I'd first seen him fight on the deck of his old ship—and I was glad to have him on my side.

From up above, I heard Preston holler, "Die, you peanut-brained, maggot infested biscuits!"

I didn't waste another second before hoisting myself over the taffrail, drawing my sword, and throwing myself into the chaos.

"Raaaa!" I screamed, drawing my pistol and firing it at a man bearing down on Pearl. He was aiming to kill. *Not on my watch, you won't.* Screaming, the man dropped to the deck, his thigh bleeding.

There were more than thirty men on this ship, but not by much. We still outnumbered them. I slashed my sword at a young man, and he caught my blade with his, looking frightened. "Surrender or die," I growled.

"So many women!" he yelped.

"Aye, you dolt. We can fight too." I knocked the man's sword from his hand with the force of my strike, then hit him over the head with my sword's pommel. As he collapsed, I risked a glance at the other frigate. Over a hundred and fifty sailors were crowded on the deck, in a panic. A nicely dressed man with a tricorne was shouting, trying to assemble them.

I moved on to the next sailor, knocking him unconscious, too. Finding myself fighting back to back with Johnny, I felt a whiff of nostalgia. *Just like the good old days.*

"You good, Cap'n?" he panted.

"Never better!" I swept a pot-bellied one off his feet and bent to render him disabled.

"Emerald!" Naomi screamed. I looked over to see her fighting like a whirlwind. "Jade! Ruby! Where's Pearl? Get your *derrières* to *The Kingston*, NOW!"

Emerald and Jade teamed up on a lanky opponent. "We can fight, *madame!*" The sailor planted a thick-soled leather boot in Emerald's chest and she toppled over as easily as a tower of playing cards.

Naomi snarled, disabling her opponent and leaping to her students' aid as gracefully as a dancer. "This is non-negotiable, girls! Find your sisters and get over there *tout de suite*, or I'll ban you from my halls forever!"

"Cass! Look out!" Alexander shouted from somewhere behind me.

I turned, and caught the blade of the attacker a moment before it sank into my flesh. A new wave of adrenaline tore through me, and I blocked and swiped, no time to think about what would've happened if Alexander hadn't warned me.

Out of the corner of my eye, I saw him dancing between his opponents, his sword a flash of brilliant silver as he parried blows from multiple attackers, easily holding his own. I had to resist a bizarre urge to stop everything and watch him.

Barnet's men were slowly dropping. Our swordsmanship was superior, as was our enthusiasm. We were a roaring beast made of dozens of voices. I grinned manically, knowing victory was imminent.

But then I saw Charles fall. My heart clenched. Why was he out fighting? *He was injured!*

New urgency filled me. We had to end this before there was any more bloodshed. I defeated my next attacker, and every man I met after I told to surrender. Soon I heard Anne and Alexander yelling the same thing.

Finally, the call was issued, and the sailors' swords clattered to the deck. We cheered and hollered in celebration. I looked around, seeing blood and bodies on the deck. A metallic scent drifted through the breeze. *How many were dead?* I looked over my shoulder to see the other ship bearing down on us, sails taught.

We had little time.

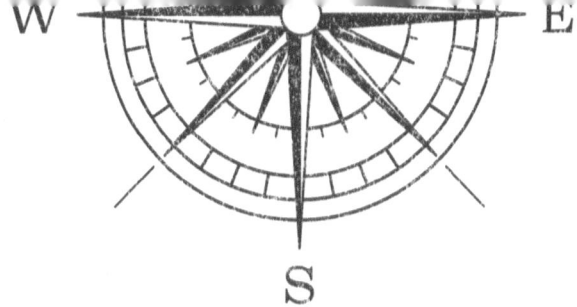

## Chapter 40

I LEAPT UP ON THE RAIL and gripped the rat lines for support. "Listen up, muttonheads," I yelled. "You must choose! Be left behind on this beach with no share in the gold and a captain who's not a man of his word. Or sail with us and share in the riches we acquire. I'll even let you have a bit of this treasure, which is more than you could ever earn from honest sailing." I looked around at them all. "What say you?"

Some shuffled their feet, others looked down.

"I'll give you five seconds to decide," I barked. "Who's with us?"

Hands crept up. Their loyalty for Barnet was as fragile as a china tea cup. A bullet whizzed past my ear, and I whipped my head around to see the other frigate closing in, not fifty yards away. We had a few moments before they club-hauled and pulled up alongside us. If we let that happen, it would be fifty of us against over a hundred of them. I jumped down to avoid being shot, then yelled some more orders. We tossed half the sailors overboard, the ones who refused my offer.

Then I ordered everyone below decks to man the cannons. We were going to sink them. My crew headed straight down, but the newcomers hesitated.

"What?" I snapped.

"You're askin' us to fire on our own ship," one of them said.

"I know some o' those fellas. I don't want to kill them," another added.

"Then tell them to abandon ship," I growled. "Now, go down there and give it everything you've got—unless it's your heads you want stuffed in the cannons?"

Without another protest, they scrambled below decks. I nodded smugly, swinging my gaze back to the opposing frigate.

We gave them a broadside.

Thirty-eight cannonballs sailed towards them, most of them missing, but the rest riddled the bow of their ship with holes. They shouted to each other, trying to turn the ship so their starboard side faced ours. Now that their flagship was shooting at them, they had abandoned their caution.

"AGAIN!" I called down the hatch.

Immediately, more iron punched through their hull.

"Aim for the waterline! Sink them!" I yelled. "FIRE!"

Realizing they were too late to board us, their captain frantically shouted new orders. Sailors rushed to the anchor wheel, spinning it furiously. The anchor dropped and caught, yanking the frigate into a desperate club-haul, but it was futile—their ship already sat lower in the water.

With another deafening blast, another volley of iron carved gaping wounds into their hull.

"Abandon ship!" the captain screamed, his order echoed by all who heard it. Sailors leapt overboard. Several dashed to the longboats, fumbling with the knots that secured them.

*No time,* I thought. *Just jump and swim for it, men!* My eyes followed the captain as he dove from the taffrail. *Leaving before your crew makes it off? Coward.*

We sent one final broadside their way. Shards of timber erupted, and the hull groaned as seawater poured in hungrily. A thrill of giddy elation coursed through me at the destruction we had wrought, and I called everyone back to the main deck to witness the spectacle.

"Adiu, my fine gentlemen! Tell Poseidon I said hello!" Preston waved.

As the frigate sank into the sea, several poor souls, longboats and all, were dragged under, swallowed by the terrible force of suction. Even our own ship lurched sideways under the pull. The rest of Barnet's sailors—a good eighty or so—escaped to shore.

I leapt down from the taffrail, and my foot crunched on something. Bending down, I picked up a small unfinished wooden lion. Its mane was of incredible detail, but the tail had broken off when I'd landed on it. *What a shame it was dropped so carelessly.* I slipped both pieces into my pocket and roved my eyes around the deck.

Wyatt carried the man I'd shot across the gangplank, where he'd have his wound treated by Dan. A few of my people hobbled that way too, supporting each other. I watched Alexander, with some difficulty, lift a sailor up and make his way slowly toward the gangplank. My gaze sharpened. Was something wrong with his gait? He passed off the man to one of my able-bodied crew, and looked around for more wounded. As he turned, my eyes landed on a nasty gash in his leg. Blood had already soaked most of his pant leg, and it was seeping farther with every passing second. Suddenly light-headed, I rushed forward.

"Alexander! You're hurt!"

He looked down, grimacing. "It looks worse than it is."

"If it causes you to limp, it's bad enough for me! Go to the infirmary and tell Dan to fix you up immediately."

"That's not right. There are many wounded, some worse off than me."

"Do I look like the kind of girl to stick to what's *right*? Excuse me for my selfishness, but you take first priority."

A smile tugged on his lips.

"If he likes to suffer, let him suffer!" Anne appeared beside me.

I glared at her angrily.

She put her hands up. "Joking! I'm only joking." She took him by the arm. "Come, boy. If ye like pain so much, ye'll enjoy Dan's needle."

As they set off, I heard someone choke out a breath. "*Please.*"

I turned to the voice. A few paces away, a man knelt over another. The injured sailor, a middle aged man I didn't recognize, spoke again. "Give this to Mary. Tell her I fought bravely." He pressed something into his friend's hands. With a final breath, he stilled. His companion bent over to close the man's eyes, his hands shaking. Only then was I able to see the dead man's last gift.

A wooden lioness, with incredible detail.

The unfinished figurine felt heavy in my pocket as I forced myself to turn away. But my eyes beheld a much more sorrowful sight. Charles lay on the deck in a small puddle of blood, while Nayomi cradled his head. Guilt swept through me. I'd nearly forgotten I'd watched him fall.

"You weren't supposed to fight, *mon cheri*. You were already injured."

"What, and let you have all the fun?"

"Charles," I whispered, coming to kneel beside him.

"I had two arms and legs. I was in fine condition to fight."

I shook my head. "That didn't mean you had to. Stronger men would've easily taken the excuse."

Charles tried to smile, but it looked more like a grimace. He gripped my hand, squeezing almost painfully. "There's a man named—" He winced and drew a long, unsteady breath. "Alaric Frost. Tell him I fought fiercely. Give him a quarter of my share. Ask him to share my story with my remaining family members, so they may know our honor is restored."

I clenched my fists, my hands warm and wet. *What did honor matter anyway?* I thought, distraught and furious. *Who is this Frost, to take a quarter of his share?* But I couldn't argue with a dying boy.

I nodded.

Satisfied, he brought his gaze back to Nayomi. "Tell my mother I'm sorry—" He heaved a ragged breath. "—that her son had to die before she did. The rest of my share must go to her."

A tear escaped her eye and landed silently on Charles's cheek. "*Oh, my boy,*" she whispered.

"Promise?" His voice was barely audible.

"*Je le promets.* I will take care of her, child. You will be remembered as a hero."

Charles closed his eyes and moved no more. Nayomi gingerly unclasped his necklace and slid it into her pocket.

I finally unclenched my hands and stared at them. They were red with Charles's blood. "How many other casualties?" I asked hoarsely, sensing my mother's presence behind me.

She heaved a sigh. "So far, on our side, just Patterson." She took a swig from a canteen.

*So far.* Only time would tell how many injuries would prove fatal. The drink in my mother's hand was looking awfully tempting. "Line the dead up and prepare them for a sea burial. Let's get this deck cleaned up."

I couldn't stop staring. *So much gold. So much silver.* There were chests full of small silver bars, and chests brimming with old Spanish doubloons. I sifted my hands through the coins, transfixed. My fingers brushed something different, and I fished out a beautiful pearl necklace, with a large teardrop shaped sapphire, as blue as the sea. It was at least twenty-five carats, and had to have been worth eight hundred pounds.

We were rich.

I couldn't help but laugh, overflowing with euphoria. We were probably the wealthiest pirates on earth!

I stood up, realizing—"I haven't appointed a treasurer." I looked around at all the eager faces, deciding who I could trust for the task. "Robin, can you read, write, and count?"

"I sure can," she nodded.

"Brilliant. Find some parchment to keep track of what everyone earned and, in the future, how much we spend, and how much we need to save. I want you, Sarah, Frieda, and Naomi to divide up the shares."

"Sure thing, Captain. And how many shares do each of us get?"

"Naomi gets twenty-five percent of the value. After that, I think we all agreed that the captain receives two shares, the quartermaster one and a half, and the rest of the crew one. And save a bit for the newcomers."

"Cass," Anne started. "We need a captain fer this ship, too."

"Indeed." I smiled, slapping her on the back. "I daresay you've earned it. Take these new pirates, since they know the ship. And a dozen more of mine." We'll be both undercrewed, but we could make it back to Tortuga. I clapped my hands twice. "Handsomely now! We're not safe yet!"

We passed over an extra Jolly Roger from *The Kingston*, and as it replaced the British colors, Anne announced that she'd rename the frigate the *Mary Read*. I thought it was fitting.

I leapt over to *The Kingston*. "Step lively, ladies and gents!" I shouted at them, and they quickened their pace. "Patch those holes, let's get her ready to make way!"

Someone shouted from the crows nest, "Barnet, ho!"

I scrambled up to the poop deck, where I could see the forest clearly. I counted five chests, and a huge crowd of men—but Barnet was easy to distinguish. He was staring at the spot where his other ship used to be. I waved, then cupped my hands to the sides of my mouth: "Thank you, Jonathan Barnet, for all you've done to assist me! We couldn't have carried all that treasure through the jungle by ourselves!"

From the *Mary Read*, Anne yelled, "An' might I add, a truly fine ship ye've given me!"

"Good luck getting that gold where you need to go!" I cackled.

Barnet roared more loudly and furiously than I thought humanly possible, and the sound echoed up and down the cove. The villagers might've imagined it was an evil beast.

I turned back to my crew. "Haul the leeward lines! Set sail for Tortuga!"

"We'll meet again, ye coward!" my mum called one last time, before dealing orders to her new crew.

I was happy for her. Anne was finally a captain. She didn't have to take orders from anyone, and she had freed her son from Barnet's clutches. I wondered what had become of Finn... maybe he found refuge with the villagers. Maybe he would eventually find his way home.

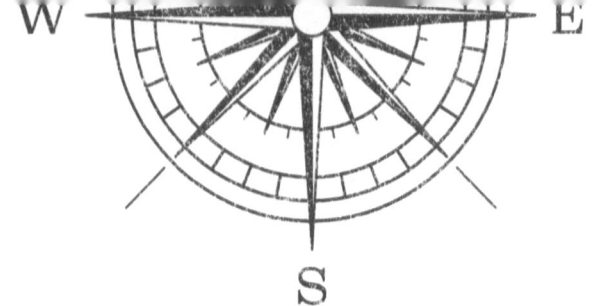

W     E

S

## *Chapter 41*

THE SUN WAS GETTING LOW in the sky as I stepped out of my quarters. It was a relief to wash up and change. My hair was brushed, my eyes were lined with kohl, and my ears were studded with diamonds I'd received as part of my share. Once land was out of sight, we had pulled our ships together and distributed the treasure. There was nearly a half ton of gold, silver, gems, and jewelry piled up in one corner of my room.

Joyful, I looked down at my outfit once more. I wore a white blouse with a black, gold-trimmed tail coat, to match the tricorn Naomi gave me. She'd suggested a corset—but it was a day of celebration, not pain!

We'd escaped the island with most of the treasure, using Barnet's manpower—and Barnet's ship. Watching him shrink into the distance, stranded on a beach with naught but a morsel of gold was the sweetest possible revenge.

We'd bought Tortuga some time. Barnet wouldn't give up—he'd hail a passing ship, spend his gold on warships, and come for us. We needed to make Tortuga impenetrable, for now the world knew where it lay.

I walked down the companionway and found Alexander leaning against the railing, looking out to sea. I came to stand next to him, resting my arms on the taffrail like him. "You're rich."

He grinned at me. "I can buy a telescope."

Laughing, I replied, "You're going to *perfect* the telescope. And then you're going to discover that there's even more stars in the sky than you thought."

He got a dreamy look in his eyes.

I poked him. "I'm in need of a first mate, if you'd like a promotion."

"I didn't know you trusted me so much," he teased.

I raised my chin. "Well, since you saved my life twice, I am still in your debt—"

Xander took a small step toward me, one arm leaving the rail. "Are you really still focused on that?"

I shrugged. "It's the way of the world."

"We don't have to follow the way of the world." He slipped his hand lightly around mine, lazily fingering the rings on my pinky and forefinger. The touch was electric. "We can make our own rules. So no, Cassandra, you're not in my debt. I'll go to the ends of the earth for you, but I'm not going to keep score." He leaned closer, his blue eyes gazing deeply into mine. "And I don't want *you* to do so, either."

I turned my head away, then nodded. *I'll go to the ends of the earth for you.* My breath caught. Never before had anyone said that to me...not even the man I'd nearly married. My hat left my head, and I looked back to see him wearing it. I grinned. It was a good look for him—but alas, a captain couldn't be without her hat. "You can't steal from a pirate."

"Says who?" he challenged, taking a step around me and bracing my hips against the railing.

A warning bell sounded in my head, reminding me of the last time I trusted someone with my heart, but as he slid his arms around my waist and met my eyes, my doubt burned away. This was a risk, for certain, but I realized I wanted it more than I'd ever wanted the treasure. *Besides, what's a pirate, if not a risk taker?*

I grabbed the front of his shirt and pulled him in, so close that our noses brushed. He still smelled of blood and sweat from the skirmish, but I didn't care. It just made him seem tougher, braver. And even though Alexander would never want to accept that he was a pirate, he was the best one I'd ever met. "*I* say there should be a trade," I whispered.

When his lips met mine, they tasted like salt. I slid my hands up his chest and into his hair, tossing my hat to the ground. He was *perfect*. The kiss was perfect: slow, and wonderful, and *real*. Because he knew who I was, and where I'd gone, and what I'd done, and still...he loved me. And that realization made it so much sweeter.

## Epilogue

B ARNET WAS MORE THAN FURIOUS as he stood watching the pirate scum sail away with his ship. He was seething with rage. He was bloodthirsty.

"Sir," a nasally voice spoke behind him. "Can I keep this necklace?"

Barnet promptly pulled out his pistol and shot the man. The other sailors gasped and cowered as he fell, his blood a stark contrast with the white sand. Barnet had a fleeting sensation of remorse—he was praised by the King, and what he had done would be considered murder—but it was soon smothered by his wrath. His other ship was nowhere to be seen, but the rest of his men, soaked from a swim, told him that she had sunk it. She had taken his eye, part of his crew, and *three* of his ships. He devoted his life to justice, but seeing her hanged would not be enough.

*Nay*, he thought, savoring the idea. *I'll rip out her eye and then kill her slowly*. And for the reward, he would bring back her head.

He knew where she would be hiding. He would tear down that filthy island rock by rock until he found every last pirate and locked them all away. And for Bonny and Rackham...he would take care of them personally.

But for all his hopes and dreams, he was stuck here. On this god forsaken beach. He had over two hundred sailors, but what good would they do without a ship to sail?

He stormed up the beach, desperately needing to get away from them. He was sure a ship would pass by, but how long would it take? Days? Weeks?

Possibly months?

He stopped short, realizing that a group of men that size... it wouldn't be long before they started complaining of hungry bellies.

Barnet closed his eyes, a new wave of rage hitting him. Rackham thought she outwitted him. She thought she had left him in ruin. But Barnet would kill *every single one of them* if that's what it took to survive until a rescue ship came.

He would live to see her die.

# Acknowledgements

I'd like to thank my family, for supporting me through this long journey and giving me hours of their time while I read them my story aloud. A special thanks to you, Mom and Dad, for getting me to the end of the road and believing in me when it got hard. And thanks, Sis, for being my most exuberant cheerleader and giving me hope that people will love this story as much as you do. You don't know how much your excitement and love of these characters meant to me during the hardest parts of the publishing process.

To Elizabeth Splaine, the writer and music teacher who believed in me, gave me invaluable advice, and connected me to an amazing editor. I don't know how to thank you enough. You really made a huge difference to me and my writing future.

To my editor, Rose Alexandre-Leach, who brought this story to the next level and really made it shine.

And thanks to YOU, the reader, for setting out on this pirate adventure and sticking with me until the end. It makes me so happy that you could get to know the characters I've loved for so many years. Hopefully I'll see you when I write book two of this series!

LILLIEANNE BROWN began writing stories when she was 12 years old. She started working on *Call Me Captain* in her junior year of high school, inspired by the ocean she adored and her favorite movie, *Pirates of the Caribbean*. She's a lover of high seas adventure, dangerous secrets, and slow-burn romance. When she's not dreaming up pirate captains or diving into historical rabbit holes, she can be found re-reading her favorite series, playing guiter with her siblings, or hiking in the forest. *Call Me Captain* is her debut novel.

FOLLOW LILLIEANNE BROWN ONLINE
@authorlillieanne on TikTok
@authorlillieanne on Instagram